THE

"Though the book is characterized by breakneck pacing, deeply developed characters and impressively intricate plotlines, it's Ryan's subtle focus on vivid worldbuilding (particularly on varied sensory descriptions) that makes this such an immersive read. . . . Readers who enjoy their fantasy fast and furious will find Ryan's latest to be an immensely satisfying, top-notch adventure fantasy." —*Kirkus Reviews*

"Features everything that we've come to love in Ryan's books. . . . From well-crafted and fascinating characters to a masterfully established world . . . *The Wolf's Call* is everything a fantasy fan could ever wish for." —BookNest.eu

"Robin Hobb meets Joe Abercrombie in a story that delivers so many gut-wrenching blows. This is fantasy with a totally legendary feel; it's epic in every regard and certainly something that needs to be added to your reading list." —Fantasy Book Review

"I've said it before and I'll say it again: 'Anthony Ryan is David Gemmell's natural successor and heroic fantasy's best British talent.'" —Fantasy Book Critic

"*The Wolf's Call* is a return to form for the world of Vaelin Al Sorna. If you're a fan of the Raven's Shadow trilogy, then you'll be thrilled with the quality of this book." —The Fantasy Inn

Ace Books by Anthony Ryan

The Raven's Shadow Novels

BLOOD SONG
TOWER LORD
QUEEN OF FIRE

The Draconis Memoria Novels

THE WAKING FIRE
THE LEGION OF FLAME
THE EMPIRE OF ASHES

The Raven's Blade Novels

THE WOLF'S CALL
THE BLACK SONG

THE WOLF'S CALL

A RAVEN'S BLADE NOVEL

ANTHONY RYAN

ACE

NEW YORK

ACE
Published by Berkley
An imprint of Penguin Random House LLC
penguinrandomhouse.com

ISBN: 9780451492524

The Library of Congress has cataloged the Ace hardcover edition of this book as follows:

Names: Ryan, Anthony, author.
Title: The wolf's call / Anthony Ryan.
Description: First edition. | New York: Ace, 2019. | Series: A Raven's blade novel; 1
Identifiers: LCCN 2019003843 | ISBN 9780451492517 (hardcover) |
ISBN 9780451492531 (ebook)
Subjects: | BISAC: FICTION / Fantasy / Epic. | FICTION / Fantasy / General. |
GSAFD: Fantasy fiction.
Classification: LCC PR6118.Y3523 W65 2019 | DDC 823/.92—dc23
LC record available at https://lccn.loc.gov/2019003843

Ace hardcover edition / July 2019
Ace trade paperback edition / June 2020

Printed in the United States of America
ScoutAutomatedPrintCode

Cover art © Cliff Nielsen
Cover design by Judith Lagerman
Book design by Tiffany Estreicher
Unified Realm map by Steve Karp, based on an original by Anthony Ryan
Kingdoms of the Far West map and Northern Prefecture map by Anthony Ryan

Dedicated to the memory of my late friend and one-time boss,
Dr. Robin Cooper, PhD, who would have made a great Aspect of the Third Order

ACKNOWLEDGMENTS

Thanks once again to my US editor, Jessica Wade, and my UK editor, James Long, for their helpful input and advice in bringing Vaelin Al Sorna's next adventure into the world. Thanks also to my agent, Paul Lucas, for all his efforts on my behalf, and Paul Field, my ever-vigilant second set of eyes.

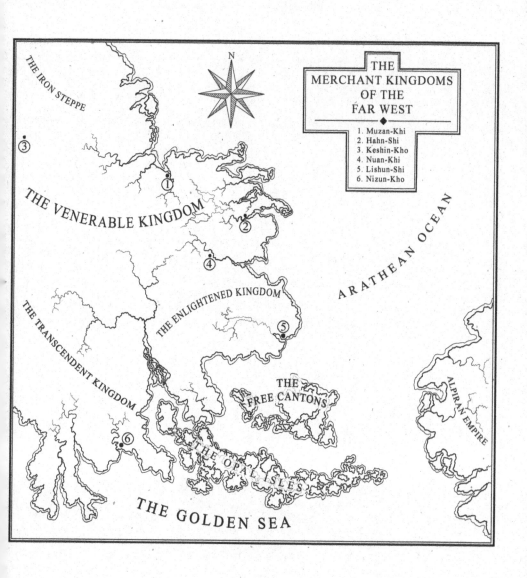

THE
WOLF'S
CALL

PART I

The raven's blade
Cuts deep,
Laying bare my sins.

—SEORDAH POEM, AUTHOR UNKNOWN

Luralyn's Account

The First Question

There are many these days who call my brother a monster. They speak of his deeds, both dreadful and wondrous, as the work of a preternatural beast that had somehow taken on the form of a man to wreak the greatest havoc upon the world. There are others, in the more shadowed and wretched corners of the earth, who still call him a god, though when they do, the word is always spoken in a fearful whisper. Curiously, neither those who think him monstrous nor those who think him divine ever speak his true name, even though they know it as well as I. Kehlbrand, my brother whom, despite it all, despite every battle, conquest and massacre, I still contrive to love. But, I hear you ask, most honoured reader, how can this be? How is it possible to harbour love for a man who bathed half the world in blood?

In these quieter days, far removed from the frenzy and terrors of war, I have the leisure to consider such questions. As the years pass and ever more grey creeps into the once-auburn mane that crowns my head, as yet more aches beset my joints and I squint ever closer at these pages as I write, it is this question I ponder most.

Honoured reader, rest assured that I know you did not open this volume to endure an old woman's complaints. No, you wish to know of my brother and how he came to reshape the world entire. But his story cannot be told unless I also tell mine, for we were bound tight, he and I. Through blood and purpose, we were bound tight. For many years it was as if we shared a soul, so mirrored was our intent, our commitment to our holy mission. But the mirror, I have come to learn, is the worst of liars, and no mirror ever remains uncracked by time.

It has taken me years of contemplation to identify the moment when I became truly bound to Kehlbrand. Perhaps it was when I slipped from the back of my first horse at age seven and spent several moments whimpering over the bleeding scrape on my knee. It was Kehlbrand, just a day or so shy of his twelfth year, who came to me. As the other children of our Skeld laughed and threw dung at the sobbing weakling, it was my brother who came and helped me to my feet. Already he was long of limb with the leanness of a born warrior, standing at least a foot taller than I, as he would for the rest of our lives.

"Druhr-Tivarik, little colt," he said, voice soft with concern as he spoke the priests' term for those who carry the Divine Blood, thumbing the tears from my eyes, "do not weep." With that, he gave a smile of apology before forming his features into the customary mask of harsh disdain and delivering an open-handed slap to my face. The blow was hard enough to send me to the ground with the iron sting of blood on my tongue.

I spent several seconds blinking in confusion, although I was surprised to find my tears had stopped flowing. Looking up through bleary eyes, I saw Kehlbrand advancing on the other children. He made straight for the tallest, a burly boy a year his elder named Obvar, who was always to be found at the forefront of my tormentors.

"Druhr-Tivarik," my brother repeated, delivering a closed fist directly into Obvar's face, "cannot be judged by the merely mortal."

The subsequent fight was both lengthy and bloody, becoming something of a legend amongst the youngsters of the Skeld. It greatly overshadowed the insult done to a child of the Druhr-Tivarik, which was soon forgotten. This, I later realised, had been Kehlbrand's intention, for the priests were given to punishing such things harshly. When it was over, Obvar lay groaning on the ground, bleeding from numerous cuts, whilst Kehlbrand, no less bloody, remained standing. As is often the way with boys, in the days that followed, he and Obvar became the closest of friends, remaining sworn saddle brothers until one particular and very fateful day some twenty years later. But, honoured reader, it appears I am getting ahead of myself.

But no, important lesson though it was, we were not truly bonded that day. Nor, strangely, the morning after I had my first True Dream. You must understand that the power of the Divine Blood is fickle. Although those of us fated to join the ranks of the Druhr-Tivarik are born to mothers with manifest gifts, such gifts are not always passed on. In many cases they lay dormant throughout childhood, only becoming apparent with the onset of puberty. So it proved with me. At the dawning of my twelfth summer, the week of my first blood, the True Dream made itself known.

You must forgive my meagre literary skills, honoured reader, for I find it hard to convey in words the utter terror of that first dream. I use this term as I find the word "vision" somewhat silly, not to say inadequate. The True Dream is a state beyond reality, although it feels completely real to one captured in its throes. The confusion and dulled sensations of a mundane dream are not present. The feel of the air on skin, the scents carried by the wind, the warmth of a flame or the sting of a cut. All these are present, and felt in full.

That night, as I lay on my mats in the tent I shared with the other favoured children of the Skeld, I found myself claimed by a sleep as deep and absolute as any I had known. It was as if a black veil had been placed over my eyes, banishing all light and sensation, and when it was drawn aside, I found myself standing amidst horrors.

I remember the screams most of all. The pain of a dying soul is a hard thing to bear, especially if you have never heard it before. I had seen people die by then. Heretics, slaves and those who transgressed the Laws Eternal were routinely bound and forced to kneel beneath the executioner's blade. But those deaths had been quick; a swift stroke of the sabre, and their heads would roll on the earth. Their bodies might twitch, sometimes their faces too. A ghastly sight for any child to witness but, still, mercifully brief. What I witnessed in that first True Dream was not lawful execution. It was battle.

The doomed man lay against the flank of a dead horse, eyes wide in terror and bafflement as he stared at the mess of entrails that had been his belly. His mouth gaped as he screamed, hands crimson with gore as they tried to stuff the gelatinous tubes back inside his body. Surrounding us was a maelstrom of thundering hooves, clashing blades and the shrill cries of distressed horses, all shrouded in a thick pall of dust.

Battle was a regular occurrence on the Iron Steppe in those days. It was a time when the Stahlhast endured a painful transition from disunited and endlessly feuding Skelds to what could be called a true nation. It seemed as if every other month the warriors would strap their bows to their saddles, and work stones over their sabres and lance points before mounting up to ride off in one great host. After days or perhaps weeks they would return, always victorious, the heads of enemies dangling from their saddles. Come the night they would drink and tell tales of their great deeds, tales I found did not match the nightmare that enfolded me now.

My eyes flicked from one horror to another, a crawling man trailing blood from the stumps of his legs, a horse thrashing in a pool of guts and shit leaking from sundered bowels, and there, amidst it all, Kehlbrand, my brother, standing tall.

As was his wont in battle, he wore no helm, the long braid of his hair whirling as he fought, beset by foes on all sides. There must have been a dozen of them, their armour embossed with the redbird sigil of the Rikar Skeld, our most hated enemy. Time after time they came for him, and time after time his sabre cut them down. My brother moved as if in a dance, sidestepping every thrusted lance, ducking every slashing blade and leaving a trail of corpses in his wake. He seemed invincible, unstoppable, making my heart swell with pride despite the continuing nightmare all around. But, as I have learned many times since, there is no such thing as an invincible warrior.

It was as Kehlbrand cut down that last of his enemies, a broad, brute-faced man with a patch over one eye, that the Rikar archer appeared out of the dust. He rode a tall white stallion at full gallop, leaning low over the saddle, face set in the concentrated stare of the expert as he aimed his shaft. I screamed a warning to my brother, but though I put all my strength into the shout, my brother heard nothing. The True Dream makes the dreamer a witness, but never a participant.

The arrow took Kehlbrand in the back of the neck, piercing him all the way through so that the steel head emerged from his throat by several inches. Had he worn a helm he might have lived. I watched him stagger briefly, staring down at the crimson arrowhead with curious detachment, his expression one of mild surprise. Then he fell, collapsing to the earth as all life fled his body.

I woke screaming, much to the annoyance of the other children. Two days later word came that the Rikar had ambushed one of our hunting parties and battle would be required to settle the insult. I sought Kehlbrand out amongst the gathering warriors. It was custom for relatives to gift tokens to those called to war, so I attracted little attention as I approached my brother. He, however, regarded me with amused surprise, knowing it was my habit to shun such things.

"Thank you, little colt," he said as I pushed the small wooden carving into his hands. It was a rendering of a horse I had crafted myself, something my modesty doesn't prevent my saying I have always excelled at. "This is very fine . . ."

He fell silent as I moved closer, standing on tiptoe to wrap my arms around him, whispering softly into his lowered ear, "Turn after you kill the man with the eye patch. Watch for the archer on the white horse." I released him and made to leave, then paused. "And you really should wear a helm in future."

I walked swiftly away, heart hammering. I had told no one else of the True Dream, nor did I ever intend to. Others might relish the onset of their Divine gifts and run to tell the priests the happy news. I knew better.

The warriors returned seven days later whilst I sat alone in the tent, staring at the open flap through teary eyes. I remember being unsurprised when Kehlbrand appeared, stooping low to sink down beside me. Instead, I felt only a grim certainty. My brother was a true warrior of the Hast, and his duty was clear. Those with manifest gifts must be taken to the Great Tor and given to the priests.

Kehlbrand regarded me in silence for a long time, his expression contemplative rather than awed. Finally, he said in a toneless voice, "I kept the white stallion. My gift to you."

I nodded, swallowing, my throat as dry as sand. "I'll ride him when you take me to the priests," I said, the words spoken in a thin rasp.

"Why," he said, reaching out to cup my face, "would I ever do that, little colt?"

"They'll know. They always know . . ."

"Hush." He thumbed away the tears welling in my eyes and reached into his pack. "I have another gift for you."

The tooth was long and white, the base fitted with a silver clasp attached to a chain. The tooth itself was inscribed with blackened script of some kind. I could read the letters of the Merchant Realms, but this was unknown to me. "Plucked from the jaw of a white tiger," Kehlbrand said. "Many seasons ago I sought out an old woman in the northern wastes said to be wise in the ways of the Divine Blood. She swore this will conceal it from the priests, and bargained me up to three horses and a nugget of gold before she would give it up. Like you, I worried the priests might come for me if the power ever quickened in my blood. Since it appears that will never happen," he said, splaying the chain and lifting it over my head, the metal chill on my neck as he settled it in place, "now, I give it to you."

But even this, though it drew us closer, made us truly brother and sister rather than just the issue of the same womb, this was not the final seal on the knot that bound us. The act that truly entwined our souls came on the day we were summoned to watch the Mestra-Dirhmar, the Great Priest, kill our older brother.

"Witness the judgement of the Unseen!" the old man canted, two bony fists gripping the knife raised above his head. "And know well their lessons! Mercy is weakness! Compassion is cowardice! Wisdom is falsehood! If the blood be weak, let it spill!"

Tehlvar, our brother, lay naked on the altar before the priest, his body a pale, six-foot-long testament to the many battles of his life with its web of scars marring the honed muscle. I remember that he barely twitched as the knife hovered above. The priest waited until the shadows cast by the jagged majesty of the Great Tor faded, bespeaking the exact moment when the sun had aligned with this precise spot in the centre of the Iron Steppe. Then, as the slightly curved blade caught the midday sun, he brought it down. One swift, expertly placed thrust directly into Tehlvar's heart. I watched my brother jerk as the blade sank home, watched him convulse with the last few beats of his sundered heart and then lay still.

"Druhr-Tivarik!" the Mestra-Dirhmar said, grunting a little with the effort of pulling the knife from Tehlvar's body before raising it high. Blood streaked down his arm to bathe his bare torso. As one of the Divine Blood, I stood amongst the ranks of the favoured between the two massive stones that formed the east-facing gateway. Consequently, I was close enough to the altar to witness my brother's murder in grim but fascinating detail. I remember watching as the blood dripped over the flaccid muscles of the priest's chest to the sharp grate of his ribs. It was strange to think so mighty a warrior as Tehlvar could be slain by one so old and weak, one who had never known battle.

He is the Mestra-Dirhmar, I reminded myself, repeating the words and lowering my gaze in concert with the thousands of others gathered to witness this most sacred of rituals. He speaks for the Unseen. Even then the words felt empty, my subservience merely the rote response of a well-trained dog. A smaller but truer thought lay beneath my obeisance, even as I and the gathered luminaries of a hundred Skeld sank to our knees and bowed our heads to the earth: *He is just a weak old man. Tehlvar was better.*

You should understand, honoured reader, that I did not love Tehlvar. At thirteen years his junior I barely knew him except by reputation, but what a reputation it was. They say he killed more than *fifty* men in combat before ascending to Skeltir. It was under Tehlvar's leadership that the pre-eminence of the Cova Skeld had been completed. It was through his courage and skill at the battle of the Three Rivers that the heretic traitors to the Divine Blood had been slain or captured. Although a good deal of discord lingered, many Skeld of the Hast now stood as allies rather than endlessly feuding rivals. But it hadn't been enough to spare Tehlvar the Great Priest's knife.

Having been called to the Great Tor, he was required to answer the last of the Three Questions, an answer that would see him receive his final blessing as Mestra-Skeltir: Great Lord of the Hast. Twice before the priests had summoned him to answer a question, and twice before he had provided an acceptable answer. Not all Skeltir are chosen for this honour, just those who have won the greatest renown. Years would pass without a question being asked and only four other Skeltir in all the long history of the Hast had ever answered two questions correctly, and none the third. Long had we awaited the coming of the Mestra-Skeltir, the leader who would ensure our ascendancy over not just the Iron Steppe but the far-wealthier lands of the Merchant Kings to the south.

But whatever Tehlvar's answer had been, spoken only to the gathering of priests far beyond the ears of the assembled throng, it had not been sufficient to secure his ascendency. Druhr-Tivarik he was, the Divine Blood flowed in his veins as it flows through mine, but it had been proven weak, and if the blood be weak, let it spill.

"Kehlbrand Reyerik!" the Mestra-Dirhmar intoned, lowering the knife to point the blade at the young man kneeling at my side. "Stand and be recognised!"

I watched my brother rise, seized by the impulse to reach out and stop him somehow. Although young and steeped in the priests' lies as I was, I still knew his choosing to be a curse and not a blessing. To restrain him at that moment would have meant death, and not the swift end meted out to Tehlvar. Interference in the priests' rituals would earn me the worst of torments. So perhaps it was fear that stilled my hand then, for I have never pretended to be the bravest *of souls. But I don't think so. I think that, like all the many others present, I wanted it to be Kehlbrand. I wanted to witness the moment the true Mestra-Skeltir took his place. So I didn't try to stop him, not then. That came later.*

"By right of blood you are now Skeltir of the Cova Skeld," the priest told Kehlbrand. "As dictated by the Laws Eternal, tomorrow morning will be set aside for challenges. Any warrior of sufficient rank who defeats you will stand as Skeltir in your place."

Kehlbrand bowed his head in grave acceptance before raising it to meet the priest's gaze with an expectant eye. I saw the old man's face flush with angry reluctance then. He could simply stay silent; having formally appointed my brother to the role of Skeltir, he had no obligation to also call him to the question, save for the fact that Kehlbrand had already achieved far-greater renown than most others who had received such an honour, as every member of the Hast well knew.

The priest's lips slipped over his yellowed teeth in a poorly concealed half sneer before his features resumed the mask of dutiful certainty. "If you live," *he said,* "return here one hour before the sun's apex to answer the First Question of the Unseen."

He let his arm fall to his side and paused to survey Tehlvar's body. I found his expression a sudden contrast to the mask from only seconds before. Now he seemed much older, sadness and regret clear in his eyes for one brief instant before he turned and walked away amidst the ranks of the lesser priests.

My people are never fond of overlong rituals, and soon the representatives of the hundred Skeld had all drifted away to their respective encampments. Kehlbrand, however, lingered and therefore so did I. Moving to the altar, he closed his eyes and placed a hand on our brother's forehead, murmuring his own soft farewell. He had been at Tehlvar's side for much of the preceding few years, gaining enough renown to justify a challenge for the Skeltir's mantle, but he never had.

A loud belch sounded behind me, and I glanced over my shoulder to see Obvar leaning against a monolith, wineskin in hand as he regarded me with a questioning glance.

"He's saying goodbye," *I said, turning away.*

"The pious arsehole's dead," *Obvar muttered, coming to my side.* "Can't hear it, so what's the point?" *The question was evidently rhetorical, for he forestalled my curt response by proffering the wineskin.* "Drink?"

Obvar was always offering me drink, and more besides. It was many years since his childhood bullying had given way to a different kind of interest. I often reflected that I preferred him as a bully rather than a suitor. However, my initial impulse to stern refusal stalled on my tongue as I noted the absence of carnal interest in his gaze. Unlike Kehlbrand, the disparity in our height had grown over the years, and I was obliged to look up to gauge his expression. For once he seemed troubled rather than lustful.

"Give it here," I said, taking the wineskin. The first sip had me blinking in surprise. Instead of the thick, floral berry wine typically drunk by the Hast, this was something far lighter on the palate. The taste was rich and complex, shot through with a pleasing earthiness and balanced by a smoothness that made it slip down the throat very easily.

"That's not cheap, you know," Obvar said, his thick brows bunching as I took another generous swallow.

"What is it?" I asked, handing back the wineskin.

"Not sure of the name. It's made from some kind of fruit grown in a land far across the sea. At least that's what the merchant I stole it from said. I let him live on the condition he come back next summer with more. Said I'd even pay him for it. Wasn't that nice of me?"

"Did you let the others in his caravan live?"

"The young ones." He shrugged and drank. "Slaves are valuable."

"What a disgusting animal you are, Obvar." The heat of genuine detestation sang in my voice, loud enough to make the wineskin pause on the way back to his lips, which broadened into a smile.

"Eighteen summers old," he said, looming over me as he stepped closer, the familiar lust creeping back into his gaze. "And still not wed. I always like the way your tongue cuts me, girl. Makes me wonder what else it can do."

I stared directly into his eyes, meeting the lust I saw there with utter disdain. I wasn't afraid and felt no need to reach for the long-knife on my belt. I was Druhr-Tivarik and, whilst childhood torments would have been punished with a beating, any insult or injury now that I was of childbearing age would earn him the lengthy death of a dishonoured warrior. However, as our gazes locked and seconds stretched into moments, I was given to wondering if this was the day when his lust finally overcame his caution.

"When your brother becomes Mestra-Skeltir," he said, voice thick and teeth bared, "we will conquer all. We will ravage the lands of the Merchant Kings *all the way to the Golden Sea, and I will be at his side for every battle. When all the glorious slaughter ends and the final drop of blood falls, he will ask me what reward I desire for my service. What do you imagine I will ask for?"*

"Luralyn."

Our eyes snapped to the altar at the sound of my brother's voice. Kehlbrand didn't look at us, standing with arms braced against the altar's edge, his gaze still captured by Tehlvar's body. "I will have counsel," he said before glancing up at Obvar. "Saddle brother, go and slake your appetite on a slave and leave my sister be. And don't get too drunk. I may have need of your blade on the morrow."

Obvar stiffened and I saw a faint twitch of resentment pass across his lean, bearded features. It faded quickly, however, and he let out a faint sigh of acceptance. Saddle brothers they were, but Kehlbrand was Skeltir now.

"Here," Obvar grunted, shoving the wineskin into my hands. "A token of esteem for my Skeltir's sister."

I watched him stomp off towards the encampment of our Skeld, feeling a brief spasm of sympathy for whichever unfortunate slave caught his interest. Slaves are not of the Hast. I inwardly recited one of the Laws Eternal as I joined Kehlbrand at the altar. Anything not of the Hast is booty.

"Have some," I said, holding out the wineskin. "It's really not too bad."

He ignored the offer, gaze lingering on our brother's slack, empty features. The lips had drawn back in death, baring his teeth in a parody of a grin. Unwilling to endure the sight of that grin for long, I occupied myself with another generous gulp of Obvar's wine.

"Do you know why the priests killed him, Luralyn?" Kehlbrand asked. As usual, his voice was soft. My brother rarely shouted. Even during the duels I had seen him fight, the few words he spoke amidst the tumult of blades were spoken in a steady, almost solicitous murmur. Nevertheless, I can recall no one ever failing to hear or comprehend a single word he said.

"He got the question wrong," I replied, wiping the sleeve of my formal black cotton robe across my mouth.

"I hear no grief in your voice, little colt," Kehlbrand said, finally turning to regard me. "Did you not love our brother? Does your heart not break at his departure from this world?"

To anyone listening, his questions would have been taken as earnest, sincere inquiries, coloured by an aggrieved note at my apparent indifference. I, however, knew my brother well enough to recognise gentle mockery when I heard it.

"We were birthed from the same womb," I said. "But not the same father. Tehlvar was a stranger to me for most of my life. But . . ." I paused to survey the corpse on the altar, struck once again by the sheer number of battle wounds it bore, some long healed, others barely weeks old. Kehlbrand's body, I knew, was almost entirely free of scars. "Still, I'm sorry he's gone. He was a good Skeltir, if a little overfond of reciting the priests' teachings."

"The priests' teachings," Kehlbrand repeated with a slow nod. "He did always love their lessons. 'I have ranged beyond the Iron Steppe, brother,' he told me once. 'The people who dwell there live lives of uncertainty and confusion. They celebrate weakness and revel in greed. They make a virtue of lies and a sin of honesty. When the Mestra-Skeltir rises, he will wash all of that away, in blood. This the priests have seen.'"

He fell silent, reaching out to place his hand over the dull gleam of Tehlvar's eyes, closing the lids. "But you're wrong, little colt. They didn't kill him for the answer he gave. They killed him because he gave no answer. He was not the Mestra-Skeltir, and he knew it."

"He made way for you," I said.

"Yes. He told me as much last night. We spoke for a long time and he told me many things, including the question I will be asked tomorrow, and the question to follow a year later should I answer correctly."

I stared at him in appalled silence, the wineskin almost slipping from my fingers in shock before I mastered myself. I found it necessary to take another drink before speaking on. "He told you? That is heresy!"

Kehlbrand's teeth, very white, very even, shone as he let out a rare laugh. "In time, dear sister, I will tell you all I learned last night, and you will come to realise the true absurdity of the words you just voiced."

His mirth subsided quickly and he lifted his hand from Tehlvar's eyes to grasp my shoulder. "Tomorrow, they will ask for my name."

"They already know your name. Kehlbrand Reyerik, Skeltir of the Cova Skeld."

"No, they require another name. A name worthy of the Mestra-Skeltir. A name the soldiers of the Merchant Kings will whisper in fear when they hear the thunder of Stahlhast hooves upon the Steppe. A name that will carry us all the way to the Golden Sea, and beyond."

His hand moved from my shoulder to my face, cupping my cheek. I saw regret in his face as he smiled at me, guilt too, for he knew the gravity of what he was about to ask. "That is what I need from you: a name. Luralyn, dear sister, it is time for you to dream again."

Although I tried to resist it, although it was something I had avoided doing ever since coming to this place, my eyes were drawn inevitably to the Sepulchre. It sat in the centre of the half-circle of iron and rock that formed the Great Tor. An unadorned, grey stone box ten paces wide and twelve feet tall with an opening in its east-facing wall. The opening was a black rectangle in the grey stone, for no light came from within. The priests never guarded it. Why bother since no soul would ever venture inside unless commanded to it?

"Do not fear," Kehlbrand said as my eyes lingered unblinking on the Sepulchre's black door. "The priests know nothing. We've made sure of that."

"They will," I said, finding it impossible to quell the tremor in my voice. Unbidden, my hand had stolen into my robe to close on the inscribed tiger's tooth, clutching it tight. "Even with this, so close . . . to that. They'll know."

"You overestimate their abilities. They possess barely a fraction of the power they pretend. Their true power lies in the illusions they spin to capture the souls of our people, and all illusions fade over time. Another lesson Tehlvar imparted last night."

"They'll know!" I insisted, hating the sudden tears in my eyes. His request felt like a betrayal, a selfish demand that undid the trust between us. For alone amongst our Skeld, alone amongst all my many siblings and cousins in the Divine Blood, only he knew the truth. Should the priests ever discover it, through the black door I would go, and what emerged would not be me.

"They'll make me . . ."

My voice failed as he drew me close, his arms enfolding me like twin branches of the mightiest tree. There were other words to come, other pledges and promises, but I have since comprehended that our bond was sealed in this embrace. It was this moment that I became truly his. In his arms all fear fled and I knew he would never allow any harm to be done to me, in body or in soul.

"I will kill every priest should they even suggest it," he told me, voice soft in my ear. "I will paint this tor with their blood and stake their heads in a circle around the Sepulchre for all the Hast to see." He drew back, thumbing away my tears as he had done so all those years ago, except this time there would be no slap to follow the kindness. "Do you believe me, little colt?"

"Yes, brother," I said, pressing my head to his chest, hearing the steady thrum of his heart. "I believe you."

◆ ◆ ◆

Summoning a True Dream is not a complicated process. Nor is it mystical or ritualistic. Contrary to the beliefs of more unenlightened cultures it requires no incantations, foul-smelling concoctions or blood spilled from unfortunate animals. In truth, as I had discovered in the years since the first manifestation of my gift, it requires only a secure and comfortable place rich in both peace and quiet. Consequently, I forsook the Cova encampment that night. The revels had begun early, customary propriety cast aside in the usual welter of drink, brain-addling snuff and undiscerning copulation.

Escorted by Kehlbrand and two of his most trusted saddle brothers, we left the din of the celebration behind and rode beyond the sprawl of tents and out into the vastness of the Iron Steppe. A five-mile ride under the stars brought us to a small rise in the otherwise unbroken flatness of the landscape. The two warriors pitched a tent atop the rise, attached the reins of their horses to their wrists with long ropes and retreated to a respectful distance. One faced east, the other west. Both had their strongbows unlimbered with an arrow nocked. I knew not if Kehlbrand had told them what would occur this night, but also knew if he had, they would also never speak of it. Loyalty was absolute amongst those who secured his friendship.

"In case you get bored," I said, handing Obvar's wineskin to Kehlbrand.

"Ah," he said after a small sip, eyebrows raised in appreciation. "I know this. Made from a fruit called a grape by barbarians across the Wide Sea. They reside in a kingdom beset by endless wars and irrational superstitions." He set the wineskin down next to the small fire he had lit. "They'll be glad of the peace we bring them in time."

"You intend to ride so far?"

"I intend to ride all the way around the world. For have not the priests foretold this as the course of the Mestra-Skeltir?"

I rolled my eyes at him and crawled into the tent. "Don't finish it all."

I divested myself of my oxen leather garb and lay on the furs his saddle brothers had set down for me. As ever the wind was stiff on the Steppe and the tent walls snapped continually. It was a familiar refrain and failed to disturb me as I sought the peaceful mind-state that would bring on the black veil and the True Dream.

After my first experience I had shunned my gift for a long time, fearful of what I might find once the veil parted. But curiosity, perhaps the hardest of all habits to break, eventually compelled me to seek it out. My attempts had been faltering at first; the True Dream brought brief glimpses of places and people so alien in dress and speech that whatever message I had been sent became meaningless. It was only after much experimentation that I discovered that the True Dream requires a purpose, a question to guide it towards truth.

My brother's name, I whispered inwardly as the black veil descended. What is it?

The veil duly parted and I found myself standing atop a low rise, tall grass whispering in an evening breeze. The sky had the darkened hues of twilight and I could see many fires burning in the shallow depression below. An army, I realised, taking in the sight of the veritable city of tents clustered around campfires where men sat or stood. Their armour and weapons were stacked, the design very different to the black iron breastplates and chain mail of the Hast. These consisted of the overlapping steel plates and curve bladed spears of soldiers in service to the Merchant Kings. It was the largest host I had ever seen, thousands upon thousands strong.

"Who are you?"

I started at the sound of another voice. The woman stood a dozen paces away, her appearance greatly surprising in its sheer unfamiliarity. Her garb, a simple ankle-length robe of black featuring a small white flame sigil on the breast, was not one I had seen before. Also, her features were different in shape and colouring to the people of the Merchant Realms, more like the Stahlhast with their blue eyes and pale skin. But what surprised me most, in fact shocked me, was that she was looking directly at me. She saw me.

"Who are you?" she repeated, gaping at her surroundings with wide and fearful eyes. "Where am I?"

I could only stare, dumbfounded. Never once during any previous True Dream had any of its denizens taken note of my presence. How could they? I wasn't actually here.

"Did you call me to this place?" the woman demanded, advancing towards me, suddenly angry rather than baffled. I failed to move, still caught in a snare of uncertainty and also distracted by the fact that the black-robed woman wore no shoes. Her feet were black with accumulated filth, and for some reason I found the sight oddly fascinating.

"This is not a vision from the Father," the woman said, lunging towards me. "It feels different. I can tell!"

My preoccupation with her feet, coupled with a consuming sense of utter surprise, forestalled any reaction as she actually took hold of my arms, her grip fierce. I remember noting the bloodshot condition of her eyes as her face came within inches of mine. It was a comely face, in truth, possessed of a smoothness that spoke of a woman somewhere shy of her thirtieth year. But it was crowned by an unruly mass of dark, unkempt hair, and her breath had a familiar acrid tinge that, coupled with her reddened eyes, provoked a singular deduction. A drunkard. My dream has been invaded by a drunkard with dirty feet.

"Do not try to fool me, witch!" she hissed. "What Dark design is this?"

It was the thin but pungent stream of her breath that roused me, twisting my features into a disgusted mask as I snapped my head forward, slamming my forehead against her nose. The desired effect was immediate, her hands slipping from my shoulders as she sank to her knees, groaning.

"You asked who I am," I said, drawing the long-knife from my belt and putting it to her neck. "I would know your name first."

I was gratified to see the edge of the blade press into her flesh. If we could touch each other here, it appeared we could damage each other too.

"I'll tell you nothing, servant of the Dark," she said, face tensed by pain as she stared up in defiance. "I will never betray the Father's love . . ."

She let out a pained squeak as I whipped the blade across her cheek, leaving a small but deep cut. "How do you come to be here?" I demanded. "How can you see me? How did you find your way into my dream?"

Her pain and animosity faded for a moment and she gaped up at me in baffled wonder. "You mean . . . you too are a seer? But . . . you cannot know the Father's love. He would not bestow so great a gift upon one such as you . . ."

"What father?" I demanded, angling the tip of my blade so that it hovered an inch from her eye. "What are you gabbling about?"

The sound of many horns swallowed my words, the pealing echo rising up from the army below in a great chorus of alarm. I raised my gaze from the drunken woman to see the army responding to the call. Soldiers ran to retrieve

stacked spears and don armour, crossbowmen gathered their quivers and cav-
alrymen hauled saddles to tethered horses.

"What's happening?" the woman asked. I realised I still had my knife poised
to skewer her eye and stepped away, suddenly feeling somewhat foolish.

"A battle, apparently," I replied, sheathing my blade.

"Where?" She got to her feet, wincing and rubbing at her nose. I saw that
the bruise was now fading, as was the cut on her cheek. It seemed any wounds
we inflicted here were only temporary. "Who is fighting?"

"I'm not exactly sure." I turned away to watch the army form ranks. "I suspect we are somewhere on the southern Steppe, not far from the border with
the lands of the Merchant Kings."

"Merchant Kings?"

I turned to her, brows creasing in consternation at the genuine ignorance
in her voice. How could she not have heard of the Merchant Kings? They possessed most of the wealth in the world entire. "I think it's time we introduced
ourselves properly," I said.

She drew herself up, chin jutting at a self-important angle. "I am Lady
Ivinia Morentes of the Western Marches," she said. "Servant of the Church of
the World Father, and Holy Seer by His blessing." She paused, I assumed for
dramatic effect. "Known as the Blessed Maiden to all who enjoy the Father's
love."

I shook my head in bafflement but nevertheless raised an open hand to form
the sign of peaceful greeting. "Luralyn Reyerik of the Divine Blood, daughter to
the Cova Skeld of the Stahlhast."

From the expression on her face it was clear she had no more understanding of my identity than I of hers. "You are . . ." she began with a doubtful
frown, "a seer to your people?"

"Seer?"

"You see . . . things. Events that will come to pass, or have already passed."

"Sometimes. I call it the True Dream."

"Dream." She let out a scornful snort, turning her attention to the mustering army. "No, girl, these are not dreams. They are gifts of insight from the
Father himself. Though why he chooses to share them with you, I can't imagine."

Her tone made my hand itch for the knife once more but I resisted the
impulse. "Where are your shoes?" I asked instead, casting a pointed glance at
her blackened feet.

"Worldly comforts are a barrier to the love of the Father," she sniffed, voice rich in pious certainty. "I shun them to live a simple and uncosseted life, as I shunned the life of wealth and indolence I was born to. Thus more easily will the Father's insights come to me."

I glanced at her bloodshot eyes, recalling the stink of her breath. "So you shun the comfort of shoes, but not drink."

A twitch of anger passed over her face and her response came in clipped, defensive tones. "The church's rituals often require wine, and the Books contain many references to its blessed properties."

"Oh"—my voice soured with recognition—"you're a priest."

She straightened a little, crossing her arms, her tone betraying a bitter edge as she replied, "Women are forbidden the priesthood, by order of the Holy Reader. But I serve the church better than any man. Whilst you"—she gave me a sidelong glance, eyes narrowed in calculation—"are plainly a heretic of savage origins. Perhaps that is why He brought you here, so that I may educate you in His love . . ."

"I have a knife," I reminded her, inclining my head at the valley. "Let's just watch the battle, eh? I suspect that is why we're here."

The army had mostly formed ranks by now, long lines of infantry interspersed with companies of crossbowmen with cavalry galloping to form up on the flanks. Daylight had almost completely faded, and the scene was lit by the mingled light of the campfires and the many torches carried by mounted officers. Despite the faint echo of shouted orders, the host was eerily quiet, covered by a pall of tense anticipation. I could sense no eagerness for battle here, only dread.

They were arrayed to face to the north, where I could see only a grassy plain stretching out into darkness. However, it wasn't long before I felt a familiar tremble in the earth soon followed by the sonorous murmur of approaching thunder.

"You asked about my people," I said to the woman. "You're about to meet them."

The thunder grew in volume, bespeaking a host of far-greater size than had ever been mustered on the Iron Steppe. I was forced to conclude that the army below was about to face the combined strength of every Skeld sworn to the Stahlhast. I must confess that, though it shames me these many years later, the prospect filled me with a keen anticipation.

So it was with some dismay that I heard the thunder suddenly diminish in volume and no Stahlhast host appeared out of the gloomy plain. I could still sense their presence, my ears detecting the mingled breath of thousands of horses and warriors. But, for whatever reason, their charge had come to a halt. Then, after a short pause, a broad line of about two hundred riders emerged into the flickering torchlight. Their horses moved at a steady walk, approaching the now fully formed ranks of the opposing army at an unhurried, even casual pace. I saw that, whilst many of the riders wore the garb of Stahlhast warriors, others were completely unarmoured and carried no weapons. Some, perhaps a third, did not appear to be Stahlhast at all, instead wearing the quilted jackets of the border folk.

This single line of mismatched riders came to a halt a few paces short of crossbow range, each regarding the assembled thousands before them with a fierce, determined concentration. I felt it then, the thrum of power I recognised from when the favoured members of the Divine Blood would make use of their gifts. Evidently, the woman felt it too.

"The Dark," she breathed, face now riven by fear.

A loud chorus of shouts dragged my gaze back to the valley in time to see a ball of flame rising from the centre of the first rank of Merchant soldiery. I could see men rolling on the ground, enveloped by flame. Fifty paces east another stretch of infantry some twenty strong was suddenly cast backwards as if punched by some giant invisible fist, armoured bodies tumbling like dolls. More shouts sounded as the entire first rank seemed to dissolve into disparate ruin. In one place soldiers simply slumped to the ground and lay still, in another a whole company turned on itself, assailing each other in a mad frenzy of mutual destruction. Yet more flames blossomed amongst it all, and the invisible fist struck again and again.

The confusion soon spread to successive ranks, officers struggling to keep order as company after company lost their discipline in the face of mounting panic. It was then that the Stahlhast appeared. The line of mismatched riders cantered aside as a huge arrowhead formation of mounted warriors came streaking out of the gloom at full gallop. At their head was a tall figure on a jet-black stallion, a long-bladed sabre raised high in his fist. He wore an iron helm crowned by a long horsehair plume and a grated visor that concealed his features, but I knew him instantly.

The wedge of Stahlhast struck the disordered centre of the army's line, piercing it like hot iron through softened leather, driving deep into the panicked ranks beyond. More Stahlhast charged from the plain to the east and west, each arrow of horseflesh and steel sinking deep. Within only a few heartbeats it was clear this great army was doomed, the entire valley floor a scene of slaughter. Somehow, despite the confusion and chaos of it all I had little trouble following the path of the tall rider on the black stallion. He traced a winding course across the battlefield, leaving dead and dying in his wake, his sabre moving in a constant whirl of destruction. Many are the moments now when I weep to think of my exultation then, the song of pride that rose within me at the sight of my brother's bloody journey.

"Father!" the woman at my side cried out, sinking to her knees, tears streaming down a quivering face. "Why have you cursed me with this vision?"

"Oh, shut up," I snapped, irritated by this distraction. "You should consider yourself privileged to witness this. For it is all as it should be. The Mestra-Skeltir will rise, and nothing will stop him. Long has it been foretold . . ."

I found my voice trailing to silence then as I watched the tall figure rein his horse to a halt. He sat regarding a group of kneeling Merchant soldiers, all with their weapons cast aside and heads bowed to the earth in a sign of utter supplication. My brother regarded them in unmoving contemplation for the space of perhaps a single heartbeat, then spurred his stallion forward, its hooves crushing the head of the nearest kneeling man as his sabre recommenced its deadly whirl.

I turned away, unwilling to watch the spectacle. The Stahlhast rarely took captives in the heat of battle, this I knew. Slaves would be harvested from the survivors in the aftermath. There was nothing unusual in my brother's actions. But still, why did he pause? Was he enjoying their fear?

"Mercy is weakness," I whispered, hoping the oft-spoken mantra would calm my pounding heart. "Compassion is cowardice."

I felt the True Dream begin to dissolve then, the black veil creeping into the edges of my vision as the woman ranted on in her sorrow. "Why, Father? Why show me this triumph of a blade in service to the Dark? This portent of utter destruction? How can the holy stand against such evil?"

Then the veil closed in and she was gone, perhaps back to the wakefulness in her own land. Or perhaps she spent eternity wailing away in the True Dream. All I know is that I never saw her again, in either the dream or the waking world.

Kehlbrand waited for me outside the tent, sitting cross-legged at a fire, his shadow cast long by the rising sun. Although the dream had seemed brief, it had in fact consumed my mind for many hours. I stood shuddering for a moment, chilled by both the dawn air and the echo of the Blessed Maiden's forlorn entreaties to her god.

"So, little colt," Kehlbrand said, getting to his feet and moving to wrap a wolf pelt around my shivering form. "Do you have a name for me?"

"Yes," I said, taking comfort in his smile, which had always possessed the power to banish uncertainty. "Yes, brother, I have a name."

◆ ◆ ◆

The next day Kehlbrand presented himself to the priests, standing naked and unarmed before the altar as ritual demanded. The lesser priests duly conveyed him to the presence of the Mestra-Dirhmar, who stood waiting before the Sepulchre.

The morning had been surprisingly uneventful. Usually, the rise of a new Skeltir would stir the Skeld's most renowned warriors to challenge, but only one stepped forward. He was a grizzled fellow named Irhnar, an aged veteran of near sixty summers and as many battles who had been mentor to both Tehlvar and Kehlbrand in their younger days.

"Why, old wolf?" Kehlbrand had asked Irhnar as he stepped forward, sabre raised at a lateral angle to indicate a formal challenge.

"It's ill luck for a Skeltir to ascend without blood," the old warrior said with a shrug. "And I'm tired of rising from my mats to piss six times a night. Let's get on with it, eh, boy?"

So they had fought and Kehlbrand honoured Irhnar with a suitably bloody and prolonged death. A swift end would have been an insult, after all.

I watched Kehlbrand stand before the Mestra-Dirhmar, seeing the priest's lips move as he asked his question. The distance was too great to detect my brother's answer. I could see the priest's expression clearly enough to discern a mixture of profound disappointment mingled with grim acceptance as he nodded. The True Dream, as ever, had not led me astray.

The lesser priests brought forward the dark green garb of a Skeltir and set it at Kehlbrand's feet. Once he had clothed himself, he and the Mestra-Dirhmar made their way to the altar.

"Here stands Kehlbrand Reyerik!" the priest intoned, raising my brother's arm. "Recognised today by the Servants of the Unseen as Skeltir of the Cova Skeld!"

A cheer rose from the Stahlhast throng, enthusiastically voiced by the Cova, whilst the other Skeld were more restrained. As the cheers continued I saw my brother turn and say something to the priest. The Mestra-Dirhmar's features hardened and he shook his head in stern refusal. I saw then that Kehlbrand had clasped the priest's wrist, hard enough to make him wince. As the cheering subsided Kehlbrand spoke again, and this time I heard his words: "Tell them, old man."

The Mestra-Dirhmar gritted his teeth, humiliation and pain twisting his face into a grimace. Even then I knew this to be a crucial moment, the moment when true leadership of the Hast had been decided.

"Here stands Kehlbrand Reyerik!" the great priest repeated, teeth bared as he called out to the throng, the words coloured by the rage of a defeated man. "To be known hereafter as the Darkblade!"

CHAPTER ONE

T he arrow slammed into the trunk of a pine an inch from his head. Vaelin Al Sorna stared at the fletching as it vibrated before his eyes, feeling a sting on his nose and a trickle of blood left by the shaft's barbed head. He hadn't heard the archer who loosed the arrow, nor had he heard the betraying creak of string and stave.

To an onlooker his reaction would have seemed swift and immediate, rolling to the right, coming to his knees, bow drawn and arrow loosed in a single smooth movement. But he knew it to be slow, even as he saw the archer, running now with his horn raised to his lips, take the shaft directly in the back and fall dead. *Slow.*

There was a soft rustle at his side as Ellese appeared out of the surrounding carpet of ferns, nocked bow in hand. "The camp, Uncle," she said, slightly breathless with eagerness as she started to rise. "We need to move quickly . . ."

Her words died as Vaelin reached out to clamp a hand over her mouth, exerting enough force to keep her crouching. He held her there until the next arrow came, arcing down from the forest canopy to sink into the earth half a dozen feet away. A searching arrow, Master Hutril would have called it. Always useful when flushing prey. But not today.

Vaelin met Ellese's dark, glaring eyes and raised his own to the treetops before removing his hand. *He won't blow his horn just yet,* he told her, hands moving in the sign language so laboriously taught to her over the preceding months. *That would reveal his position. I'll run to the right.* He turned, tensing in anticipation of a sprint, then paused to add, *Don't miss.*

He surged to his feet, boots pounding on the forest floor as he ran, describing a winding course through the trees. This time he heard the bowstring's thrum and threw himself behind the broad trunk of an ancient yew, glimpsing an explosion of splintered bark in the corner of his eye. A second later came the sound of another bowstring, the note deeper, possessed of an almost musical precision that bespoke the power of the weapon and the skill of its wielder. A brief pause, then the thud of a body falling from a tall height to the forest floor.

Vaelin remained crouched behind the yew, eyes closed as his ears drank in the song of the forest. It wasn't long before the chitter of birds, stilled by the unwelcome intrusion, began to return and the wind carried no more trace of sweating, fearful men.

He emerged from his refuge to find Ellese busily searching the body of the outlaw her arrow had plucked from the treetops. Her movements were swift and practised, hands betraying no sign of a tremble despite having just wrested the life from a man. He knew she had killed before in Cumbrael, during a brief and quickly crushed resurgence of the ever-troublesome Sons of the Trueblade. *It doesn't vex her at all,* Reva had written in the letter she sent north along with her adopted daughter. *Which vexes me greatly.*

He saw scant resemblance to Reva in this girl, hardly surprising given the fact that they shared no blood. Her hair was black and her eyes dark, and she was perhaps an inch shorter, if a little thicker of limb. However, the apparent immunity to the effects of killing was a recognisably familial trait she had clearly picked up somewhere along the road. One she shared with the man she called uncle.

"Bluestone," she said, tossing aside the dead man's purse and holding up a handful of gleaming azure pebbles. "Wrapped in cotton so they wouldn't clink." She angled her head as she surveyed the outlaw's corpse. "Knew his business, at least." She glanced up at Vaelin before adding with a grin, "Not well enough, though."

Vaelin crouched to retrieve the man's bow, a flat-staved hunting weapon typical to all fiefs of the Realm, except Cumbrael. Had the fellow possessed a longbow and the skill to use it, Vaelin knew he would likely be dead now.

"Check his scalp," he told Ellese, who duly whipped away the man's woollen cap, revealing a shaven head. Vaelin used his boot to turn the corpse's head until he found it, a crude tattoo forming a dark crimson stain amidst the grey stubble. "The Bloody Sparrows," he said, moving away.

The outlaw he had killed lay some twenty paces off, facedown with Vaelin's arrow protruding from his back at a near-vertical angle. Vaelin worked the shaft loose, grunting with the effort of extracting the barbed head from the bony trap of the man's spine, before turning him over.

"Jumin Vek," he said after a brief survey of the blotchy, pockmarked face.

"You know him?" Ellese asked.

"I should. I arrested him up on a Queen's Warrant four years ago. He left a trail of murder, rape and thievery all along the roads of Renfael before fetching up in the Reaches. I packed him off on a ship to face the noose in Frostport."

"Seems he managed an escape."

Or bribed his way clear, Vaelin thought. It was an all-too-common occurrence these days. With so much money to be made stealing and smuggling the bounty of the Northern Reaches, it seemed as if every outlaw had the means to buy their way out of trouble. As Tower Lord, and therefore the queen's appointed warden of this land, the frequency with which Vaelin was obliged to recapture the dregs of the Realm made him less than scrupulous in observing her royal edict against immediate execution.

"Another Bloody Sparrow?" Ellese asked.

"No." Vaelin tossed away Jumin Vek's cap to reveal a shock of thick, greasy hair. He grasped the man's chin and turned it, revealing a more accomplished image inked into the sallow flesh of his neck. "The Damned Rats. They're mostly disgraced former Realm Guard."

"So we face two gangs today?"

"I doubt it. Lord Orven wiped out most of the Bloody Sparrows last winter. It seems the Rats found room for some survivors."

He relieved the unfortunate Jumin Vek of his purse, finding it to contain two nuggets of gold along with a few bluestones.

"Your nose is bleeding, Uncle," Ellese observed as he rose.

Vaelin took a rag from his belt, soaked it with a small bottle of corr tree oil and pressed it to the cut on his nose. He swallowed a grunt of pain as the concoction seeped its fiery way into the wound, unable to suppress the sense that it hadn't stung quite so much in his youth.

"Fetch the others," he told Ellese, dousing his face with water from his canteen to wash away the residual blood. "Meet me at the canyon's edge. And, Ellese," he added as she turned away. "The bluestones."

He held out his hand, meeting her gaze until she gave a huff of annoyance and handed over the stones, griping in a low mutter, "You have me hunting scum for no pay."

"Your mother sent you to me for an education. If you want paid work, there's plenty to be had in the North Guard, or the mines. Until sold, under law bluestone and gold belong to the queen. You know that." He pocketed the stones and jerked his head in dismissal. "On your way."

◆ ◆ ◆

It transpired that the outlaw camp was in fact a stockade formed of a semi-circular enclosure arcing out from the eastern wall of a canyon known as Ultin's Gulch. The place had been named in honour of the Reaches' most famed miner, a man Vaelin remembered fondly from the Liberation War.

Ever a cheerful soul, Ultin had returned to the Reaches bearing the queen's order to scrape all the wealth he could from the mines, thereby filling the royal coffers to meet the escalating costs of war. Honoured for his efforts as a Sword of the Realm with a generous accompanying pension, Ultin had politely refused Vaelin's offer of a position as Lord Overseer of Mineworks. Instead, he retired to a smallholding near North Tower where, over the course of the next three years, he proceeded to drink himself to death. *It was the war, my lord,* his widow had told Vaelin the day they gave her husband's body to the fire. *All those murdered souls, murdered children. The men he lost at Alltor . . . all of it. He could never get it out of his head.*

Vaelin spared a brief thought for Ultin's memory before focusing his attention on the stockade. It was plainly new built, the timbers forming its defensive wall still green and unseasoned, although they seemed solid enough. The occupants had constructed a lookout post atop the canyon wall, providing a no doubt fine view of the surrounding landscape. Vaelin knew the ground to the east consisted of a half-mile-long expanse of bare rock, across which no attacking force could expect to approach undetected.

The canyon floor was similarly lacking in cover but also narrower, allowing for a rapid assault. Even so, he didn't relish the prospect and found this new tactic of fortification troubling. Usually, the various outlaw and smuggling gangs would establish temporary camps deep in the forest or the more inaccessible crags from which they would raid the caravan routes. Now it appeared this particular group had opted for a permanent home. *Are they getting bolder?* he wondered. *Or just more desperate.*

He detected only the smallest sign of the Cumbraelin's approach, just a faint scrape of buckskin on grass before the man appeared at his side, lying flat as Vaelin did.

"My lord," he said.

"Master Tallspear." Vaelin glanced behind to see the war party of Bear People emerge from the forest at a crawl, spears and bows held low so as not to break the silhouette of the skyline.

"You can see it's as we said," Tallspear said, nodding at the outlaws' stockade. Over the course of recent years Vaelin had often pondered the fact that Tallspear's face possessed only the most meagre vestige of the man who had once tried very hard to kill him. The Cumbraelin's features were still the hardened, weathered mask of a lifelong hunter, but the fiery glint of fanaticism had long since faded from his gaze. Apart from the longbow he carried, his garb was that of the Bear People and he spoke their language, still beyond Vaelin's skills to master, with an easy fluency. Although Vaelin still couldn't help thinking of him as Cumbraelin, in any way that mattered he was now a hunter of the Bear People clan, evidenced by the name they had given him. Vaelin knew he would probably never learn the man's birth name, and found himself content in his ignorance.

"You said you found this a month ago?" Vaelin asked.

"Twenty-five days, to be precise. It wasn't here two weeks before. Our people come here fairly regularly, plenty of beavers to be trapped in the river."

"So they saw you?"

Tallspear responded with a frown that was both amused and faintly insulted.

"Apologies." Vaelin turned his gaze back to the stockade. "How often do they raid?"

"That's the curious thing, my lord. They don't, as far as we can tell. Very few tracks in the surrounding country, except what you'd expect from the occasional hunting party. For the most part they just stay in there. Truth be told, we were tempted to leave them be, but the elders felt we should honour our treaty with the Tower Man."

Vaelin inclined his head in thanks. Since being granted leave to settle in the Reaches after their forced migration from the icy wastes to the north, the Bear People had consistently proven themselves loyal if insular subjects of the Realm. "Be sure to tell them their consideration is appreciated."

"I will, my lord. Also, two-thirds of the spoils when we're done would also greatly emphasise the honour in which you hold the Bear People."

Vaelin bit down a sigh. After being spared execution and finding a home with the Bear People, Tallspear had forsaken the god-worshipping fanaticism that had brought him to this land intent on assassinating its Tower Lord. Instead, these days the Cumbraelin's reserves of zeal were now fully employed in the role of chief bargainer for his adopted tribe, keen to protect them from the greed of the Realm-born.

"Half," Vaelin said. "Including profits from the sale of any gold and bluestone we recover."

The hunter seemed about to argue the point but fell silent at a loud click from behind. Vaelin turned to see a diminutive young woman crouched nearby, a small black bear at her side. The woman's name was Iron Eyes, and it was easy to see where she got it in the scowl she directed at Tallspear. As the only shaman remaining to the Bear People, she was the closest thing they had to an overall leader. She was also Tallspear's wife and mother to their three children.

She clicked her tongue again before telling her husband, "Don't be rude," in clipped but well-spoken Realm Tongue. "Half is acceptable, Tower Man," she added, turning to Vaelin. "But there must be a blood price for any hunters called to join the Green Fire."

"Of course." Vaelin inclined his head before returning his attention to the stockade. He counted a dozen sentries on the wall, each bearing either bow or crossbow. Once they realised an attack was under way more would surely join them, meaning a charge across the floor of the gulch would inevitably cost lives. In addition to the forty or so Bear People, he also had another sixty North Guard, surely enough to put the matter beyond doubt regardless of how many arrows the outlaws cast their way.

"Best wait for darkness, my lord," Tallspear said, evidently following his line of thought. "We can easily get within fifty paces of that wall come midnight, put up a volley to cover a charge for the gate. A few blows from a decent-sized ram should be enough to gain entry."

"They'll be expecting their scouts to return come nightfall," Vaelin said, shaking his head. "Waiting for midnight will take too long." He thought a moment longer before nodding at the small bear at Iron Eyes' side. "Does he have a name?"

"Little Teeth," Iron Eyes replied, running a hand through the beast's thick fur. He let out a contented huff and nuzzled her side in return.

"Wise Bear's beast was called Iron Claw," Vaelin recalled. "He carried him all the way across the ice to the land of the Dark Hearts. There we fought a great battle. You know this?"

Iron Eyes scowled again, nodding cautiously. The old shaman had never returned from the ice and neither the Bear People nor anyone else had discovered his fate. Vaelin knew they still hoped for his return and that his continued failure to do so was a decidedly sore point. "I know this," the shaman said.

"Iron Claw was brave," Vaelin told her. "How brave is Little Teeth?"

◆ ◆ ◆

They set out the moment the sun dipped behind the eastern peaks. Vaelin, in company with Tallspear, Iron Eyes, Ellese and a dozen North Guard, made a silent descent into the gulch. They forded the narrow but swift flowing river running through the centre of the canyon and crawled the remaining few hundred paces to a shallow depression within bowshot of the stockade. Once halted, Vaelin nodded to Iron Eyes. The shaman briefly ran a hand over Little Teeth's snout before fixing her gaze upon his. After a short pause both bear and shaman blinked in unison before the animal loped away into the gloom, making for the south-facing stretch of the stockade wall.

"What now, Uncle?" Ellese asked in a whisper that drew a sharp glance from Vaelin.

Use your hands! he signed in annoyance.

She lowered her head, hands moving in reluctant contrition. *Sorry.*

Now we wait, he told her, nodding at her bow. *Be ready.*

He watched her nock an arrow to the string, slender but firm hands grasping the intricately carved stave. The weapon was a true thing of beauty, fashioned from wych elm decorated in various martial motifs carved by an expert hand. *A bow of Arren,* Reva had called it. *Quite possibly the last in the world. I lost her sister in the Boraelin Ocean. There's a standing reward of a hundred golds for anyone who brings me another. As yet, no one's claimed it.*

He knew the weapon was said to possess some form of divine blessing, the more ardent followers of the World Father and his Blessed Lady ascribing preternatural power and accuracy to what was, in essence, a length of shaped wood. However, the feats he had seen Reva and her daughter perform with this bow often gave him cause to wonder.

He turned back to Iron Eyes, seeing the empty cast to the woman's gaze as she lay immobile at her husband's side. Her mind, he knew, was elsewhere. The sight provoked a rush of memory, another woman sitting on a hillside far away in both time and distance, her eyes empty as her soul soared free of her body . . .

Vaelin turned away, flexing his fingers to banish a sudden tremble before nocking an arrow to his bowstring.

"He climbs . . ." Iron Eyes said a few moments later, eyes still unfocused and voice little more than a hiss in the darkness. "He reaches the top . . . There is a man . . ." A spasm passed over her features, her lips drawing back from her teeth in an echo of a snarl before the placid mask returned. "Now there is not . . . The air smells of drink and five leaf . . . Men sleep and snore, others walk the walls . . . All eyes are turned out, not in."

Lines creased her brow and she cocked her head a little, as if straining to hear something. "Voices . . . two men in argument . . . They speak of scouts . . . of men who should be here but are not."

"The gate," Vaelin said, although he doubted she could hear him in this state.

Iron Eyes lapsed into a silence that seemed to stretch for many minutes when it could only have been seconds. Vaelin nudged Ellese to silence as she let out a soft groan of impatience.

"He is there . . ." Iron Eyes whispered finally. "The gate is sealed with thick rope . . . His teeth are little, but they are sharp, his jaws are strong . . ."

Vaelin's hands moved in front of Ellese's eyes. *First and second from the left,* he told her before pointing at the sentries on the wall. Moving to Tallspear's side he put his mouth close to the Cumbraelin's ear, speaking in a low murmur. "The two on the right. Loose when I do."

As Ellese and Tallspear rose to a crouch, Vaelin readied his own bow, fingers hooking the string on either side of the arrow's base. He focused on the two men standing directly over the gate, still arguing and oblivious to the bear busily gnawing through the ropes below. The distance was a little under a hundred paces. He may not be the finest archer ever to emerge from the House of the Sixth Order, but he was far from the worst.

He heard Iron Eyes let out a soft sigh followed by the creak of the gate swinging open to reveal Little Teeth contentedly chewing on a length of rope. Vaelin, seeing the men on the wall suddenly forget their argument, drew and loosed an arrow at the tallest. Ellese and Tallspear both loosed a fraction of a second later, arrows streaking through the night air to send the sentries tumbling from the wall. The shorter of the two outlaws reacted quickly, subsiding into a crouch but not before Vaelin's second arrow took him in the shoulder. He fell from the wall, landing heavily on the other side of the open gateway and shouting in shock at the sight of the bear who greeted him with an inquisitive growl. The man's shouts died as Vaelin lowered his aim, sending his third arrow through the gateway and into the stricken outlaw's chest, muttering a curse as he loosed. He had hoped to get inside without raising an alarm, but rarely did any battle conform to a plan.

"North Guard up!" Vaelin called out, rising and reaching over his shoulder to draw his sword. He ran for the gate with the North Guard close on his heels, hearing Tallspear's hunting horn pealing out a summons to the others waiting in the forest.

A few outlaws came stumbling from the shadows in various states of undress, attempting to form a barrier across the portal. Their aim was quickly frustrated by Little Teeth, who began to whirl, lashing out with his claws and sending the outlaws into confusion. One man staggered back from the beast, clutching a bleeding arm, placing himself directly into Vaelin's path as he reached the gate. He made the mistake of drawing the knife on his belt and died for it, Vaelin jabbing the tip of his Order blade neatly through the ribs to pierce his heart, leaving him kneeling as blood swelled his mouth.

The remaining would-be defenders were quickly cut down by the North Guard, though the obscenity-laden defiance they screamed out in the course of the brief but frenzied fight ensured any last vestige of surprise had now vanished. Looking around, Vaelin saw the interior of the stockade featured only a few huts and no structure large enough to accommodate the kind of numbers that must dwell here. However, his gaze soon alighted on an opening in the canyon wall. It was a typical mineshaft common to the Reaches, buttressed with timber and wide enough to allow entry by five or more men at once.

They didn't come here to raid for riches, Vaelin surmised. *They came to dig for them.*

He could hear a rising tumult from within the shaft, accompanied by a flicker of torchlight that grew in brightness with every passing second. Working a mine, he knew, required many hands, probably a good deal more than he had reckoned to find in this place.

"Line out!" he barked to the North Guard, then turned to Ellese and Tallspear, jerking his head at a nearby ladder. "Get on the wall. Loose as soon as they emerge, see if we can choke them at the entrance."

He nocked another arrow to his own bow and took up position in the centre of the guardsmen's line. A glance behind showed the remaining North Guard and Bear People moving rapidly across the canyon floor. Judging by the sounds emerging from the mineshaft, Vaelin doubted they would arrive before this battle began in earnest.

"Lay it on thick, lads," he told the guardsmen. "Don't want me to tell your families you fell to a scum-blade, do you?"

He received a chorus of grim affirmation in response, even a few chuckles. Those with bows nocked arrows, and the others took a firmer grip on their swords. They were mostly veterans of the Liberation War. Having fought all the way from the Realm to the gates of Volar, witnessing countless horrors in the process, they weren't about to succumb to fear in the face of outlaws, however many they might face this night.

Vaelin half drew his bow, eyes locked on the tunnel, now glowing brightly with burgeoning torchlight. He frowned at the sounds emerging from within. At first he had thought it the clamour of desperate men girding themselves for a fight, but now realised it to be a discordant chorus not unlike the din of battle. It continued on for some time as no new foe emerged from the shaft, rich in screams and rage and, as it wore on, terror.

Abruptly, the cacophony ended, heralding a short interval of eerie silence before two figures appeared in the shaft entrance. They were silhouetted by the glow, one standing tall, the other kneeling. Vaelin noted that the standing figure appeared to be holding the kneeler by the neck. As the kneeling man struggled, the other jerked him to stillness, Vaelin detecting the distinct clink of a chain as he did so. Hearing the creak of a drawn bow from the wall,

Vaelin stepped forward, raising his hand. "Hold!" he called out, glancing up to see Ellese lowering her bow and frowning at him in bemusement.

"Wait here," Vaelin told the North Guard, tossing his bow to the nearest one. He approached the shaft with his sword held low and to the side, his free hand raised and open. He came to a halt when he could make out the two figures clearly, finding he recognised one but not the other.

"Termin Resk," he said, squinting at the kneeling man. He was a stocky fellow of middling years, a former Realm Guard sergeant, now leader of the Damned Rats, with a dire reputation to match. Resk gasped out something in response; his words, either a plea or an expression of defiance, were quickly choked off by a tightening of the chain around his neck. The outlaw's stubby fingers clawed at the iron links to little effect, his head increasingly resembling a quivering, reddened blob.

Vaelin's gaze tracked along the chain to the manacle on the wrist of the man holding Resk. Taking the full measure of the fellow, Vaelin found him to be taller than himself by an inch or more. The man's bare chest was broad and impressively muscled if marred by numerous scars, some recent, and Vaelin recognised the telltale mark of a whip. The sweat of recent exertion shone on the man's dark skin and he met Vaelin's gaze with a cool, appraising stare beneath brows marked by a series of pale, precisely placed scars.

"You are far from the empire," Vaelin observed, speaking in Alpiran.

The man's eyes narrowed at the words. From his colouring, Vaelin knew him to be of the southern provinces where the Emperor's tongue wasn't always known, but he saw comprehension in his face.

"It is not my empire," the man replied, his Alpiran accented but clearly spoken. He jerked the chain, causing Resk to grunt in pain, eyes bulging now. "You are this one's enemy?" he asked.

"He is a . . . bandit," Vaelin replied, using the term most commonly ascribed to outlaws in the Alpiran Empire. "I enforce the law in these lands."

"Then you serve *her*." The tall man's eyes betrayed a small glimmer Vaelin recognised: hope. "You serve the Queen of Fire."

"She doesn't like that name." Vaelin gave a formal bow. "Vaelin Al Sorna, Tower Lord of the Northern Reaches by the grace of Queen Lyrna Al Nieren. And you are?"

He saw the tall man's hope joined by another emotion then, his brows bunching with a particular sense of recognition Vaelin hadn't seen for many years. "Alum Vi Moreska," he said, the muscles of his forearms bunching as his fists tightened the chain. In response Resk let out a final, choking gurgle and fell limp, all light fading from his bulging eyes. "I request safe harbour," Alum Vi Moreska said, unfurling the chain from Resk's corpse with a skillful flick of his wrists. "For myself and my people."

Vaelin nodded at the mineshaft. "There are more of you in there?"

"Many." The man met Vaelin's gaze once more, letting out a hard, shame-filled sigh as he sank to one knee. "On behalf of the Moreska Clan, I pledge our allegiance to the Great Queen in the hope she will bestow upon us the gift of her renowned mercy and compassion."

CHAPTER TWO

In all, they had taken six outlaws alive; the rest, over a hundred in number, had perished in either the stockade or the mine. Captain Nohlen, commander of the North Guard contingent, reported a total of four hundred and twenty-three people in chains in the mine, plus another thirty-two corpses besides the outlaws'.

"Bad business, my lord," the man advised Vaelin in his typically clipped tones. "They didn't die easy. Those that didn't perish in the fight had been worked to death, I'd say."

The slaves were all of the same clan as Alum, the Moreska, and Vaelin could find none with an unscarred back. There were no children or old people amongst their ranks.

"The pirates took them away," Alum said after describing how their ships had come under attack by a flotilla of pirate vessels in the Arathean Ocean. "We know not where. If the gods are kind, they were given a swift death. If not . . ." A shadow passed across the man's face, and his nostrils flared as he fought to master himself.

"When did this happen?" Vaelin asked him.

They sat together at a fire pit where the outlaws had cooked their meals, the embers still warm and littered with bones. Alum had taken a spear from one of the dead and used it to describe a series of intricate symbols in the ashes as he spoke. "Six months, maybe more. A man loses sense of time when he labours beyond sight of the sun."

"The pirates? Do you know which port they called home?"

"They spoke a language not known to us, but had the eyes and faces of those from the lands of the Merchant Kings. Many bore fresh scars, and their ships had plainly seen recent battle. They had the look of desperate men, so desperate they didn't hesitate to kill any who cast a defiant glance their way. After weeks at sea they brought those of us still alive to this land of damp and cold, where they sold us to these dogs so that we might dig into this mountain for the metal they craved."

"Why were your people sailing the Arathean?"

Alum's spear paused in the ash as an even deeper sadness crept over his face. "This," he said, jabbing the spear at the symbol he had drawn, "is the sign of Malua, Lord of Sand and Sky. These"—the spear shifted to the smaller symbols on either side—"are his children, Jula, Lady of the Rains, and Kula, Lord of the Winds."

"Your gods," Vaelin said.

"A word we do not use. In our tongue they are 'Protectors.' Since the time of the first feet upon the sand, we have held true to Malua and his children. The Emperors always respected this. As long as we pledged loyalty with the dawn of each new season and sent our warriors to join their host when they called, we were left in peace. The Empress"—Alum's jaws bunched and his lips twitched in restrained anger—"feels differently."

"Empress Emeren wanted you to worship the Alpiran gods?"

Alum nodded. "She tried to sunder us from the loving arms of the Protectors. She sent envoys that spoke of unity, of how all subjects of the empire must now come together because the Queen of Fire, having seized all the lands of the Volarians, now looked upon ours with envious eyes. More than that the Empress sent people to settle lands that had always been ours, lands the Emperors had long shielded from outsiders. They scraped furrows in the sacred earth to grow crops, hunted all the animals they could find, leaving none for the next season, claimed the wells as their own. When we drove them off she sent soldiers. We are fierce but they were many. Long we fought but the blood of our clan seeped away with every battle."

Alum paused to look around, pointing as his gaze alighted on Captain Nohlen. "That man has skin like mine," he said. "The old ones told stories of another tribe that had once fought against the Emperor and fled across the sea to find refuge in the north lands. We sought to follow their example."

"The exiles came here four generations ago, it is true," Vaelin said. "They were made welcome, as are you." He gestured at the symbols in the ashes. "And your Protectors. As for your children, the Merchants' Guild in North Tower keeps a ledger of all pirate sightings. Perhaps some clue to their home port can be found there. You're welcome to accompany me on my return."

"I will. As for my people?"

"They are now free subjects of the Greater Unified Realm and may do as they wish within the confines of the law. However"—Vaelin raised his hands, gesturing at their surroundings—"Captain Nohlen tells me the seams are rich here. If you wish, it's within my power to grant licence for you to remain. All gold mined within the Reaches belongs to the queen, but you will receive one-quarter of the price gained for every shipment sold."

"We are hunters, not miners."

Vaelin glanced at a huddle of Moreska nearby. Unlike Alum, most were stick thin and hollow cheeked from lack of food, many with glistening wounds from recent whippings. "Your people need a home," Vaelin said. "At least for now. As for hunting, the surrounding forest is yours as far as the broad river to the north. Beyond that the land belongs to the Bear People. They're a generous folk, but jealous in guarding their hunting grounds."

Alum looked away, his furrowed brow bespeaking both puzzlement and contemplation. "I am not Clan Chief of the Moreska. He died fighting the pirates. But we were brothers in war if not blood. Together we answered Emperor Aluran's call when your people came to steal the ports on the Erinean coast. Together we marched with the host and together we witnessed the night when the man they called the Hopekiller came out of the desert to wreak fire and fury upon us." He blinked and met Vaelin's gaze. "The name they gave you, it doesn't seem to fit."

A small laugh escaped Vaelin's lips, surprising in the bitterness he heard in it. It all seemed so long ago now, and yet the name Hopekiller still lingered like a ragged, stinking cloak he could never cast off. "It fit well enough then," he said. "But I've earned a few more since."

"I consider any blood debt settled by your actions this night," Alum said, his voice possessed of a grave note that implied a sense of formal agreement. "But still, I feel the scales are weighed in your favour. Even so." Alum's gaze tracked to the small cluster of captive outlaws. "I find I must ask for one more thing."

◆ ◆ ◆

"You can't hang this one, Uncle. He's far too pretty." Ellese favoured the captive outlaw with a smile, running a finger along the youth's jaw to the tip of his chin. "Can't I keep him? As a pet, I mean."

The outlaw stared up at Vaelin, pleading eyes bright in a pale, delicate face that contrasted with the brutish aspect of his fellow captives. "This is the one?" he asked Alum.

The Moreska nodded. "It was him."

Vaelin moved closer to the captive, watching him tense in fearful anticipation. "Name?" Vaelin demanded.

The outlaw swallowed and coughed before forming a thin, barely audible reply, Vaelin detecting the broad vowels of southern Renfael in his voice. "Sehmon Vek, my lord."

"Kin to Jumin Vek?"

"My cousin."

"Your cousin's dead. My niece killed him in the forest."

Sehmon Vek glanced at Ellese, who replied with a broad smile. "Then she saved me a job, my lord," the youth said, narrow shoulders moving in a shrug.

Vaelin grunted and inclined his head at Alum. "This man tells me you aided his people. Gave them extra rations, brought water when it was forbidden. He also says you unshackled their chains upon hearing our attack. Is that true?"

At this the other outlaws stirred, an angry murmur rising and one attempting to get to his feet, raising his bound hands in an effort to club the young outlaw. "You treacherous little fucker!"

One of the North Guard stepped forward and slammed the pommel of his sword into the man's face, sending him sprawling and bloody to the ground. The others soon quieted as Vaelin's gaze tracked over them.

"Never wanted any part of this, my lord," Sehmon Vek said. "My family's been outside the law for as long as any can remember, that's true enough. But the Veks have always been smugglers, not slavers. After my pa died, Jumin came back from the north with promises of more gold than we'd ever seen." He paused, casting a glance at Alum, rich in shame. "Didn't tell us we'd be knee deep in filth whipping folk raw every day. It weren't what I was raised for. But I did my part in it and I'll take my due. It's said the Departed take a dim view of those who die with lies on their lips."

Vaelin searched Sehmon's face for some sign of deception, some artifice hidden beneath the mask of his contrition. He found nothing, only the misery of guilt and the knowledge of impending death.

"The Queen's Word decrees that slavery has no place in her Realm," he said, addressing the outlaws as one. "Any found engaged in this vile practice are subject to execution without trial. Captain Nohlen."

The captain stepped forward, saluting smartly. "My lord."

Vaelin pointed at Sehmon Vek. "Release this one. Hang the others."

"Yes, my lord."

The youth's bonds were cut whilst the remaining captives were dragged towards the gate. A couple shouted pleas for clemency; the rest either struggled vainly and hurled obscenities or slouched dumbly towards their end.

"Alum Vi Moreska has asked for your life," Vaelin told the young outlaw. "I am minded to give it to him. This is my sentence for you, Sehmon Vek. You now belong to him. You will serve him as he sees fit until the day he decides to release you. This is not slavery, merely indentured servitude, which is within my province to impose. Under law you do, however, have the right to refuse." Vaelin gave a pointed glance at the gate where the noose was being thrown over the lintel.

"I . . ." The lad faltered, swallowed hard and tried again. "I most happily agree, my lord."

◆　◆　◆

"Could've just given him to me," Ellese admonished Vaelin as he stood in the centre of the compound to watch the executions. "I saw him first." She fidgeted for a moment, her agitation increasing as a noose was slipped over the first outlaw's head. "Do we really have to watch this?"

"*You* don't," Vaelin said. "*I* do. And if your mother had ordered it, she would watch too. When you order a killing, you need to see it, lest it becomes too easy."

Tallspear appeared at Vaelin's side with his typical absence of noise, his gaze dark as he watched a trio of North Guard haul on the rope. The outlaw's desperate sobs for mercy died as he was dragged aloft, legs kicking in a frantic dance.

"I recall a time when your heart was more merciful, my lord," the hunter said. "Even at the dawn of war."

"That war ended," Vaelin replied. "Whereas this one never seems to."

"Was I any less wretched than these men? Any less deserving of death?"

"Perhaps not. But then I . . . knew there to be a chance for you. If the Bear People found you, there was a path to peace. Such insights are beyond me now, and the queen's justice is all I have to offer."

Ellese let out a small whimper at the sight of the outlaw's body spasming, the crotch of his trews becoming sodden as his bowels loosened in death. *Just a child after all,* Vaelin mused, watching the blood drain from the girl's face. *The thrill of the hunt and the fight is one thing, this is another.*

The outlaw's legs kicked a few more times before he slackened. Piss mingled with shit to cover his boots before dripping to the ground where it steamed in the chilled night air. Ellese gagged and turned away, hurrying off to a shadowed corner to loudly disgorge the contents of her stomach.

"She will truly be Lady Governess of Cumbrael one day?" Tallspear asked, eyebrow raised to a dubious angle.

"As is her mother's wish," Vaelin told him.

"I did so much in service to the World Father and the Fief." Tallspear shook his head, a new depth of sorrow in his voice. "It all seems like a dream now. An old nightmare that troubles me only rarely. Sometimes I wonder if I deserve this life. Iron Eyes, our children, the people who took in a starving madman they found wandering the woods. It feels like gifts to an unworthy soul. I suppose that's when I lost him, the Father. For why would he ever reward one such as me?"

Vaelin found himself seized by sudden anger. This man he had spared, this former assassin and fanatic bemoaning his lost god. He had an urge to beat this self-pitying fool to the ground. As it often did, anger carried Vaelin back to the craggy hilltop in northern Volaria, the wind and the rain beating at his benumbed flesh as he held Dahrena, her body a small, limp thing in his arms. *She spoke of how much she loved you,* the Ally had said. *But mostly she worried for the child you made together . . .*

"My lord?"

Vaelin blinked, realising Tallspear had retreated a step, face wary. Vaelin turned back to the gate, where another outlaw was being dragged towards the noose, feet scrabbling at the muddy ground, his face rendered childlike by desperate sobs. "Captain Nohlen!" Vaelin called out.

"My lord?"

"This is taking too long. Behead the rest and have done. I'm keen to be gone from here."

◆ ◆ ◆

He left Nohlen and half the North Guard at the gulch as security against any outlaw gangs who might attempt to seize the mine. At Alum's urging the Moreska agreed to remain, though most seemed disinclined to keep working the seams. Only half the gold ore accrued by the outlaws could be packed onto the mules they found in the stables. Vaelin told Nohlen he would send a suitably well-protected caravan for the remainder on return to North Tower.

Before setting off he watched Alum consult with a small group of Moreska. There were six of them, four men and two women comprising the oldest souls to be found amongst the freed captives. They joined hands to form a circle with Alum kneeling in the centre, head lowered as he spoke in a tongue Vaelin didn't know. He was struck by the sadness of the other Moreska, each face drawn in sorrow, tears visible on their cheeks.

When Alum had finished speaking, one of them, a woman marginally older than the others, raised her eyes to look at Vaelin. Like Alum, her brows were inscribed with a series of precisely placed scars, but hers were more numerous. Vaelin found her gaze uncomfortably direct, possessed of a piercing quality that he knew saw a great deal. A faint, plaintive echo of something lost stirred in his heart as the woman continued to regard him, making him wonder what tune the blood-song would have sung at this moment. The loss of his gift was several years distant now, but there were occasions when he felt its absence keenly, like an old wound aching on a cold morning. There were even times like this, when he fancied he still heard it, a faint tune just out of reach, a tune that brought insight and surety, a tune that had saved him more times than he could count. *A tune lost in the Beyond*, he reminded himself, straining for it once again but failing to grasp more than the faintest echo that may have just been born of his yearning. But, blood-song or not, he somehow still sensed this woman's gift. *What does she see?*

As if hearing his unspoken question, the woman blinked and returned her gaze to Alum, speaking softly in their shared language. It had a melodi-ous quality, possessed of a near-musical cadence that made it seem as if she were reciting poetry. When she fell silent she and the other Moreska all unclasped their hands and turned their backs on Alum, walking away with neither glance nor word as he continued to kneel on the ground.

"If you would, my lord."

Vaelin looked down from his horse to find Tallspear proffering a piece of parchment. "The name of our factor in North Tower," the hunter explained. "He'll oversee receipt of payment for our efforts here."

"The Bear People have a factor now?" Vaelin asked.

"As you know, the Reaches are full of rogues keen to cheat the unwary. Last winter a merchant came to the Sound offering strings of beads for all the beaver pelts we could provide. He was lucky to be chased off with only a spear jab to the arse."

"I'll see to it." Vaelin pocketed the parchment. "I would ask that you have a care for these people," he added, gesturing to the Moreska. "Provide food until they can hunt for themselves."

"It's not our way to shun those in need." Tallspear smiled tightly and moved back, then paused, a cautious look in his eye. "Hunting outlaws is not truly a war, my lord. Merely the management of vermin. The wars are over. You do know that, I trust?"

Vaelin gave a very small laugh as a long-remembered phrase came to mind. "There's always another war."

"Only if you go looking for it." Tallspear gave a formal bow of farewell and strode away.

◆ ◆ ◆

"Your walls aren't big enough," Alum observed eight days later as they reined in atop a hill from which the whole of North Tower could be seen. Vaelin had to concede the man had a point. In the years since his return to the Reaches a once-small but bustling port had transformed into a minor city. Homes and storehouses now extended a good distance beyond the walls. Some months ago, Vaelin had commissioned plans for a new defensive barrier, much to the objections of the Merchants' Guild, dismayed at the prospect of a levy to cover the costs, despite their ever-more-swollen coffers. But such greed-inspired grumbling hadn't been the reason he put the plans aside; at the rate the place was expanding, any new walls would soon also be rendered obsolete.

"Gold is like water in this Realm," he told the Moreska. "It makes things grow."

Alum gave a rueful shake of his head, both amused and baffled. "Those born to the sands will never understand the allure of a shiny yellow metal too soft to even make a decent spear-point." Vaelin detected a wistful note to his voice that told of a profound longing for lands now lost, perhaps forever.

"The world is ever changeable," he said. "Perhaps one day . . ."

"No, my friend." Alum smiled and shook his head. "There will be no return to the sands for the Moreska. The Protectors do not live there any-more, so neither will we."

Vaelin thought back to their departure from Ultin's Gulch, the sight of this man kneeling in the circle of elders. "What did it mean?" he asked. "When your people turned their backs?"

"It meant that as our clan can no longer return to the sands, I can no lon-ger return to them, not until I have found our children, be they dead or be they living."

"You do know that may not be possible?"

The question seemed to baffle Alum, and Vaelin realised it genuinely hadn't occurred to him before. "I have never failed in a hunt," he said. "I will not fail now."

Vaelin opted to enter the town via the north-western road where the new-built housing was thinnest. Even so, people still came to watch the Tower Lord's arrival, dozens emerging from homes to offer shouted greet-ings although most simply bowed. These days, over half the population of North Tower were immigrants from the wider Realm. Almost all seemed to have their share of dark memories of the Liberation War and a frequently annoying level of reverence for the man who wrought the Miracle of Alltor and stormed the docks of Varinshold. Consequently, Vaelin took every opportunity to absent himself from the tower and did his best to ensure his departures and arrivals occurred in the hours of darkness. Sadly, with the need to get the gold under lock and key, that hadn't been possible today.

"I thought your people worshipped the dead," Alum said, squinting at the passing crowd.

"They do, after a fashion," Vaelin replied. "Though some worship a single god and others . . ." He trailed off with a sigh. "Suffice to say, when it comes to matters of worship, the Realm is a complicated place."

"Not so complicated." Alum bared his teeth in a grin. "These people seem to worship you."

The North Guard were soon obliged to take the lead in order to clear the road of over-enthusiastic welcomers, ensuring a reasonably swift passage to the western gate and into the town proper. Here the people were mostly Reaches-born and less inclined to gather in welcome, though a few Vaelin knew by name called out a greeting as they navigated the narrow streets to the tower. In times past it had been custom for the North Guard garrison to parade upon return of the Tower Lord, but Vaelin had long since discontinued the practice. In fact the only sign of a welcoming party was the blond woman and the girl standing on the tower steps. Both seemed nervous and keen to avoid his gaze, something that caused his heart to plunge. *Not again.*

"You'll be provided a room," he told Alum as they dismounted. "It would be my honour if you would join me for a meal tonight."

"Of course. The Merchants' Guild . . ."

"First thing on the morrow." Vaelin glanced at Sehmon Vek clumsily disembarking the back of a mule, much to Ellese's amusement. "Your servant will sleep in the stables."

The blond woman greeted him with a formal bow as he climbed the steps, something he had told her not to do more times than he could count. However, she had always been keen on propriety, evidenced by the unadorned gown she wore, which still bore the black ribbons of mourning for a husband near six years dead.

"My Lady Kerran," he greeted her, bowing in return before extending a hand to the girl at her side. "No kiss for your uncle, Lohren?"

"Sorry," she said, coming forward to hug him tightly as he planted a kiss on the top of her head. The fierceness of her embrace told him a good deal, as did the faint tremble in her limbs.

"My lord," Kerran began. "It grieves me to raise a somewhat difficult matter so soon upon your return . . ."

"Just tell me," Vaelin cut in, frowning at the sight of her tightly clasped hands, the knuckles pale with tension. "He hasn't killed anyone this time, has he?"

Kerran gave a very weak smile before replying. "Not for want of trying, my lord."

CHAPTER THREE

Lord Nortah Al Sendahl sat on the floor of his cell, head slumped and back propped against the wall. He didn't look up as the door swung open, though Vaelin detected a faint grimace under his beard. The cell lay deep in the bowels of the tower, the only illumination a small candle in an alcove. The space reeked of unwashed flesh and stale drink, the foul humours enhanced by the contents of the bucket in the corner. The stench did little to alleviate Vaelin's already darkened mood.

He told the guard to close and lock the door, then stood staring at Nortah in silence until he finally raised his head. The amused glint in the reddened eyes visible through the veil of unwashed hair made Vaelin glad he had removed his weapons before coming here.

"What happened to your nose?" Nortah asked.

"An outlaw's arrow," he replied. His gaze shifted to a patch of dried blood on Nortah's forehead, picking out the small black knots stitched into his scalp under the reddish brown stain. "Brother Kehlan says they'll live." Vaelin stooped to peer at Nortah's wound. "You're out of practice, brother."

"This was Master Hollish, proprietor of the White Stag," Nortah replied, his chains rattling as he lifted his hands to gesture at the injury. "Now there's a fellow with a strong arm. He was at Alltor, you know."

"So were many."

Vaelin moved to the low wooden bunk with its straw mattress and sat down, allowing the silence to descend once more. Nortah had never been comfortable with silence.

"Three dim-witted sailors talking about the war," Nortah said finally. "Bragging about the battles they'd been in. They'd never been in a fucking battle, I could tell. I thought they might benefit from a taste of what it's really like."

"Actually, one of them served aboard the *Queen Lyrna* at the Battle of the Beacon. Brother Kehlan says he'll be lucky if he keeps his eye."

Nortah looked away, tongue playing over his lips and fists bunching in his manacles. Vaelin knew his moods well enough by now to read the signs; he was starting to sober up, meaning he was also getting thirsty.

"My sister came begging, I assume?" Nortah asked, a certain resentment colouring the discomfited note in his voice, just a notch shy of desperation. "I didn't ask her to."

"No, you never do. And yet she comes anyway. This time she brought Lohren, but not Artis. Why is that?"

Nortah shrugged. "The boy wishes to carve his own path."

"The boy is barely twelve years old. Having lost his mother it seems he's also lost his father."

"Kerran cares for him, and Lohren and the twins. They get all of my pension save a small pittance."

"For which the innkeepers of this town are very grateful."

For a second Nortah glared at him, then laughed. "All right," he said with a rueful shake of his head. "What will it be? Another thirty days in the mines? Sixty? Fair enough. Miners always have plenty of grog. I will, of course, pay due restitution to the injured parties. Even buy that sailor a glass eye if he needs it."

"No." Vaelin shook his head. "No, brother. Not the mines. Not this time."

"Then what? A flogging in town square? Hang me in the old gibbet for a few days?" His mouth twitched as he smiled, voice quavering as the thirst took hold with a vengeance. "As you wish, my lord." He closed his eyes, running a palm over his bunched brows. "Just a small cup of wine first, is all I ask."

"I am not currently minded to accede to any request you might make, Lord Nortah." Vaelin got to his feet, moving to the door. "You will receive adequate food and water. Brother Kehlan will visit every few days to check on your health."

"You're just going to leave me here?" Nortah forced a laugh, bracing himself against the wall as he got unsteadily to his feet. "I have a right to trial, don't forget. As a Sword of the Realm . . ."

"You have all the rights I choose to grant you," Vaelin snapped, pausing to glance around the cell. "For now, I choose to grant you the hospitality of my home."

Nortah's tongue snaked over his lips again. "For how long?"

"However long it takes Brother Kehlan to tell me you're no longer a drunkard." Vaelin turned back to the door, raising his fist to knock for the guard's attention. "By then perhaps you'll have remembered you're a father."

The attack came without warning, Nortah's bulk slamming Vaelin against the door, his chain looping over his head, drawing tight. "What do you know of fatherhood?" he hissed in Vaelin's ear, his breath acrid enough to sting the eyes. "What do you know of family? Just because you used to fuck my sister . . ."

Vaelin's head snapped back into Nortah's nose. He followed with a hard elbow to the ribs before ducking loose of the chain. Nortah retreated a step, eyes bright above his bloodied beard as he snarled and charged again, aiming a double-fisted blow at Vaelin's head. Vaelin stepped close before it could land, driving a knee into Nortah's midriff, forcing the air from his body. Nevertheless he kept trying to fight, reaching for Vaelin's throat with chained hands. He may have been more than a match for three drunken sailors the night before, but in the midst of his thirst, his weakness was pitiable. Vaelin shrugged his hands aside and clamped his own about Nortah's neck, pressing his head hard against the wall.

"What do I know of family?" he grated, teeth clenched. "I know what I lost. Sella was my family too, and so are you, you self-pitying fool!"

Nortah stopped struggling as Vaelin's hands tightened on his throat, the animosity draining from his face to be replaced by a grim, hungry acceptance. "Do it," he whispered. "They're all gone. Caenis, Dentos, Barkus . . . Sella. All gone. Send me to them. Send me to her."

Vaelin's hands slackened and he moved back, finding he couldn't meet the desperate plea in Nortah's eyes. This man was a ghost, a tired echo of the overly proud scion of Renfaelin nobility Vaelin had met the day they were taken into the House of the Sixth Order all those many years ago. A decade of harsh tutelage and war had transformed that boy into a man of deep compassion and great courage, ensuring his elevation to the highest rank in the pantheon of heroes to arise from the prolonged nightmare of the Liberation War. But, as Vaelin had often observed, in peacetime the rewards of courage were often meagre.

"I told you before," he said. "The Beyond is not . . . was not what they told us. She won't be there."

"You can't be sure," Nortah insisted. "You told me that too. There is something there, something on the other side. You've seen it . . ."

"She won't be there!" Vaelin rounded on Nortah, fully intending to beat him down, try to pummel some sense into his addled brain. He stopped upon seeing the undimmed hope in his brother's gaze. As much as he thirsted for drink, it was plain he thirsted more for death.

"Our brothers died," Vaelin said, straightening and putting as much surety as he could into his voice. "Dentos and Barkus in Alpira, Caenis in Volaria. And your wife died, brother. Sella died of a tumour in her breast two years ago. Brother Kehlan and all the healers in the Reaches tried but couldn't save her. The memories carried by those she loved are her Beyond. She is truly gone, but your children are still here and I'm not yet prepared to make them orphans."

Nortah's strength seemed to seep away in an instant and he subsided back to the floor. "Dreamt about him again last night, y'know," he said in a low mumble as Vaelin's fist rapped on the door. "Caenis, I mean. It's always the same, we stroll around that blood-soaked temple where we saved the queen, stepping over the bodies as if they're not there. I don't always remember on waking what he tells me, but this time I did. Want to hear it, brother?"

Vaelin paused as the guard heaved the door open, glancing back at Nortah's slumped form. He wondered how it was possible to barely recognise a man he had known since childhood, his last brother transformed into a pathetic remnant, a stranger.

"Yes," he said. "What did he say?"

"Said we should listen for the wolf's call." Nortah's head swivelled towards him, red eyes blinking with the exhaustion that told of an imminent faint. "Any notion of what he meant?" he asked before passing out.

◆ ◆ ◆

Petition Day was another reason Vaelin did all he could to absent himself from the tower. As Appointed Delegate, Lord Orven would deal with most of the myriad requests and complaints, but there were always some that required the Tower Lord's personal attention. The tedium was shot through with an underlying sadness born of a realisation that, had she survived the Liberation War, Dahrena would have been much better suited to this role. Although none had ever dared voice such opinions, he could recognise a similar sentiment in the often irked faces of the more long-standing denizens of the Reaches who came seeking his judgement. As adopted daughter to the previous Tower Lord, Dahrena had been accepted as one of them whilst he, even after so many years in the chair, was often still seen as an interloper. When presented with the more complex cases, she would have drawn on a wealth of knowledge and experience, not to mention personal attachments, that could ease the sting of a negative judgement. Vaelin, however, found himself continually striving to extend his patience in the face of convoluted disagreements that, in his experience, invariably involved three principal ingredients: money, tears and a good deal of shouting.

"Vile seducer!" Mistress Ilneh cried out, her pointed finger stabbing at the young man on the opposite side of the Lord's Chamber with all the energy of a spear thrust. "Dark-empowered stealer of daughters!"

Standing beside the young man was a girl perhaps eighteen years old, her hands clasped together over a swollen belly. She flinched at the woman's words, face flushing in embarrassed exasperation.

"No one stole me, you daft old cow!" she yelled at Mistress Ilneh. She seemed about to yell something else but fell to silence as Lord Orven slammed the butt of his staff on the flagstones. The girl flushed and bowed to Vaelin in the Lord's Chair. "Forgive me, my lord, but I know my own mind."

"I'm sure," Vaelin said, shifting his gaze to the young man at her side. "This man does not possess the power to alter a person's thoughts, not through use of the Dark, at least." The young man inclined his head in response, offering a grin that disappeared as Vaelin added, "How is your wife these days, Master Lorkan?"

The girl stiffened at this whilst Lorkan merely winced before offering an empty smile. "My wife, as I believe you know, my lord, has made her wishes quite explicit. Consequently, having not set eyes on her in several months, I have no notion of how she is."

Lorkan's voice betrayed a clear resentment, however polite his phrasing. Much as Vaelin could barely recognise Nortah, he increasingly found little resemblance in this man to the fearful if ultimately resolute youth who had journeyed with him across the ice. What had once seemed like charm, albeit shot through with a fair amount of guile, now struck him as self-serving manipulation. Lorkan and Cara had appeared so devoted in the aftermath of victory, their union forged in the frozen wastes and the fires of war. Perhaps that was why it hadn't lasted. Devotion was easy when every day brought new dangers. Then they had each other to cling to. With the security of peace there was less need to cling, and so they hadn't.

"I understand," Vaelin went on, "the Council at Nehrin's Point have banned you from returning there, though they failed to enlighten me as to why. Perhaps you could explain?"

"Families tend to take sides during . . . marital disputes, my lord. Cara always enjoyed closer friendships than I."

"True," Vaelin conceded. "But then I never recall her being accused of thievery or fraud."

Lorkan straightened, forcing an aggrieved sniff. "All blatant lies, fuelled by prejudice against the Gifted."

"As I understand it, these allegations were made by the Gifted."

"Hah!" Mistress Ilneh barked, letting out a triumphant laugh as her finger stabbed anew, this time at her daughter. "See, Olna, even his own kind don't want him." She moved towards the Lord's Chair, bowing low. "Please, my lord. I beseech you. Command my daughter to return to the embrace of her family—"

"Embrace?" Olna shouted in return. "When did you ever embrace me, you loveless old hag!"

Another slam from Lord Orven's staff, louder than before, brought both the girl and her mother to silence. "If I understand the particulars of your petition, Mistress Ilneh," Vaelin said, glancing through the clumsily inscribed scroll the woman had presented at the start of the audience, "you seek compensation for the grave insult done to your family's reputation by Master Lorkan Densah and the immediate return to your household of your daughter Olna."

"I do, my lord." The woman bowed lower, hands raised in supplication. "By taking up with an adulterer she has shamed us. Bad enough we'll have to care for his bastard but, as he is still bound by lawful marriage, he will not even pay a customary dowry."

Tears, shouting and money, Vaelin thought. *Always the same.* "I see," he said, keeping the weary note from his voice as he shifted in his seat, turning to his right where Ellese sat. The future Lady Governess of Cumbrael had propped her elbow on the arm of her chair, chin rested on her upraised palm, face and eyes dulled by boredom. She stirred only a little as Vaelin spoke.

"Do you have any counsel to offer here, my lady?"

"Certainly, my lord," she replied, stifling a yawn as she gave Olna a vapid smile. "In future, keep your legs closed or find a wise woman with the right mix of herbs. You," she added, smile disappearing as she turned to Lorkan, "be prepared to cough up for the consequences if you're going to tumble on the other side of the blankets."

Like her mother in some respects, after all, Vaelin thought, fixing Ellese's uncontrite visage with a hard glare. He recalled that Reva didn't like Petition Day any more than he did, but she had at least developed the capacity to pretend otherwise.

"My niece's point is valid if crudely made," he said, turning back to Lorkan. "Does Cara wish to remain married to you? And know well that I will take a very dim view of a dishonest reply."

Lorkan seemed about to offer another smile, but the lingering weight of Vaelin's gaze evidently made him think better of it. "No, my lord," he said with a sigh. "She has told me as much in terms that left little room for doubt."

"Then it appears at least one part of this complaint can be settled forthwith. Under the powers delegated to me by Queen Lyrna Al Nieren, I hereby annul your marriage." He turned to the scribe seated off to his left. "Draft a formal order for my signature and register it with the Fourth Order by the end of the day."

The scribe nodded and refreshed the ink on his pen. "I will, my lord."

"Mistress Olna," Vaelin said, turning to the pregnant girl. "How many years have you?"

"Seventeen and ten months, my lord," she replied promptly, clamping her jaws against another outburst as her mother let out a somewhat unconvincing whimper.

"Oh, my despoiled child," the woman moaned, face in her hands.

"Have you a trade?" Vaelin went on, choosing to ignore the woman. "Skills?"

"I am a seamstress, my lord." Olna shot her mother a sour look. "Just about the only useful thing she taught me."

"You expect to raise a child alone on only the income of a seamstress?"

"I am not alone." Her jaw took on a defiant angle as she turned and clasped Lorkan's hand. "My child's father will provide for us."

"Through thievery and fraud?" Vaelin asked, fixing his gaze on Lorkan.

He saw an angry retort die on Lorkan's lips, though the long-standing resentment still shone in his eyes. Although he had entered into the Liberation War willingly enough, it had been his love for his now-estranged wife that compelled him to suffer the great travail on the ice as they journeyed to Volaria and the battles that followed. Vaelin's refusal to release Cara from her obligation and spare him an epic of suffering, albeit one he had ultimately survived to great acclaim, had clearly birthed a grudge. "As you know, my lord," he said. "It was through your good graces that the queen herself granted me a pension in recognition of my service in the Liberation War."

"She did," Vaelin conceded. "I also know it is currently paid to various merchants, gambling houses and lenders the moment you receive it. Only last week Lord Orven was obliged to deal with a petition for your immediate arrest for non-payment of a long-standing and substantial debt, one he settled out of his own pocket."

"For which I am grateful, my lord," Lorkan told Orven with a bow.

"Lord Orven was driven by sentiment for an old comrade," Vaelin said. "I am not. I am, however, minded to settle all your remaining debts and, once the annulment of your marriage is formalised, stand witness to your marriage to Mistress Olna. In return," he added, seeing the burgeoning smile on Lorkan's lips falter somewhat, "you will be enrolled in the North Guard for a period of five years, where your particular ability will be fully utilised."

Lorkan's smile had disappeared now and he stood regarding Vaelin with a naked animosity. "I've had my fill of war, my lord," he said.

"Very well," Vaelin told him, gesturing to the chamber entrance. "You are free to go. Be aware, however, that I will today issue an order forbidding any ship from carrying you away from the Reaches. You, sir, will stay here and provide for your child and its mother, even if I have to flog you into the mines to do it." He held Lorkan's gaze. "Honest service in the North Guard is preferable, wouldn't you agree?"

Lorkan's jaw bunched as his face reddened in anticipation of a no doubt highly unwise outburst. Whatever words had boiled up from within died when Olna clasped his hand tighter, moving close to whisper in his ear. Lorkan closed his eyes, exhaling slowly as the girl's whisper grew fierce.

"My lord," he said finally as Olna drew back, offering Vaelin only a fractional bow, "I duly accept your most kind offer."

"Report to the barracks at first light tomorrow," Vaelin told him. "Lord Orven will begin your training. Also, two-thirds of your pay will be allotted to Mistress Olna for the duration of your service, regardless of whether you marry or not. Mistress Ilneh," he said, turning away before Lorkan could say anything else, "you will receive a discretionary payment of . . ." He paused for a moment's consideration. "Three golds for the distress and embarrassment caused to your family." He forestalled the woman's objections by inclining his head at Orven. "Next case, my lord."

Mistress Ilneh had to be bustled out by two North Guard, despite her voluble protestations, whilst Lorkan and Olna left quietly. The young Gifted's shoulders possessed a slump of defeat, though the guarded look of pure enmity he shot at Vaelin before leaving the chamber made him wonder if it wasn't another example of his capacity for deception.

"He'll most likely run," he told Orven. "Best put a triple guard on the docks tonight. Make sure at least one is Gifted."

"I will, my lord." The North Guard commander moved back, slamming his staff onto the flagstones once and raising his voice. "The embassy of the Merchant King Lian Sha will come forward!"

The embassy consisted of two principal ambassadors and a retinue of a dozen, all men. Vaelin felt the ambassadors to be a mismatched pair, one dressed in richly embroidered silks and somewhere close to his sixtieth year with an elegantly coiffured steel-grey moustache and a narrow beard. The man at his side was shorter but considerably broader, dressed in a much more simple quilted jerkin emblazoned on the breast with a circular wheel-like design. He was also younger by several years, but his blunt, weathered features told of a much harder life than his companion. Even if the man hadn't worn a sword on his belt, Vaelin would still have known him instantly as a warrior.

"Great lord of wide renown," the bearded man said in near-perfect Realm Tongue, he and the warrior both bowing. "On behalf of Lian Sha, Ruler by the Grace of Heaven of the many lands of the Venerable Kingdom, I, Kohn Shen, offer greetings and gifts."

A member of the retinue, plainly attired in garb of black cotton, moved forward in a low crouch. He kept his eyes averted as he approached the dais to set a small chest down on the first step. "Please," Kohn Shen went on, "accept this most unworthy offering as but the first of what we hope will be many tokens of esteem between our kingdoms."

"This is not a kingdom," Vaelin said, getting up from the Lord's Chair to retrieve the box. "Merely a province, and all gifts presented here are the property of my queen." He opened the box to find four jewels set into a velvet cushion, each one different in colour.

"Ruby, sapphire, emerald and diamond," Ellese said, coming to his side, her face suddenly alive with curiosity. "Each one at least twice the average weight, I'd say." Vaelin had noted before how her interest became piqued by only three things: the prospect of combat, handsome young men and anything related to money. He supposed she had Reva to thank for the first, Lady Veliss to thank for the second and no one for the third.

Lyrna always likes jewels, he thought, returning his gaze to the chest as he thought of the various trinkets with which the queen adorned herself. *Though she'd probably consider the size vulgar.*

"A fine gift, Ambassador Kohn," he told the bearded man, closing the chest and beckoning a guard forward to take it. "I'm sure she will be pleased."

He saw a slight hesitation in the ambassador's response. Vaelin knew the notion of a woman holding authority over men was largely alien in the Far West, even sacrilegious in some places. The ambassador, however, was willing to suffer the ignominy today. "As will our king, I'm sure," he said bowing again before extending a long-nailed hand to the warrior at his side. "May I present General Gian Nuishin, commander of the Seventh Cohort of the Venerable Host."

Vaelin gave the man a courteous nod. "General."

"I regret the general has only a partial understanding of your language," Kohn Shen said. "Therefore, I shall be our king's voice at this meeting."

Vaelin pursed his lips and smiled at General Gian before addressing him in Chu-Shin, the Far Western dialect most commonly spoken by merchants and officials. "If you can't talk to us, why did your king send you?" he asked, giving a pointed glance at the man's sword. "Was it to fight us?"

He saw a flicker of amusement in the general's face before he grunted a response. "If I was here to fight you, I wouldn't have bowed first. An enemy deserving of war requires neither respect nor mercy."

It was, Vaelin knew, an old saying drawn from the works of one of the innumerable philosophers to feature in Far Western history, but not one he could name. His education in such things was far from complete.

"You speak Chu-Shin well, my lord," Ambassador Kohn said. "We were not aware your accomplishments extended so far."

Vaelin gave a small shrug. "My tutor tells me my accent is somewhat variable and my vocabulary still lacking. I do continue to learn, however. Every year more and more people arrive here from the lands of the Merchant Kings, seeking to discuss all manner of business. It seemed churlish not to converse in their own language."

The man began to voice another compliment but Vaelin waved him to silence. "You, however, are too high in rank to be here on business of a purely mercantile nature, and you bring a soldier. This I find very curious."

This kind of indirect allusion, he had learned from prior dealings with Far Western officials, was the expected when conversing with emissaries from the Merchant Realms. Simply asking, "What do you want?" would have been a considerable affront to the ambassadors' dignity.

"My lord is as insightful as he is valiant," Kohn said. "Although, there is in fact a commercial aspect to our mission. We are here to negotiate a purchase, but it does not concern the many riches found in these lands."

He waved forward another member of his retinue, this one bearing an intricately engraved tubular bronze case. The man's pose was identical to his colleague's, crouched and eyes averted to display a level of servility even the Volarians might have balked at. He attempted to place the tube on the first step of the dais but stopped when Vaelin reached down and took it from him with a soft murmur of thanks.

The man started, eyes wide as he raised them briefly, Vaelin noting the thin scar that traced from the man's brow to his severely combed and lacquered hair. *Another warrior?* he wondered as the servant quickly lowered his gaze, head bobbing as he retreated back into the ranks of the retinue. It seemed unlikely such an embassy would travel without some kind of body-guard.

Turning his attention to the tube, Vaelin removed the ornate cap to extract the scroll within, unfurling it to reveal two carefully crafted, if some-what fanciful drawings. At the top was a crossbow-shaped device, twice the height of a man, casting forth a torrent of bolts like a fountain. Beneath it an even-larger contraption shaped like a giant bottle spewed a thick cascade of flame onto the deck of a ship.

"I see," he said, handing the scroll to Orven with a raised eyebrow. The North Guard commander scanned it briefly before letting out a faintly amused snort.

"We believe the rendering to be accurate," Ambassador Kohn said.

"Your dimensions are off," Vaelin told him, resuming his seat.

"You know these devices?" General Gian asked.

"I should. They were crafted by my own sister."

The man exchanged a brief glance with Kohn, a doubtful frown on both their brows. *Women rulers, women artificers,* Vaelin thought. *How strange we must seem.*

"But they work as depicted?" Gian asked.

"The first is a type of ballista that can cast fifty bolts at a target in less than a minute. The second can issue a jet of fire capable of consuming any ship within seconds. Yes . . ." Vaelin's voice faded as he recalled the many times he had held Alornis's shuddering form after she woke from yet another nightmare. *They keep asking me why,* she would whisper. *Even as they burn, they want to know why. It wouldn't be so bad if they just screamed . . .* "Yes, they work very well."

He gave an apologetic smile before continuing in a brisk tone. "Good sirs, it grieves me to inform you that your journey has been wasted. By order of the Queen's Word these devices are not for sale, at any price."

Both ambassadors responded differently, General Gian's blunt features bunching in a frown whilst Kohn pasted an empty smile on his face. "You have not yet heard the price we are willing to offer, my lord," he said. "The gift we have already provided is but a small token in comparison, a mere symbol of our king's intent."

"I am not governed by your king's intent," Vaelin replied. "But by my queen's, and she has decreed these weapons remain solely in the hands of her own host. I am sure a man of your intellect will be quick to understand her reasoning."

General Gian let out a sigh, his lips forming a sardonic grin. "Sell a neighbour a dog and he'll train it to bite you," he muttered in an accent far more coarse than before. The general, it seemed, was not of noble origins.

"Quite so, good sir," Vaelin said.

"If the devices cannot be purchased," Kohn continued, Vaelin detecting a suppressed note of desperation in his voice, "then perhaps the expertise to craft engines of equal effectiveness could. Is your sister here? I should greatly enjoy making her acquaintance."

"My sister currently resides in Varinshold," Vaelin told him, voice hardening into a less than courteous tone. "Where she serves as Principal of the Royal College of Arts. I assure you any approach you might make to her will be swiftly refused. She has no desire to ever craft another weapon of any kind."

Kohn's smile faltered, a narrowing of his eyes bespeaking the level of insult he had suffered. Nevertheless, he recovered quickly, forming his long-nailed hands into a symmetrical clasp Vaelin recognised as a gesture used in calming meditation. "In that case, my lord, I must request that we be permitted to appeal directly to your queen. If you will allow us to continue to enjoy your hospitality for a few more days, I will compose a formal proposal."

"As you wish," Vaelin said. "The queen is currently touring her Volarian dominions so it may be months before you receive a response. I should caution you, however, that I find it highly unlikely she will accede to your request."

"Nevertheless, as you are bound by your Queen's Word, I am bound by my king's." Kohn bowed again, then paused, a flicker of irritation passing across his lined features as Gian murmured an unfamiliar word. It sounded to Vaelin much like the Chu-Shin word for "whore," but with a more prolonged inflection.

Does he expect me to procure him a woman? Vaelin wondered as Kohn forced another smile.

"If you will allow me to raise another, hopefully less contentious matter, my lord," the ambassador said. "The renown of the warriors in your Realm is acclaimed across the world entire, particularly the archers of the southern lands and the horse-folk of the northern plains. Our king is highly desirous of witnessing their skills with his own eyes. If we could be permitted to invite some to return with us to the Venerable Kingdom, it would be greatly appreciated. They will, of course, receive generous compensation."

First weapons, now mercenaries, Vaelin mused. *The Venerable Kingdom is troubled, it seems.*

"All subjects of the Realm are free men and women," he said. "And may go where they wish. However, I should advise you that, whilst you will surely have some success in recruiting archers from Cumbrael, the Eorhil rarely venture from the plains unless in direst need. Still, some of them may be curious to see what manner of horses you breed in your kingdom. A moment, if you will, good sirs."

He beckoned Orven closer, speaking in Eorhil. "They want to recruit mercenaries from amongst your wife's people."

"Then they'll be wasting their time," Orven replied with a bemused frown.

"I know, but I'm keen to find out why and I doubt I'll get a straight answer from the old man. The warrior, however . . ."

Orven gave a nod of understanding. "But I don't speak his tongue, my lord."

"A ruse. I suspect he speaks Realm Tongue just as well as the old man does. Perhaps he'll demonstrate how well after you share some wine at the campfire."

Vaelin turned to the ambassadors, switching back to Chu-Shin. "Whilst Ambassador Kohn composes his missive to the queen, perhaps General Gian would like to journey forth to meet with the Eorhil. Lord Commander Orven here will make the introductions. He knows them very well."

The general exchanged a brief glance with Kohn before bowing and offering a gruff agreement. There were more effusions of gratitude from Ambassador Kohn, accompanied by more bowing, before the embassy finally made its exit and Vaelin decreed Petition Day at an end. The few remaining petitioners exuded a low grumble of disappointment as they filed out, but knew better than to make any overt protestations. To Vaelin's surprise, Ellese remained in her seat as the chamber cleared, a rare contemplative frown on her brow.

"Something wrong?" he asked her.

"The man with the scroll," she said. "He had a scar."

"Yes, I saw. You did well to spot it. He's a warrior of some kind, or more likely a spy. The Merchant Kings are well known for their fondness for espionage. Don't worry, we have our own spies. Lord Orven ensured they've been closely watched since their arrival."

"It wasn't just the scar . . ." She trailed off, shaking her head and rising from her chair. "It seems I can never escape my suspicious nature. Mother's influence. I'll forgo dinner, if you don't mind, Uncle. Delightful as I find your company, I really should check on Scrapper. She's still a youngster, gets jittery if she's on her own for too long."

Scrapper was Ellese's horse, which meant she intended to visit the stables where Sehmon, the outlaw turned indentured servant, would be bedding down for the night. The urge to order her to her room was strong, as was the desire to nail it shut for the next few years, but Vaelin knew such tactics had failed before. *The tighter I bind the leash,* Reva's letter had said, *the more delight she takes in breaking it.*

He was tempted to remind Ellese of her words to Olna but stopped his tongue. In all likelihood she had already sought out a wise woman with the requisite herbs. Instead, he said, "Be back before the changing of the midnight watch."

"I will." She stepped close to peck a kiss to his cheek before hurrying off. "Love you, Uncle. Thanks for taking me hunting."

CHAPTER FOUR

T his one." Alum's finger tapped at the symbol depicted in the ledger,
a shield enclosing two crossed sabres beneath a cracked and bleeding heart. "The ships all bore this flag."

"The Forlorn Blades," Kerran said, peering at the recently penned script
alongside the symbol. "A fairly troublesome lot, to be sure. Until recently
that is. This is the first report we've had of them for some months." She
pointed to a red X inscribed below the symbol. "This indicates the Merchants' Guild believes this particular group to have been wiped out. A not
uncommon occurrence these days." She waved a hand at the other entries
on the page, Vaelin counting another ten Xs below the various pirate motifs.

"They're feuding again," he concluded. "Piracy has dropped off recently,
but I assumed it was due to the increased number of warships escorting the
convoys."

"Some kind of power struggle seems to be playing itself out," Kerran
agreed. "We keep hearing rumours of a new pirate alliance far to the south
in the Opal Isles. However, firm intelligence eludes us. Pirates are ever a
secretive lot and surprisingly loyal."

"The Opal Isles?" Alum asked.

Kerran reached for a map and unfurled it on her desk. It was a sailor's
chart, inscribed with numerous lines and notations beyond Vaelin's understanding, but he did recognise the long, varied coastline of the southernmost
regions of the continent that Realm Folk referred to as the Far West.

"Here," Kerran said, pointing to an archipelago of numerous islands sprawled across the lower Arathean Ocean that stretched between the Far West and the western extremity of the Alpiran Empire. "It's a mostly lawless region, despite repeated attempts by both the Merchant Kings and successive Alpiran Emperors to bring it to heel. The plentiful channels and inlets make for excellent hiding places. The isles are dotted with pirate settlements, some quite large and well populated."

"So these Forlorn Blades could have sailed there?" Vaelin asked.

"Possibly," Kerran said, "but if they had slaves to sell, it's more likely they'd head for one of the ports in the Enlightened Kingdom." Kerran's finger tracked to the mainland north of the Opal Isles. "The Merchant King dynasty here has a long-standing tolerance for the slave trade not shared with their brother kings in the north. It's thanks to this that the queen forbade Realm merchants from trading with the Enlightened Kingdom three years ago."

"I remember," Vaelin said, recalling an unusually tense meeting with an ambassador from the court of the Enlightened Kingdom. Unlike Ambassador Kohn, the man hadn't known a word of Realm Tongue, and his clumsy attempts to have his interpreter translate an offered bribe had been an embarrassment to all present.

"Therefore," Vaelin continued, "no ship in this port will carry you to the Enlightened Kingdom. However, many vessels sail to the other kingdoms in the Far West every day. Here." He took a heavy purse from his belt and handed it to Alum. "For your passage and expenses once you reach the Far West. One man alone cannot hope to free so many by force. You'll have to buy them back."

Alum eyed the purse, a puzzled frown on his face. "You will not be sailing with me?"

Vaelin glanced over the map once more, taking in the vastness of the region and realising Alum most likely faced an impossible task. Even so, he couldn't deny a severe temptation to join the Moreska's search. *I could just leave it all behind*, he thought. *For a time, at least. Petitions, outlaws, Ellese's lessons . . . Nortah.*

"I have duties here," he said.

Vaelin took hold of Alum's wrist, planting the purse in his palm and nodding at Kerran. "The Lady Guild Mistress will find you a suitable ship. Come and eat with me again before you sail."

"We will sail," Alum said. "Together."

"I told you . . ."

"My cousin spoke the true word." The coins in the purse jangled as Alum's fist tightened on it, a hard insistence colouring his words. Vaelin recalled the eyes of the Moreska woman at the mine, the piercing, knowing gaze. "We will sail together," Alum repeated. "The path to our children lies with you. Until you are ready to sail, I must remain here."

"Well," Kerran said, breaking the silence that followed. "I'll let Cook know we have one more for dinner tonight."

◆ ◆ ◆

Artis scowled into his soup, maintaining a sullen silence as he ate, which was matched by his sister, although she seemed more distracted than angry.

"No next course if you don't finish that," her aunt chided from the head of the table.

Lohren gave a small grimace and dutifully spooned some soup into her mouth. Vaelin noted how her eyes kept straying to the portrait over the fire-place. It depicted a middle-aged man in the garb of a sea captain, standing with sabre in hand against a background of smoke-darkened skies and burning rigging. Vaelin had never met him, but by all accounts Kerran's husband hadn't been quite so tall and slim of waist, nor the hair on his head so plentiful.

He was a good man, my lord, Brother Kehlan told Vaelin once. *Quick of wit and generous of heart for a merchant. But he had no business commanding a warship. They do say he died bravely, nonetheless.*

To Vaelin's eyes the dining room was, like the rest of Kerran's home, overly large. The husband for whom she still wore the mourning ribbons had been a rich man, although Vaelin suspected much of his wealth had resulted from the acumen of his wife. Following his death, the profits of the Honoured Trading House of Al Verin had doubled and then tripled. Kerran was now one of the ten wealthiest individuals in the Reaches and the much respected head of the Merchants' Guild. But still, the mourning ribbons remained firmly sewed to her bodice and he knew it wasn't simply to ward off unwanted suitors, even though there were many.

"The twins aren't joining us?" Vaelin asked, glancing at the empty chairs to his left.

"I find it best to let them eat in the kitchen," Kerran replied. "They can be a bit fractious, even more so lately."

"They miss Father," Lohren said, which drew a derisive snort from her brother. "Well they do!" she insisted with a glare that she immediately turned on Vaelin. "As do I, Uncle."

"Your father is where he needs to be," Vaelin told her. "For now."

"Leave the piss-stained drunkard there to rot for all I care," Artis muttered, his first words of the evening.

Vaelin's fist came down on the table, hard enough to make the cutlery rattle. He stared at Artis, letting the silence stretch until the boy eventually raised his eyes, defiant but also a little fearful.

"Your father," Vaelin said in a soft but intent voice, "travelled across half the world fighting the worst war this Realm has ever known. He waded through fire and blood to save the life of our queen and watched our brother Caenis die in the process. He didn't do this out of lust for glory or expectation of reward. He did this to keep his family safe, and it cost him more than you can imagine. Regardless of his crimes, your father requires your respect and you will show it."

Artis glared back, Vaelin finding the boy's face a disconcerting mirror of Nortah's at the same age. He also possessed much the same capacity for acting without due thought.

"That man is no longer my father!" Artis shouted, getting to his feet, defiance overcoming his fear. His spoon skittered away as he flung it down on the table. "And you're not even my real uncle."

"Artis!" Kerran said, a rare scowl of anger on her brow as she rose from her seat, casting a pointed glance at Alum. "We have a guest!"

"And you're not my mother!" Artis yelled, whirling away and rushing to the door. "My mother died, remember?"

The door slammed as Artis fled the room, leaving a thick silence in his wake.

"You should send him to a hut in the hills," Alum told Kerran. He seemed unruffled by the disturbance and continued to partake of his soup, lips smacking in appreciation. "Once I was disrespectful to my grandmother so my father sent me to the hut for a whole summer, with only a knife and no food or water. I ate snakes and scorpions." He gave a nostalgic chuckle and took another mouthful of soup. "Or you could just beat him."

"That's a thought," Vaelin muttered, drawing a hard glance from Kerran.

What had passed between them had been a brief thing, born of mutual loneliness in the months after the war's end when the absence of those they had lost felt like a raw, bleeding wound. They had both known it would never last. Close as they became, their shared affection was not the kind that blossoms into something that could endure. It had ended amicably, at her insistence. She blamed it on the minor scandal and burgeoning gossip their less-than-discreet nightly liaisons had engendered, though he had known that to be an excuse; throughout it all the mourning ribbons never went away. Even so, these five years later, Kerran continued to enjoy a certain leeway with the Tower Lord not afforded to others.

"Perhaps," she said, "he would be better behaved if his uncle spent more time attending to family instead of endlessly scouring the countryside for more outlaws to hang."

"He misses home," Lohren said, voice soft and eyes distant as she stirred her mostly uneaten soup. "Our friends are all at the Point. Cara teaches school there now Father's gone. She is firm but kind and they love her, which makes her heart hurt less. She misses Lorkan but won't say so, even to herself."

Kerran stared at her niece, face suddenly pale. "You're doing it again," she said in a thin whisper. "You said it didn't happen anymore."

"It doesn't, mostly. But sometimes it comes back. I don't tell you when it does, but Uncle Vaelin needs to know something."

Lohren gave a wan smile and raised her face to Vaelin, eyes wide and unblinking. He knew she wasn't seeing him, or anything else in this room. "Last night I dreamt of a wolf. He was very big and very beautiful. Also, old. So old. He's showed me many things. One was a man, also old but not nearly as old as the wolf. He's worn many faces, lived many lives. Done so many things. He's come such a long way, Uncle. He has something to tell you." A line appeared in Lohren's smooth brow as she frowned, a shadow passing over her small face. She blinked and he saw a tear trace down her cheek. "But he has people to kill first."

The wolf. It had been so long since he last saw it, but the memory was as sharp and real as if it had been moments before, in the Great Northern Forest when its mighty howl summoned the Seordah Sil to war against the Volarians. All the other encounters tumbled through his mind in a rush. That first glimpse in the Urlish Forest before it had intervened to save him from the assassins, a vision of silver-grey predatory beauty licking blood from its jaws. Its snarl in the Martishe that had made him step back from the brink of outright murder. Outside the walls of Linesh during the Alpiran war before it summoned the sandstorm that saved him, but failed to save Dentos. *Said we should listen for the wolf's call,* Nortah had said, words spoken to him by a dead man in a dream. Vaelin well knew the wolf's call often brought salvation, but it also brought death.

"Where?" Vaelin said. He moved to crouch at Lohren's side, laying a hand on her shoulder. "When?"

"The tower," she said and he felt her shudder. "Now." Her shudder abruptly turned into a convulsion, her face bleaching of colour as she fought down a retch. "Part of him . . ." She grimaced in confusion. "Someone he used to be . . . wants to meet his daughter again. It was a delightful surprise to find her here. He never got to kill her when he was alive. Something he's always regretted."

Someone he used to be . . . his daughter . . .

Vaelin tore himself from Lohren's side, unhooking his sword from the back of his chair before rushing to the door. The realisation sang in his mind with all the force of a scream. *Ellese!*

◆ ◆ ◆

Vaelin dragged his horse to a halt in the courtyard, leaping down from the saddle and sprinting for the stables. He drew his sword and forced himself into a walk before entering the shadowy interior, ears alive for any sound beyond the snorting of many annoyed horses.

"Ellese!" he called out, moving towards the rear of the stables. "Show yourself!"

"Uncle?"

He turned to find her framed in a doorway, blanket clutched around her unclothed body and an aggrieved scowl on her face. Beyond her, Vaelin could see the pale form of Sehmon Vek frantically struggling into his trews.

"Get dressed," Vaelin told Ellese.

"Much as I appreciate your concern," she said with a sigh, "I am not yours to command . . ."

"Get!" Vaelin broke in, moving towards her, staring into her eyes with unmistakable intent. "Dressed!"

She blinked and stepped back, her eyes flicking to the sword he held and scowl fading as she gave a nod of understanding. "Of course."

The North Guard sergeant who had charge of the night watch hurried into the stables, two poleaxe-bearing guardsmen at his back. "Trouble, my lord?" he asked.

Alum appeared behind the guardsmen, breathing heavily. He wasn't an experienced rider and Vaelin had quickly outpaced him in his dash to the tower.

"You," he said, nodding at one of the guardsmen and gesturing to Alum. "Give this man your poleaxe."

"Yes, my lord."

"Sergeant," Vaelin went on. "Rouse Lord Orven, and the entire garrison. There is an intruder in the tower. It's to be searched from top to bottom."

The sergeant, a veteran of many years' service, gave only the slightest hesitation before saluting smartly and turning about, voice raised to bark out the requisite orders.

"What's happening?" Ellese asked, Vaelin glancing over to see her now mostly clothed, hands moving rapidly as she laced up her boots.

"You have your weapons?" Vaelin asked her.

"Always."

"Good. Get them."

"Your pardon, my lord." Sehmon appeared at Ellese's side, bowing low, voice strained with panicked contrition. "If I have offended in any way . . ."

"Oh, shut up, you!" Ellese snapped. She strapped on her belt with its two hunting knives, one long and the other short. "Here," she said, handing him the shorter blade. "Might as well make yourself useful."

"Stay close," Vaelin told them, heading back to the courtyard.

"Where are we going?" Ellese asked, nocking an arrow to her bow.

Lohren's words played through his mind. *He's come such a long way . . .* "We need to check on our visitors."

◆ ◆ ◆

Ambassador Kohn had at least received a quick death. He lay on the voluminous bed in the large chamber reserved for the most honoured guests, steel-grey beard stained red below the chin and the sheets on either side soaked with fresh blood.

A single cut, Vaelin saw, teasing aside the beard to peer at the wound, an almost surgical one-inch incision severing the main artery in the neck. His attendants hadn't been so lucky. Four of them lay around the chamber, each body featuring at least three stab wounds to the chest. The blood sprayed onto the walls, and the general state of disorder indicated a frenzied slaughter.

"This all happened very quickly," Alum said, surveying the carnage with a practised eye. "The old man was killed first, probably in full view of these others." His foot nudged the hand of one of the slain attendants, the fist slack around the hilt of a knife. "No blood on the blade. They tried to fight, but it did them no good."

"He's not here," Ellese said, moving from one corpse to another, face set in the predatory tension of the hunt. "The one with the scar." She straightened and turned to Vaelin. "He knew me. That's what I saw ... what I failed to see. It's *him*, isn't it?"

"In here, my lord!" Lord Orven's voice called from an adjoining chamber.

He found Orven crouched beside the bloodied, wheezing form of General Gian. Another three attendants lay close by, all dead. The general clutched his sword tight in his fist, Vaelin noting the red stain on the blade.

"You wounded him?" he asked in Chu-Shin, crouched at the man's side.

"Leg ..." Gian gasped, a cloud of blood accompanying the word. He convulsed, letting out a shout that was both enraged and despairing. "Known him since ... he was a boy ... practically raised the little bastard ..."

"Send for Brother Kehlan," Vaelin told Orven. "The assassin's wounded in the leg. Have the guards look for a blood trail, and get the hounds out of the kennels."

"Yes, my lord."

"Wait ..." Gian groaned, dropping his sword to reach for Vaelin's cloak as he made to follow Orven from the chamber. "The weapons ..."

"A concern for another time, sir," Vaelin said. He tried to pry Gian's hand loose but the man held on, staring up at him, a fierce plea for understanding in his gaze.

"We *need* them ..." Gian convulsed again, a thick torrent rushing from his mouth to bathe the flagstones. He dragged air into his lungs and spoke on, fighting through the pain. "They're coming, thousands upon thousands of the fuckers ..."

"Who?" Vaelin leaned close as Gian's voice descended into a ragged whisper. "Who is coming?"

The word emerged in a wet sibilant rasp, Vaelin seeing a familiar dimness creep into Gian's eyes. "S-Stahlhast . . ." He groaned, a brief flare of life returning to the gaze he fixed on Vaelin. "Coming for us . . . then you . . . then everything . . ."

"General?"

Gian's eyes continued to stare into his, but the glimmer of life had gone and his hand slipped from Vaelin's cloak. "General of the Seventh Cohort of the Venerable Host," Vaelin murmured, reaching out to close the man's eyes. "I suspect you deserved a better end."

"Blood here," Alum called from the corridor outside. Vaelin cast a final look at the general's corpse and left the chamber, finding the Moreska crouching to inspect a small red spatter on the flagstones.

"He's bound the wound," he said, fingers tracing through the still-wet blood. "This was moments ago." His brows bunched in concentration as he rose, reaching out to pluck a torch from an iron bracket on the wall. "Strange," he murmured, casting the light over the floor and the walls.

"What is it?" Vaelin asked.

"The blood, the mark it leaves, like a shooting star." Alum paused to point at a single elongated drop on the wall. "Like the trail left by a wounded cheetah. But surely no man can move so fast."

"This is not truly a man," Vaelin said. He followed Alum to the end of the corridor where it met the tower's western stairs. The hunter's torch revealed more blood on the steps leading to the tower's lower reaches but none leading up.

"Wait," he said as Vaelin started down. "No more shooting stars, see?" His torchlight played on a series of small rounded drops.

"It's a false trail to be sure, my lord."

Vaelin glanced up to find Sehmon standing alongside Ellese. "Really?"

The youth blanched a little but straightened, finding the resolve to meet Vaelin's gaze. "It's an old trick," he said. "One I learned young. People always expect you to go down," he inclined his head at the stairs to the left, "when it's usually better to go up. Rooftops are an outlaw's friend."

Vaelin gestured for two North Guard to follow the descending trail, then started up, eyes scanning the stonework for more blood but finding nothing. He paused at a doorway to an open walkway overlooking the North Guard barracks, but saw nothing of interest. He was about to move on when Alum stopped him with a touch to the arm, moving out onto the walkway to run his hand along the stones of the low battlement.

"Here," he said, raising a hand to display a small drop of blood on his finger. "Still fresh."

"Then where . . . ?" Vaelin's gaze roamed the walkway. The door it led to guarded the tower's secondary armoury and was consequently secured with no less than five locks. The wall above offered no handholds, nor did the wall below.

"Uncle," Ellese said softly. Vaelin turned to see her raising her bow, eyes focused on something below. Following her gaze, he could see only the shadowed angles of the barracks roof. The tower was loud with alarm now, the shouts of the North Guard punctuated by the excited yapping of the hounds. Many torches had been lit and cast a shifting flicker of shadow that only made it harder to discern the object of Ellese's interest. Then he saw it, a small shape crouched near the western edge of the barracks roof, as still as any statue but undoubtedly the form of a man. The barracks lay within the walls of the keep, but the gap between the roof and the outer battlement was an easy jump even for a man without Dark-born speed.

"I need him alive," Vaelin told Ellese as she drew the bow.

He heard the mirthful anticipation in her voice as the arrow's fletching brushed her cheek. "So do I."

The shadow moved the same instant she loosed, becoming a blur in the flickering torchlight. Ellese let out a curse as her arrow careened off the roof tiles and spun away. She immediately nocked and drew again, body moving with a speed and skill that could match the best archers Vaelin had seen. The shadow, moving faster than any man ever could, streaked across the apex of the roof and leapt just as Ellese's bow thrummed once more. Vaelin saw the shadow twist as the shaft struck home, the blurring form seeming to slow in midair as it tumbled, colliding with the outer battlement of the keep before plummeting to the ground beyond.

Vaelin jumped up onto the battlement, resisting the impulse to leap down onto the barracks roof, knowing all he would accomplish would be two shattered legs. Instead, he cupped his hands around his mouth and bellowed to the North Guard in the courtyard. "Get the hounds through the gate! Make sure they don't kill him!"

He turned and leapt down from the battlement, descending the stairwell and emerging into the courtyard in a sprint, with Ellese and the others close behind. He ran through the gate, following the barking cacophony of the hounds until he caught sight of the pack. They were all Renfaelin hunting dogs, each standing three feet tall at the shoulder with long snouts and strong jaws. The pack whirled in a cluster about a blurred, thrashing shape. Dogs repeatedly darted forward in an attempt to bite their quarry, without apparent success. Vaelin saw three cast away by the blurred shape, the hounds tumbling through the air and coming to rest several yards distant with a pained whimper. But the pack was fifty strong and tireless.

As he drew closer Vaelin noticed how the shape became less blurred, resolving into a man. It blurred a few more times, casting another brace of dogs into the air, but came to a sudden halt as four hounds leapt in to clamp their jaws on its limbs.

"Easy now," Sergeant Jolna called out as the pack closed in for the kill, the man in the centre of the pack jerking in pain as ever more teeth sank into his flesh. Jolna had held the position of Master of Hounds for many years, rearing all of these dogs since birth. They shrank from him as he waded amongst them with his cane whipping the air. The enraged snarls of the pack slowly descended into growls, though those holding the man continued to do so.

"Sorry, my lord," Jolna said as Vaelin halted nearby. "Their blood's truly up tonight. Not often they get to hunt all together like this."

"And fine work they did, Sergeant," Vaelin told him. He fixed his gaze on the assassin, the hounds parting as he moved closer. The broken stub of Ellese's arrow jutted from the man's shoulder, and a heavily stained bandage was wrapped around his thigh. He shuddered in suppressed pain as he raised his face, Vaelin finding it masked in a thick sheen of blood. He noted it was thickest around the eyes and nose, a clear sign of prolonged use of a gift. Despite the blood, Vaelin could make out the scar on the man's forehead.

"Brother . . ." the assassin gasped, grimacing in pain before offering Vaelin a broad grin, his teeth gleaming red and white in the gloom. "It's been far too long." His eyes flicked to Ellese as she came to a halt at the edge of the pack. Despite the recent exertion her face was bleached of colour and devoid of expression as she stared at the scarred assassin.

"And my lovely daughter," he said. "Have you missed me?"

She moved too fast for Vaelin to stop her, the hounds scattering as she charged, a scream of fury escaping her throat. The sound produced by her fist as it connected with the assassin's face reminded Vaelin of a hammer striking hard stone. He managed to catch her wrist as she drew her arm back for another blow, pulling her into a close embrace.

"I am owed this!" She thrashed in his arms, legs kicking. "For what he did to my mother! What he did to me!"

"I know." Vaelin's arms tightened on her, holding her close until her struggles ceased and she subsided into sobs. "You'll get what you're owed, I promise," he whispered, letting her fall to her knees before turning his gaze back on the assassin. He sagged in the hounds' clutches, blood dripping from his bowed head. "But first I need to hear what he has to tell me."

Vaelin nodded to Sergeant Jolna. "Tell Brother Kehlan he has another patient. And fetch chains. The heaviest you can find."

CHAPTER FIVE

Ellese stationed herself outside the cell door and refused to leave whilst Brother Kehlan tended the captive's wounds.

"You should sleep," Vaelin told her, which earned him a withering glance.

"Could you?" she asked. "Knowing that thing is still alive and in this tower." Her voice slipped into a sibilant hiss as she stared through the slat in the cell door. "He might wear a different face, speak with a different voice, but I see it now, that smile. He wore it the day he killed my mother."

Vaelin eased her aside to peer through the slat. The man chained to the wall favoured Brother Kehlan with a grateful smile as he finished fixing a bandage on his wounded shoulder. Like Ellese, Vaelin had seen that smile before, on Barkus's face when the mask finally slipped and all the malice of the Ally's servant stood revealed. For years this thing had worn his brother's form like a cloak, along with so many others: Ellese's father, who had plotted with god-worshipping fanatics to orchestrate the downfall of Cumbrael; the blind shaman who brought the Bear People to the brink of extinction; the Volarian slave soldier who had taken Dahrena from him.

How many times, he wondered, *will I have to kill it before it no longer feels as though I'm murdering my brother?*

Brother Kehlan emerged shortly after, his lean features beset by a mix of disdain and curiosity. "I must say I find him strangely polite, my lord," he told Vaelin. "Given his . . . nature."

Vaelin had never told Kehlan the full details of Dahrena's death. The healer had loved her like a daughter so it seemed kind to spare him, an impulse Vaelin was now grateful for. Had Kehlan known the creature in the cell was responsible for her demise, he would never have treated him, regardless of the strictures of the Fifth Order, which required all those in need to be cared for with equal diligence.

"Will he live?" Vaelin asked.

"If properly tended," the brother replied. "However, he seems somewhat convinced that he won't survive to see another dawn, and that his death is likely to be highly prolonged. Is that the case, my lord?"

Ellese let out a very small chuckle. "He'll be lucky to see noon, never mind the dawn."

Kehlan's jaws bunched in annoyance but he kept his gaze on Vaelin. "My lord is fully aware of my concerns regarding torture . . ."

"Your compassion, as ever, does you credit, brother," Vaelin cut in, clapping the older man on the shoulder. "Rest assured, I am certain such measures will not be required here."

He reached for the door, then paused as Ellese moved eagerly to his side. "No," he said, shaking his head, voice firm.

Ellese glanced at Kehlan before leaning closer to reply in a harsh whisper, "You made me a promise."

"And I'll keep it. But not yet. Wait here."

Going inside he dismissed the two North Guard in the cell and closed the door behind them. Ellese's bright, angry eyes glared at him through the slat, narrowing in consternation as he slid it closed. At his instruction two chairs had been placed in the cell. The scarred man sat in one, thick chains tracing from manacles on his wrists and ankles to brackets in the walls.

"They used to call you the Messenger, as I recall," Vaelin said, moving to take the other chair. "But it occurs to me that I never learned your name. Your true name."

The scarred man's chains clinked as he shifted, meeting Vaelin's gaze with placid indifference.

"The witch who brought you into this world must have named you," Vaelin prompted. "Even monsters have names."

He watched the creature's face closely, hoping his taunts might provoke some betraying reaction. Instead he saw only faint, bitter amusement.

"Gone," the Messenger said, chains clinking again as he shrugged. "For years I had no urge to recall it, now I couldn't if I tried. What you see here"—he grimaced with the effort as he raised a manacled wrist to gesture at his face—"is just a remnant."

"What about her name?" Vaelin asked.

This provoked a twitch of genuine puzzlement. "Who?"

"Your mother. You might have forgotten your own name, but who could forget their mother's?"

The chains rattled before drawing tight, the Messenger lunging forward in his chair, face abruptly transformed into a reddened mask. "I am not here to talk about my fucking mother!" he snarled. Vaelin saw the power of his gift now, the way his body vibrated, his hands producing a thrum like two giant bees as they blurred fast enough to stir a breeze in the cell.

Vaelin stared into the Messenger's enraged eyes and smiled. "There are a great many books in the tower library," he said. "I've been collecting them since the war. The role of Tower Lord affords a generous salary but my needs are small, so most of it is spent on books. Especially those that concern the old stories. It shouldn't surprise you to hear that you crop up here and there in different incarnations. 'The Tale of the Witch's Bastard' is an old one, and it's changed a good deal over time."

A trickle of blood emerged from the Messenger's flared nostrils, tracing over his quivering lips, his entire body straining against the chains now.

"But," Vaelin went on, "the further back in time I go the simpler the tale becomes. A raped woman gave birth to a child who grew into something vile and murderous. But, sadly, I could never find her name, or yours. Strange to think that people of such importance to history have no testament beyond a tale that changes with every passing year. Whilst you linger on like a stain that never washes out."

The Messenger's hands fluttered into stillness and he slumped in his chair, shaking his head as a soft laugh escaped his lips. "Is this all the torment you have for me? I must say, I was expecting more."

Vaelin sent a meaningful glance towards the door. "There's a young woman waiting outside who'll be glad to fulfil your expectations. Shall I invite her in?"

"Ah, yes. My vengeful daughter. Do you really think this is any kind of threat? I know you'll allow her to sully her soul with torture, nor do you need to. Ask any question you like and I'll answer honestly."

Vaelin stopped himself from exhibiting the sudden anger birthed by a realisation that the power in this meeting had now shifted from him to his prisoner. The Messenger had no fear of pain, no concern at all for what torments Ellese might inflict, even if Vaelin allowed it. It made his hands itch as he fought the urge to bunch them into fists, made him want to summon Dahrena's face as he beat this creature again and again until its body was nothing but pulped bone and sundered flesh.

"I'm not lying, brother," the Messenger said, head tilted at an angle that indicated he had no difficulty in reading Vaelin's change in mood. "Ask and I'll answer."

Vaelin clasped his hands together and reclined in his seat. "Very well. How is it you are here? I was told the body you last inhabited died in Alpira years ago. The Beyond is supposed to be a snare for your kind and it died with the Ally at the end of the Liberation War. You were the Ally's slave, sustained in this world by his will alone. With him destroyed, there should have been nothing to keep you here."

"The Beyond," the Messenger repeated, voice coloured by a note that mingled scorn with pity. "You've never really understood it, have you? What it is. What it actually means."

"The Ally told me it was a scab covering a wound."

"A somewhat colourful description, but he always was a pretentious fucker. Can't say I miss him much. Oh yes," he added, seeing the glint of concern in Vaelin's eye, "unlike me, he is truly gone forever. As for the Beyond, it's not something that can be destroyed, not truly, merely . . . disrupted, disordered for a time. That is what you accomplished. No more than a ripple in the fabric of something that joins this world with . . . something else."

He fell silent, a shadow passing over his bruised features. "Don't misunderstand me. What was merely a ripple in the Beyond caused great pain to those souls obliged to endure it. Some slipped away into the blessed release of the void; others were rent to pieces, left as little more than maddened fragments tormented by memories of what they had been. That was my fate, brother. That was what you did to me, and it was far worse than any torture you or that little bitch outside could ever contrive. I know now it lasted for years, but it felt like eternity. Time is malleable in the Beyond, stretched or contracted seemingly at the whim of chance. Imagine screaming forever, Vaelin. Then imagine something finding you, collecting all the pieces left of you and putting them back together. Not whole, not anymore. But made the Messenger once again."

The Ally's last words came back to Vaelin then, his stricken, terrified eyes as he stared at the black stone. In the years since, Vaelin had often reflected how so much discord and slaughter could have been caused by so non-descript a thing. It was finely carved but lacked decoration of any kind; no ancient, unreadable script marked its surface, nor any pictogram that might give a clue to the power it held. It had sat in its chamber beneath the great arena of Volar for centuries, kept hidden by the persecuted servants of the suppressed Volarian gods who imagined it divine. It had all begun with this simple, unadorned plinth of black stone, just one touch of the Ally's hand in the far-gone days when he had still been contained within his own body. Then, Vaelin knew, he had been hungry for the gifts it held, but had whimpered like a child at the prospect of laying hands on it once more.

When I touched it, he had said, eyes moist and wide as they pleaded for mercy he must have known would never come. *When I received my gift, I looked into that world . . . and something looked back, something vast, and hungry.*

The Ally had been an ancient soul of sufficient malice, resolve and intellect to bend the entire Volarian Empire to his will and use it to bring the world to the brink of calamity, and yet when presented with the black stone beneath the arena, he had been rendered pathetic by his terror.

"What something?" he said.

The Messenger stared back in silence for some time, his face now rendered strangely serene, apparently lacking animus. However, when he spoke again, Vaelin recognised the familiar note of malice. "You don't know," he said, leaning forward. "You don't know what you did when you made the Ally touch that stone. You don't know what you awoke. But you will, brother. It saw you, it saw everything, and it grew hungrier than ever."

"What is it?"

A faint shrug and a raised eyebrow as the Messenger leaned back. "I only know what it can do. Not what it truly is. But its intent." A smile played across his lips. "That I know very well. It's been setting the pieces on the board for a very long time, and the first moves have already been made, such as placing me in this shell."

"What for?"

The Messenger lapsed into silence. Vaelin once again felt the itch in his hands. He could just get up and open the door, let Ellese have her way with this thing. Hearing its screams echo along the corridor as he walked away would have been shamefully satisfying, but it was clear there was still more to learn.

"General Gian spoke of the Stahlhast," he said, opting for a different approach. "What are they?"

"Merely a tool," the Messenger replied. "As am I. I was placed in this shell in order to win the general's confidence. It wasn't easy; he was a clever man who had long learned the value of suspicion. But eventually I gained his trust so that I might whisper the right suggestions in his ear. I first proposed our visit here over a year ago, when the Stahlhast overran the hill country south-west of the Steppe. But it was only when they destroyed the army the Merchant King had sent to oppose them that he began to listen."

"You persuaded him to sail across an ocean just to kill him under my roof?"

"Thereby sowing doubt and discord between the Far West and the realm of the Queen of Fire. Besides, if I hadn't, I would have been denied the chance to speak with you again, brother. So you see, I am here in part on my own agency."

The Messenger's face lost its serene cast, Vaelin finding himself disconcerted by the genuine regret he saw in it. "It's strange," the Messenger went on, voice now lacking the malice from before, "but when I was suffering in the Beyond, it was the most recent memories that stayed with me. I remember the havoc I wrought amongst the Ice People, all those years plotting with the Sons of the Trueblade and"—the malign tone returned briefly as his eyes slid towards the door—"all those happy days with the wife and daughter of poor old Lord Brahdor. It was such a pleasant surprise to find her here with you . . ."

Vaelin's reaction was immediate and instinctive, a red haze colouring his vision for a second before it cleared and he found himself standing over the Messenger, hand stinging from a hard backhand cuff to the man's face. The Messenger spat blood and coughed out a laugh. "Oh, brother," he said, shaking his head with a rueful chuckle. "Always so easy to play you, like plucking strings on a mandolin. I am going to miss it."

Vaelin closed his eyes, taking a deep breath before forcing himself to retake his seat. "I tire of this," he said. "If you have something to tell me, get it said."

The Messenger coughed up more blood, then settled in his seat, his face taking on a reflective cast. "As I said," he continued, "much was lost except for the most recent lives, one in particular, one stream of memory out of so many others, when I was big, bluff, honest Brother Barkus and we were bound together in the Order, the five of us, brothers united against all the ills of the world. I came to realise, using what meagre reason was left me, that if the Ally's will hadn't bound me so absolutely, I would have stayed in that shell for all the years I could. I learned grief then, not the maddening rage of injustice and vengeance I knew so well, but the ache of losing those you love."

He blinked, meeting Vaelin's gaze with a sad smile. "Hurts doesn't it? When you're alone in the dark and the ghosts come to whisper their awful truths. And they do come, don't they, brother? All those many, many ghosts. Who whispers loudest, I wonder? Caenis? Dahrena? Me?"

Feeling the red haze descend once more, Vaelin rose and moved to the door. "Enough of this. You can rot here. I'll not kill you so your new master can put you in another body. I suggest you spend the years in contemplation of your many crimes . . ."

"Sherin."

The cell was small and possessed no echo. Nevertheless, the name lingered in the air, halting Vaelin's hand as he reached out to rap on the door. Slowly, he turned, finding the Messenger regarding him with head tilted in curiosity rather than cruelty.

"I told you I was here on my own agency," he said. "I came to deliver my final message. My last service to you."

Vaelin moved to stand over him, staring into his upturned gaze. "Speak plainly," he instructed, "because I have no more patience for riddles. What do you know of Sherin?"

"I know she now resides in the Venerable Kingdom. Despite being a mere woman, she has become a physician of great renown. Even the Merchant King himself has had cause to call upon her talents. I know the Stahlhast will sweep across the border within months, and I know Sherin will be one of the first to perish, for she has placed herself in great peril. You sent her to the Far West expecting her to be safe. You should have known there is no safe place in this world. Conquerors come and go in history but the Stahlhast are different. They intend to remake the world and will kill any soul who doesn't fit their mould."

Vaelin saw it then, the growing loss of focus to the Messenger's gaze, the sheen of sweat covering his forehead. He gripped the man's face as his head lolled, shaking him until clarity returned to his gaze. "You have taken poison," he said in realisation.

The response emerged in a hissing echo of a laugh. "Of course I have. Took it before I sliced that old fool Kohn's throat. Timed the dosage just right, brother. But I've had plenty of practice in such things . . ."

His eyes dimmed again, face going slack in Vaelin's grip. Vaelin shook him again, leaning close to shout his demand. "Where do I find her? Where is Sherin?"

"Gone to minister . . ." the Messenger murmured back, his voice barely a whisper, ". . . to the Jade Princess . . ." He spasmed, the movement violent enough to shake him loose from Vaelin's grasp. For a brief second life returned to his features and he looked up at Vaelin with open, fear-filled eyes, tears streaming down his bleached skin. "Don't worry," he rasped, shuddering with the effort of talking, Vaelin watching a matrix of swelling veins spread across his eyes as his skin grew ever whiter. "There will be no more shells for me . . . This time, it will finally rip the remnants of my soul to nothing. Think . . . better of me, brother . . . if you can . . ."

He closed his eyes and his head slumped forward, the chains clinking a final time as his limbs slackened. Vaelin stood in silent regard of the corpse as a cavalcade of memories played through his mind. All the horrors crafted by this creature, all the torments he had suffered at its hands. The moment should have conveyed a sense of finality, he knew, an epilogue to the epic of malice. But instead he knew it to be a beginning, for the memory that came most to mind was not of murder or cruelty, but the face of a woman he had last seen over ten years ago. Her features had been slack in the sleep of the drugged as he placed her in the stonemason's arms, her skin warm as he smoothed the hair back from her forehead. Despite the eventful years since, the memory of her face hadn't dimmed at all, nor had the guilt . . . *Betrayal is always the worst sin.*

Does she hate me? he wondered, a question that had bedevilled him ever since he watched the ship take her away. What would he see in her eyes when she beheld him once more? Scorn? Despair? Somehow, he doubted it would be joy, and yet, she always possessed the most compassion of any soul he had met. *Perhaps forgiveness?*

He straightened as the decision took hold, moving to the door and knocking for the guard to open it. "Burn that," Vaelin told him, jerking his head at the Messenger's corpse. "No rites are needed."

Vaelin strode away along the passage and ascended the stairs to the courtyard, deaf to the questions Ellese shouted in his wake. Whatever Sherin chose to show him when he looked upon her once more, he would accept it as his due. He would sail for the Far West, find her and see her safe, regardless of any risk or cost, for that was the least of the debt he owed her.

Chapter Six

L ike North Tower, Nehrin's Point had grown since the war. What had once been a small cluster of somewhat dilapidated houses fringing a shallow bay was now fast becoming a substantial settlement. Unlike North Tower, however, the inhabitants felt obliged to construct and maintain a sturdy defensive wall.

"This is a garrison town?" Alum enquired as they crested a low rise a half mile short of the main gate.

"No," Vaelin said. "Merely home to people with a well-justified sense of caution." He paused, unsure of how to explain the peculiarity of this place. "My people have a phrase," he went on after some brief consideration. "'The Dark.' You know of this?"

Alum's scarred brows bunched in bafflement and he shook his head.

"Your cousin's . . . ability," Vaelin went on. "In the Unified Realm it would be called a manifestation, or an affliction, born of the Dark. In recent years, however, the term 'Gifted' is preferred, and enforced under the Queen's Word."

"In the wider empire they call it 'the Shadowed Path,'" Alum said, understanding dawning on his features. "Amongst the Moreska we do not name it. Those born with it are watched closely, for we know it does not hail from the Protectors, and who can say how such power will twist the heart?" His gaze narrowed as he surveyed the settlement once more. "All of the people here are . . . Gifted?"

"No, just most of the adults, and perhaps half the children."

The Moreska shifted in his saddle, Vaelin noting how he clutched the reins tighter and his horse began to stir as it sensed his discomfort. "I see," was all he said.

"Perhaps," Vaelin ventured, "you would prefer to spend the day hunting. The hill country to the north is rich in wild goats . . ."

"Goats! Yes!" Alum straightened, reaching for one of the spears he had chosen from the tower armoury. "You have given me these fine weapons. It would be insulting not to furnish meat by way of thanks." He turned his horse to the north, then paused. "If you do not emerge from this dread place within two days," he told Vaelin in a grave voice, "be assured I will rescue you."

With that he spurred his mount into motion and galloped away, Vaelin noting how he kept his gaze firmly averted from Nehrin's Point.

Vaelin approached the gate at a canter and reined in to dismount. "Master Rentes," he greeted the burly, staff-bearing Cumbraelin who came forward to take charge of his horse.

"Good day, my lord. Shall I send word to convene the Council?"

"That won't be necessary. I assume Mistress Cara is at the school?"

"That she is, my lord. Be another hour before she lets the little 'uns loose, though."

"I'll wait." Vaelin nodded his thanks and proceeded inside. Walking the broad streets to the schoolhouse, he was reminded of why he liked coming here; the people were always scrupulous in avoiding his company. Some offered a muted greeting or a bow before hurrying on their way, but most just averted their gaze and busied themselves with various chores. *The Queen's Word protects them*, he thought. *But still they fear me, even though I was once one of them.* It occurred to him that the loss of his gift was why they feared him, perhaps suspecting such misfortune might be contagious.

Most of the inhabitants came from all corners of the Realm, and a sizeable minority from yet more distant shores. Each had their own tale of persecution at the hands of their own people and therefore valued the security offered by this refuge. Aside from the long-standing risks posed by the ever-suspicious non-Gifted, the years since the war had brought the added threat of the Blood Reavers. The knowledge that drinking the blood of the Gifted would prolong human life had been suppressed under the Queen's Word.

Nevertheless, this hadn't prevented it becoming widely known amongst the upper echelons of society throughout the Greater Realm. A select few criminal gangs had made themselves rich by abducting Gifted in order to drain their blood and sell it to a select clientele. Any caught doing so were subject to immediate execution but the potential profits were sufficient to overcome the fears of many an outlaw. The wall around Nehrin's Point was not for show, nor was it a manifestation of paranoia.

So far, there had only been one serious attempt at abduction in the Reaches. A teenage boy and girl had ventured beyond the walls for a midnight tryst only to be captured by an opportunist band of cutthroats. Vaelin had handled the matter with swift and merciless efficiency, hunting down the band with the aid of the tower's hounds. He ordered those not killed in the brief skirmish paraded through the streets of North Tower before executing them in the square, the hangman having been ordered to make sure the spectacle lasted as long as possible. However, Vaelin was not so naive to think the threat had disappeared, and a garrison of twenty North Guard were on permanent station at Nehrin's Point.

Since Nortah's tenure as teacher, the original schoolhouse he constructed had been given over as a nursery for the youngest children. Classes for the older students were now held in a large two-storey building constructed from the red sandstone common to the Reaches. Both buildings sat close to the longhouse where Nortah and Sella had made their home. It sat empty now, the windows boarded up and a chain on the door. Vaelin cast a critical eye over the roof, finding numerous tiles missing, and grimacing as he pondered the likely state of the interior. He had been a frequent visitor here in the years before Sella's illness. Even then Nortah's increasing appreciation for the bottle had become apparent, his evening conversation full of morose musings on the war that gradually descended into slurred and potentially treasonous commentaries on the nature of their queen. Sella, ever a patient soul, had forborne it all with a stoic good humour and Nortah, despite greeting most mornings with a befuddled and aching head, had attended to his teaching duties with a determined diligence. The building of the new schoolhouse had been his idea, paid for with a grant of monies from the Tower Lord. For a time his drinking diminished as he oversaw the construction, but it had only been partially complete when Sella fell ill.

Promise me, she had said when Vaelin sat by her bedside for the last time.

Her face was tense with pain as she made the signs, hands still gloved even then. *He is your brother,* she told him, seeing the reluctance he hadn't managed to keep from his face. *Promise me. You will not let him destroy himself.*

"My lord?"

Vaelin blinked, finding Cara standing a few feet away. She wore a plain gown and shawl of dark fabric, hair bound up although a few wayward coils twisted in the stiff sea breeze. Vaelin was struck by the contrast she made to the often frightened but determinedly brave girl who had followed him across the ice. As one of the more celebrated Gifted in the Realm, she enjoyed a position of considerable respect at the Point, not to say authority despite the fact that she continually refused to serve on the Town Council. In contrast to her fellow townsfolk, she always greeted Vaelin with an open smile of genuine welcome, but not today. Instead, her expression mixed forced solicitude with guarded expectation.

"Cara," he said. "I've told you before, there's no need for formality when we're alone."

She glanced over her shoulder at the gaggle of children emerging from the schoolhouse. Most were hurrying home amidst a chatter of horseplay and laughter, but a few lingered to stare in blank curiosity at the Tower Lord conversing with their teacher. "Off with you lot!" Cara called to them with an impatient flick of her wrist. "Don't stand and gawp when your parents are waiting with food on the table."

From the way they fled in the face of her strident tones Vaelin divined that Cara's style of teaching was something of a contrast to Nortah's. His brother had always enjoyed an effortless ability to capture the attention and respect of his pupils. Cara, it seemed, felt the need of a more commanding approach.

"You have something for me, I believe," Cara said, turning back to him and extending her hand.

"I do." Vaelin took the scroll from his pocket and handed it to her. "Word flies quickly, it seems."

"And gossip flies quickest of all, especially when one's husband takes up with a slattern."

Vaelin concealed a wince at the hard edge of bitterness in her tone, watching her unfurl the scroll and give a satisfied nod upon surveying the contents.

"So, I find myself a spinster by order of the Tower Lord," she said with forced humour.

"I was assured you would have no objection. If that's not the case . . ."

"Oh no." She rolled the scroll into a tight cylinder and consigned it to the inside of her shawl. "I certainly have no objection. You pressed him into the North Guard. I'll wager he hated that. The prospect of war was almost as likely to make him take to his heels as the prospect of chores. Still, can't say I relish the memory of it much either." She turned, inclining her head at the schoolhouse. "Come, I've got stew on the boil. Won't have it said the Tower Lord went away from my door with an empty belly."

"I'll eat with you," he said. "And gladly. But I have other business first." He directed his gaze to the stretch of beach beyond Nortah's abandoned house. He could make out the dark huddle of a hut amidst the dunes, although there was no sign of smoke from the chimney. "Is he . . . ?"

"Still there, don't worry," Cara assured him, exasperation in her voice. "I keep telling him to move in with me, but he won't. Says he likes the quiet." She started back to the schoolhouse, speaking over her shoulder. "See if you can get him to come and eat with us, will you?"

◆ ◆ ◆

He found Erlin hunched over a book on his porch, apparently deaf to the scrape of Vaelin's boots on the sand. He sat at a small desk with a book in one hand whilst his other held a pen, poised with predatory expectation over a sheaf of parchment.

"A lustrous mane of golden hair!" Vaelin heard him exclaim in a mutter rich in judgemental satisfaction, his pen scratching ink on the parchment. "Lakril's hair was brown, you fool."

"Aspect Dendrish got it wrong again, I take it?" Vaelin enquired.

"The fifth error I've found." Erlin reclined in his seat, rubbing at his eyes. "If he wasn't dead I'd be minded to write him a very lengthy and sternly worded letter."

"I doubt he'd have read it. He was never fond of criticism."

Erlin slowly lowered his hand from his eyes, which had taken on a glint of cautious curiosity. "Wasn't expecting you for a few weeks. Got another language to learn?"

"I'm not here for language lessons." Vaelin moved to lift the book from the table, reading the title on the spine: *Madness and Royalty—The Reign of* the *King Lakril* by Dendrish Hendrahl, Master of the Third Order. "This time it's your favourite subject," he said. "History."

"Your library is nearly as rich as mine," Erlin pointed out.

"Not with regards to the Far West. For that, I need you."

"And what's in the Far West that concerns you so?"

Someone I loved . . . "The Stahlhast," Vaelin said, setting the book down. "And the Jade Princess."

Erlin stroked his increasingly fulsome beard. When he had first taken up residence on this beach, it had been black shot through with grey; now it was grey shot through with ever-diminishing threads of black. There was also a stoop to his shoulders that hadn't been there a year ago, and he was given to groaning and rubbing his back whenever he got to his feet. Vaelin did his best not to stare as Erlin rose from the table, teeth bared in a grimace, but witnessing the rapid onset of age in one who had been ageless stirred a deep well of guilt. *He lost his gift at my behest,* Vaelin reminded himself, his self-reproach unalloyed by the knowledge that there had been no choice. Trapping the Ally in a physical body required a vessel possessed of sufficient power to lure him from the Beyond, but the price had been high. A man who had walked the earth for more years than he could remember now knew death to be but decades away, if not sooner. For all that, he remained a surprisingly cheerful soul and content in his labours.

"Faith," Erlin breathed. He spent a few seconds massaging the base of his spine before moving to the shed. "I'll make tea. This isn't a short tale."

The hut's interior was even more filled with scrolls than at Vaelin's first visit here years before, though in a much less orderly state. They lay piled in each corner amidst the stacks of books, which Erlin preferred. "Never could get on with Harlick's penmanship" was his excuse for the disregard he displayed towards the hut's previous occupant. Vaelin suspected it had more to do with a basic dislike of the author, an attitude with which he had some sympathy.

"You were supposed to check his work," he pointed out, taking a seat at the table whilst Erlin poured the tea. "He writes me letters enquiring as to your progress every few months. Apparently, the shelves of the Grand Library yearn for these tomes."

"They can yearn a bit longer," Erlin replied. "Not my fault Harlick chose the most boring twaddle to transcribe, is it?"

He pushed a steaming cup across the table and sat down, sipping his own beverage, brows creased in thought. "It's been quite a long time since I heard mention of the Stahlhast," he said. "Can't say they've made a huge mark on Far Western history."

"I believe that may be about to change." Vaelin went on to describe the events of the previous few days. He left out nothing, reasoning that of the two of them, Erlin possessed by far the greater number of secrets.

"General Gian." Erlin's bushy eyebrows rose in surprise. "Him I have heard of. Must've been near twenty years ago, but he had a fine reputation even then. As I recall, he made his name defeating the Black Banner Fleet during the wars with the Northern Pirate Alliance, a feat that had eluded a dozen predecessors. Not a man to scare easily."

"The Stahlhast scared him enough to make him sail across the Arathean in search of novel weapons. What are they?"

"A people best avoided, by all accounts. One of the horse tribes that range across the Iron Steppe, though their customs are unique and they're said to differ from the other horse-folk in appearance and language. I can't attest to this myself, since I never clapped eyes on one. But I did hear many a tale of their rituals and they sound far from pleasant."

"Rituals? So they're god worshippers?"

"After a fashion. It's said they worship something they call the 'Unseen,' whatever that is. There are various clans, called Skeld, each competing for dominance with the other, but they all owe obeisance to their priests." He paused for a moment of contemplation as he sipped more tea. "And General Gian indicated they now pose a threat to the northern border of the Venerable Kingdom?"

"With his dying breath."

"The one thing all sources agree on about the Stahlhast is their martial prowess. I remember one Far Western cavalry officer calling them the finest horse-borne warriors in the world."

"Better even than the Eorhil?"

"Hard to believe, I know. But, skilled as they are, the Eorhil have no armour and make little use of steel. The Stahlhast are renowned for the quality of their armour and their blades. Some sources refer to them as the Steel Horde. If someone has managed to unify them, the kingdoms of the Merchant Kings could well be in for a very difficult time."

"Gian seemed to think his kingdom faced utter destruction, and that the

Stahlhast wouldn't stop there." Vaelin paused before adding, "The Messenger said something similar before he died."

A shadow passed across Erlin's face and he set down his teacup, lowering an unfocused gaze to the tabletop. Mention of the Messenger led inevitably to thoughts of the Ally, thoughts Vaelin knew Erlin did everything in his power to suppress.

"I'm sorry but I have to ask," Vaelin said. "The Ally. He spoke of something before we made him touch the black stone. Something vast and hungry, he said. Do you know what he meant?"

Erlin stayed silent for a long time, so long in fact that the steam rising from his teacup had thinned to nothing before he spoke again. "No, but I do remember his fear of it. Much of his emotions had been worn away over the many centuries of his existence, leaving only his desire for it all to end, and his terror of what he had seen the second time he touched the black stone. The memory is vague, just a swirling mist of sensation, none of it pleasant. In truth, I don't think he knew what he was seeing, but he did understand what it meant, what it wanted."

"What did it want?"

Erlin shrugged and reached for his cup, giving a sour grimace at the cooled contents. "Everything. It wants everything, and even then it won't be sated." He rose and went to the stove at the far end of the hut, lifting the kettle onto the hob. "You also made mention of the Jade Princess," he said, evidently keen to change the subject.

"There was a woman," Vaelin said. "You never met her, but we were . . . very good friends . . ."

"Sister Sherin," Erlin interrupted. "Your lost love, sent far away so that she might be spared your fate at the end of the Alpiran war. The story is fairly well known."

"It is?"

"Of course." Erlin chuckled and shook his head. "There are very few aspects of your life that aren't. The price you pay for becoming a legend, I suppose."

"In any case," Vaelin said. "Sherin was . . . is a healer. The Messenger intimated she had cause to minister to the Jade Princess, and placed herself in grave danger as a result."

"Then you can safely dismiss his words. The Jade Princess is even older than I am. She doesn't get sick."

Vaelin arched an eyebrow at Erlin's mostly grey beard. "Things change, even for the Gifted."

"You don't understand. She is . . . different. When I say she's older than me I don't mean by a few decades, or even a few centuries. She had such stories." A distance crept into Erlin's gaze, his lips forming a faint smile of remembrance. "Of a time before the cities rose, of great beasts lost to the vagaries of time and climate. Of wars and kingdoms and empires, the names of which no one save her can now recall. Next to the Jade Princess, I am but an infant. If Sherin went to her, it wasn't as a healer."

"Then why?"

"The people of the Far West have always sought out her counsel, believing her to possess wisdom and insight far beyond the most sage of scholars. For this reason she has long secluded herself in various refuges, moving on when they inevitably crumble under the weight of time. The High Temple is merely the most recent. It lies deep in the northern mountains of the Venerable Kingdom and is not an easy place to get to. I should know, I travelled there twice. But, however arduous, there are those who continue to come in search of her wisdom. Perhaps Sherin did too."

He paused, eyeing Vaelin carefully. "I can see what you're thinking, my friend," he said. "And I urge you: don't."

Vaelin's thoughts returned to Kerran's dining room and Lohren's vision. *Last night I dreamt of a wolf.* "I'm not sure I have a choice," he said. "If she's in danger . . ."

"How do you know she would even welcome your help?" Erlin cut in. "After what you did?"

Playing his fingers through her hair, placing her in Ahm Lin's arms, watching the ship take her away . . . *Betrayal is always the worst sin.* "I don't," Vaelin said. "But welcome it or not, I can't just linger here, not now. Also, the way the Messenger spoke of the Stahlhast, he made it clear there is a greater threat here than merely the rampaging of an obscure horse tribe, a threat Queen Lyrna may need to be warned against."

"They lay far across the ocean. What threat could they pose here?"

"Any ocean can be crossed, as our queen demonstrated and the Volarians discovered to their cost. They imagined themselves safe from us. They were wrong."

"The lands of the Merchant Kings are not the Realm. Nor are they Alpira or Volaria. In the Far West they were printing books and plotting the course of the stars whilst we were still working out which end of a spear to poke a deer with. There you have no legend. There you will be no more than a barbarian foreigner, little more than a savage in their eyes."

Vaelin grimaced and nodded at the kettle. "It's boiling."

Erlin let out a sigh and lifted the kettle from the hob. "Always the same with you. Never content. Never able to settle, not when there's another calamity to embroil yourself in. Haven't you travelled far enough? Haven't you seen enough blood?"

"I have, and if fortune smiles, I'll see no more however far I travel. But I am resolved on this, Erlin. And I need your help. I need to know all you can tell me about the Far West. And I need a map to guide me to the High Temple and the Jade Princess."

"I can't teach you what you need to know in mere days." Erlin's shoulders sagged a little as he sprinkled fresh leaves into his teapot, his next words emerging in a weary sigh. "I'll have to come with you. You've always been a bit lost without me, anyway."

"No." Vaelin's voice was firm. "I'll not ask this of you."

"Why not? Because I'm old now, and getting older by the day?" Erlin's gaze took on an amused twinkle. "Rest assured, I'm spry as ever when I need to be. And a map won't be of any use to you without me to guide you clear of the Merchant King's soldiers." He stirred the leaves with a long-handled spoon and placed the lid on the teapot. "So, when do we leave?"

Chapter Seven

So, *his cousin spoke the true word after all,* Vaelin mused, watching Alum ascend the gangplank to the deck of the *Sea Wasp.* The ship sat low in the waters of the North Tower harbour, her holds filled with a mixed cargo of Cumbraelin wine, Asraelin iron ore and Alpiran spices. She had been built during the Liberation War and her martial heritage was clear in the clean lines of her hull and the old scars marring the timber of her rails and masts.

"The fastest vessel owned by the Honoured Trading House of Al Verin," Kerran assured Vaelin as they stood together on the quayside. "Every year I award a bonus to any ship that makes the fastest crossing of the Arathean. The *Sea Wasp* has won for the last four years in a row."

At Lord Orven's insistence, two dozen North Guard were arrayed in ranks nearby as a farewell honour guard, adding a sense of ceremony to this occasion that Vaelin could well have done without. The morning had already provided a sufficient trial in the form of Ellese's violent reaction to being told she had to stay behind.

"I'll go wherever I bloody well want!"

The plate she hurled at him missed his head by less than an inch, shattering on the wall of the meal hall where they had, up until this moment, shared a fairly convivial breakfast.

"By order of your mother and, I might add, our queen," Vaelin told her in a shout that brooked no argument, "you are under my command, Lady

Ellese! And you will follow your instructions or I'll have you bound and gagged!"

She blanched a little in the face of his anger but stood her ground, hands twitching as she presumably resisted the urge to reach for another projectile. Amidst the fury, he detected an additional sting of rejection. It hadn't occurred to him she might react this way, and he reminded himself once more how much the wounded child she remained. *Reva packed her off to the Reaches; now I abandon her for months.*

"Lord Orven will see to your lessons in my absence," he said. "You will also study healing with Brother Kehlan. Come winter you will journey to stay with the Eorhil until the turn of the year, after which you will spend a month with the Seordah. There will be plenty to occupy you."

"You heard what that thing said," she replied, her voice calmer now but still betraying a harsh quaver. "It wanted to kill me, after hurting me all over again. I know you're going to the Far West to find whoever sent it here. You promised me a reckoning, Uncle, and I didn't get it."

"That thing is dead, in any way that matters. There is no reckoning to be had and I will not take the heir to the Fiefdom of Cumbrael into unknown dangers. You will remain here and I'll hear no more on the subject."

There had been further angry words, and a few inventively profane insults, before she stormed off to her rooms. He had decided it was best to leave her there, hoping she might have calmed herself come the late morning tide. However, she remained conspicuously absent from the throng on the quayside.

"Are you sure this is an altogether good idea?" Kerran asked him, her gaze fixed on the trio of North Guard carrying an unconscious figure aboard the ship.

"He was always a better man when he had a task to perform," Vaelin replied. "Although, I'll admit the voyage is likely to be a trial."

He held out his arms to Lohren and Artis. The girl came to embrace him immediately, Artis after a moment's sulky hesitation. "Take care of your aunt," he told the boy, drawing back. "I've appointed Captain Embi to take over your lessons with the sword. He's a fine teacher, but not so forgiving as I so don't forget to duck."

Artis blinked and lowered his gaze. "I won't, my lord."

"Will Father be all right?" Lohren asked him, eyes bright with tears. "Will you?"

Vaelin resisted the impulse to lie, knowing such kindnesses were wasted on her. "The road is long and the future ever uncertain," he said, cupping her cheek. "Even for you, I suspect. Any . . . special insights to offer your uncle?"

She smiled and shook her head. "It went away again, much to Auntie's relief."

He wasn't sure if she was lying. Kerran's fear of the Dark had always been palpable, and consequently it had taken her years to form a true bond with her niece. Vaelin pulled Lohren close once again, whispering into her ear. "If it comes back and you happen to learn something of importance, go straight to Lord Orven. He has instructions to hear you out and act accordingly."

Releasing her he exchanged a brief bow with Kerran—an embrace would have been unseemly—and moved to the gangplank where Orven waited to offer a salute. "I wish you would reconsider, my lord," he said. "Just a small escort of North Guard . . ."

"You have need of them all," Vaelin broke in. "Besides, stepping ashore in the Venerable Kingdom with soldiers in service to a foreign crown would be certain to attract the wrong kind of attention."

"There is . . ." Orven hesitated, shifting in discomfort. "A small matter of law, my lord?"

"Law?"

"The original charter set down by King Janus authorising the settlement of the Northern Reaches stipulated that the Tower Lord is forbidden from absenting himself from these lands without express royal consent."

"I see. And the penalty for transgression?"

Orven did some more shifting. "Death, my lord."

"A serious matter then. I suggest you write to the queen with all urgency. I'm sure she will be swift in sending a response. It may even arrive here before I return."

Orven sighed and gave a weary nod. "I will, my lord."

Vaelin glanced back at the assembled folk who had come to see him off, mostly faces he knew mixed with a few gawpers. Apart from that unfortunate business in the Outer Isles four years ago, he hadn't been beyond the confines of the Reaches since the end of the war.

"I have a sense of trouble ahead," he told Orven. "I think it best if you recall the militia early for training this year. Also, increase the pay by another few coppers a day. See if we can't persuade some more recruits to join the ranks."

"As you wish, my lord. And as for petitions?"

Vaelin gave a small grin. Orven had no more liking for the ritual than he did. "I've asked Lady Kerran to attend, in an advisory capacity only, of course. I strongly urge you to listen to her counsel."

"I'm sure it will be most welcome."

Vaelin held out his hand and the guardsman clasped it, his grip strong. "Much as I cherish my family, I'd give almost anything to come with you. It seems such a long time since our last foray."

"Miss it, do you?"

"Sometimes. As a boy I dreamt one day I would join the King's Guard and do great deeds in a just cause. It's hard to believe it all came true. For all we lost, all the horrors we witnessed, things were simpler then."

"Battles are simple. It's what comes before and after that's complicated."

Vaelin gave his hand a final shake before starting up the gangplank.

◆ ◆ ◆

"You poxed bastard!"

Nortah's punch was a testament to his diminished faculties. Vaelin ducked easily under his flailing arm and stood back to watch him spin into an untidy heap on the deck. He lay there, eyes glaring out from unwashed and bearded features.

"Are you quite finished?" Vaelin enquired.

"I am a Sword of the Realm!" Nortah climbed unsteadily to his feet, raising his voice to address the crew of the *Sea Wasp*. "I will pay gold to any man who rows me to shore."

Most of the crew paused to regard him with either bafflement or amused contempt before returning to their duties.

"Take a look, brother," Vaelin said, moving to the rail and gesturing to the ocean stretching away to the misted horizon on all sides. "We've been at sea for three days," he explained. "Brother Kehlan's sleeping draught is evidently quite something. I don't think trying to row home is a particularly good idea, not that the captain will be willing to part with a boat in any case. You're welcome to try swimming though."

Nortah closed his eyes and let out a groan, head slumped as he subsided against the rail. "I assume the crew have been ordered not to supply me with grog," he muttered.

"In fact they've been paid not to do so," Vaelin assured him. "You have to admit, it's preferable to a cell."

"How long?" Nortah opened his eyes, favouring Vaelin with a gaze deeper in resentment than any he had shown before. "Until we reach the Far West. How long?"

"Three weeks with a fair wind, four or more without."

"I hear they have a wine there made from fermented rice. I assure you, brother, the first thing I do upon landing will be to seek it out. I shall also, from that moment on, consider whatever brotherhood exists between us to be at an end."

"That will be your choice. Although, how you'll make your way with no coin and no knowledge of the language will be interesting to see." He clapped Nortah on the shoulder and moved towards the ladder to the hold. "I dine with the captain at the seventh bell. Please feel free to join us."

◆ ◆ ◆

Sehmon was quick and lithe with a keen eye for both risk and opportunity. He nimbly evaded the first two thrusts of Vaelin's wooden sword before delivering a slashing reply with his own. It was here that his lack of expertise with a long blade became obvious, the blow delivered with a stiff arm and his wrist at too sharp an angle. Vaelin's parry caught the outlaw's wooden blade close to the hilt and sent it spinning out of his grasp.

"Nicely done, my lord," he said with a rueful grin that promptly disappeared when Vaelin slapped the flat of his sword against the side of the youth's head.

"A fight doesn't end when you lose your weapon," he said, drawing the ash blade back for a second blow. Sehmon reacted swiftly, dipping into a forward roll that brought his hand in range of his fallen sword. He snatched it up in time to deflect the thrust Vaelin jabbed at his midriff.

"You seem to think this a game, Master Sehmon," Vaelin said, advancing on the now-back-pedalling outlaw. "I assure you it is not."

Sehmon leapt as Vaelin slashed at his legs, landing atop the starboard rail, then leapt again to avoid another blow that would have sent him into the sea. He caught hold of some rigging and swung, bringing his body round in a wide arc to deliver a two-footed kick to Vaelin's hip. He managed to keep his feet but the force of the impact sent him to his knees.

Three ways, he thought as Sehmon landed close by. *Three ways in which a skilled adversary could kill me now.* Unfortunately for Sehmon, he chose the wrong way. His sword came down in a hefty vertical swing that thudded into the deck as Vaelin moved his head aside. Sehmon let out a groan of mingled pain and defeat as Vaelin's lunge took him in the belly, leaving him gasping on the deck on all fours.

"Deep breaths," Vaelin told the youth. "Remember, a kneeling man turns slower than a standing man. Best to come at him from the side."

Sehmon fought down a retch. "My thanks for the lesson, my lord."

Helping the outlaw to his feet, Vaelin heard Alum let out a low chuckle. "The dance of the long blades, my people called it," he said, smiling at them from his perch atop a dense coil of rope. "We always found the attachment of others to such things strange. This," he said, reaching for the spear propped close by, "is all a man needs in a fight, or a hunt. Here." He tossed the spear to Sehmon. "Put that twig down and learn the true art of combat."

Sehmon cast a questioning glance at Vaelin. "Your master's commands take precedence in this," he said, moving aside.

He spent an hour or so watching Alum tutor his servant in the basics of the spear, gaining a true appreciation for the Moreska's skills in the process. He had already assessed him as a skilled hunter with the strength and resolve to kill a man with only a set of chains. Now, seeing the fluid economy of his movements and the way the spear blurred and seemed to change shape in his hands, he was forced to judge Alum as a man he hoped he would never have to fight. It raised the question of how it had been possible for him to be captured.

I was captured once, he reminded himself. The notion inevitably led to reminiscences about his time in the Emperor's dungeons, and the visions of Sherin brought to him by the blood-song. They had just been brief glimpses at first, growing in detail and duration as he honed his ability with the song. Always he saw her healing; a sailor with a broken arm, a sickly child in a hovel, a woman in an opulent mansion suffering through a difficult birth. In time the glimpses began to fade as he felt her drawing beyond his reach, but the final vision remained clearest of all. *She had been happy,* he remembered, recalling the deep regard of the man she had been greeting. *Who is he? Friend? Lover? Husband?*

A loud commotion from belowdecks broke through his rumination, Alum and Sehmon's practice coming to a halt at the volume of the disturbance.

"It'll just be a brawl, my lord," Sehmon said as a chorus of upraised voices continued to emerge from a nearby hatchway. "Never met a sailor that couldn't find something to fight about."

The babble of conflict seemed louder than any mere brawl and, as it continued, Vaelin detected an odd note, one voice pitched higher than the others. A female voice.

Muttering a curse, he ran for the hatchway and quickly scaled the ladder into the hold. The source of the commotion wasn't hard to find, a dense knot of men near the stern, repeatedly closing on and then retreating from something in their midst. One of them reared back with a shout of pain, Vaelin glimpsing blood on his face. The other sailors, six in all, closed in again, kicking and punching at a struggling figure on the deck.

"Stand fast!" Vaelin barked, pushing his way through the knot of men. All but one responded immediately, moving back, heads lowered in the face of the Tower Lord's ire. The man with the bloodied face, however, continued to drive his boot into the belly of the figure on the deck. Vaelin stepped forward to pull him away, then halted as a swift shape emerged from the shadows beyond the prone man to drive a punch into the face of his assailant. The sailor staggered from the blow, remaining upright and licking at the blood streaming from his nose until the figure from the shadows delivered another blow to his temple that left him senseless on the boards.

"That's enough!" Vaelin met Ellese's gaze as she moved towards the man she had knocked to the deck, knife in hand.

"Filthy bastard put his hands on me," she hissed, drawing the knife back for a thrust. Vaelin stepped between her and the fallen sailor, snaring her arm in a tight grip.

"I said, that's enough."

"I'm fine, incidentally," Nortah groaned from the deck, wincing and holding his stomach as he sat up.

"He tried to keep them off me," Ellese said. "This lot"—her voice took on a snarl as she regarded the other sailors—"thought they could have their way."

"She's a stowaway, my lord," one of the sailors said. Vaelin found he didn't like the resentful defensiveness in the man's bearing as he shot Ellese a dark glare. "Stowaways got no rights. It's tradition . . ."

His words died as Vaelin delivered a hard backhand cuff to his jaw, sending him reeling. "Get yourselves up top," he told the sailors, jabbing the toe of his boot against the skull of their unconscious shipmate. "And take this one with you."

They possessed enough wisdom to mute any grumbling as they gathered up the fallen man and climbed the steps to the upper deck. "Can you stand?" Vaelin asked, stooping to take hold of Nortah's arm. He jerked it away and got slowly to his feet.

"Had to hide in the rum store, didn't you?" he asked Ellese before shaking his head and stumbling off into the gloomy recesses of the hold.

Vaelin turned to Ellese. Her body seemed to thrum with frustrated anger and she met his gaze with an unrepentant stare. "How?" he asked simply.

"Swam the harbour from the northern mole and climbed the anchor chain when you were saying your goodbyes." She shrugged. "It wasn't difficult."

So much like Reva, he thought. *But not entirely.* "Your mother would have killed at least two before I got here," he told her.

Her stare turned into something more guarded. "I'm stiff from crouching behind barrels for three days."

No, he decided, studying her face carefully. *You knew I'd stop you.* "Did Lord Nortah partake of any rum?"

She shook her head. "He was about to, sure enough. Tried tapping a spile into one of the small barrels and knocked it onto my foot. That lot heard us arguing." She hesitated. "Are you going to hang them?"

"Do you want me to?"

She was calmer now, the anger leeched away into a nervous uncertainty. "They were a bit free with their hands, but I doubt they were really going to do anything. If that matters."

"They outraged the person of my niece, who also happens to be the heir to the Fiefdom of Cumbrael. It can't go unanswered. But neither can your disobedience."

She gave a derisive snort. "Going to flog me, are you, Uncle?"

He stared at her wordlessly until the grin slipped from her lips and she began to fidget as he let the silence stretch. "I've been indulging you, up until now," he told her, hoping she heard the soft sincerity in his voice. "Because of the love I bear for your mother. I have tried to be gentler in your education than my masters were in mine. I used to see their harshness as cruelty, an unnecessary adjunct to the wisdom they imparted. Now, I see I was mistaken. You have learned nothing from me, because I have not taught you properly."

He stepped closer to her, keeping her eyes trapped in his. "So I will give you a choice. Submit to my training or don't. If you don't, you will be confined on this ship and returned to the Reaches once I have disembarked in the Far West. You will return to your mother, explaining my failure to teach you. Or"—he stepped closer still, lowering his voice to an intent whisper—"agree and I will allow you to journey with me. I offer nothing but hardship, judgement and pain from here on in and you may well hate me by the time we're done. But at least you might have a chance at surviving this world, for I suspect it has many dangers in store for you."

He watched her throat bulge and resentment steal over her features. He knew she was fighting the impulse to strike at him, hurl yet more abuse and declare her scornful rejection. But, if he had any real chance of teaching her, she would have to master her impulses.

After a few seconds of staring at him with bunched jaws and reddening skin, she gave a jerky nod of acceptance.

"I need your word," Vaelin said. "State your agreement, Lady Ellese."

"I . . ." She faltered and cleared her throat. "I agree to submit to your training, Lord Vaelin."

He glanced over her shoulder at the shadowy confines of the rum store. "These quarters aren't suitable. From now on you'll sleep on the upper deck, regardless of the weather."

◆ ◆ ◆

Captain Veiser of the *Sea Wasp* was a tall, taciturn Renfaelin with a face that resembled a mask of weathered stone but for the occasional twitch. From the cowed demeanour of the transgressing sailors arrayed before him, Vaelin was struck by the realisation that they were more afraid of their captain than their Tower Lord. Veiser listened in silence to Vaelin's account, which included a fulsome apology for the actions of his niece, before turning a cold eye on the sailors.

"Your punishment, my lord?" he enquired.

"It's your ship, sir," Vaelin said. "And they're your men." He glanced at Ellese, who stood nearby trying vainly to conceal her apprehension. It was clear to him she had no desire to witness another hanging. "Lady Ellese has indicated a desire for clemency," he added. "However, I leave any punishment in your hands."

"Lady Ellese is to be commended for her compassion," Captain Veiser replied, his eyes never wavering from the sailors. They were arrayed in a line parallel to the beam of the ship, flanked on either side by the bosun and the third mate, both large men bearing cudgels. "However," the captain went on, "in addition to the insult they dealt her, these men have also transgressed the ship's rules as set down by the Honoured Trading House of Al Verin. All stowaways are to be brought immediately to the captain."

He stepped closer to the sailors, voice hardening as he walked along the line. Vaelin noted how his face twitched with increasing energy as he spoke. "The *Sea Wasp* is a respectable vessel. She is not some flagless tub crewed by scum. Once my crew were all fine men. Once we sailed across half the world and did great service at the Battles of the Beacon and the Cut. But many were lost to the fires of war, and these days I am increasingly obliged to take on wretches such as this."

This last was punctuated by a hard openhanded blow to the last man in line. From the way the man whimpered in response, Vaelin was forced to ponder the manner of Veiser's command.

"The last man to breach house rules received ten strokes of the Crimson Duchess, as you may recall," he said, stepping back, a contemplative frown on his brow as he turned to Vaelin. "Are you familiar with the Duchess, my lord?"

"I've heard of it. A many-thonged whip fashioned from the hide of the red shark, I believe."

"Quite so. Cuts the skin of man like a dozen razors at once. The sight is really quite affecting. And not always fatal. Still." He thought for a moment longer. "Since the good lady has made a plea for clemency we'll leave it at a caning." He turned to the bosun. "Ten strokes each. And no rum for the rest of the voyage. Any further transgressions and it'll be a dozen strokes of the Duchess."

The punishment took an hour to administer, each man taking his turn at being tied to the main mast to receive ten strokes of an ash cane. The bosun did his work without obvious relish, but also with a diligent efficiency that left each man on their knees with blood seeping from the welts on their back, weeping and gasping in pain. As the fifth transgressor was led to the mast, Ellese turned away and started towards the stern.

"Stay," Vaelin ordered, his glare sufficient to freeze her in place. "Watch." She stood, flinching with every stroke as the bosun set to work on the next sailor. "Consider this your first true lesson," Vaelin told her. "All actions have consequences."

CHAPTER EIGHT

S o, the Emerald Empire existed for a thousand years before the rise of the Merchant Kings?" Vaelin asked.

"Closer to nine hundred, give or take a few decades," Erlin said. "I must say, in all my travels I never heard tell of a single dynasty that lasted so long. But everything fades with time. What was strength becomes weakness. So it was with the Emerald Empire."

Vaelin glanced over at Ellese as she came to a halt a few feet from their perch close to the ship's prow. The sun was high in a cloudless sky and sweat shone on her brow and the bare skin of her arms as she laboured to drag air into her lungs. Sehmon, who had opted to take an equal part in her training, stumbled to her side an instant later, his breathing even more ragged.

"Was that six laps?" Vaelin asked Erlin, who shrugged.

"Wasn't counting."

"In that case we'd better make it another two, just to be sure." He met Ellese's gaze and jerked his head in dismissal. She swallowed a sigh before filling her lungs and setting off on another full-pelt lap around the deck, Sehmon following a few paces behind.

"Strength became weakness?" Vaelin prompted, turning back to Erlin.

"Quite so. Before the empire the Far West was just a clutch of competing kingdoms in a near-perpetual state of war, rather like the Realm before King Janus came along, but on a much grander scale. Mah-Shin, the First Emperor, wiped out the old monarchies, killing every member down to the fourth generation, and declared it his intention to craft a dynasty that would achieve the perfect harmony between Earth, Heaven and man. This so-called harmonic principle was an old idea even before Mah-Shin's birth, the goal of the many ambitious conquerors that preceded him. However, only he ever came close to putting it into practice, founding the Emerald Empire on the twin pillars of an extensive bureaucracy and a canon of written law."

A brief drum of footfalls and Ellese stumbled to a halt once more, back bent and chest heaving. Sehmon took another second to arrive, sinking immediately to his knees, groaning with every breath.

"One cup of water each," Vaelin told them. "Then climb the mainmast."

"How . . . many . . . times?" Ellese enquired between breaths.

"Until I tell you to stop."

She nodded and started towards the water barrel, pausing when Vaelin spoke her name. "Would you leave your brother lying there?" he asked, pointing to Sehmon.

For the first time in days a glimmer of defiance flickered across her face. "He's not . . . my brother."

"He is now."

He held her gaze until she set her jaw and moved to Sehmon, taking hold of his arm and dragging him to his feet. "Get up, you lazy sod." She prodded him towards the water barrel. "And don't even think about calling me 'sister.'"

"Heaven," Vaelin said to Erlin. "The home of the Far Western gods, I assume?"

"They don't really have gods, not as we would understand them. Rather, Heaven is the source of all fortune, good or bad, and also the wellspring of what we term the Dark."

"The Music of Heaven," Vaelin murmured, recalling Ahm Lin's tale of how he had been conscripted to serve one of the Merchant Kings once his blood-song had been revealed.

"A rare gift," Erlin said. "One of many, as we well know. Those that possess them are said to enjoy the blessing of Heaven and are thereby elevated above the rest of humanity, for when they die their souls will take their place in Heaven. The spirits of the non-blessed will remain earthbound, contained within tombs and placated with offerings from their descendants, lest they become restless and disturb the balance."

"And did the First Emperor achieve his goal? This perfect harmony."

"Many a Far Western historian will insist he did. It was under Mah-Shin that military and civil appointments were made on merit rather than privilege. He established laws that banned arbitrary imprisonment and guaranteed rights for all from the lowliest peasant to the wealthiest landowner. He also began construction of the great web of canals that even today links all corners of the Far West. Prosperity and justice were his legacies, at least that's what the official record would have us believe."

"And the truth?"

"He was a tyrant who ruled as much through fear as wisdom. It's said he went mad in his later years, believing himself to be a living vessel of divine grace and therefore infallible. On his deathbed he decreed that no word of the laws he had set down were ever to be altered. And so, as lesser sons sought vainly to match the glory of their forebear in ever-changing times, they found themselves increasingly constrained by the laws that had once seemed so vital to the empire's well-being."

"And yet it lasted for a thousand years."

"Yes, with many wars, famines and bloody dynastic feuds along the way. Theories differ as to why the Emerald Empire eventually fell apart, but I tend to subscribe to the notion that the imperial bloodline had become so corrupted by inbreeding and luxury it simply lacked the ability to produce an heir capable of effective rule. The last emperor was widely rumoured to have never actually walked on his own two feet or been taught to read. However, it was a series of floods, droughts and subsequent famines that brought the ultimate crisis. Above all else, the favour of Heaven is said to reside in the weather. Faced with so many submerged cities and ruined crops, who could doubt that the emperor had lost its blessing?"

"And so the empire split into the realms of the Merchant Kings."

"After two decades of chaos. The provinces of the empire were each governed on a tripartite basis consisting of a civil governor, a military commander and a financial minister. When the empire collapsed, power coalesced around the financial ministers since they held not only the keys to the provincial treasury, but the knowledge of how to administer the tax system. In time, these masters of coin became masters of all, and the realms of the Merchant Kings were born. There was another decade or so of warfare as small regions were gobbled up by the larger neighbours so that today there

are three Merchant realms: the Venerable Kingdom in the north, the Enlightened Kingdom in the south-east, and the Transcendent Kingdom to the
south-west. Technically, the Free Cantons that comprise the major islands of
the Golden Sea could also be termed a kingdom, but they govern themselves
according to old imperial law rather than Merchant statutes."

Hearing a shout from above, Vaelin glanced up in time to follow Sehmon's untidy fall from the mainmast. The youth's descent was partly arrested
by some rigging before he collided with a crossbeam and tumbled into the
sea off the port side. Vaelin went to the rail to see the outlaw thrashing in the
ship's wake. The winds were strong today, swelling the *Sea Wasp*'s sails, and
he was soon swept towards the stern. Vaelin looked up at Ellese standing in
the crow's nest and gestured expectantly at Sehmon's struggling form.

"Will you leave your brother drowning?" he called to her.

He watched her head tilt back in a brief spasm of annoyance before she
bent to retrieve a coil of rope from the base of the crow's nest. She quickly tied
one end around her waist and fixed the other to the mast before clambering
down to the crosstrees below and sprinting forward to propel herself into the
air, arms sweeping out and down to form a spear-point. She left a small splash
as she completed her dive, surfacing quickly and striking out for Sehmon.
Reaching him after a few strokes, Ellese wrapped her arms around his waist,
sputtering out some colourful language to quell his struggles.

"Make ready to haul 'em in, lads!" the bosun called, taking hold of the
taut rope.

"Leave that a while, if you please," Vaelin told the man as a trio of sailors
ran to join him.

"You want us to leave them in the water, my lord?" the bosun asked, his
heavy features bunching.

"I do."

"For how long?"

Vaelin glanced at the sky, judging the sun at an hour past noon. "Until
it gets dark," he said. "Or it looks like they might drown. Whichever is
soonest."

◆ ◆ ◆

Ellese's hand shook as she spooned stew into her mouth, chewing and swallowing with a somewhat mechanical determination. Since being hauled
from the sea she had kept her gaze firmly averted from Vaelin's, he assumed

in order to avoid any temptation towards unwise words. She had lasted over an hour before finally losing her grip on Sehmon, whereupon the bosun had ordered her hauled in and another line thrown to the outlaw. Vaelin was struck by the lad's lack of animosity, his pallid and chilled features betraying a strange impression of acceptance, as if nearly perishing at the whim of the Tower Lord were some form of honour.

"Your lessons are hard," Alum observed to Vaelin as they ate together at the far end of the table.

"Yes," he agreed. "And yet still kinder than those I was taught at a far younger age."

"You were one of the blue-cloaked beasts, were you not? Tell me"—he leaned closer, voice dropping a little—"is it true they kill in order to sate the shades of the dead with blood?"

Vaelin started to laugh, then saw the seriousness on the Moreska's face. "Is that what you were told?"

"The Empress's agents tell many stories these days. And often they concern the Hopekiller and his vile brethren."

Vaelin recalled his last encounter with the woman who had since been named Empress Emeren, the Trust of the Alpiran People. *Your apology is as empty as your heart, Northman. And my hatred is undimmed.* He remembered the hard gleam of utter sincerity in her eyes as she faced him on the quayside in the Meldenean capital. In that moment the blood-song had made it clear her lust for vengeance was far from over, but its tune failed to reveal that she would one day hold sway over an entire empire.

"No," he told Alum. "The Sixth Order does not kill to sate the shades of the dead. They fight in service to the Faith and the Realm and, on occasion, have done good in so doing."

"But you no longer serve them," Alum said. "Why?"

Vaelin reached for a tankard and sipped some watered-down wine as he pondered his answer. "It's often said that doubt is the enemy of faith. But I have found the real enemy of faith is truth. I left the Order because I had heard and seen too many truths to stay."

"So you have no gods? No . . . faith?"

"I've yet to be convinced that any god is more than a fable. As for faith, I still have it. In myself, in those I'm privileged to call friends." He glanced over at Nortah, who sat at the opposite end of the table, head bowed and face blank as he ate. "And in my family, what remains of it."

Alum's brow creased in puzzlement, as if the notion of navigating life without recourse to gods was an imponderable notion. He began to voice another question but the words died as the urgent tolling of a bell sounded through the deck boards above.

"Stand to arms!" came the muffled cry of the first mate. "Pirate vessel approaching!"

"Fetch your weapons," Vaelin told Ellese and Sehmon, rising and hefting his sword.

He found Captain Veiser at the stern, spyglass trained on the northern horizon. The seas were heavy today, painted slate grey by an overcast sky, the waves whipped high by a stiff easterly wind. Vaelin could make out the dim shape of a sail in the swirling haze, but not much more.

"How many ships?" he enquired, coming to the captain's side.

"Just one, my lord. But she's about our size and therefore I'd wager she'll be a sight slower, but she does have the wind in her favour."

"No chance of outrunning them?"

Veiser shook his head, eye still pressed to the spyglass. "Can't make out the flag at this distance. If she's one of the affiliated clan ships, we might be able to buy them off. If not . . ." He trailed off with a meaningful shrug.

"If you can't see the flag, how do you know she's a pirate?"

"Three red lines on the mainsail. Lets us know they mean to board us. That might be a good sign, suggests they're not spoiling for a fight."

Vaelin looked back at the deck, watching those sailors with bows climb the rigging whilst the first mate and the bosun marshalled the others into two companies, positioned fore and aft. Vaelin gained a quick impression of a marked lack of expertise from the way most of the sailors held the swords and billhooks they had been given. "Has this crew been in battle before?" he asked Veiser.

"Only the handful I sailed with in the war. Must say, my lord, at this juncture I'm sorely glad to have you aboard."

Vaelin watched the approaching sail grow in size, the darker shadow of the hull beneath resolving into view as the minutes passed. A large black flag flew from her mainmast emblazoned with a white motif showing a shield shot through by a bolt of lightning. Beside him, the captain gave a grunt of relieved recognition. "Seems we're in luck, my lord."

"How so?"

"Ships bearing that flag first appeared about two years gone, and they never trouble Realm vessels. The rest of the world aren't so lucky. No one's exactly sure why."

His words were quickly borne out when Vaelin saw a fresh gout of white water erupting on the starboard side of her pirate's hull as she began to veer away. Within moments she had slipped into the haze of the northern horizon.

"Pity."

Vaelin turned to find Nortah standing close by. He wore a seaman's oil-skin cloak, his face pale and thoroughly miserable in the chilly drizzle that swept the deck. Vaelin took a small measure of satisfaction from the fact that his brother had chosen to arm himself with a billhook, though the absence of either fear or anticipation on his face was less encouraging. "I thought at least a pirate might give me a last swallow of grog before tossing us to the sharks."

"Sorry to disappoint you, brother."

He expected Nortah to scowl and slouch away but instead he lingered, voicing an uncomfortable cough amidst the lengthening silence. "I'm bloody bored," he said finally. There was a tension on his colourless features, an impression of a favour asked only with the greatest reluctance. "Sea life is tedious without grog, or something to do," he added with forced and unconvincing levity.

"Lady Ellese is skilled with the bow but still has room for improvement," Vaelin said. "And the lad lacks stamina."

"I'll see to it." Nortah paused, grimacing as he forced himself to ask another question. "I no longer own a sword . . ."

"Your sister bought it back from the blade monger you sold it to," Vaelin said. "It's with my gear, along with your bow." He started towards the ladder to the lower deck. "I'll fetch them."

"I'm still going to get drunk when we make landfall," Nortah called after him, voice diminishing to a bitter sigh when Vaelin didn't turn. "I'm just bored, that's all."

CHAPTER NINE

W hat is that smell?"

"A city."

Alum's nostrils flared and his lips formed a disgusted grimace. "I once journeyed to Alpira. It didn't smell like this."

"Alpira is constantly swept by the desert winds," Vaelin replied, recalling
the days towards the end of his five-year confinement when he had been
allowed out of his cell for a short period each day. The easterly wind would
stiffen each morning with remarkable regularity, bringing a daily pall of
dust along with a warm breeze that did much to banish the worst of the
capital's aroma. To Vaelin the scent seeping through the morning fog enfolding the *Sea Wasp* wasn't especially unpleasant. It consisted mainly of smoke
with a few sharper notes that told of the fish market and the tannery. He
found it no more objectionable than Varinshold on a summer's day, although
the fact that it had reached them at such a remove from the port indicated a
place of far-greater size and population.

"Trim sails!" the bosun called, sending a dozen men aloft whilst others
heaved ropes across the deck. "Prepare to haul away the boat."

"This may not be the best place to disembark, my lord," Captain Veiser
told Vaelin as the lights of the city began to shimmer through the haze. "If
it's your object to remain unnoticed, there are smaller ports to the south
where the authorities are not so scrupulous." He rubbed his thumb and fore-
finger together in the universal sign of the bribe.

"Master Erlin tells me this is where we'll find our guide," Vaelin replied. "Besides, I've often found that the larger the city the easier it is to evade notice."

"As you wish. The *Sea Wasp* will call at this port on our return journey in two months. If you're not here . . ."

"Then sail home with my thanks. Your full fee for this voyage has been lodged with Lady Kerran." Vaelin clapped him on the shoulder and moved to the rail as the crew finished hauling the boat over the side.

"A fee I'd happily forgo to see you safely returned." There was an uncharacteristic intensity to Veiser's gaze that made Vaelin pause. "The Reaches needs you, my lord," he went on. "As does the Realm. We lost too much in the war. I have met Queen Lyrna, and don't relish standing before her to explain why I carried Vaelin Al Sorna to his end."

"Tell her I commanded it. I'm sure she'll understand."

Vaelin joined Ellese at the rail, watching Nortah and the others climb into the boat. He took a moment to survey her, noting how her face had become leaner over the weeks at sea. The daily regimen of punishing exercise, sword practice, Nortah's lessons with the bow, not to mention the nights spent sleeping on deck, had all been borne with wordless acceptance. Her gaze still betrayed the occasional flash of resentment but at no point had she refused a command, no matter how injurious to her pride it might be. He wondered if she were trying to prove something to herself rather than him. *Or is it Reva?* he thought. *Is it her measure she wishes to match?* The thought provoked a small pang of sympathy, for he knew that to be a height none could ever hope to reach.

"Your last opportunity, my lady," he told Ellese. "You can still turn back, go home. I feel your mother will be satisfied with your newfound discipline . . ."

She turned away and vaulted over the side, landing in the centre of the boat and drawing a soft curse from Sehmon as it rocked in the placid harbour waters. Vaelin smothered a laugh and climbed down the rope to join them. He pointed Ellese and Sehmon to the oars and joined Erlin at the prow as they began to row.

"The name of this place, again?" Vaelin asked him.

"Hahn-Shi," Erlin replied. "The greatest port in the Venerable Kingdom. Second only to the capital in size and population."

"So, I assume finding the guide you spoke of will not be easy?"

A faint smirk crossed Erlin's face and he shook his head. "Oh, I don't think so. Unless someone's finally managed to slit his throat that is."

◆ ◆ ◆

Although the hour was barely past sunrise, as was the way with ports the quayside was busy with people when they came ashore. Fishermen prepared their nets for the day, and merchant crews traced uneven courses back to their ships after a night of drink and carousal. As Erlin led them from the docks into the densely packed streets beyond, Vaelin was surprised by the lack of interest they aroused in the inhabitants, drawing only a few glances and most of those directed at Alum due, Vaelin supposed, to his height.

"The docks are the foreigners' quarter," Erlin explained. "The only place in the entire kingdom where they are allowed to live for any length of time, having purchased license to do so from the Merchant King, of course. Some Realm-born and Alpiran merchants have lived here for years."

"What's to stop them upping sticks and moving somewhere else?" Nortah enquired, Vaelin noting how his eyes scanned the various passing shop signs with keen interest.

"The threat of immediate execution," Erlin said. "And the fact that there's a fairly large wall enclosing the quarter. You'll find the people of the Far West are nothing if not thorough."

The streets narrowed as they moved deeper into the city. Erlin turned this way and that with an unconscious familiarity that bespoke an undimmed memory regardless of any bodily failings. Vaelin soon gained an appreciation for the marked difference in architecture here, almost all the houses being constructed from wood rather than stone and hardly any standing higher than two storeys. The roofs sloped at a more shallow angle than those in the east, each densely covered in terra-cotta tiles that dripped swollen dewdrops onto their heads as they passed beneath.

"What a place for a thief this would be," Sehmon commented. Vaelin glanced over his shoulder to see the outlaw gazing up at the encroaching rooftops with a wistful eye. "Each house no more than a few yards apart, and if you slipped, the fall won't kill you."

"No," Erlin told him, coming to a halt and nodding at a symbol painted in red on the wall of a corner house. "But the Crimson Band would if they caught you. I advise you to curb your urges, young man. No one steals here without permission."

"The Crimson Band?" Vaelin asked, moving to Erlin's side to peer at the symbol. It was round with an intricate curved character in the centre.

"All cities have their underside," Erlin said. They had come to a junction between five streets, and he peered into each one in turn with a tense, wary expectation. "And those that govern it. We'll need their assistance to get beyond the wall."

"So that's our destination? The den of this gang."

Erlin let out a derisive snort. "'Gang' is far too inadequate a term. And as for their den, I couldn't find that if I wanted to."

"Then where have you been leading us?"

"Not so much where as when." Abruptly, Erlin's gaze snapped to the nearest rooftop. Vaelin saw nothing but his ears detected the faint tick of a disturbed tile. In the space of a few heartbeats, he heard several more from the surrounding houses.

"When what?" he demanded.

"Whenever they chose to take notice of a bunch of armed foreigners wandering their streets without permission. Don't!" he snapped as Ellese reached for an arrow. "All of you, make no move that could be taken as a threat."

Vaelin's gaze roamed roofs, shuttered windows and walls as a thick silence descended on the junction. His eyes slid over an empty street, then froze as a woman appeared from a shadowed corner. She stood a dozen feet from them, features faintly inquisitive and lacking alarm or suspicion. She wore a plain jerkin and trews of loose-fitting dark brown cotton and possessed no weapon that he could see. However, the surety and lack of concern she exhibited made him conclude she was far from defenceless.

It was Erlin who broke the silence, voicing a polite good morning in Chu-Shin and bowing low. As he straightened he formed his hands into a curious gesture, the left positioned above the right in a fist with small and fore fingers extended.

In response the woman tilted her head a fraction, her gaze sliding from Erlin to Vaelin and then the others. Her face possessed a youthful smoothness that jarred with the experience he saw in her narrowed gaze, no doubt gauging the threat each of them posed. Her survey complete, she blinked and focused again on Erlin, speaking in a soft, almost melodious voice, "It will be the scorpion's kiss for all of you if you have spoken falsely."

With that she turned and started along the street. Erlin hurried to follow, gesturing for Vaelin and the others to do the same.

"I take it the scorpion's kiss is not to be relished?" Nortah asked in a grim murmur.

"I shall do you a service by not even describing it," Erlin replied. "Except to say that I once saw a man chew off and swallow his own tongue to avoid it."

◆　◆　◆

The subsequent journey was even longer and more confusing than the course traced by Erlin. The woman moved at a rapid pace, turning corners with a regularity Vaelin knew to be intentional as his gaze picked out landmarks they had passed at least once before. Apparently, she wished to ensure they weren't being followed before leading them to her destination. From the continued tick of disturbed tiles from above, they remained under continual if unseen observation.

The woman finally came to a halt outside the doorway to a nondescript shop. A continual pall of steam emerged from the doorway and windows, Vaelin recognising the Far Western symbol for tea inscribed on the sign hanging over the lintel. The woman bowed and gestured for them to enter, continuing to hold her pose as they hesitated.

"Never precede a stranger through an unfamiliar door," Nortah said. His eyes roamed the surrounding streets and Vaelin recognised the anticipatory clench to his hand that told of an urgent desire to reach for the sword on his back. *At least he's fearful rather than thirsty,* Vaelin decided.

"If you want to find what you came for," Erlin said, a strained smile on his lips as he returned the woman's bow, "then there is no choice. The only onward path is through this door."

Vaelin mirrored Erlin's bow before moving to the door. The interior was clouded with a sweetly scented steam that concealed much of the detail, and presumably rendered any visitor vulnerable to attack. He glimpsed a few shapes in the swirling mist, all seated at tables where long spouted porcelain teapots added yet more steam to the atmosphere. None of the seated figures turned to regard the tall foreigner as he passed by, Vaelin gaining a sense of studied indifference.

A dozen steps brought him to a counter even more shrouded in steam than the rest of the shop. It billowed from a dozen or more copper kettles, much of it escaping through a wide aperture in the ceiling. A lone figure moved amongst the kettles, arms bare and torso clad in an apron as he went from one shiny receptacle to another, lifting and pouring the boiling water into a row of teapots on the counter.

"Wait here," the woman told Vaelin, moving to the counter to stand with her hands clasped together and head lowered. It took a prolonged interval for the man to take notice of her, repeatedly emerging and disappearing into the steam to fill his pots. A succession of waiters came and went from the counter to convey them to the customers. Like the clientele, they were scrupulous in paying no heed to the foreigners in their midst.

"You're old," the man behind the counter said, his voice startling in its stridency, and surprising in his words; they were spoken in perfect Realm Tongue.

He filled another pot, then set the kettle down, bracing his arms on the counter to regard Erlin with a steady gaze. Vaelin found it hard to judge the man's age. His head was completely bald and his face clean shaven. His bare arms were not broad but were rich in finely honed muscle, scarred here and there with the pale, jagged stripes that told of injuries suffered in combat. Only the faint lines around his eyes and the depth of careful scrutiny they held told Vaelin this was a man with several decades of hard experience at his back.

"My grandfather named you Kho-an Lah," the man went on. "The 'Ageless One.' And now you return to make him a liar."

"Age comes to us all," Erlin replied, a tentative smile on his lips. "Even me, old friend." He gestured at Vaelin. "May I present . . ."

"Vaelin Al Sorna," the man interrupted. "Tower Lord of the Northern Reaches." He blinked and focused his piercing scrutiny on Vaelin. "You are very far from home, and not here by the Merchant King's invitation."

"Your perception was always a thing of wonder," Erlin said. Dropping his voice, he stepped closer to the counter. "We have business to discuss, Honoured Pao Len. Business of both a private and lucrative nature."

Pao Len's eyes flicked from Erlin to Vaelin and back again. His face remained impassive but Vaelin sensed a reluctance in the slow nod he gave before snapping out a curt command to the woman in Chu-Shin. "The back room. Tea for these others." He paused and addressed his next words to Vaelin. "They will be killed if they try to leave before our business is concluded."

He was still speaking Chu-Shin, although Vaelin had no notion of how the man knew he could speak it.

"Understood," he said in a neutral tone. "Wait here," he told the others as the man disappeared into the misty recesses of the shop.

"And do what?" Nortah enquired.

"Drink tea, brother." Vaelin followed Erlin as the woman lifted a slat in the counter and gestured for them to enter. "Perhaps you'll like it."

◆ ◆ ◆

"I once had a cousin who journeyed to your Realm." Pao Len sat on a stool at a small round table on which a teapot sat next to three cups. He poured a dark, floral-scented liquid into each cup as he spoke, Vaelin noting how he never spilled the slightest drop. "He stood high in the ranks of the Crimson Band," Pao Len went on, setting the teapot down, "and was our eyes and ears in your country for many years. Sadly, he was tortured to death some time ago by an agent of your late king, and our reports have been fragmentary ever since."

He gestured for Vaelin and Erlin to take a seat and sat in silent expectation as they regarded the steaming teacups before them. Erlin lifted his after only a slight hesitation, blowing gently on the liquid before taking a small sip. "Flying Fox," he said, eyebrows raised in surprised appreciation. "You honour us, Pao. Enjoy this, my lord," he said as Vaelin sniffed his own cup. "The finest blend of leaves to be found in the Far West. One pound of it would fetch the same weight in silver."

Reasoning that Erlin wouldn't have tasted his cup if he suspected poison, Vaelin followed suit. He found the tea pleasing with a slight tingle to the tongue, but not sufficiently remarkable to justify its supposed price. "And yet," he said to Pao Len as he sipped, "you possess sufficient knowledge to know me by sight, despite the loss of your cousin."

"A man who has charge of such riches can expect only fame." Pao Len shifted his gaze to Erlin, speaking on with barely a pause. The Crimson Band, it appeared, had little use for the courtesies of Far Western official-dom. "Why are you old now? When first I saw you, I was a boy. The next time I was a man, and you were no older. Now we are both old men."

Erlin's face clouded and he took several more sips of his tea before reply-ing. "The blessings of Heaven were taken from me. I find I don't miss them." He smiled, straightening into a businesslike posture. "But I won't trouble you with a long tale of woe, Honoured Pao, for I recall you were always a man of commerce above all. Lord Vaelin, his companions and I require passage to the High Temple. And we do not wish to trouble the Merchant King with the burden of our company. Lord Vaelin commands riches, as you so sagely note. You will be richly rewarded."

"The High Temple," Pao Len repeated. "So you wish to make another pilgrimage to the Jade Princess. Why? Do you imagine she will restore your blessing?"

"No, old friend. I am not so naive. Though, I must confess, I would sorely like to hear her song once more before I fade from this world."

"Then why?"

"Is it necessary for you to know our reasons?" Vaelin asked. "We require your services and are willing to pay for them. Our purpose is our own."

He saw Erlin's face twitch in warning, although Pao Len betrayed no particular offence. "Necessary?" he asked, his tone mild. "No. But certainly desirable, advantageous. All knowledge brings advantage. It is through knowledge that the Crimson Band prospers. For example, we know to within an ounce the weight of gold mined in the Northern Reaches over the course of the last five years. We know that you rule there but fail to enrich yourself in the process. We know that you were once a warrior monk in service to a religion that worships the dead and that you spent five years in an Alpiran dungeon for killing the heir to their emperor's throne. We know that you were your queen's general during a war that made her conqueror of the Volarian Empire. And we know she spends the gold you mine from your domain to rebuild the lands she has conquered and grow armies to conquer more. Now you are here."

"My business in these lands is personal," Vaelin told him. "In fact I am here without my queen's knowledge or permission. Under the laws of the Unified Realm this makes me an outlaw, and I will face an accounting when I return."

"You risk so much for the merely personal. Strange for one so mired in sentiment to rise so high, or is it all due to your skill in battle?" Pao Len angled his head as he studied Vaelin closer still, his eyes seeming to gleam with scrutiny. "Mostly, perhaps. But not all. There is more to you than just the killer. Your presence here is a disturbance, another grain to tip the scales and upset the balance that keeps the Far West in harmony. But the Crimson

Band has never prospered through harmony. The Harbingers of Heaven are abroad, it is said. Portents and rumours abound, and word comes to us of a great battle on the Iron Steppe. War is coming and the scales will soon tumble, and when they do the Crimson Band will harvest its reward from the chaos that follows. It has always been so. From the earliest days of the Emerald Empire to the rise of the Merchant Kings."

He lifted his cup and drank, draining the contents in a few gulps. "So," he said, setting it down and pouring more tea. "I will agree to facilitate your journey to the High Temple. But the price will be high."

"I have gold," Vaelin said, reaching for the purse on his belt. "If more is needed it can be sent for . . ."

"I do not require your gold. I require your word."

"My word?"

"Yes. Your word is true, is it not?"

"I've never broken it, if that's your meaning."

"Good. Therefore, Vaelin Al Sorna, Tower Lord of the Northern Reaches, I require your word that when the Crimson Band next asks you for a service, you will provide it. You will make no argument. You will hold no scruple. You will simply do what is asked of you. *Whatever* is asked of you."

He lifted his teacup to his lips once more, holding Vaelin's gaze as he drank.

"Lord Vaelin has access to many treasures," Erlin said. "Not just gold. Bluestone, fine gifts garnered from all corners of the world . . ."

"His word." Pao Len's cup made a slight, almost musical chime as he set it down on its saucer. "No other price is acceptable."

Erlin turned to Vaelin, speaking in Seordah, a language Vaelin knew well enough for only basic communication. However, from Pao Len's frown it appeared he knew it not at all.

"Refuse," Erlin said. There was a weight to his gaze that left no room for doubt as to the gravity of the moment. "This is no small thing."

"You said there is no other way."

Erlin gave a helpless shrug. "Hire another ship. Find a secluded cove to put ashore . . ." He trailed off, shoulders slumping in resigned defeat. "No. This is the only way."

"I have to find her," Vaelin said. "But your concern is appreciated."

He turned to Pao Len, dipping his head in a brief bow. "My word is given to the Crimson Band."

Pao Len inclined his head and raised a hand in a beckoning gesture. The woman who had led them here emerged from the shadows at his back, head once again lowered in servile respect. Vaelin found himself both chilled and impressed that he had failed to discern her presence in the room until now.

"Chien will be your guide," Pao said. "She speaks your language well and possesses the most current knowledge of the patrol routes favoured by the Dien-Ven."

"Dien-Ven?" Vaelin asked.

"The 'Coin Guards,'" Erlin translated. "They oversee all internal travel in the Venerable Kingdom. All roads in the Far West carry a toll, and all travellers must give their name and destination at each gate. The Merchant Kings are ever keen to track the movements of their populace. Hence our need for a guide."

Pao glanced at the woman and spoke two words in Chu-Shin: "Black knot."

She moved her head in a swift nod and the tea maker grunted in satisfaction before getting to his feet. "You leave tonight. There is a cellar below where you and your companions can rest. Food will be provided."

He sketched a brief bow and left the room, the woman coming forward to clear the teapot and cups from the table. "Black knot?" Vaelin asked, making her pause and regard him with a gaze that betrayed the only emotion he had yet seen in her, hard bitter resentment.

"I'll fetch the other foreigners," she said in Realm Tongue that was well spoken but lacked the accentless precision of Pao Len. It also lacked any note of respect. "Remain here." With that she exited the room leaving his question unanswered.

"It means a mission that cannot fail," Erlin said. "If she doesn't guide us safely to the High Temple, she is required to kill herself." He grimaced, shaking his head. "Pao Len must put a great deal of stock in your word if he's prepared to risk his daughter's life to secure it."

Chapter Ten

They spent several hours in the vault-like cellar beneath Pao Len's teashop. The space was musty with the scent of tea piled in sacks all around. A meal was duly provided, consisting of boiled rice and chicken stewed in a thick peppery sauce. Much to Nortah's evident annoyance the silent, expressionless men who served the meal seemed content to ignore his clumsily phrased requests for wine. Chien returned after several hours when night had descended on the streets above. She wore a leather pack on her back and carried a plain staff. Her loose cotton garb had been exchanged for sturdier quilted trews and jacket.

"Put these on," she told them as the silent men returned carrying bundles of similar clothing. "And these," she added, tossing a broad conical straw hat to Vaelin. "Keep your face lowered when we get above ground."

Rolled blankets were also provided to conceal their weapons and other non-Western accoutrements. Once they had dressed she surveyed them all with a glance possessing none of the placidity from before. Muttering a disdainful "foreigners look like mules and stink like oxen" under her breath, she turned and strode towards an apparently bare wall at the rear of the cellar.

"No talking," she instructed, pressing her hands against two separate bricks, one high and one low. There was a loud click within the wall, and Chien began to push against it, grunting with the effort as it slid back on an unseen hinge, unleashing a wave of foul-smelling air in the process.

"By the Father's arse!" Ellese said, voice muffled as she pressed her sleeve against her face. "What a stench!"

"Sewer," Sehmon said. His features wrinkled with disgusted familiarity as he squinted at the damp tunnel beyond the false wall. "The route of outlaws the world over, it seems."

"No talking!" Chien repeated, turning a glare on Vaelin and continuing in Chu-Shin. "Make your servants obey or this is pointless."

He inclined his head in contrite acceptance before barking out a command for the others to remain silent. Chien seemed only slightly mollified as she tied a kerchief about her face and started into the sewer, beckoning for them to follow.

The tunnel she led them through was narrow and long. Vaelin was soon obliged to follow Chien's example and tie a rag around his nose and mouth to diminish the stench raised by their feet sloshing through a channel of filth-thickened water. It connected to a broader channel after a hundred paces or so, Chien turning right after a cautious glance at the ceiling. Faint moonlight streamed through a series of circular iron grates in the passage roof, the light dimming at irregular intervals as feet trod the streets above. From the steady rhythm of the footfalls and the dim snatches of clipped conversation, Vaelin quickly divined they lurked beneath a guard post of some kind.

Seeing Chien had come to a halt at an opening in the passage wall, he moved to her side, finding the portal blocked by a thick iron gate. "The guard wall lies above," she explained in a murmur, glancing up at the nearest grate before reaching out to take hold of the iron railings. A small squeal sounded as they swung back, Vaelin's eyes making out a hinge where they met the curved ceiling. He expected Chien to swing it all the way open but she waited, gaze still locked on the grate in the ceiling.

"Be ready to move quickly," she whispered. "We won't have long."

"For what?"

The answer came an instant later, the loud toll of a bell sounding through the grates to echo the length of the sewer. Chien lunged forward, swinging the railings up, the loud clang as the metal connected with the brickwork swallowed by the continued tolling of the bell. She held the railings up and jerked her head urgently at Vaelin. He waved his hand at the others and scrambled through into the most constricting tunnel yet. It was barely three feet high, obliging him to crawl on his hands and knees as the others pressed in behind. He heard the clang of the railings falling back into place just before the bell's toll faded.

"Keep moving," Chien ordered in a harsh whisper. "The midnight chime is loud, but that doesn't mean they didn't hear us."

It took over an hour of crawling to get clear of the tunnel, Vaelin continually fighting the harsh, rasping gag in his throat from the unabated miasma of foulness. Finally, the air began to clear and he clambered his way out onto a broad ledge. The illumination was dimmer here, coming from a small opening far above. He could see that the ledge extended away on either side for a good distance. Before him lay a long downward slope of smooth stone, streaming with water. It descended into the gloomy depths without apparent end, birthing a brief wave of dizziness that made him take a careful step back.

"Keep your feet together and pointed into the shadow," Chien advised as she followed the others out onto the ledge. "And your arms crossed. You'll be tempted to use your hands to slow your fall. Don't, unless you want the flesh ripped down to the bone."

Vaelin began to enquire as to her meaning, but the question died as she crossed her arms and leapt clear of the ledge, sliding down the slope and disappearing into the waiting darkness in the space of a heartbeat. Erlin followed her almost immediately, muttering, "It didn't seem so steep all those years ago," before closing his eyes and jumping clear of the ledge.

"I don't want to do that," Sehmon said quietly, breaking the silence that followed.

"If an old man can do it, so can you," Ellese said. She took a breath, crossed her arms and leapt, Vaelin catching a muffled curse as she slid rapidly from view.

Alum went next, voicing a soft chuckle as he did so, although Vaelin detected a small, wary note to it before the Moreska slipped into the gloom.

"Master Sehmon?" Vaelin said, raising an eyebrow at the outlaw. He swallowed and crossed his arms but failed to jump as he continued to stare into the depths.

"I'll be along, my lord," he said. "Just need a moment . . ."

His words transformed into a terrorised yell as Nortah's boot connected with his rump, sending him into an untidy, flailing tumble. Vaelin watched Nortah count off the seconds until the youth's screams came to an abrupt end.

"A hundred feet or so." Nortah gave a bland smile. "Unnerving but hardly fatal. After you, brother."

"I assume you've calculated a return route through the sewers," Vaelin said. "And a likely source of wine."

"What would be the point? I have no coin, as you said."

"Then you won't object to going first."

He met Nortah's gaze. The long-standing resentment that had so possessed him during the voyage was dimmed now, replaced by something Vaelin felt to be worse. *Shame and defeat,* he concluded, turning away. They could fight, he knew that. Nortah had recovered some strength and skill on the *Sea Wasp* but he was still far from his former self. It would be possible to send him tumbling in Sehmon's wake. But then what? The road they faced was long and he couldn't spend every step of it worrying his brother might seek out a drink.

"Have a care of the tea seller," Vaelin sighed, crossing his arms. "He's likely to take exception to your presence."

"No more persuasion for me?" Nortah enquired in genuine surprise. "At least a punch or two."

"I've brought you as far as I could. I was a fool to think I could save you. Before she died Sella made me promise to try. And I did, brother. But a drunk is a drunk. It's time I allowed you to be what you are."

He crossed his arms and leapt, legs straight as a spear-point as the slope carried him into the gloom.

◆ ◆ ◆

His descent ended in a splash and the chilly embrace of water deep enough to cover his head. A short plummet brought his boots into contact with something hard and he kicked, propelling himself upwards. Breaking the surface he found himself in a pool of rushing water, the current conveying him towards a broad cave-like opening. The force of it was too great to swim against and, seeing no other avenue of escape, he allowed himself to be carried into the open air. The water flowed into an oddly straight river with banks of shaped stone rather than earth. He was propelled along it for sev-

eral yards until the current began to abate and he saw the dim shadow of
Alum on the bank, crouching with his hand extended. Vaelin caught hold of
the Moreska's wrist, grunting his thanks as the hunter helped haul him from
the water.

He surveyed his companions, taking note of how badly Erlin, Sehmon
and Ellese shivered in the night air. "We need to light a fire," he told Chien.
"Dry off."

"No time," she said, settling her pack on her shoulders and hefting her
staff. "Walk until dawn, then the sun will dry us."

"W-where's Lord Nortah?" Ellese chattered.

Vaelin smoothed a hand through his hair to work out the damp, glancing
back at the opening in the base of what he saw to be a sheer granite cliff at
least seventy feet high. "He won't be . . ."

A faint splash sounded and Nortah emerged into the moonlit flow a few
seconds later. Vaelin and Alum hauled him from the river, where he spent
several seconds retching on his knees. "Think I may have swallowed some of
that shit water," he gasped.

"Then vomit as you walk," Chien told him before setting off along the
riverbank at a brisk pace. "And do it quietly."

◆ ◆ ◆

Chien allowed no rest, maintaining a punishing pace along the riverbank.
By the time the sun rose above the broad expanse of cultivated fields to the
east, Vaelin reckoned they had covered at least ten miles. During the trek,
the course of the river hadn't altered by a single inch.

"It's not a river," Erlin said when Vaelin asked about its curiously straight
appearance. "Merely a minor branch of the canal network connecting Hahn-
Shi to the lake lands twenty miles north. They in turn feed the canals that
trace all the way to the capital."

"So we just follow this to our destination?" Vaelin asked.

Erlin winced as he looked at the rising sun. "Not for much longer. The
Dien-Ven don't bother patrolling the minor canals, but we'll soon be nearing
the locks. Then I suspect things will start getting complicated."

Chien finally came to a halt about an hour past sunrise, climbing the
grassy verge fringing the canal, shading her eyes to peer at something to the
north. Vaelin joined her, drawing up short at the sight that confronted him.

It appeared to be a town of some kind, buildings and bridges clustered together in a confusing maze descending in tiers towards the shore of a huge body of water. To call it a lake seemed foolishly inadequate. It was more of an inland sea, the placid waters stretching away to a northern shore too distant to be glimpsed.

"Nushim-Lhi," Chien said, nodding to the oddly configured town.

"Lock bridge?" Vaelin asked after puzzling over the translation.

"More like Lock Town," Erlin said. "Any town with a bridge bears the name 'khi,' and this one has many. The canals come together here. Boats are conveyed to the lake by a series of locks. It's quite a marvel of engineering, one your sister would surely find fascinating."

"Will you look at that?" Sehmon breathed in awe. Vaelin turned to see him gazing towards the south. The source of his wonder wasn't hard to find. The port city of Hahn-Shi stretched away to east and west, filling the horizon for at least fifty miles. Suburbs extended into the surrounding fields in dark masses, birthing roads that snaked across the orderly green landscape like the tendrils of some giant beast that had crawled from the sea.

"You could fit ten Varinsholds into that," Sehmon said, "and still have room for more."

"How many people live in this land?" Ellese asked Erlin, her expression more troubled than awed.

"So many the Merchant Kings have a great deal of difficulty counting them," Erlin replied. "When I last came here the census estimated some thirty-five million in the Venerable Kingdom alone."

"A million is a thousand thousands, yes?" Alum asked Vaelin.

"It is."

The Moreska shook his head, letting out a grim laugh. "If my cousin hadn't told me to follow you, I would now be insisting we turn back and find a ship to the Opal Isles. We cannot hope to remain hidden in such a land."

A faint snort came from Chien as she started down the bank and into the fields below. Vaelin heard her mutter, "Foreigners have the wit of pigs," as she set off towards the east without looking back.

"So, we're not going to town," Nortah observed.

"Faith no, the Dien-Ven would catch us in minutes," Erlin said, descending the bank and following in Chien's wake. "Come along. As I recall it's only a seven- or eight-mile walk from here."

◆ ◆ ◆

Their destination turned out to be an unedifying ramshackle mill-house on the lake-shore. The aged planks that formed its walls bowed inwards and the roof sagged. A waterwheel turned slowly in the current flowing into a broad irrigation channel, and a thin stream of grey smoke rose from the chimney. Chien came to a halt some thirty paces from the mill-house, motioning for Vaelin and the others to do the same.

"Say nothing," she cautioned, continuing to stand as the seconds grew into minutes. Finally there came a rustle of disturbed vegetation and two men rose from the half-grown wheat stalks close by. They were each festooned with concealing leaves and faces blackened with earth. They also both carried crossbows, drawn and loaded with wickedly barbed bolts.

"You are not expected," the man on the left told Chien. He squinted in deep suspicion as his gaze tracked over her companions.

"No, I am not," Chien agreed. "Crab is inside?"

Although her tone lacked any emotion, something about her bearing seemed to increase the pair's agitation. They exchanged a brief glance before stepping back, crossbows lowering to point their bolts at the ground. Chien walked past them without another glance, hefting her stick at Vaelin in a beckoning gesture. He gained a keen sense of being closely observed as she led them to the house, although the windows remained shuttered and no further rustling could be heard in the wheat stalks.

The door opened the moment Chien reached it, an old, stick-thin woman bowing low and standing aside. Following Chien inside, Vaelin blinked in surprise at finding himself in a brightly lit interior. Paper lanterns hung from the ceiling to illuminate a large space lacking stairs or rooms. Where the floor should have been there was a water-filled dock in which sat a narrow hulled boat some thirty feet from bow to stern. The mill-house, it was clear, was just a shell to conceal a hidden dock.

"Esteemed sister!" a stocky man called from the stern of the boat, raising a hand in greeting as he stepped onto the walkway lining the wall. His grin was cheerful as he approached, Vaelin noting how he bowed to Chien before she bowed in return. The official status of women in this land, it seemed, was not mirrored amongst its outlaw society.

"Esteemed brother," she said. "Esteemed Father sends greetings, and a gift." Her hand disappeared into her jacket and emerged with a small red lacquer box.

The stocky man said, taking the box and removing the lid to sniff the contents, "Ah, Firebloom Balm." He patted the small of his back and inclined his head in gratitude. "My old bones thank you." For all his apparent affability, Vaelin saw a keen and possibly dangerous calculation in his gaze as it slipped from Chien to the foreigners at her back. "And you bring interesting company. A gift in itself, I always say."

"We require passage across the lake," Chien told him. "Esteemed Father has given his word."

The man's eyes betrayed another moment's calculation before sliding back to Chien. "And his word will be honoured," he said, bowing once more. "I am called Crab," he went on, raising his voice and speaking in slow deliberate tones to the foreigners, as if addressing lackwit children. "I need no other name and have killed men who asked for it. This is my boat." He pointed at the narrow-hulled craft in the water. "We go across the water when it gets dark. Until then, you eat." His blunt-fingered hands mimed the passage of invisible food to his mouth before he rubbed his stomach. "Mmmmm."

"This one's an idiot," Nortah said in Realm Tongue, drawing a faint snicker from Ellese.

"Quiet," Vaelin said, smiling and bowing at the man who called himself Crab. "I suspect it might be to our advantage if he thinks we're the idiots."

"Can't risk a daylight run these days," the boatman told Chien as they ate a short while later. The food, a pleasantly spiced pork and vegetable broth, was prepared by the old woman who had answered the door. From the energy with which she moved from one steaming pot to another, Vaelin was forced to wonder if she was as old as she appeared. Apart from her and Crab, no others had joined them, but the occasional creak from the shadowed rafters above made it clear they were still under close observation.

"Too many folk coming south," Crab went on. "More folk on the water means more Dien-Ven keen to tax what they've brought with them. Been going on since the spring rains. Soldiers go north, people come south. More by the day, and not all peasants either. I've had to remind some newcomers that these lakes belong to the Crimson Band, but not all are likely to heed the lesson, no matter how many ears I cut off. Esteemed Father should know this."

"Then send word," Chien said. "There was news of a battle in the border-lands. What have you heard?"

"Mostly just rumours and nonsense from beggared peasants. Lots of tales of the Harbingers of Heaven, of course, but that's always the way when trouble brews. As for the battle . . ." He shrugged. "Some horde or other come out of the Iron Steppe for a good old rampage. They'll piss off home when their saddlebags are full of booty and they've garnered enough slaves. That or the Merchant King will find a general to beat them. It happens every few decades. Ask her." He turned to the old woman, raising his voice to a shout. "Seen it all before, haven't you, Old Snake? Rampaging barbarians and such."

The old woman spooned broth into a bowl, barely glancing at him as she spoke in a dry, cracked voice, "You are a fool."

Crab let out a hearty guffaw at this, slapping his knee. "She loves to berate me, and what man would begrudge his great-grandmother her pleasures?"

His merriment died when the old woman spoke on. Apparently, voicing more than a short insult was not her custom. "They called it the Year of the Tiger," she said, the rasp of her voice soft but still easily discernible in the still air of the mill. "When the Steppe tribes rode all the way through the Vener-able Kingdom to sack Hahn-Shi."

"The Merchant King was weak then," Chien said. "A drunken wastrel they say."

"No." The old woman shook her head. "He was just a man, as all kings are. Wise in some ways, foolish in others. And it is a fool who fails to heed the Harbingers of Heaven. Warning was given, but he did nothing and so the barbarians came to take all we had."

"Not for long," Chien said. "The Merchant King was deposed and a great army raised by his successor, the grandfather of Lian Sha himself. The bones of every single barbarian who invaded these lands now lie beneath the Black Cliffs. So it will be if any come again."

The old woman sprinkled salt in her bowl and handed it to Ellese. She had already quickly downed one bowl and seemed grateful for a second. The woman gave her a fond smile, which faded as she turned to Chien. "Then you are also a fool to think anything in this world is eternal."

She took up Ellese's empty bowl and, moving with a disconcerting speed, hurled it at Chien. The old woman's speed, however, was mirrored by her target, who jerked her head aside, the bowl missing by a whisker to shatter on the wall behind.

"All that is made can be unmade," the old woman told Chien with a bow that didn't match the evident disrespect in her eyes. "As you would do well to remember, esteemed sister."

"Great-grandmother earned her name well," Crab told Chien as the old woman returned to her pots. "Quick as a cobra with a temperament to match. My father said he lost count of the bodies she sent to the bottom of the lake when we were still fighting the Silver Thread for control of the water."

Chien kept her face free of emotion but Vaelin glimpsed the small tic of fury in her cheek before she shrugged and returned to her own meal. "When do we leave?"

◆ ◆ ◆

Once the moon had reached its peak Crab's men lit a fireboat five miles to the west and set it loose upon the lake.

"That should draw the gaze of any Dien-Ven on the water tonight," the boatman said from the tiller. Vaelin and Alum had taken up the oars to propel the boat from the shadowed confines of the mill. Once they had reached clear water, a sail constructed of wicker and bamboo was raised and a stiff southerly breeze carried the craft towards the heart of the lake.

"Deeper the water the better," Crab said. "Smugglers keep close to shore, easier to beach and run for it if the soldiers show up." He turned to Vaelin as he and Alum shipped their oars, raising his voice once more and pillowing his hands under his cheek. "You sleep now. Need rest for tomorrow. Understanding?"

"Rest," Vaelin repeated with a good-natured nod. "Yes."

"Good fellow." Crab patted him on the shoulder and returned to the tiller.

"Don't be offended," Chien said, catching sight of Ellese's sour expression. "It's commonly believed that foreigners possess brains only two-thirds the size of those born to these lands."

"And do you share this belief?" Vaelin enquired.

"Oh no. I'd say . . ." She paused for a moment's consideration. "Four-sixths, at least." With that she disappeared into the roofed mid-deck of the boat.

◆ ◆ ◆

Vaelin dreamt of the Battle of Alltor that night, something he hadn't done for a long time. The images conjured by his slumbering mind failed to match his true memory of the event but that was ever the way with dreams. This time the Volarians failed to react when he charged towards them, standing in their orderly ranks as unmoving and indifferent as any statue. They made no effort to fight as he cut them down, regarding him with impassive faces rendered pale as alabaster in the dim light seeping through the smoke rising from the ruined city. Free Swords, Varitai and Kuritai all fell before him like wheat before a scythe, not even voicing a scream as blood gushed from wounds and stumps. This time Flame, the mount that had carried him all the way from the Reaches, didn't fall to an arrow. Instead the warhorse bore him through the carnage he carved through the silent ranks and into the city.

He expected to find Reva in the square, overlarge sword in hand as she greeted him with a smile, but today someone else was waiting for him. A slim, diminutive woman standing amidst a carpet of corpses, her black hair twisting like a wraith in the wind. As he picked his way through the surrounding bodies, he saw each bore a familiar face. Here was Dentos, an arrow jutting from his chest, lips drawn back from his teeth in a grimace of death. Here was Barkus, head severed from his body and features frozen in a final taunting grin. Ultin lay with a rope around his neck, face swollen and purple. Linden Al Hestian stared up at him with pleading eyes that begged for release from his pain . . .

He froze at the sight of the next one. It peered into the smoke-clouded sky with dim eyes set in a face rendered near unrecognisable by the multiple slash and stab wounds that covered it. He hadn't been there when Caenis met his end but had imagined it many times. However, the horrors crafted by his imagination hadn't come close to matching this. *His pain must have been unimaginable,* he thought, staggering with the sudden weight of once dulled grief. *I'm sorry, brother . . .*

"You couldn't save them."

Vaelin's gaze snapped to the slim woman. Her face was turned from him but he knew her voice as well as he knew the surrounding dead. When she turned, her eyes were white in the bleached angular mask of her face, the eyes that told of a spirit flying free from her body.

"You couldn't save me," she went on. The thin robe she wore blew away like chaff in the wind, leaving her naked. There were no marks on her body, for she had died by a single touch. Nevertheless he could see no beauty in her now. Her skin he knew would be like ice to the touch, bled of all life.

"What makes you think you can save *her*?" Dahrena enquired. "Is it because you loved her more? Was she the one you always really wanted? Is that why you let me die?"

Her words sank into him with all the force of a hundred arrows, robbing him of strength, sending him to his knees, lips moving in whispered, non-sensical entreaties, for he had no words for her. All he had was guilt and sorrow.

Dahrena blinked her white eyes at him as a pitying frown passed across her mask of a face. "Poor Vaelin," she said. "Why didn't you just stay in your tower? It wouldn't have saved you either, but at least you would have had a few years of peace."

He breathed deeply, the smoke thick in his throat, making him cough as he sought to calm his racing heart. "The wolf . . ." he gabbled. "It called . . ."

"The wolf." She laughed, a sound harsher than anything he had ever heard in her voice in life. "For one who shuns gods with such fervour, you seem happy to abase yourself before a dying remnant of the Nameless. It called, that's true." She walked towards him, the thickening pall of smoke wreathing her naked form like a cloak. He stared up at her, as frozen as the Volarian army he had slaughtered, staring in terror at the hand she lowered to caress his cheek, her touch a blade of ice on his skin. "It called you to an early death . . ."

◆ ◆ ◆

"Brother!"

He came awake with the scent of smoke still in his nostrils, blinking at Nortah's tense features. "What is it?" Vaelin asked.

"Trouble, by the looks of it." Nortah had unfurled the blanket that concealed his weapons and was busy stringing his bow. "And the smell."

Vaelin retrieved his sword from his own blanket and shook Ellese and Sehmon awake before leaving the cabin. Alum was already perched atop the roof, one hand gripping the mast as he gazed at something to the west. Catching sight of Vaelin he gave a grim smile and said, "It seems I have a talent for finding pirates, even far from the sea."

Dawn had risen to paint the surface of the lake a pale pink beneath a lingering haze, and it was easy to make out the object of Alum's interest. A pall of smoke rose from a burning boat about a mile away. It was similar in dimensions to Crab's vessel but appeared to be adrift, flames licking the length of its sail and covering its deck from stern to bow. Beyond it Vaelin could make out a confusion of other boats, two large like the first, surrounded by a dense cluster of smaller craft. The accompanying sounds were faint but Vaelin's ears were well attuned to shouts of struggle and terror.

"The Silver Thread," Crab said from the tiller. He was speaking to Chien, both of them watching the distant turmoil with an aspect of professional disdain. "What's left of them these days. They've taken to preying on the peasants fleeing south. Haven't seen so many of the bastards in one place for a long time. Still, three boats full of swordless yokels was probably too tasty a meal to pass up."

"What do we do, Uncle?" Ellese asked, appearing on deck with bow in hand.

"We do nothing, girl," Chien told her before glancing at Crab. "Best to steer east for a time. No need to invite attention."

"We can't just leave those people," Ellese insisted, her gaze veering between Vaelin and Chien. "Uncle?"

The doubt and confusion on her face was a hard thing to see, but it was the scream that decided him. Full of pain and despair, it rose from the beleaguered boats to echo across the water like a battle horn, plaintive and irresistible in its summons. Vaelin turned to Nortah and they exchanged a wordless nod.

"Stand with Lord Nortah," Vaelin told Ellese. "He'll tell you where to aim. Master Sehmon, have a care for my back if you please."

The youth tightened the buckle of his sword and straightened. "Of course, my lord."

"Take us there," Vaelin told Crab in Chu-Shin, inclining his head at the boats.

The boatman blinked in momentary surprise at the fluency of Vaelin's words, then let out a dismissive laugh. "Only I command this boat, foreigner . . ."

His mouth clamped shut as Vaelin stepped to him, drawing his hunting knife and pressing it to the ample flesh of his neck, all done with a smooth lack of hesitancy that forestalled any reaction.

"This is unwise," Chien said, voice rich in warning. "The Crimson Band has a treaty with the Silver Thread . . ."

"I don't." Vaelin pressed the edge of his blade deeper into Crab's neck, the man's nostrils flaring in a mix of fury and fear. "Take us there. Now."

CHAPTER ELEVEN

Nortah's bow began to sing as soon as the swirling cluster of boats drew within range. His first arrow followed a high arc as it plunged down into the back of a man on the foredeck of the nearest boat. He was an easy target to identify, having been engaged in ripping the clothes from a frantically struggling woman before the arrow slammed into his back. It had been the woman's screams that called to Vaelin, screams that fell to silence as her attacker reared up and staggered, trying vainly to reach for the shaft protruding from his back. Ellese's arrow took him in the chest, pitching him into the water.

"That puts the knot on it," Chien said in bitter resignation, hefting her staff. "We have to finish them all," she told Crab. "If word of this reaches their brothers, war will follow."

The boatman gave a reluctant nod, gaze still locked on Vaelin's. "That isn't necessary now," he grated, flicking his eyes at the knife still pressed against his neck.

Vaelin grunted in satisfaction and withdrew the blade, sliding it into the sheath on his belt and turning to watch the fast-approaching chaos. The flames consuming the larger boat blossomed higher as they drew nearer, birthing an even thicker cloud of smoke that robbed Nortah and Ellese of further targets. As Sehmon and Alum worked the oars to close the distance, Vaelin's ears detected the snapping chorus of multiple crossbows being loosed in unison.

"Down!" Nortah barked, throwing himself flat as a hail of bolts came streaming out of the smoke to rake the boat. Ellese let out a curse as one plucked at her sleeve before she rolled clear of the roof. "Just a scratch," she said as Vaelin inspected the wound. It bled far more than a mere scratch and would need stitching, but there was no time for that now.

"There's still work to do here," he told her, inclining his head at the stern.

She frowned at his flat tone but, as had become her habit these days, kept any retort to herself. Nocking an arrow, she bobbed up, drew and loosed, ducking back down as a trio of crossbow bolts whined overhead. "Well, that's one less at least," she said.

"Alum," Vaelin said, making his way to the prow. "If you would care to join me. Master Sehmon, remain here and have a care for Master Erlin. Also." He paused to glance back at Crab before returning his gaze to Sehmon. "Make sure our captain doesn't decide to take himself off."

"As you wish, my lord."

Vaelin crouched low behind the sturdy block of timber that rose from the prow. It bore many old scars, presumably as a result of occasions much like this one. He waited until the prow butted against another hull, then hauled himself up, launching himself onto the deck of the adjoining boat, drawing the sword from his back as he did so. To his right a man immediately surged out of the smoke, a broad-bladed, cleaver-like weapon raised high above his head. Ellese's arrow whined past Vaelin's ear to slam into the man's chest before he could strike, piercing him from sternum to spine. Vaelin stepped over his rapidly expiring body, sword flicking up in time to parry the thrust of a curve-bladed spear stabbing out of the acrid murk.

The spear bearer withdrew the weapon and tried again, this time aiming a slashing thrust at Vaelin's eyes. He was swift and evidently practised, his bunched, outraged features smeared with the gore of recent slaughter, but anger made him clumsy. His thrust was delivered with too much energy, causing the weapon to swing wide as it missed its target, leaving his face and neck exposed. Vaelin's stroke cut him from chin to forehead, rending his already garish features into ruin. He clung to life, however, whirling away with blood spiralling from his bisected features, gibbering in panic. His flailing had the beneficial effect of impeding four of his fellow outlaws, forcing them to dodge his wayward spear as they attempted to charge the newcomers. The pause was sufficient for Nortah to claim two, each with a precisely placed shaft to the chest. A third outlaw cursed and shoved his still-flailing comrade aside, sending him tumbling over the rail into the lake.

Alum leapt into the path of the two remaining outlaws as they resumed their charge. The Moreska's spear blurred as it whirled left then right, laying open the neck of one outlaw and slicing deep into the arm of the other. The man's narrow-bladed sword fell from nerveless fingers as he yelled in mingled pain and fury, turning and attempting to flee into the smoke, then falling dead as Vaelin's throwing knife took him between the shoulder blades.

"Please . . ."

The woman from the foredeck crouched at his feet. She clutched the tattered rags of her clothes against her thin frame. Vaelin winced at the sight of her spine, the bones jutting from flesh denuded by starvation. Clearly, she had suffered much even before falling victim to outlaws.

"Stay low," Vaelin told her, crouching to put a hand to her shoulder. "This isn't done yet."

She shook her head, hair parting to reveal a face hardened by privation, her brows knotted in consternation rather than fear. "The cargo," she said, pointing to a gap in the deck boards. "If the flames reach it . . ."

Peering through the boards Vaelin saw a sizeable stack of large clay pots, also several pairs of bright eyes staring out of the gloom. Leaning closer he made out the huddled forms of half a dozen children, all as thin as the woman kneeling at his side.

"What is it?" he asked her, pointing to the pots.

"Naphtha. We brought it from home, all this way. It would buy us a new home, my husband said." She let out a bitter laugh that quickly turned into a cough. Vaelin flared his nostrils, tasting the smoke which he realised held a thick, oily tinge very different from woodsmoke. Recalling the way the fire that claimed the first boat had suddenly blossomed, he cast his eyes over the deck, finding several patches of flame on the ropes and woodwork.

"Alum," he said, rising. "We need water . . ."

"Uncle!"

Ellese's shout drew his gaze to the east in time to see a dozen small boats emerging from the smoke, each bearing five men or more, many of them aiming crossbows directly at him. He threw himself to the deck, hearing the overlapping thud of dozens of bolts tearing into timber. When the volley faded he looked for the woman, finding her unharmed and huddled against a grain sack. Hearing a muttered curse, he glanced at Alum as the hunter tied a rag over a cut in his forearm.

A chorus of angry shouts came from the outlaws, and Vaelin raised himself up to see one tumble into the lake with an arrow in his neck. More arrows followed in quick succession as Nortah and Ellese, presented now with a wealth of targets, began a steady barrage. Three more outlaws fell before four boats peeled away from the pack, oarsmen labouring to bring them alongside Crab's boat. The remainder kept heading for Vaelin, crossbowmen working frantically to reload their weapons. By his estimation he and Alum would soon face combat with thirty outlaws or more. Whilst the Vaelin Al Sorna of popular myth would have seen scant challenge in such odds, he had never fallen victim to the folly of believing his own legend.

Vaelin's gaze went to the naphtha pots below as a notion sprang to mind, a lesson his sister had once taught to the Volarians. "Get your children on deck," he told the woman. "Be ready to jump to our boat when I tell you."

She cast a bright, fearful glance at the approaching outlaws, then nodded, moving to the hatchway and calling for the children below. As she shepherded the whimpering infants to the foredeck, Vaelin climbed down into the hold to retrieve as many pots as he could carry.

"Are we to drink to our own death?" Alum enquired with a bemused grin, watching Vaelin remove the stopper from a pot. He ripped off a strip of coarse fabric from a grain sack, dousing it with a splash of naphtha before stuffing it into the pot's spout. Spying a tongue of flame licking at a coil of rope, he held the pot to it, setting the soaked rag alight.

"I'd fancy you have the better arm for this," he said, holding the flaming pot out to Alum.

The Moreska eyed the pot doubtfully for a second before his brows rose in comprehension. Taking it from Vaelin, he straightened from his crouch, ducked down to avoid the instant hail of crossbow bolts before rising again. Alum launched the pot into the air with a swift overhand sweep of his arm. Flame trailed from the makeshift wick as the pot arced towards the oncoming outlaws, landing squarely in the middle of the lead boat and exploding in a bright ball of yellow flame. Screams rose as the occupants thrashed in the resultant conflagration, beating at the flames that ate through clothing to the flesh beneath. Within seconds the boat was empty and adrift, the surrounding water filled with struggling men and rising smoke.

"A jackal's cunning indeed," Alum said in approval, holding his hand out for another pot.

They worked at a steady rhythm, Vaelin preparing the pots and the Moreska launching them with an unerring eye. He threw six in the space of a few minutes, the water off the port rail soon filled with screaming men and flaming boats. Vaelin watched the surviving two boats turn swiftly about and disappear into the smoke, the outlaws marking their departure with a plethora of shouted, rage-filled insults and a parting volley of crossbow bolts, none of which found a target.

Any sense of victory faded when Vaelin heard a clash of blades from Crab's boat. One of the four outlaw craft that had veered off from the pack was adrift, its crew feathered with arrows and lying dead or dying. The remaining three had managed to press home their attack, a dozen outlaws scrambling onto Crab's boat with weapons in hand. Vaelin saw Ellese deliver a solid kick to the head of one, sending him back over the side. She dodged a cleaver blow from another, the man falling dead to Nortah's sword thrust a second later.

A warning shout rose in Vaelin's throat as he saw a pair of outlaws leap up behind his brother, but it faded as Chien appeared at their rear. Raising her staff above her head, she twisted it, the wooden pole parting to expose a yard-long length of steel. Chien's arm seemed to blur then, the revealed blade flickering as she sank to one knee. The two outlaws staggered back and fell, blood flowing freely from near-identical slashes to the neck.

Chien whirled about to face the stern where Vaelin could see Sehmon and Crab frantically fending off the bulk of the attackers. Sehmon had managed to kill one, his blade red down to the hilt as he parried the slashes of his enemies. The rest were kept at bay by Crab, who had armed himself with an axe, sweeping it back and forth with a speed that displayed more strength than skill.

Vaelin watched Chien leap into the midst of the surviving outlaws, her whole body seeming to blur now as her blade flickered once more. Within seconds it was over, three outlaws lying dead and the only survivor on his knees, hands empty and head bowed all the way to the deck in an obvious pose of surrender. Vaelin saw Chien's lips move, perhaps in an apology, before she stabbed the tip of her blade into the base of the kneeling man's skull.

"Hurry!" she called to Vaelin, beckoning urgently before pointing her reddened steel in the direction of the fleeing boats. "We have to finish the rest!"

• • •

"The Stahlhast first came last spring." The thin woman's name was Ahn-Jin and she spoke in an accent very different to Chien's, her voice possessing a softness that belied the tale she had to tell. A denizen of the hill country close to the northern border, she sat close to the stern with her five children, relating how her people had been forced to flee their village.

"There were only a hundred or so, that first time," she went on. "They stole the naphtha we harvested from the earth, and some of our young folk, killing those who tried to fight."

"So, that is their sole object?" Vaelin asked. "Theft and slaughter?"

She gave a grim shake of her head. "They made it clear this was just the first cut of many. They told us their god had been made flesh and now rode at the head of their horde. Soon he would sweep south to claim all the wealth of the Merchant Kings. When they stole and killed they had been laughing, but when they spoke of their god there was no laughter. Each bowed their head when one spoke his name, and it was spoken in a whisper."

"His name?" Vaelin asked.

Ahn-Jin nodded and spoke a short phrase in Chu-Shin that caused Vaelin to straighten in surprise.

"Brother?" Nortah said. "What did she say?"

"The Stahlhast have a leader," he murmured in response. "A man they think of as a living god, apparently. His name . . ." He let out a soft laugh, shaking his head. *Simple coincidence, surely.* "His name translates literally as 'Darkblade.'"

Ellese let out a laugh at that, something he hadn't heard her do for many days now. "How rude of him not to ask your permission, Uncle." Seeing Alum's puzzled expression she added in slowly phrased Realm Tongue, "As far as my people are concerned, *he*"—she nodded at Vaelin—"is the Darkblade. Named in the Prophecies of the Maiden as a great and terrible scourge visited upon all those who enjoy the Father's love, since redeemed by the word of Blessed Lady Reva, as inscribed in the Eleventh Book." She closed her eyes, reciting the words with practised accuracy, "'And so did the Darkblade come to Alltor in its time of direst need and with his steel and his fury did wash away his sins with the blood of our enemies.'"

She opened her eyes to regard Vaelin with unusually sincere gravity. "This simply won't do, Uncle. There can't be two of you. It's blasphemy."

Vaelin gave her a withering glance and turned back to Ahn-Jin. "So, that is why you fled?" he asked.

"We didn't flee right away," she said. "The Merchant King's soldiers came a day later, the officer telling us it was just a raid and we should have fought harder to defend the king's property. We were also fined for falling short on our quota for the season. The Stahlhast raided other villages in the months that followed, always in greater numbers, always taking more, killing more. In time the Merchant King sent his army, who also took from us. 'Soldiers need to eat,' they told us, 'so they can fight in your defence.' Weeks later they came back, what was left of them, a few dozen starving, terrified wretches who tried to steal from us again. The men of the village killed them with pickaxes. We tried to stay, some of the elders reasoning that conquest had come and gone before, that even the hated tribes that had rampaged all the way to the capital could be bought off with gold or naphtha. But then"—her expression darkened further—"the others came."

"Others?" Vaelin prompted.

"Others in thrall to the Darkblade, but they were not Stahlhast. They were like us, from the northern villages, still like us in language and dress, but . . . changed. Most had no horses and carried only sparse weapons and armour, and they spoke only of *him*, their love for *him*. 'You will all be redeemed in the sight of the Darkblade,' they said, then they hung the monk who tended our temple from the gatepost and cut his belly open whilst his legs were still kicking. After that, we knew we couldn't stay. I wanted to head east, to the coast, use our oil to buy passage on ships to take us far away. My husband knew better."

She cast a hard glance at the two drifting boats now several hundred yards to their rear. The fire had evidently found the cargo of the second, for a bright blossom of flame could be seen in the heart of the pall. "He always thought he knew better," she murmured.

"Idiot peasants," Crab muttered from the tiller, his gaze fixed on the northern horizon as he scoured it for sign of their prey. "Should've sold your oil to the first merchant you found. The further you travel the more likely someone like me will take it from you." He turned a baleful glare on Alum and Sehmon, who were working the oars. "Faster, you foreign filth! If they make the shore, we'll have the whole Silver Thread down on us by nightfall, and they won't be in a forgiving mood."

"What was that?" Alum asked Vaelin.

"We need more speed." Vaelin rose and nudged Sehmon's heaving back with his boot. "Get some rest. I'll take over."

He and Alum hauled on the oars for over an hour, the speed of the boat increased by the sail Crab skillfully angled to make best use of the wind. "Hah!" the boatman exclaimed from the tiller, teeth bared in a predatory grin. "They're making for Heron Cove."

"And that's good news?" Vaelin asked, grunting as he continued to work his oar.

"The current flows west here." Crab jerked his head at the sail. "We have the wind to counter it, they don't. You and you." He flicked his hand at Nortah and Ellese. "Go forward. Kill them when they get close enough. All of them, mind."

After Vaelin translated the order, the two archers duly took up position at the prow of the boat, nocking arrows and waiting for the outlaw craft to come into range. After perhaps another twenty minutes of rowing, Vaelin heard Ellese say, "Is that . . . a ship?"

The uncertainty in her voice made Vaelin pause in mid-stroke. Standing, he turned his gaze to the prow, ignoring Crab's barked command to stick at it. He could see a very large shape resolving through the mist a few hundred yards away. It was indeed more a ship than a boat. Water swelled before a dark hull as it cut through the lake, a dozen oars on either side propelling it forward. Instead of one sail it had three, the foremost emblazoned in white with a symbol Vaelin had last seen when Ambassador Kohn presented his credentials: the seal of the Merchant King Lian Sha.

He could see a dense knot of men on the huge boat's foredeck, clad in red and standing with bows raised and drawn. As he watched, the archers all loosed as one and a cloud of arrows rose, arcing high before plunging down onto the two outlaw craft. The lake surface turned white as the arrows fell, covering both boats in a thicket of shafts that surely left no outlaw alive.

"Heaven shits on me once more!" Crab cursed, hauling hard on the tiller whilst tugging on the rope that controlled the sail. The boat duly heaved to starboard, wallowing for a moment before settling. "Get back on your oar," the boatman instructed Vaelin curtly. "If we can get to shore in time..." His voice faded and his eyes grew large as they alighted on something to the west. Vaelin turned to see three more boats emerging from the haze. They were smaller than the first but well crewed by oarsmen and all bearing the same symbol on their sails. It was obvious they were moving far too swiftly to allow any escape.

Crab's hand slipped from the tiller and he exchanged a sour glance with Chien. "Black knot?"

She nodded, lips twitching in an expression somewhere between a smile and a grimace. "The rule is clear," she said, her voice betraying only a slight note of apology.

"If I haven't said it before," the boatman began, "I've always found your company singularly unpleasant..."

Chien's staff divided with a snick, and the blade flicked across his throat. Crab sank to his knees, gurgling as blood flowed freely from the gaping wound beneath his chin. He fell face-first to the deck and lay still after a few shuddering spasms.

"You they might spare," Chien said, turning to Vaelin. She jerked her head at where Ahn-Jin crouched, clutching her terrified children. "Tell them these were our captives and they might spare them too."

Taking a deep breath she reversed the grip on her blade, placing the tip just below her sternum, teeth clenched in anticipation of the thrust. Vaelin lashed out before she could drive the blade home, striking just below her nose with his fore-knuckles. Her head snapped back and she staggered, rapidly dimming eyes finding the strength to regard him with a glare of pure hatred before she slipped senseless to the deck.

"Now what?" Nortah asked, breaking the silence that followed.

Vaelin raised a questioning eyebrow at Erlin, who offered a weak smile in return. "We allied ourselves with outlaws," he said. "We also gave succour to smugglers and travelled the Merchant King's domain without licence. All offences punishable by death."

Vaelin looked at the rapidly approaching ship-sized boat, drawing closer by the second with every sweep of its many oars. It was close enough now for him to note that the archers on the foredeck all had arrows nocked to their bows, although he took a morsel of comfort from the fact that they hadn't yet raised them.

"Put your weapons down," he told the others, unbuckling his own sword and letting it fall to the deck. Climbing up onto the roof, he gave a precisely measured bow to the oncoming vessel, head lowered by three inches and chest only fractionally forward, hands raised level with his waist, held open and out to the sides. It was a bow Erlin had taught him on the *Sea Wasp*, insurance against a circumstance such as this; the greeting of a noble emissary to the court of the Merchant King. His uncertainty as to its effect was not enhanced by the spontaneous ripple of laughter that came from the assembled archers on the foredeck.

"I'd guess that's not a good sign," Nortah muttered before the prow of the Merchant King's craft slammed hard into the hull, sending them all sprawling.

PART II

Fear the man with a spear more than you fear the man with a sword.
Fear the man on a horse more than you fear the man with a spear.
Fear the man with a crossbow more than you fear the man on a horse.
Most of all, fear the old woman who comes with a knife as you lie
bleeding at the battle's end, for she fears you not at all.

—SOLDIER'S PROVERB, EMERALD EMPIRE, C. EARLY THIRD CENTURY
OF THE DIVINE DYNASTY

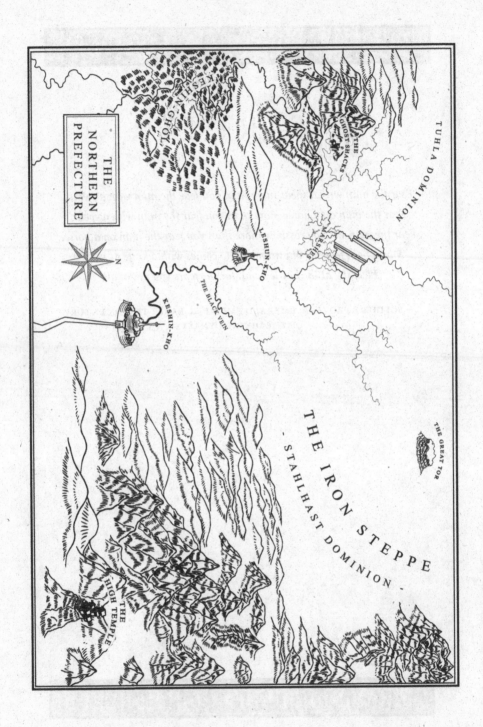

LURALYN'S ACCOUNT
The Second Question

Having read several accounts of my brother's life from those who flatter themselves with the title "historian," I find myself struck by how often they employ the phrases "reign of terror" and "path of destruction," particularly in relation to the commencement of his conquests. Whilst I emphatically reject any suggestion that I would ever style myself as my brother's apologist, it is my intention to provide an honest account in these pages. Therefore, it is my duty to relate that the first steps of Kehlbrand Reyerik on the road to godhood were neither terrible nor destructive. Throughout history many conquerors have built their power through a combination of military might and subsequent subjugation of a cowed and fearful populace. Others, like my brother and the fabled Fire Queen of the Barbarous East, are wiser, for they knew that, for power to endure, the conquered must be given reason to love their conqueror.

Kehlbrand's ascension to Skeltir of the Cova had been followed by a year-long period of consolidation. Rivals were summarily dealt with through a measured employment of battle or personal challenge. Alliances with many of the other Skeld were secured through marriage, Kehlbrand taking four daughters of fellow Skeltir to wife and marrying off his half sisters and cousins to various sons and Stahlhast luminaries. By the time he was called to the Great Tor to answer the Second Question, he was without doubt the most powerful Skeltir who had ever lived, although full dominance had not yet been achieved.

This time there was no drama when the Mestra-Dirhmar made his pronouncement, although I once again detected a distinct reluctance in the old man's demeanour. Also, I noted how the assembled lesser priests all turned their back and walked swiftly away at the completion of the proclamation, once again confirming the success of Kehlbrand's second step towards recognition as Mestra-Skeltir.

The Mestra-Dirhmar lingered for a brief second before following his brethren into the confines of the Great Tor and I managed to catch his softly spoken words to my brother. "Abandon this path, Kehlbrand Reyerik. We both know the third question will be beyond you. You love yourself far too much to answer it."

Other Skeltir would have bridled at the insult but Kehlbrand just laughed. "No, you venal fool. I love myself far too much not to."

"What was it?" I asked him as we rode back to our encampment. Whilst he had shared a great deal with me regarding what our brother had told him, much still remained hidden. "What was the second question?"

"It was a simple thing really," he said. "He asked me, 'What is a god?'"

"And the reply?"

"All in good time, little colt." He laughed and spurred his horse to a gallop. "All in good time."

Kehlbrand's masterstroke in securing eventual dominance of the Hast came the following spring when he persuaded the other Skeltir to cede to him control of their tors. Kehlbrand had long understood that the true wealth of the Stahlhast has always resided in the tors from where we source our iron and smelt our steel. Each tor had its own cluster of hovels and workshops where the slaves laboured to craft the metal into weapons and armour, whilst others are set to work in the pens where we breed the finest horses in the world. Such labour has long been considered beneath the dignity of those born to the Hast. In fact, the raids we launched into the southlands were often driven by the need to replenish the enslaved workforce who had a tendency to perish after barely a dozen years of productive use. The whole enterprise was undoubtedly effective in producing steel of good quality, but it was also massively inefficient.

"Every season you must leave half your warriors behind to guard your tors and whip your slaves," Kehlbrand explained to the assembled Skeltir. "If we are ever to sweep to the Golden Sea, this must change. Place your tors in my hands. They will still belong to you, all the slaves and steel will be yours, but I will oversee them, and the rewards will be great."

"But who will guard them?" the Skeltir enquired. "And who will whip the slaves?"

"Soon the Stahlhast will be one," Kehlbrand replied. "And Skeld will not steal from other Skeld. As for the slaves . . ." He paused then and I remember a small smile playing across his lips as he lowered his head, muttering something in the language of the southlands, a tongue unknown to all present save me. "What god need whip his supplicants?" The smile disappeared as he raised his head once more, face forming the purposeful glower expected of a Skeltir as he replied, "They will come to fear the merest glance of the Darkblade far more than the kiss of your lash."

There were objections, of course, voices raised in condemnation of one who would undo centuries of tradition, one who would lead us away from the path set down by the Unseen countless years ago. This obliged Kehlbrand to engage in another brief round of battle and challenge, and within the space of another year the tors were in his grasp.

"What do you see, little colt?" he enquired as we toured the hovels clustered around one of the largest tors in the Iron Steppe. It had been named the Fist of the Unseen by some long-forgotten ancestor, and generations of Stahlhast had fought to possess it ever since, it being so rich in ore. Until recently the Fist had rested in the hands of the Wohten Skeld, whose Skeltir, a stubborn man with an unfortunate attachment to his name, had chosen death rather than subservience. Tacitly, the Fist remained the property of the Wohten, but any fool could see that only my brother's will held sway here now.

"I see a den of slaves," I replied, surveying the ramshackle huts. Filth ran in shallow channels through the narrow streets, and the place stank of smoke and human waste. Most of the inhabitants were at work in either the mines or the pens, the few who remained careful to seclude themselves in their hovels as we passed by. Here and there a body lay in a shadowed corner, stripped of clothing and shrouded by flies. Whilst I would dearly love to claim some welling of compassion at this juncture, the unpalatable truth is that the plight of the slaves had never troubled my thoughts to any great degree. They were not of the Hast, and their bondage and labour were necessities blessed by the priests. It had always been this way.

"I see disease and death," I added, swallowing and holding bundled silk to my nose. "Also little reason to remain. Unless it's your desire to watch your sister lose her breakfast."

"Look closer," he told me, pausing at one of the huts. Pushing the door aside he revealed a dirt floor and a few meagre possessions: a blanket, an old iron skillet. It took a second before I discerned the two emaciated figures crouched in the unlit recesses of the hut, a woman and a girl. They both had their eyes closed and heads lowered, as was required of their kind when looked upon by their betters.

"What do you see?" Kehlbrand pressed.

I took note of the fierceness of the woman's grip on the girl, the closeness with which she held her. As my gaze lingered the girl shuddered, a whimper escaping her lips and causing the woman to smooth a hand through her unwashed, greasy hair, lips moving in barely audible words of comfort.

"A mother and child," I said. "They fear us."

"And are they right to do so?"

"Of course. A fearless slave is not a slave."

"True." Kehlbrand spoke softly to the woman and child in the language of the southlands, it being the most common tongue amongst the slaves: "Pardon our intrusion."

He closed the door and we resumed our stroll, Kehlbrand leading me towards the workings in the base of the Fist. "Fear is as much a necessary part of what happens here as the slaves' labour," he said. "But it is expensive, for the production of fear also requires labour, on our part."

The hovels soon gave way to the expanse of bare stone that surrounded the tor, revealing the sight of the massed slaves at work. The Fist resembled half of a giant, rotted apple, its flanks eaten away by the quarries where the slaves toiled. Like maggots in the flesh, I thought, surveying the multitude. An exact count of their number was never taken as they died so frequently. The only measure of their worth was in the amount of ore they dug from the rock. When the tally fell, the Wohten would raid to replenish their workforce.

"As you see." Kehlbrand gestured expansively at the works, from the quarries to the long lines of slaves pushing carts or carrying ore-laden baskets towards the smoke-shrouded buildings where the smiths worked. Warriors were everywhere, several hundred at least, mostly mounted and sitting in silent vigilance. Every few minutes one would turn his mount towards a line of slaves moving fractionally slower than the others. This increased scrutiny was usually sufficient to compel them to greater efforts. If the warrior found their response unacceptable, or succumbed to boredom, they would unhook the long oxhide whip from their saddle. These whips produce a particularly vicious crack as they snake through the air with deceptive slowness. Most warriors were content to leave a bleeding lash mark or two on faces or arms of tardy slaves, whilst others were more inventive.

"That man, for instance." Kehlbrand pointed to where a warrior had skillfully looped his whip around a slave's ankle in order to drag him across the stone. The warrior's features were set in a mask of determined anger rather than cruelty, the face of a man engaged in a bothersome chore. "He would rather be galloping across the Iron Steppe with a falcon on his wrist," my brother went on. "Or charging lance in hand into the heart of the battle, hungry for renown and the favour of the Unseen. But here he finds no more renown than a common herdsman, and our great mission suffers for it."

The warrior's mount came to an abrupt halt as Kehlbrand called out to him, striding across the stone with hand raised. "Mestra-Skeltir," the warrior said, swiftly dismounting to sink to one knee. The title hadn't as yet been formally bestowed upon my brother by the priests, but even then it had become commonplace for the Hast to refer to him as such.

Kehlbrand ignored the kneeling warrior, instead moving to the slave and crouching to unfurl the whip from his ankle. "Are you hurt?" he asked in the southland tongue as the man gaped at him in mingled terror and mystification. "Sister!" Kehlbrand called out to me, voice rich in urgent compassion. "Fetch water!"

I did as I was bid without hesitation, accustomed by now to my brother's liking for unexpected theatrics. Going to a nearby barrel I scooped water into a bucket and carried it to Kehlbrand's side, watching as he used his hands to convey the liquid to the slave's mouth. I took in the sight of the raw, bleeding scrapes on his forehead and limbs, deep enough to lay bare the muscle beneath his skin. Such injuries would normally entail a swift execution since they would render him unfit to work for several days.

"Fear not," Kehlbrand told the slave, spooning more water into his mouth. Rising he called out to the two warriors who had escorted us through the hovels. "Ride to our camp, bring the healer!"

"Healer?" the warrior who had inflicted the punishment asked in evident bafflement. The incident had attracted the attention of several of his fellows and I kept the wariness from my features as we found ourselves in the centre of an encircling ring of riders. They were all Wohten, until recently fierce and hated enemies of the Cova. I could see no aggression in them, however, just a shared depth of incomprehension.

"What was this man's offence?" Kehlbrand demanded of the dismounted warrior.

"He met my gaze, Mestra. It is death for a slave to look into the eyes of one born to the Hast. So have the priests ordained."

"Do not speak to me of priests," Kehlbrand rasped, face reddening. I watched as he made a show of mastering himself, breathing deeply and running a trembling hand through his hair. "This is not your fault," he said, voice faint as if experiencing a sudden realisation. "Too long have those who stand between the Hast and the Unseen led us along the wrong path."

My unease deepened as I saw the warriors exchange uncertain glances. Fortunately, Kehlbrand was ever skilled in not allowing the thoughts of his audience to dwell on uncomfortable notions.

"You are needed here no longer," he told them. "Return to your Skeld. Hunt, practise your skills, teach your young. Tell all, the great ride to the Golden Sea will soon be upon us."

"But . . ." one of the warriors began, gesturing to the quarries. "The slaves, Mestra-Skeltir."

"Slaves?" Kehlbrand looked down at the injured man at his feet, his smile as full of warmth as it was of guilt. "There are no slaves here now. Leave this tor and these people to me, for now their labour will be my labour."

It took a great deal more inventive rhetoric before the warriors of the Wohten tied their bows and lances to their saddles and rode off towards the encampments of their Skeld. By Kehlbrand's order they each left one weapon behind. The oxhide whips were all piled atop the largest quarry, where he stood to address the assembled slaves. They stood in bedraggled ranks below, staring up at the strange, tall Stahlhast with a voice that seemed to reach every ear with unnatural ease.

"These," Kehlbrand said, pointing to the piled whips, "will never touch your flesh again. This I swear. Many are the crimes that brought you here and great is my pain at all you have suffered. Know this, today the Darkblade has taken you under his protection and I will cherish you as I cherish my own blood. Henceforth all labour will be rewarded. None will go hungry. Before another pick touches this tor, we will build real houses where families will live in warmth and safety. For now, go and rest. Tomorrow we build, and so that you know my word is true, the Darkblade and his beloved sister will stay and build with you. We will not leave this place until all is made right and all wounds are healed."

The cheering was unexpected, perhaps because I assumed none of the people gaping up at us possessed the strength for it. But cheer they did, a thin, tremulous thing at first, like a chord struck to the strings of a lyre by untutored hands, growing by the second to something full and vibrant. Hands raised in gratitude, people went to their knees, others wept, but they all called out in worship to the Darkblade.

"I don't want to stay here," I said when he finally turned away from the supplicant throng. I recall his expression as being strangely lacking in either triumph or exultation. Instead he wore a small smile of satisfaction that reminded me of when my mother put the final stitch in a well-crafted jacket.

"Oh, cheer up, little colt," he told me. "After all, I just made you sister to a god."

◆ ◆ ◆

And so we stayed amongst the slaves, or the artisans, as my brother insisted they now be called. Although we were two amongst many, no hand was raised against us. I soon came to understand that Kehlbrand had captured them that first day; his words now bound them tighter than any chain. We lived in their huts and suffered their stink whilst he organised the construction of sturdier homes, finding those amongst the artisans with building skills and setting them up as foremen. Hovels were duly torn down and new houses were crafted from the great piles of rubble that surrounded the tor. Every night we would eat with a different family and my brother would speak to them of our great mission.

"Your enslavement was a crime," he would tell them as they listened, gazes rapt and tongues stilled by awe. "A crime visited upon you by a cabal of wicked men who call themselves priests. Long have they led the Stahlhast astray, long have they shielded us from the true word of the Unseen. Your liberation is but the first step towards the day when the crimes of the priests will be punished. For now we must build, craft something of such greatness they can never pull it down."

At his insistence I spent most of my time tending the sick or teaching the Stahlhast tongue, always with a kindly smile on my lips I knew rarely touched my eyes. The artisans never regarded me with the same awe as they did my brother. Instead, I was treated with a wary respect, sometimes even reverence due to the blood I shared with their divine liberator.

"What am I doing here?" I asked him one evening as we sat together in the mean hut he had chosen for us. Kehlbrand had forbidden a move to one of the new houses until they were all completed. He had spent the day at work, as was his wont now, labouring under the guidance of a master builder who only weeks before had been nearly whipped to death for dropping an ore basket. Every day my brother rose with the dawn and worked until dark, although he never seemed to tire. I, however, sat slumped by the fire, wearied by a day that had made me witness the prolonged death of an infant boy from the flux.

"You don't need me for this farce," I added. "It's you they worship."

"I do need you," he insisted. "I will not always be in their midst. In my absence you will be the Darkblade's eyes. And more than that." His expression grew more intent, voice lowering a notch. "You will also be my hunter."

"Hunter? For what."

"How many thousands reside in the shadow of the Fist? How many more will we find at the other tors?"

I gave a tired shrug. "A great deal, I suppose."

"Yes, a great deal. And amongst so many, is it not reasonable to assume there are others like you?"

My weariness dissipated as understanding dawned, replaced with a growing unease. "You wish me to hunt out slaves with the Divine Blood."

"We no longer use that word, dear sister. But yes. You will find them, and bring them to me."

I lowered my gaze as unease gave way to fear. "The Laws Eternal dictate . . ."

"Any not of the Hast found to have the Divine Blood are to be killed, I know." Sensing my fear, he shuffled closer, laying the hard muscular branch of his arm across my shoulders. "Since when have the Laws Eternal troubled us?"

"If they find out . . ."

"When they find out, you have my assurance it won't matter."

"How can you be so certain of everything? How can your path be so clear? I have dreamt none of this."

His arm tightened, drawing me into the comforting heat of his body. "Because I answered the second question, remember?" he said, fingers playing through my hair. "Would you like to know the answer now?"

To my surprise, I didn't. I recall a sense of disorientation in that moment, as if the world had shifted around me bringing change and knowledge I neither wanted nor understood. Even so, I had to know, for my fate was ever bound to his. "Yes, brother," I said.

He hugged me tighter for a moment before gently easing me away and turning my face towards his. "'What is the true nature of a god?' That's what the old bastard asked me. It is, of course, a ridiculous question. You can no more discern truth from the divine than spin gold from water. That was our brother's answer, incidentally. Possessed of sufficient vagary and basic insight to be acceptable, for the priests are not interested in elevating a Mestra-Skeltir with genuine wisdom. They care only for power, cherishing their petty luxuries and privileges won through the blood and toil of the Hast and these beggared creatures."

He paused, a reflective smile playing on his lips. "I could have just given them Tehlvar's answer, or some variation of it that would have satisfied the Great Priest, alleviate his growing suspicion. But I find I enjoy his discomfort far too much to do that. And so I told him. 'Fear,' I said. 'Gods are not born of love, sacrifice, scripture or faith. Gods are born and succoured by fear. Take you, for example. Your service to the Unseen is absurd. You shun the company of women, at least publicly, and spend your days grovelling to something you have never set eyes on, a voice you have never heard. All because you fear the chance it might actually exist.'"

Kehlbrand's smile turned into a laugh, soft and short. "He surprised me then, little colt. I had expected rage, you see. I had expected, even wanted him to rail at me, call me a blasphemer, a vile heretic. Had he done so, I would have laughed at him for a time and walked away, for I am tired of their rituals. I have long suspected that shunning the priests might provoke discord amongst the Hast, but there are no Skeld who can now stand against me, so what does it matter? But he didn't rage or rail. Instead he grew very still and pale of face. 'What causes you to imagine,' he said, 'that I have never heard the voice of the Unseen?'

"For a time we just stood and stared at one another. I heard truth in his words, Luralyn. Disgusting old hypocrite he may be, but in that moment he was not a liar. To him the Unseen remains real, as real as you and I. And so I found a new answer to the second question. What is the true nature of a god? Fear is part of it, yes. But also power. The power that comes with belief. The power to render slaves into willing servants through carefully applied kindness, coupled with the fear that it might all be taken away. Power that could bind the Stahlhast to a bunch of grasping old men for centuries through promise of the Unseen's favour and fear that its loss will bring the crushing shame of defeat. But their power is limited, made pitiful by their failure to realise its potential. To wield such power so that it might change the world, I must not merely believe in a god, but become one."

He frowned at the troubled scowl on my face and reached out a large, warm hand to cup my cheek. "Have no fear for me. My mind is not broken, merely enlightened. You ask the source of my certainty. This is it. For what manner of god would I be if I couldn't divine the future?"

◆ ◆ ◆

The first I found was a girl. No older than fifteen and born to the tor. A lifetime of squalor and infrequent rations made her appear little more than a child. Her head barely reached my shoulder, and her limbs poked like pale, unwashed spindles from the sacking she wore.

"Your name?" I asked her in the southland tongue, receiving only a fearful shake of her tousled head in response. She kept her eyes lowered, rendered incapable of meeting my gaze by a lifetime of subservience. She shuddered as I reached through the veil of matted hair to cup her chin, gently but firmly raising it until the greasy tendrils fell away to reveal her face. It was a soot-smeared white oval, striking in its resemblance to a porcelain-faced doll I had once owned as a child.

"Look at me," I told her, keeping hold of her chin until, slowly, she opened her eyes. Tears streaked through the soot on her cheeks as she gazed at me, terror plain in the wide, black pupils.

"You must have a name," I said, and she shook her head once more.

"Girl," she murmured, soft as a breeze. "They only call me girl."

"Your mother? Father?"

Another shake of the head, accompanied by a shift in her bony shoulders. "Never knew 'em."

She spoke just loud enough for me to discern an accent this time, a coarse echo of the dialect native to the borderlands. I saw a tic of annoyance pass across her face as my hand lingered on her chin, and sensed a small flicker of something inside her, the same something that had led me to her. A fractional widening of her eyes told me she had sensed the same thing in me.

"You are very special," I said. "I shall call you Eresa. It means 'jewel' in the Stahlhast tongue."

"Jewel?" she asked. The genuine puzzlement on her besmirched brows brought a smile to my lips, the first real smile in weeks. I have come to understand these many years later that this was when it began, when my heart began its long journey away from my origins. This small, wretched girl and her simple curiosity had stirred something new within me, something not of the Hast.

"A shiny precious stone," I said. "Very rare, like you." I took her hand and led her away from the midden where she had been picking bones from the accumulated muck. "Come along. I believe it's time for you to have a bath."

Eresa, it transpired, had the power to conjure sparks from thin air. They were little more than small flowers at first, brief fluttering blue embers lighting the gloom of our hut much to our mutual delight and my brother's satisfaction. In time, with a judicious amount of coaxing and encouragement, her flowers grew into sustained and powerful bursts of pure energy. This wisp of a girl was soon capable of birthing flame in any combustible object or stopping the hearts of rats and, some years later, the soldiers she would face in battle.

I found another a month later, a tall youth who had gained considerable muscle thanks to the improved diet Kehlbrand provided. I felt his power blossom as he worked the pick into a slab of stone in the quarry, the tool biting deeper than the others, too deep in fact to be the result of his improving frame.

"It only works with stone, mistress," he said, shuffling uncertainly under my careful scrutiny. "I just look at it and it crumbles. Kept it hidden all this while. It seemed for the best."

"Indeed it was," I assured him. "Don't call me mistress. My name is Luralyn, and it's the only name you need address me by. What is yours?"

It shames me to say I cannot recall his true name now, for at the time it scarcely seemed to matter. I named him Varij, the ancient word for "hammer." Following this it became my habit to name all those I found. Casting away their former titles was a way of binding them to the Darkblade. "You are reborn," I would tell them, words that soon became a mantra. "You are made new in the sight of the Darkblade. You will be his shield and his lance in the battles to come."

I could find no more Divine Blood at the Fist, despite three months of searching. By then the transformation of those who toiled in the quarries from slaves to artisans was complete. The provision of improved housing and better food had succeeded far better in increasing the amount of ore hewn from the tor than any amount of terror or whipping. But I knew it was more than just full bellies and sound walls that spurred them to such feats of labour. I could see it on every face as the Darkblade made his farewells with the promise of a return the following year: complete and utter devotion. Truly, he had made himself a god.

I watched Kehlbrand prepare to leave with a dull ache in my chest and a familiar cloudiness in my head that came from a troubled sleep. "You dreamt last night, didn't you?" he said, pausing in the act of strapping his quiver to his saddle. "You always get the same look on your face when you dream. Like you've eaten a sour apple but can't remember where you found it."

"It found me," I said. "I didn't go looking for it this time."

He raised an eyebrow at the gravity in my voice, sensing more than just my frequently expressed bitterness at being left behind. I was to take Eresa and journey to the other tors, freeing the enslaved and spreading the Darkblade's word, whilst also searching for more jewels with particular talents. He would take Varij and the warriors of five Skeld south into the borderlands.

"There's an outpost of the Venerable Kingdom we've never been able to storm," he told me the night before. "Walls too high to scale. But with our new brother"—he gave a meaningful glance at Varij—"I believe they won't stand so high for much longer. Once it's gone we'll have a hundred miles of border country to raid at will."

Now I watched him tug the ties on his quiver tight, regarding me with a faint but discernible resentment. As the years went by the certainty with which he pursued his plans increased, but so did his dislike of anything that might disrupt them. "So, what did you see?"

I gave a small shake of my head, which did little to dispel the clouds. It is always this way with unbidden True Dreams. The unasked-for gifts of Heaven are often vague but always troubling.

"A man," I said. "Tall, like you. Strong like you. I saw him fight, and he fights well."

"You've watched me kill men who stood a head higher than I," he responded with an amused snort. "Stronger too. As for fighting well, who can fight as well as a god?" His voice held a mirthful note, but not, I noted, as mirthful as when he first began to describe himself as such.

"It wasn't just that." I closed my eyes, trying to recall the details of the vision. It had been partially formless, the figures ghostlike, insubstantial, except for the tall man. "He was on a boat, killing men," I said. "He saved a woman, children . . ."

"How noble." Kehlbrand's hand slapped against the pommel of his saddle as he prepared to haul himself onto the back of his horse. "I'll be sure to compliment him if I ever meet him . . ."

"I heard his name," I cut in. "It is also your name. The name I found for you."

Kehlbrand stopped, his foot lowering slowly from the stirrup as he turned back to me. The moment I began my journey away from the Stahlhast had come when Eresa's besmirched and puzzled face brought a smile to my lips, but this was when I took the first true step away from my brother. It was a backward step, in fact, provoked by the depth of malice made stark in the suddenly ugly mask of his face. It was a face thousands would behold in years to come, some with love, more with terror. This was my first glimpse of the Darkblade and it brought tears to my eyes, for I hadn't known until this moment that my brother could ever be rendered so ugly.

"And where do I find him?" he asked, voice mirthless now and soft with lethal certainty. "This thief of names."

It took me the space of several hard, chest-aching heartbeats to answer, so transfixed was I by his expression. "He bore the name long before you did," I said, my voice shot through with a tremor I detested almost as much as his transformed face. He had never made me afraid before, and I found I had to cough before speaking on. "And you will not find him. He will find you."

CHAPTER TWELVE

The carriage heaved beneath him before taking on a sustained tremble as its wheels shifted from the smooth brick surface of the road to something rougher. *Cobbles perhaps?* Vaelin wondered. If so, it might mean they had come to a city and this journey could finally be at an end.

He was alone in the carriage save for a small mouse that had somehow contrived to gain entry during one of the nightly rest stops. Vaelin would feed it crumbs from the bread shoved through the slat in the base of the carriage door once a day, along with a small amount of water in a wooden bowl. The mouse never came close enough for him to reach, its small but apparently keen mind having calculated the length of his chains. They were heavy and short, fixed to an iron bracket in the floor. On the first day of the journey, he had tested his strength against the bracket, promptly concluding it would take the strength of ten men to have any hope of dislodging it.

This mobile prison featured wooden walls of thick timber. Like the door they had no window, and he could discern only faint glimmers of daylight through the tiny gaps in the planking. He kept track of the days by counting the meals, now amounting to fifteen. In that time he had seen no other living soul nor heard another voice beyond the muffled conversations of the guards and drovers.

His years in an Alpiran dungeon had habituated him to both solitude and confinement, also the folly of dwelling on the fate of friends. But in those days he had still possessed his song, and the walls that held him were no barrier to its reach. Now he had only his memories and the nagging, persistent need to know what had become of Ellese and the others.

He hadn't caught a single glimpse of them since his capture on the lake. The soldiers of the Merchant King had swarmed Crab's boat with staves in hand, displaying little hesitation in their use. Ellese had made the mistake of swatting away the hand of a soldier as he made to bind her wrists and been clubbed to the deck for her pains. Vaelin had suffered his own flurry of blows when he tried to step to her side. As he lay on the deck, gasping from pain and clutching ribs he suspected might be broken, a sackcloth bag was thrust over his head and his wrists were bound with thick twine. There had been a few hours of lying in what he assumed was accumulated bilge water in the bowels of the ship-sized boat. He heard Nortah's voice raised at one point but whatever witticism he had intended to bestow was rapidly drowned by a harsh shout and the dull thwack of hard wood on flesh.

Eventually he had been dragged from the damp into the open air. Harsh prods propelled him across solid ground as he peered through the weave of the sack at what he took to be some form of dockside. Then came the gloomy interior of the carriage and the jangle of chains followed by the feel of cold iron on his wrists. The bag was whipped away, and he caught a fleeting glimpse of a soldier's armoured back before the door slammed shut.

"Is this how you treat a noble visitor?" he had muttered to the gloom with a weary laugh, reflecting on the uselessness of Erlin's lessons in etiquette.

"I don't suppose," he asked the mouse now as the carriage's wheels continued to rattle over what he hoped were cobbles, "you know the name of this place?" He accompanied the question with a few bread crumbs. The mouse, however, appeared unimpressed. The black beads of its eyes gleamed as it paused to regard him for a second before hopping closer, gathering the morsels to its mouth with tiny claws.

"No." Vaelin sighed. "I doubted you would."

He strained to peer at one of the larger gaps in the planking. It was barely the width of his small finger and revealed only a variety of passing light and shadow, although from the increased pitch of noise, it was clear the carriage was indeed now navigating some kind of city. The sheer number of accumulated voices he could hear, coupled with the hours it took for the carriage to come to a halt, convinced him this was a far more substantial place than a mere town.

He reckoned it took a total of four hours before the vibration of the wheels gave way to something far smoother and the carriage came to a halt. A hard metallic clanking and the door swung open. Vaelin blinked watery eyes in the harsh daylight until his vision cleared to reveal a hard, frowning face that, he realised, was one he had seen before.

He judged the man's age at a few years more than his own, his smooth shaven features marred by lines at the corners of his eyes and mouth. His black hair was drawn back into a topknot revealing a forehead marked by a trio of old scars, two of which hadn't been there when Vaelin last saw him. Also, his expression had been very different. *The face of a man in love,* Vaelin recalled. Also, whilst his memory increasingly contrived to discard some details as he grew older, the visions conveyed to him by the blood-song never dimmed, especially those concerning Sherin.

The man's eyes narrowed as Vaelin's gaze lingered on him, nostrils flaring in a disdainful sniff. "Fetch a bucket," he said, glancing to the side. "He cannot assault the king with such a stink."

With that he stepped back and two soldiers in red-lacquered armour climbed into the carriage. They removed Vaelin's chains and one barked out a command to get up. Vaelin groaned as his muscles stretched for the first time in days, getting unsteadily to his feet only to be shoved towards the door. It was clearly a push calculated to cause harm, forcing Vaelin against the metal-bracketed edge of the doorway with sufficient force to provoke a pained grunt. Hearing the man who had shoved him let out a snicker, Vaelin groaned again and sank to one knee, head sagging in exhaustion.

"On your feet, you barbarous ape," the shover said, meaty hand clamping hard on Vaelin's shoulder. He sagged lower, forcing the guard to stoop and slightly unbalance his stance. Vaelin's head snapped back in a blur, connecting with the soldier's nose, producing a satisfyingly loud crack. As the man reeled, Vaelin twisted, catching hold of the hand on his shoulder whilst simultaneously lashing out with his foot, sweeping the soldier's leg away. He collapsed onto Vaelin, trying to tear his hand free as his companion loomed closer, reaching for Vaelin's arm. He rolled, taking the soldier with him, hands moving with brisk, practised efficiency, screams filling the musty confines of the carriage. In the time it took for two more soldiers to climb into the carriage and drag them apart, he succeeded in breaking three of the shover's fingers.

"Enough!"

Vaelin felt the cold kiss of steel under his chin and found the man with the familiar face standing over him. He held the tip of a sword to Vaelin's skin with a precise but firm grip, a deep temptation to use it plain in his gaze.

"Kill me," Vaelin said, "and who will you take to meet your king?"

"I strongly suspect," the man said as the sword tip pressed harder, Vaelin feeling a trickle of blood on his neck, "he may well be satisfied with just your head."

Vaelin gave a bland smile and released his grip on the soldier, letting the man scrabble away, cursing and clutching his ruined hand.

"Shut up!" barked the familiar man, the note of authority in his voice marking him as an officer of some kind. Sheathing his sword, he spared the soldier a disgusted glance before turning away. "Short rations and no wine for a month. You were warned he was dangerous." Turning to Vaelin, he inclined his head at the door. "No more trouble. Understand me, barbarian?"

"I have companions," Vaelin said. "I would know where they are before I go anywhere."

"Any questions will be answered by the king, if he deigns to sully his tongue by conversing with you. Now get up or I will happily deliver you to him in chains."

Climbing down from the carriage, Vaelin found a bucket full of soapy water waiting at the foot of the steps. A few paces beyond stood a soldier holding a bundle of plain but clean clothes.

"Strip," the officer said, gesturing at the bucket. "Then wash, then dress."

Vaelin took a moment to scan his surroundings. He stood amidst a ring of a dozen red-armoured soldiers in a courtyard he would have taken for a field were it not for the smooth slate tiles that covered it from end to end. It was bordered by three-storey buildings with low-angled roofs, the corners and edges of which were richly adorned in statuary. Beyond the buildings he saw towers rising into the pale cloudy sky. They were almost as tall as the towers of Volar, but thinner, each one crowned by a structure that resembled a miniature fortress. *Watch-towers*, he concluded, finding himself impressed. *No army could approach within fifty miles without being seen.*

THE WOLF'S CALL · 165

"Strip, wash and dress!"

Vaelin glanced at the familiar man and gave a courteous bow before divesting himself of his clothing. The sweat-matted fabric peeled away from his skin to birth a miasma that even he found strong enough to sting his eyes. "You haven't asked my name," he commented once fully naked, moving to the bucket. "Is that because you already know it?"

He gave the officer a sidelong glance as he lathered himself, seeing a determinedly rigid composure in his features. This was a fellow well practised in concealing emotion. "Or my business in the Venerable Kingdom," Vaelin went on. He dipped his head into the bucket and soaked his hair before working his fingers through the tangled strands. "Don't you wish to know why I am here?"

The man said nothing, face just as rigid as before.

"Sherin Unsa," Vaelin said, watching for any reaction and finding none. "A woman of my former acquaintance. Sister Sherin Unsa to be precise, formerly of the Fifth Order of the Faith. Although I imagine she dropped the title years ago."

Still nothing beyond a slight twitch to the eyes. "She's an easterner," Vaelin added, hefting the bucket. "A barbarian you would say. Like me." He upended the receptacle and emptied the contents over his head, enjoying the sensation of cleanliness despite the chill. "Strange that you would have no knowledge of her." He tossed the bucket aside and took a moment to shake the moisture from his hair. "I had heard she achieved some renown in these lands thanks to her healing skill . . ."

"I know of whom you speak." The man's expression had hardened once more, Vaelin seeing the same hunger for violence in his gaze. "And, yes, I do know who you are. She is nothing like you."

He's never met me, yet he hates me, Vaelin concluded. *What did she tell him?* He turned away as the question provoked a shameful bitterness. *The truth would be cause enough, if he loves her.*

"If the Merchant King wishes to know my business in his realm," he said. "She is the sole reason . . ."

"Don't speak of her again!"

The surrounding soldiers tensed as their officer took a step towards Vaelin, fist tightening on the sword at his belt. He mastered himself quickly, however, stepping back and nodding at the soldier with the clothes. "Dress and be quick. This tardiness is only adding to the insult you have dealt this kingdom."

The clothes were a simple set of grey cotton trews and jacket. Shoes were not provided so, once Vaelin had dressed, he was obliged to walk on bare feet as he followed the captain from the courtyard. The soldiers marched on either side, rarely taking their eyes off him. Vaelin was led through a series of gates and along successive walkways, guards snapping to attention as the captain passed by. People Vaelin took to be servants from their plain garb and the bundles they carried would scurry aside and bow low. By contrast, those of more opulent dress, presumably courtiers or officials of some kind, would either stare at Vaelin in open curiosity or pointedly avert their gaze as if the mere sight of a barbarian were somehow injurious.

Eventually they came to a gate far taller and more ornate than the others, its massive doors grinding on iron hinges as they swung open to reveal a broad pleasing panorama. Low hills of vibrant green surrounded placid pools of clear water whilst cherry blossom trees scattered petals across the vista. Vaelin recalled Lyrna's liking for gardens and the extensive royal parks she reputedly funded in her new dominions. However, he doubted she had as yet crafted anything to match this for sheer scale and beauty.

"Wait here," the captain told his soldiers, starting through the gate and gesturing for Vaelin to follow. The great doors swung closed the instant they stepped through onto the lush pasture. There appeared to be no pathways here, and Vaelin enjoyed the feel of the grass on his feet as he followed the captain up one hill and down another.

"You know my name," he said, labouring to keep up thanks to the depredations of his confinement. "Will you not tell me yours?"

The captain remained silent for some time before replying in a tone of weary necessity, "Sho Tsai. Commander of the Red Scouts."

"A mere scout?" Vaelin scoffed. "And not even a general? Surely a man of my standing should be escorted by someone of equal rank."

It was another calculated barb, one that seemed to strike deeper than the others. Sho Tsai came to a halt, turning in a slight crouch, one hand on the scabbard of his sword whilst the other gripped the handle. "Rank?" he asked in a low murmur. "You have no more status here than a worm wriggling in shit."

Anger, Vaelin thought in satisfaction as he began to voice another insult, one he hoped would guarantee an attack. He would disarm this prideful scout and force information from him. *He knows where the others are. He knows where Sherin is, and I'll have him tell me.*

A high-pitched chime sounded across the park, drawing Vaelin's gaze from Sho Tsai's glowering visage. The sound had originated from a small island in the centre of the nearest pool. It was linked to the bank by a stone pier and featured a slope-roofed structure supported by four pillars. A tall man with long silver hair stood beneath the roof, repeatedly striking a baton to a broad bell of some kind. A little girl capered about in front of him, her giggles mingling with the chimes.

Sho Tsai let out a deep sigh as he straightened, gesturing to the island. "The Merchant King Lian Sha commands your presence."

He turned and strode off, leaving Vaelin to briefly consider and then discount the notion of subduing him now that his back was so conveniently turned. A brief scan of the surrounding park revealed no sign of other guards or attendants, but he had an intuition that such emptiness was an illusion. Surely no king would leave himself so defenceless. He was also increasingly aware of his dangerous lack of caution since leaving the Reaches. As Tower Lord Al Sorna he would never have baited Sho Tsai so. *Brother Vaelin, however, was always far too accepting of risks.*

The chimes and the little girl's giggles fell silent as they traversed the pier to the island. She abruptly abandoned her dance to hide behind the tall man's robe, peeking out at Vaelin with a fearful scowl.

Sho Tsai came to a halt at the end of the pier and sank to one knee. "Most Favoured of Heaven," he said in strident but respectful tones. "I bring the interloper as per your command. And"—he glanced over his shoulder at Vaelin—"will be greatly honoured to administer your swift and wise judgement."

The tall man favoured the soldier with a kindly smile but said nothing, his gaze lingering expectantly on Vaelin. *The brother might not have bowed,* he thought. *But the Tower Lord would.*

He repeated the bow that had failed so conspicuously on the lake, embellishing it by lowering his head an inch or two further than etiquette required. The tall man evidently found this amusing for he gave a hearty laugh before turning to Sho Tsai.

"My thanks, Captain. Return to the shore if you would. I will speak to this man alone." His voice was soft, possessed of a melodious quality very different from any accent Vaelin had yet heard in this land. Nevertheless he found it to possess a certain effortless authority that reminded him of Aspect Arlyn, another man who rarely felt the need to raise his voice above a murmur.

"Forgive me, Most Favoured." Sho Tsai bowed lower, a hard reluctance in his voice. "But the barbarian should be considered a dangerous beast. He attacked one of my men . . ."

"Really?" the Merchant King interrupted, silver eyebrows raised in surprise. "Did he kill him?"

"No, Most Favoured."

"Could he have, if he wished?"

Sho Tsai's shoulders hunched a little. "Yes, Most Favoured."

"Then he cannot be termed a beast, can he?"

Sho Tsai hesitated a moment longer, then dipped his head lower before rising. Turning smartly about, he favoured Vaelin with a glance full of dire warning before marching along the pier to the shore.

"We shall speak in your tongue," Lian Sha told Vaelin in precise Realm Tongue coloured by his musical tones. "So there is no misunderstanding between us."

"As you wish, Highness," Vaelin replied. At the sound of his voice the little girl sheltering behind Lian Sha's robes let out a tiny squeak and hid her face in the cascade of silk.

"A moment, please," the Merchant King said before crouching and gently easing the girl away. "He is just a man, blossom of my heart," he told her, using his sleeve to wipe away her tears. "Such foolish notions your mother teaches you. Play now." He pointed to a collection of dolls and sundry toys close by. "Your grandfather has business to attend to. And what is business?"

"Business is the sun and rain," the girl replied promptly. Lian Sha stroked a finger across her cheek and she scampered to her toys without further hesitation.

"My youngest grandchild," the Merchant King told Vaelin. "Only four years old and already my favourite. Do you have a favoured child?"

"I have no children, Highness."

"Yes, I was forgetting. Vaelin Al Sorna, Tower Lord of the Northern Reaches and most famed sword of the Unified Realm, has never married.

What a curious people you are. A man born to any of the Merchant King-doms who remains unmarried beyond his twenty-first year would find himself shunned, even subject to fines in certain Prefectures. Is it lust for the flesh of men that prevents you choosing a wife?"

"No, Highness."

Lian Sha's dark eyes seemed to twinkle as they regarded him. Whereas the Merchant King's voice reminded Vaelin of Aspect Arlyn, his eyes evoked sour memories of King Janus.

"No insult suffered, I see," Lian Sha mused. "A man possessed of a broad mind, or at least broad experience. Of course, I know why you have no wife, as I know what brings you to my kingdom without invitation. You come in search of the healing woman, in memory of the love you shared and lost."

"Your Highness is well informed."

"An ill-informed king will soon find himself a beggar, or dead. It will not surprise you to know that I became aware of your presence here within two days of your stepping onto the docks of Hahn-Shi. A remarkably efficient intelligence and messenger network was one of the more useful legacies of the Emerald Empire." The twinkle faded and the king's eyes took on a sudden hardness. "I would know the fate of my emissaries to your tower."

"They were murdered by a member of their retinue."

"The weapons I sent them to purchase?"

"Will not be forthcoming, at least until my queen rules on the matter, which will take months and even then, I fully expect the answer will be no."

"Her response might be altered were she to learn her most favoured general is now a guest in my palace."

"I assure you, Highness, it will not. When it comes to negotiations, Queen Lyrna will not suffer any disadvantage and I caution you against rousing her anger. Not long ago, an entire empire was crushed for making the same mistake, as I suspect a well-informed king would already know."

A steely glint crept into the Merchant King's eyes and his voice became a low, steady murmur. "For the sake of a pleasant outcome to this meeting, make no assumptions as to what I do and do not know." He held Vaelin's gaze and blinked, the murmur abruptly replaced by a brisker, more businesslike tone. "What became of the assassin?"

Vaelin considered some form of obfuscation, finding it doubtful that most men, even a king, would find the truth believable. But he had a sense that this man possessed a very keen ear for dishonesty. "He possessed abilities derived from what my people term the Dark and your people call the Blessings of Heaven," he said. "Using these abilities he killed Ambassador Kohn and General Gian before being captured. He died as I questioned him, having taken poison before carrying out his mission."

"And what information did you glean from him before he did so?"

"That our kingdoms are under threat from the creature he served."

The king's eyes narrowed, a slight shift in the angle of his head telling Vaelin he may actually have told him something he didn't already know. "The Stahlhast and their living god," he murmured. "That is who he served."

Vaelin shook his head. "I don't think so. He said the Stahlhast are just a tool but that they served the same master. What its nature is, or where it resides, I know not."

Lian Sha's granddaughter let out a loud "hah!" Vaelin glanced over to see her miming out a fight with two of her dolls. The larger doll was evidently some kind of mythical monster with the head of an orange-striped cat and a man's body, whilst the other wore a soldier's uniform. The cat-headed doll appeared to be winning.

"You may be wondering," Lian Sha said, smiling at the child's antics, "why you are not dead. Why I have not punished you for your most heinous crime."

Vaelin's gaze lingered on the battling dolls, watching as the monster pummelled the soldier to the ground before the girl let out another "hah!" and swiftly brought him back to full height. Within a few seconds he had laid the monster low and stood with arm upraised. "You won!" his owner congratulated him. "Now you get *all* the cakes."

"I imagine," Vaelin said, "Your Highness has use for me. I find it is often the way with kings."

Lian Sha smiled again, inclining his head. "You travelled deeper into my domain than I expected," he said. "Perhaps you might actually have made it to the High Temple if I hadn't sent the Red Scouts to intercept you. You were correct in not formally presenting yourself to me on arrival. It would have taken weeks to navigate the web of bureaucrats I employ to protect me from unwanted or unfamiliar petitioners. And what would have been achieved once you had done so? Only a brief audience and a polite refusal. A foreign barbarian requesting leave to traverse my realm on personal business? I could never publicly countenance such a thing. But now, you are my prisoner. By the laws of this land you belong to me, and I may use you as I will."

"I did not come here to fight your war."

"No, but come you did. You came for the Healing Grace. That's what they call her, this woman you seek. A woman so skilled in curing ills and mending wounds it is claimed she too has the Blessing of Heaven. I heard about her some years ago when my daughter lay close to death as she sought to bring another life into this world. My court physicians were appalled, of course. Allowing a foreigner access to a princess of the royal line. A near-blasphemous act in their eyes. I had to execute two or three before they stopped grumbling."

Vaelin's eyes returned to the little girl. Her dolls lay forgotten now as she batted a leather ball around with her small hands, tongue poking from her lips as she frowned in concentration. "Sherin delivered her," he said.

"And saved her mother. By way of reward I offered her riches, enough for her to live out her days in luxury had she wished. But she declined, instead asking for funds to build a healing house in the town where she had made her home. I funded it of course, but still the debt I owe her is substantial. I now consider it partially settled in sparing you."

Business is the sun and rain, Vaelin remembered. *Everything here is measured in debts owed and paid.*

"If you would permit me to take her back to the Unified Realm," he said, "you would repay her in full. If you would but tell me where she is . . ."

The old man laughed, the sound as rich in surprise as mockery. "What a shambling, clumsy people yours must be. So lacking in guile, so devoid of subtlety. It mystifies me as to how your dread Fire Queen conquered so many lands so quickly."

"Because many who live in those lands consider themselves to have been freed, not conquered. Can any of your subjects say the same?"

He had expected some form of angry retort but the Merchant King merely laughed once more. "Freedom, eh? The freedom to do what? Pay taxes to their queen? Serve in her armies when she commands it? My people realised long ago that freedom is an illusion, a notion best left to the rumination of philosophers. My subjects do not look to me for freedom, they look to me for two things above all else: opportunity and protection. It is to the latter that I now principally concern myself, and why I have use for you. Tell me, what do you know of the Jade Princess?"

"She's said to have lived for countless years, thanks to the Blessing of Heaven."

"Quite so. I was a boy when my father sent me to hear her song. Thirty years later I returned and whilst my belly had grown and my beard turned grey, she was as young and fair as before, even her song hadn't changed. That is what she represents, you see: stasis. She does not change and neither do we. It has long been a belief of my people that the Jade Princess is the embodiment of Heaven's favour. As long as she resides in the High Temple, our lands, our cities, our songs and wisdom will endure. Wars and famine may have beset us through the ages, the Emerald Empire may have crumbled, but the people of the Far West have always continued to grow and prosper. But now the Stahlhast menace our borders and the Jade Princess is gone."

Vaelin recalled the final moments with the Messenger, the odd mix of regret and malice. *Sherin, gone to minister to the Jade Princess . . .* "And the woman I came to find," he said. "The Grace of Heaven . . ."

"Gone with her. The healer was summoned to the High Temple. A strange request since the Jade Princess is immune to illness, but it was assumed one of her beloved servants had been taken ill so the local Prefect issued the required travel warrant. Within days a messenger arrived informing me the Jade Princess and the Grace of Heaven had vanished. I had the Prefect flogged and dismissed from my service."

"And all your spies and messengers have no notion of where they went?"

"Just a vague report they were seen travelling north by way of a mountain track. If true, this route will soon take them into the borderlands, where the Steel Horde now raids freely. I simply cannot imagine what could have compelled them to such a course."

The Merchant King fell silent and moved towards the edge of the island, pausing to play a hand over his granddaughter's head. She had lost interest in the ball and now amused herself with a wooden top decorated with colourful designs that blurred into a mesmerising spiral as she spun it.

"This park was built at my father's order," Lian Sha said, causing Vaelin to blink and look away from the spiral. The old man stood with arms crossed as he regarded the placid waters of the pool and the verdant hills beyond. "It was necessary, for it was here that the greatest damage had been inflicted upon the old palace. The savages of the Iron Steppe came before, you see. A coalition of tribes from the eastern plains. Ironically, it later transpired they had been forced to migrate when the Stahlhast expanded into their lands. So they came for ours, leaving a scar of blood and ash across the Venerable Kingdom that reached all the way to this palace.

"They didn't understand it, this huge camp of stone that never moved. To them it was sickening, abhorrent, so they sought to destroy it. It's said three thousand courtiers were herded into the complex of temples that once stood here, to have their throats slit, whereupon the savages set the whole place on fire. When my father eventually vanquished the tribes and deposed the dullard who held a throne he didn't deserve, he found it odd that this ruined part of the palace had since grown rich in grass and flowers. My scholars tell me it's thanks to the bones of the courtiers. Somehow in their deaths they managed to enrich this soil. So instead of rebuilding the temples, my father ordained that a park be crafted instead. It didn't endear him to the monks but he was never of a particularly spiritual bent. 'The monks clutched their beads and beseeched Heaven for deliverance,' he told me once. 'But only steel and cunning will be your saviour when the savages are at your door. Remember that when they come again, for they will, my son.'"

Lian Sha paused, silver moustache twitching as his lips formed a smile of fond remembrance. "And so my father is proven once again to have been a very wise man. A war unlike any before is upon this kingdom. The Steel Horde will not stop at our border. The other Merchant Kings delude themselves, imagining the horde will oblige them by destroying a competitor before scurrying back into the Steppe with their spoils. But only a fool thinks the tiger is ever sated. A storm of evil design has come, and to fight it my subjects must believe victory is possible. I have lost an army fighting the Stahlhast, it is true, but by the dawning of the summer months I will have half a million fresh recruits ready to march. The question is, how will they fight?"

"It's my experience," Vaelin put in, "that soldiers will fight well if they are well trained and well led."

"Even if they know the favour of Heaven has been taken from them?" The old man shook his head. "I know the temper of my own people. There have been too many omens of late, too many unseasonal storms, too many sightings of the Harbingers of Heaven."

"I have heard this phrase before. What exactly are these harbingers?"

"Beings sent by Heaven to warn of impending doom, or so it's believed. They tend to appear in times of crisis or calamity. For example, a swarm of winged foxes was seen flying over the Qan Li estuary the night before a tidal wave destroyed most of the villages along its banks. In my father's time a huge bear was witnessed prowling the northern hills shortly before the tribes won their first battle against us."

"Winged foxes and giant bears." Vaelin pursed his lips. "I see."

Lian Sha squinted at him, his eyes betraying a faint glimmer of annoyance. "Is that scorn I hear in your voice? Does the barbarian imagine himself more rational than the people of the Far West? I know a great deal of you and the land you hail from. It is a place where for centuries people have killed each other in the name of ancient scribblings and imagined gods. Do not presume to test my patience with your judgement."

He turned to Vaelin, his face taking on a masklike immobility that told of a man speaking with utter sincerity. "You think I wish you to fight my war, lead my armies perhaps? What arrogance. I would no more put my soldiers in your hands than place my granddaughter in the clutches of a baboon. No, you will be my hunting dog, Vaelin Al Sorna. You will go in search of the Jade Princess and return her to me. I sent the best trackers in the Northern Prefecture to find her but they scoured the mountains for days with no result. I suspect you might have better luck. If you happen to find the healer with the Princess, then all to the good. I shall even allow you both to depart my kingdom. That is the use to which I will put you, and I will entertain no pretence of refusal. We both know you have no choice."

More Janus than Arlyn, Vaelin concluded, jaws aching as he clamped his mouth shut to confine any unwise words. *Although, Lyrna would have tangled him in her own web. But I am not her.*

"I travelled with several companions," he said when the ache in his jaw receded.

"Yes, and they currently enjoy my hospitality. Take them with you if you wish. If you like, you can even have that vicious bitch from the Crimson Band. I'm afraid I was obliged to send agents to deal with her father. A certain tolerance of the criminal element is a necessary aspect of governance, but his transgression was too great. Like you, she has been left in no doubt that she now belongs to me."

The Merchant King Lian Sha gave a barely perceptible bow Vaelin recognised from Erlin's lessons: the dismissal of a noble but minor functionary. Turning, he beckoned to Sho Tsai. "I'll send the Red Scouts with you," he said. "My best troops and their commander have a keen interest in the success of this mission. You see, when my daughter lay near death, it was he whom I sent to fetch the healer. He's been quite terribly in love with the Healing Grace ever since."

CHAPTER THIRTEEN

"Tsai Lin." The young soldier bowed low as he introduced himself, Vaelin judging it the deepest bow he had been afforded since arriving in these lands. "Dai Lo to the Red Scouts."

"Dai Lo?" Vaelin asked. "I do not know this term."

"Apologies, lord." The young man's head dipped an inch lower. "A Dai Lo is . . . an apprentice, you might say, a student awaiting confirmation as an officer in the king's army."

"I see." Vaelin glanced around the courtyard, his gaze tracking over the three dozen soldiers preparing their mounts for the journey. Sho Tsai moved amongst them, checking gear and ensuring the packhorse loads were securely tied. "Tsai," he said. "You share a name with the commander."

"I am honoured to be his son, lord."

"The third egg in the nest, more like," one of the soldiers said in a low but audible mutter that drew a snicker from the others. Vaelin was impressed by the fact that the young man's composure didn't falter, though he discerned from the rigidness of his features as he straightened that some insult had been suffered.

"The commander has appointed me your bodyguard and liaison for the duration of this mission," Tsai Lin went on.

"Bodyguard?" Vaelin raised an eyebrow, taking guilty satisfaction from the sudden discomfort on the youth's face.

"A formal term only," he stammered, bowing again. "All foreign dignitaries are allotted a bodyguard. Naturally, I would never presume . . ."

"My companions," Vaelin cut in. "I was assured by the Merchant King . . ."

His enquiry was proven unnecessary by a chorus of cursing from the far end of the courtyard. "Get your hands off me, you heathen fuckers!"

Ellese appeared as the Red Scouts made way for a company of blue-armoured soldiers. She struggled in the grip of two guards, hair an unruly tangle and besmirched features set in a snarl. She quieted on catching sight of Vaelin, however, sagging in the guards' grip until they released her.

"Thought you were dead," she said with a chagrined smile, coming forward to embrace him. He didn't return the embrace or allow it to linger. Her training was still incomplete after all. A spasm of hurt passed across her features as he eased her back, but she regained her composure quickly, standing straight and fixing her face into a neutral mask.

Nortah arrived shortly after, quickly followed by Alum and Sehmon, all equally unkempt and unwashed. Erlin came next. The depredations of confinement seemed to have taken the greatest toll on him, moving with a bowed head and slumped shoulders as the soldiers conveyed him to the courtyard. *Truly an old man now*, Vaelin thought, taking note of the additional streaks of grey in Erlin's hair and beard.

Chien was the last to appear, escorted by four guards instead of two and her wrists manacled. She moved with a stiff-backed, blank-faced composure that turned into an icy glare as she caught sight of Vaelin. The stare didn't waver as the guards removed her manacles, and Vaelin decided it would be an inopportune moment to offer a greeting.

"Dai Lo!"

The young soldier snapped to attention at the voice of his commander, turning and saluting with a closed fist to his chest. "Yes, Dai Shin!"

Horseshoes clattered on the tiles as Sho Tsai guided his horse through the throng, a tall dappled stallion with the long legs of an animal bred for the hunt. "Get the foreigners mounted up and let's be on our way," the commander ordered.

"My people need a moment," Vaelin said, nodding to his companions. "Refreshment and time to wash."

Sho Tsai regarded him in silence before nodding to a horse trough. "Wash then," he said, setting his mount into motion. "And be quick about it. The Merchant King has commanded a speedy resolution to this mission and I have no intention of disappointing him."

He cantered from the courtyard with the fully mounted company close behind, riding in two neat files. There was a clatter of wood and metal, and Vaelin turned to see a blue-armoured soldier dumping a canvas bundle onto the ground. Upon landing, the canvas fell away to reveal their weapons.

"Well, that's something," Nortah observed, retrieving his bow. "At least they didn't break anything."

"Lord, if you would," Tsai Lin said, gesturing to where grooms held the reins of seven saddled horses. "We cannot linger."

Vaelin nodded, halting Ellese and Sehmon in their tracks as they moved to the trough. "Get your gear and mount up," he instructed. "Wash later. A bit of stink won't kill you."

◆ ◆ ◆

"Is this whole country just one never-ending city?" Alum wondered, gazing around at the unceasing maze of close-packed buildings. The hour was early but the streets were still busy with people, all quick to shuffle to the side with bowed heads as the soldiers rode by. It had been over an hour since the Red Scouts departed the Merchant King's palace and there was still no sign of an end to the city.

"Muzan-Khi is the largest city in the Far West," Erlin said. "Which makes it probably the largest city in the world." He spoke in a tired drawl and sat hunched in the saddle with a decidedly grey pallor to his sagging features.

"Are you all right?" Vaelin asked.

"Of course not." Erlin grimaced and let out a very faint laugh. "I'm old."

Morning had become afternoon by the time the walls came into sight. The outer districts were on a lower elevation to the centre of the city, so Vaelin was afforded a clear view of the forty-foot-high barrier stretching away for several miles on either side. Unlike the port of Hahn-Shi, there appeared to be no further conurbation beyond the walls, only a vast patchwork of cultivated fields in various hues of green.

"It is forbidden to build beyond the walls, lord," Tsai Lin explained when

Vaelin raised the question. "The Merchant Kings have long decreed Muzan-Khi to be an eternal jewel, as unchanging as the sun."

"But the number of people here must grow by the year," Vaelin said.

"Muzan-Khi is often called the nest of the kingdom. All second sons and daughters are required to move to another city or town upon reaching the age of twenty-one, and are happy to do so, for opportunity waits for those who seek it out. Thus is the Venerable Kingdom bound together."

"What about third or fourth sons and daughters?"

"Such a thing is forbidden in the cities, lord. Only in the provinces are families permitted more than two children. From the earliest days of the Emerald Empire it has been known that too many mouths means famine in the long run."

They rode through a north-facing gatehouse that had the dimensions of a minor castle, and found themselves traversing a road of remarkably straight construction. Only in Volaria had Vaelin seen a road to compare, although it lacked the slightly elevated centre and drainage ditch that made the arteries of the now-former slave empire immune to the depredations of the weather. As in the city, people made way for the soldiers of the Merchant King, carts and people hurrying aside at the first glimpse of the Red Scouts, with one notable exception.

"Must've left a pot on the boil," Sehmon commented as a man ran past at a pace barely below a sprint. He wore a light, sleeveless shirt of black cotton and a white scarf on his head and ran with a long-practised stride. Unlike the other folk traversing this road, he paid no heed to the soldiers, his gaze fixed determinedly on the city. He also carried no burden apart from a cylindrical case slung on a strap across his back.

"A messenger?" Vaelin asked Tsai Lin.

"Yes, lord. Judging by his pace, he's probably worried over losing his scarf."

"His scarf?"

"The distance between each messenger post is exactly three miles. The time each messenger sets off is noted, as is their time of arrival. Every week their average speed is calculated and any considered too slow will lose their scarf. They are given one week to win back their scarf by increasing their speed and will suffer the cane if they fail to do so. Six strokes for the first offence, ten for the second. A third offence will earn dismissal and disgrace."

"So, not a sought-after role, I assume?"

"Actually, lord, there is fierce competition to enter the messenger service. The Merchant King hosts a grand race every year and only those who can run a three-mile course in the fastest time are chosen. The pay is high and the honour great."

They came to the messengers' outpost soon, a small building that was somewhat dwarfed by the banner of the Merchant King rising from its roof. As the company trooped by, Vaelin saw a messenger arrive from the city. Before coming to a halt, he unslung the cylinder from his back and tossed it to another man who had already set off for the north at the same measured but impressive pace.

"Wouldn't horses be faster?" Vaelin asked Tsai Lin.

"Horse messengers are used for the northern routes where the roads are not so good," the Dai Lo replied. "Here men are used. They require less food, and a horse does not fear the cane in the same way as a man. Strangely, it does not affect the speed of the message very much at all. A study conducted by the Merchant King's Master of Calculation concluded that a message can be carried by foot over a distance of two hundred miles and reach its destination within fifteen hours in fair weather." He spoke with a keen enthusiasm that put Vaelin in mind of Caenis; he too had always loved numbers.

"Two hundred miles in less than a day?" Vaelin shook his head in wonderment, recalling how it often took even a royal messenger a full week to traverse the Realm. *I'll write to Lyrna of this,* he decided. *Should I get the chance.*

◆ ◆ ◆

They passed another five messenger posts before the light began to fail and Sho Tsai called a halt for the night. The Red Scouts encamped close to a larger outpost that appeared to double as a barracks for the local contingent of Dien-Ven. From the way they stoically ignored one another, Vaelin divined a certain animus between the two groups.

"They are not true soldiers, lord," Tsai Lin said with a faint curl to his lip. "Merely tax farmers in uniform. I've seen them run from bandits."

The determination of the Red Scouts to ignore the Dien-Ven seemed to be matched by their indifference to those they had been commanded to escort. They pitched their tents at a notable remove and clustered around their fires, leaving provision of supplies to Tsai Lin, who went about his duties with an aura of forced affability. *Always the way in any army,* Vaelin decided. *The youngest are given the worst tasks.*

"Leave that," he told the Dai Lo as he filled a cooking pot with rice. "Lady Ellese and Master Sehmon will cook from now on."

He didn't turn upon hearing Ellese let out a thin sigh between clenched teeth. "I am bound to say, Uncle," she grated, "I have never cooked a thing in my life."

"Learn." Vaelin rose and started towards where Chien sat alone, hearing Sehmon murmur, "I'll show you. It's not so hard. Done it sacks of times."

"I'm sorry about your father," Vaelin told Chien. She hadn't lit a fire and huddled with her staff cradled in her arms.

"As head of the Crimson Band he knew the risk of aiding you," she replied, not bothering to raise her head.

"And yet he accepted it," Vaelin said, sinking to his haunches. "I am curious as to why."

"He weighed the likely profit against the risk. The only reason for any man to do anything in these lands." She blinked, eyes focusing on him with a dangerous intensity. "Is it guilt that compels you to speak to me? Be assured it means nothing. My father's own decisions led to his end, but I live in defiance of his authority because of you. I live in disgrace because of you. Now I am a mere slave to the Merchant King. Because of you!"

She had half risen in her anger, staff clutched in a tight grip, but froze at the sound of a sword hissing from a sheath to her rear.

"Has this criminal offended you, lord?" Tsai Lin asked, moving to stand over Chien with his sword raised in a two-handed grip. Vaelin judged his stance to be perfect, the blade held at just the right angle to sever Chien's head from her shoulders.

"Not at all," Vaelin said.

The Dai Lo gave a cautious nod and retreated a few steps, lowering but not sheathing his sword. Vaelin watched Chien settle back, deliberately forcing her gaze away from Vaelin.

"If you wished death," he said, "why not simply refuse the Merchant King's command?"

"I have three younger sisters. Unlike me they were not required to undertake employment in the family enterprise. Instead, my father sent them to an expensive school in Hahn-Shi where they will be prepared for marriage to husbands of high rank and wealth. The Merchant King agreed to fund their education and left me in little doubt as to their fate should I refuse to accompany you on this absurd mission."

Debts owed and paid, Vaelin thought. *Profit weighed against risk.* "Was that his only command?" he enquired. "I imagine there was more to his bargain."

"If you die without recovering the Jade Princess, then so do I, and so do my sisters."

Janus would've been impressed, Vaelin decided. *Though he would probably have threatened just one of the sisters.*

"I did not speak to you merely to express my guilt," he said. "I spoke to you because you are part of my company. You may hate me all you wish, but we are bound together on this course and I have little doubt as to the danger that awaits us." He leaned closer to her, speaking softly in Realm Tongue. "And I'll make you a bargain of my own. When this is done, there will be a place for you in my lands, and for your sisters."

He got to his feet. "Come and sit by our fire, eat with us. Though, I make no claims for the quality of the food."

◆ ◆ ◆

It required a three-day ride before the increasingly monotonous patchwork of fields gave way to verdant hill country. A succession of villages nestled between the hills, rendered picturesque by the numerous clusters of maple and cherry blossom that dominated the landscape. Vaelin was impressed to see that the quality of the road didn't diminish when it began to snake between the tall grass-covered mounds. The foot messengers continued to pelt past with steady regularity, and the traffic of carts and porters barely diminished.

He resumed Ellese's lessons every evening, spending two hours teaching her the sword or the bruising intricacies of unarmed combat. Sehmon was a willing sparring partner although Alum insisted he spend at least half the time learning the spear. The Red Scouts regarded all of this with either amusement or open contempt, which occasionally turned to anger at the sight of Ellese wielding a blade.

"A girl with a sword," one said, a stocky man whose lips had been untidily disordered by an old scar. As a consequence his every word was accompanied by a cloud of spit. "What's next, barbarian? A pig with a spear?"

Ellese paused in mid-parry, Vaelin watching her features flush with suppressed rage. She still possessed only a rudimentary command of Chu-Shin, but knew enough to recognise an insult, especially when it was accompanied by so much jeering. Taking a breath she resumed her stance, stoically ignoring the ongoing taunts of the spitting man and his fellows.

Vaelin lowered his own sword and stepped close to her, speaking softly, "Sufferance of an insult is sometimes necessary, but not always obligatory."

She met his gaze, a brief smile of gratitude playing over her lips, before stepping away. She reversed her grip on the yard-long ash stave used in these practice sessions and strode towards the spitting man. His face grew dark at her approach, the jeering of the other Red Scouts fading as they exchanged outraged glances.

"Get you gone," the spitting man said. "I'll have no truck with foreign whores . . ."

Ellese blurred into a pirouette, her stave lashing out to strike the spitter across the face. He staggered back, blood streaming from his nose, then fell hard onto his back as Ellese spun again, the stave sweeping his legs away. She retreated as he let out a roar, shoving away the hands of his fellow soldiers as he scrambled to his feet, his sword coming free of its scabbard. He lowered himself into a crouch, advancing towards Ellese with deadly intent writ large on his bloodied face.

"Corporal Wei."

The scout came to an abrupt halt at the sound of Sho Tsai's voice. The commander stood with his arms crossed, his gaze fixed on Vaelin rather than the now-stalled confrontation.

"Dai Shin!" the corporal said, coming swiftly to attention, a reaction mirrored by the other scouts.

"Do not embarrass yourself or this company further." Sho Tsai's gaze remained fixed on Vaelin as he spoke. *He sees this as a calculated insult,* Vaelin concluded. *Perhaps he's right.* The commander hadn't spoken a single word to him since leaving Muzan-Khi, ignoring questions and leaving all contact with the foreigners in the hands of his son. Consequently, Vaelin remained unenlightened regarding the man's knowledge of Sherin, something Tsai Lin proved equally unwilling to discuss.

Corporal Wei quickly returned his sword to its scabbard before turning to bow to his commander, another gesture copied by his comrades. "Apologies, Dai Shin! No excuse, Dai Shin!"

Sho Tsai's gaze lingered on Vaelin a fraction longer, then flicked to the corporal. "You will sleep in the open for the next three days. Consider yourself fortunate I don't demote you."

The corporal's bow deepened. "Yes, Dai Shin."

Sho Tsai ignored him and switched his gaze to Tsai Lin. "Dai Lo, if these barbarians insist on cavorting so, find somewhere beyond civilised eyes for them to do it."

Tsai Lin's bow was even deeper than the corporal's. "I will, Dai Shin."

The commander turned and walked back to his tent without another word. A shamefaced Corporal Wei quickly strode off, head lowered and apparently deaf to the supportive murmurs and backslaps of his comrades. "They won't have the Merchant King's favour forever, brother," Vaelin heard one of them mutter.

"If you would, lord." Tsai Lin bobbed his head at Vaelin, the shame on his face matching that of the corporal's. "I believe there is a field beyond that hill . . ."

"Oh, don't worry," Vaelin said, clapping him on the shoulder. "I think we're done for the night." He nodded at the bloodied stave in Ellese's hand. "Clean that. It'll be practice for when I find you a real one."

CHAPTER FOURTEEN

T he High Temple stood atop the summit of a mountain rising from the northern extremity of a shallow river valley. It remained shrouded in cloud as they approached, the covering apparently immune to the heat of the noonday sun.

"Can't remember it looking any other way," Erlin said, peering up at the misty flanks of the peak. "The temple can only be seen once you get above the clouds." His expression was mainly one of fond nostalgia but also tinged with a frown of trepidation. "I must say my legs don't relish the climb."

"Is there any point coming here?" Nortah enquired. "She's gone after all."

"To catch prey you have to find its trail," Vaelin replied. "And this is where it starts."

Sho Tsai ordered the company to halt at the base of the mountain where they were greeted by an old man in the red and black robe of a Monk of Heaven. He had emerged from a small but richly decorated house situated alongside a small arched gateway of ancient stone. Beyond the gateway an equally aged and weathered stairway, no doubt carved from the flesh of the mountain countless years ago, traced its way into the misted sky. The old man bowed a shaven head at the captain, the small bells that adorned his staff tinkling as he raised it in what Vaelin took to be some form of blessing.

"The Keeper of the Gate bids you welcome, Brother of the Spear," the monk intoned in prolonged, sonorous tones.

Vaelin saw Sho Tsai stiffen at the unfamiliar title, his response clipped and cautious. "You were not here when last I came, yet you know me."

"All who study at the temples are known to the Servants of Heaven. The Temple of Spears keeps us enlightened as to the progress of its students. How gratifying it is that, amongst all his soldiers, the Merchant King has sent you, for grave is our need and dark the hour . . ."

"It need not be so dark," Sho Tsai cut in, voice hard in reproach, "if the Keeper of the Gate had lived up to his name."

The old man drew back, rising from his bow with shock palpable on his face. "This temple is under the authority of the Servants of Heaven," he sputtered. "Leave to enter is ours to give or deny . . ."

"Because *she* let you." Sho Tsai dismounted and called out an order for the Red Scouts to do the same. "And now she's gone. Step aside, old man. The Merchant King's authority is all that matters here now, and I haven't studied at the Temple of Spears for a very long time." He turned his back on the still-sputtering monk to address his sergeant. "Make camp. Full watch tonight. We're too far north to allow for any complacency."

"Of course, Dai Shin." The man bowed and strode off, orders issuing from his mouth in a commanding torrent typical of sergeants the world over.

Sho Tsai's jaws bunched before he fixed his features into a rigid mask and turned to Vaelin. "Lord Al Sorna," he said, gesturing to the gate and the stairway beyond. "Shall we?"

◆ ◆ ◆

"Brother of the Spear?"

Sho Tsai kept his eyes on the stairs ahead, face as rigid as before. They had climbed in silence for close to a half hour and Vaelin felt no optimism that his question would be answered, so it was a surprise when the captain grunted, "A title given to all who study at the Temple of Spears."

"It's a school? A place where warriors are trained?"

"In part. The lessons are . . . varied." He paused, lowering his gaze with a frown. "But always valuable, even if their wisdom takes time to reveal itself."

"Do all the Merchant King's officers attend this school?"

Sho Tsai gave a faint snort. "Hardly. If they did, our current situation would be very different. The monks will accept able-bodied boys or men who present themselves at the gate. After one week they will either ask you to leave or allow you to stay."

"It must be a hard week."

"No, it is in fact a very easy week. They give you a mop and bucket, then set you to cleaning the courtyards. The temple has a lot of courtyards. No questions are asked of you and you are permitted no words, with either others or yourself. In my first week there were twenty others, all older than me by several years. I was the only one permitted to stay, and no word of explanation was ever given. Things became . . . more difficult after that, but I have never once regretted stepping through those doors." He paused to glance at Vaelin, eyes narrowed. "Sherin told me of the school you attended. Can you say the same?"

"It wasn't a school, it was an Order, one of six in service to the Faith. Brothers of the Sixth were charged with protection of the Faith, and such protection requires use of weapons. I imagine she told you of the many hardships I suffered in its service. As for regrets, I have too many to easily count, but I can no more regret joining the Order than a sailor can regret the storm that sweeps his ship into calmer waters. I was a child. I knew no better."

A dense wall of mist descended shortly after, reducing the view of the staircase to barely a few feet ahead. Sho Tsai's steadily climbing form became ghostlike, although Vaelin was able to discern that he moved at a slower, more deliberate pace, maintaining a carefully measured distance between them. *Close enough for a swift sword stroke, or a hard shove,* he judged, eyes flicking to the edge of the stairway. There was no balustrade or other barrier, and the drop beyond was dizzying in its sheerness. *He'll tell Lian Sha of the unfortunate accident, the clumsy barbarian losing his footing on the way to the High Temple.*

"One of your soldiers called Tsai Lin the third egg in your nest," he said. If they were destined to fight on this mountainside, then he saw only one of two outcomes and therefore little need to restrain his questions. "I assume that means you have two other children."

The captain's wraithlike silhouette stiffened a little but he kept walking. "I did. A son and a daughter. They died beside their mother when the red sickness came."

Vaelin bit down on a sigh. He had intended to enquire why a married man would dishonour himself by falling in love with a foreigner, but suddenly the cruelty of it shamed him. He didn't hate this man; he envied him. "The Merchant King told me you have been in love with Sherin ever since you escorted her to his court," he said. "Was your love returned?"

Sho Tsai came to a halt, hands slipping to his sides as he turned to face Vaelin. "That is not your concern." The captain's tone was mostly void of emotion save for a grim sense of purpose.

"You wanted to marry her, I assume?" Vaelin went on. He also stopped, positioning himself three steps below the captain, a fair distance to evade the attack he knew to be imminent. Even though the mist concealed Sho Tsai's face, Vaelin had long attuned himself to the posture of those intent on his death. "But the Merchant King forbade it, didn't he?" he enquired, maintaining an affable tone. "One of his favourite officers sullying his honour by marrying a foreigner. Unthinkable, yes?"

Sho Tsai's gathering rage showed in the hunch to his shoulders and the slow shift of his hands. "Unthinkable," he agreed, voice clipped. "As unthinkable as me allowing her to set eyes on you again. You ask about her love? What do you know of it? Do you have any notion of what you did to her? The wound you opened in her heart?"

"I did what I had to . . ." Vaelin trailed off, the words fading under the weight of truth, a truth he had always known but rarely allowed himself to hear. "I was a coward," he said. "And a fool. I allowed myself to fall victim to the folly of prophecy and the arrogance of believing destiny actually possesses any meaning. My only defence is that in that time and place, I had no doubts. She had to leave and I had to stay." *The blood-song allowed only certainty.* "I am not here to regain her love. I know I lost it many years ago. I am here to preserve her life, for that is what I owe her."

Sho Tsai's hands paused in their course, his occluded form taking on a stillness that made him appear part of the indifferent rock of the mountain. "Know this," he said, the anger in his voice replaced by an unnerving, implacable sincerity. "She is paramount to me. She is above all else and I will allow no further injury to her, in body or in soul. If the Stahlhast have her, I will kill them all to retrieve her. If you reopen her wounds, I'll kill you too even though she may hate me for it."

He turned away and resumed his climb, moving with a renewed swiftness and surely deaf to any reply Vaelin might offer.

◆　◆　◆

The High Temple lay under a bright sun that dappled its tiled roofs with gold. Vaelin thought it as impressive an example of architecture as he had ever seen, in the sheer unlikeliness of its construction if not in scale. The various buildings, large and small, seemed to blossom out from the mountain's summit like the petals of a monumental flower. Balconies and roofs extended out above the surrounding mantle of cloud around a raised centre where a tower six storeys tall rose into the sky.

"Who built this place?" he asked Sho Tsai as his gaze roved the marvellous spectacle of it all.

"Many hands over many years," the captain said. "Warlords, emperors and kings all contributed wealth and labour to craft the home of the Jade Princess. It has changed with the passage of years. She was the only eternal thing here."

Sho Tsai led him through an outer ring of gardens towards the central tower, passing a number of gardeners along the way. Vaelin took note of the manner in which they went about their duties, each one grim faced and stooped as they clipped bushes or swept leaves, offering only cursory bows to the two visitors and vaguely curious glances at Vaelin. Once he and Shao Tsai were within the confines of the temple proper, the atmosphere grew yet more sombre. Plain-robed servants swept floors with desultory dutifulness, one even weeping openly as she worked her broom across the stones. *Grief,* Vaelin thought, recognising the pitch of her sobs.

A woman awaited them at the top of the stairs leading to the central tower. Like the gatekeeper she wore a red and black robe, her grey-streaked hair swept back from handsome, angular features that betrayed a faint but apparently genuine pleasure at the sight of Sho Tsai.

"Brother of the Spear," she said, bowing. Her tone was one of forced conviviality and shot through with a poorly suppressed quaver. "Twenty years absence and yet you barely look any older."

"Mother Wehn." Sho Tsai offered a bow an inch lower than hers. "Some may say your dishonesty shames your robe, but it is welcome nonetheless. This"—he straightened with a strained smile as he gestured to Vaelin—"is Lord Al Sorna from the east. We are here on the Merchant King's business."

"Of that I have little doubt." Mother Wehn exchanged bows with Vaelin, her eyes surveying him with a keen scrutiny. "You are from the healer's land, are you not? You possess the same colouring."

"I am."

"But"—her eyes tracked from his face to the sword on his back—"you are no healer."

"No, lady, I am not."

She gave a short, tight smile and stepped aside, opening a hand in welcome. "No doubt you have questions. I will do my best to answer, though what use it may be I know not."

She led them along a wide, torchlit hallway, which soon opened out into a broad circular chamber with high windows. The shutters were open to allow a stiff mountain breeze to pervade the room, which somehow failed to chill the skin. Vaelin found himself drawn to the nearest window, his gaze captured by the view. He could see beyond the enclosing cotton blanket of cloud to the foothills to the south and the grasslands beyond. A journey that had taken over two weeks was now rendered to minuscule proportions.

"Has anything been touched?" Sho Tsai asked, drawing Vaelin's attention from the window. The captain stood at the edge of a slightly elevated dais in the centre of the room. It held a richly embroidered carpet upon which sat a small couch. A porcelain teapot rested on a table alongside several cups. Beside the couch a stringed musical instrument of some kind rested in an ebony stand. It vaguely resembled a harp but with an asymmetrical frame and a more elaborate arrangement to the strings.

"Nothing," Mother Wehn replied. "It is all exactly as she left it."

Sho Tsai seemed mostly preoccupied with the musical instrument, his eyes lit with fascination as he tentatively extended a hand towards it, the fingers coming within a hair's breadth of the string before he clenched his fist. "She left it behind," he said, his fascination now coloured by incredulity.

"She left everything behind," Mother Wehn told him. "Save for her favourite coat and the shoes she wore when she toured the gardens." The woman gave a helpless shrug. "I am sorry, Brother Sho, but I fear there is nothing here that will assist you. The healer came. They talked alone for a time until dusk, then retired for the night. In the morning they were gone and no eyes in this temple saw them leave."

"Perhaps," Vaelin said, "if we knew what they talked about it could offer some clue as to their destination."

"I regret I cannot tell you, lord. The Princess insisted on talking to the healer alone. Whatever passed between them is lost." Mother Wehn's fingers trembled a little as she played a hand along the couch's delicately carved armrest. "I simply cannot imagine what words could have compelled her to . . . abandon us in such a manner."

"The healer was sent for," Vaelin said. "There must have been a reason."

He saw the tremble in the woman's fingers take on an increased agitation before she too, like the captain, clenched her fist. She concealed both hands in the sleeves of her robe and stood with her brow furrowed in indecision until replying in a soft murmur. "She coughed."

"Coughed?" Sho Tsai's voice was suddenly loud and he stared at Mother Wehn as if she had spoken some form of blasphemy. "The Jade Princess coughed?"

Mother Wehn nodded and swallowed. "It happened only once, but I heard it, as did the servants who brought her tea at the appointed hour. One of the girls dropped the tray and began to weep. Silly little whelp. The princess, however, seemed unperturbed despite our fussing. In the end she allowed us to send for the Healing Grace, for who else could better tend to the Jade Princess? Now, of course, I wish she had ignored us."

"I assume," Vaelin said, "she had never coughed before?"

"Illness is beneath her. As is hunger or cold. She drank and ate but only in deference to the lesser souls who inhabit this temple. I was but a novice of sixteen summers when I came here to serve her. In all the years since, I never heard her cough nor sniff nor groan, even as I groan ever more with each passing day."

Did you ever hear her lie? Vaelin left the question unsaid, suspecting Mother Wehn might well faint at the implication. *A truly sick soul never coughs only once. The Jade Princess is not above subterfuge, it seems. She wanted Sherin to come here. But why?*

"The world beyond this temple is troubled," he said. "Enemies menace your borders. Did the princess know of this?"

Mother Wehn nodded. "Every week a messenger comes from the Prefecture capital bearing a scroll listing all major events in the kingdoms, and beyond. It has been this way for a very long time. The bowels of the temple are full of scrolls dating back centuries."

"A valuable archive for any historian," Vaelin mused, pondering just how much Brother Harlick would pay for access to such knowledge.

"Only she is ever permitted to read the scrolls," Mother Wehn said. "Countless scholars have sent letters begging to be allowed just an hour in the archive, but they are always refused."

She must have the clearest picture of history of any living soul, Vaelin surmised. *Even more so than Erlin. And yet she guards her knowledge jealously. Something she doesn't want the merely mortal to know, perhaps?*

"Did she seem alarmed by the recent news?" Sho Tsai asked. "If she feared for the security of the kingdom, perhaps she felt compelled to flee." From his increasingly furrowed brow, Vaelin deduced he was as confused by what had occurred here as Mother Wehn.

They don't see her as human, Vaelin realised. *To them she is a fixture of this temple, like a statue.* The notion summoned memories of a huge weathered stone head he once found amidst the ruins of the Fallen City in the Lonak Dominion beyond the Realm's north-eastern border. Ages past it had been carved to commemorate a great man who would in time become a monster. *But all statues turn to dust in the end.*

"She does not fear any more than she hungers," Mother Wehn replied with a faintly offended sniff. "She read the most recent scrolls with the same assiduous care but no particular sign of concern."

"There must be something," Sho Tsai insisted. "She was not taken from this temple. She clearly chose to leave. There must be more to this than a single cough."

Mother Wehn began to shake her head but then stopped, the crease of her brow deepening. "There was one thing," she said. "But it happened months ago. Her song . . . She perfected her song."

Vaelin watched Sho Tsai's gaze shift back to the harp, his confusion briefly transforming into outright fear before he reimposed his usual rigid mask. "Her song," he repeated, voice soft. "The Song of the Ages."

"Quite."

Vaelin recalled the first tale Erlin had told of the Jade Princess some years ago during the advance through the mountains of northern Volaria. *Uncounted years spent in practice of voice and harp. Her song is not perfected, she hasn't finished, perhaps she never will.*

"Song of the Ages?" he asked.

"She knew many others," Mother Wehn replied. "And would play them for our amusement when the mood took her. But the Song of the Ages she would play every day, often several times a day. No matter how many times I heard it, I never grew tired of the tune or the words. It was almost as if she were singing a different song with each rendition."

"The words. What do they say?"

"The song was crafted so long ago the language is indecipherable to the modern ear."

"And she never provided a translation?"

"Such is not her way, and it is not our place to ask."

"But she told you she perfected it?"

"Not in so many words. But it was clear enough. I was in this chamber the last time she played it. This time the tone, the mood of it was very different. More sombre somehow. I must confess I shed tears at the beauty of it, and the sadness. There was something about the sound, the notes, they seemed to . . ." Mother Wehn trailed off, shaking her head. "I am a foolish woman."

"Please," Vaelin pressed. "What was it?"

"It was almost like being . . . cut, being opened. But there was no pain, only a sense of revelation. Memories I hadn't recalled in years spilled into my mind. So many faces, so much pain, so much joy. I thought perhaps some treacherous servant had slipped a befuddling concoction into the tea, but no, it was the song. Joyous as it was, I say honestly that I hope I never hear it again."

Mother Wehn blinked tears and turned away, taking a moment to re-assert her composure before speaking again. "When the last note faded the Jade Princess set her harp upon the stand and said, 'Well, so it is done.' From that day on she didn't play another note."

The cough was her final note, and her farewell. "Thank you, lady," Vaelin said.

She nodded and then fixed him with a bright, beseeching gaze. "Can you . . . will you return her to us? Without her, this place is nothing. Without her, these lands face ruin. I know it in my heart."

Vaelin had long ago learned the folly of making promises but in this he felt an obligation to at least provide a partial truth. "I will find her," he said. *Whether she will ever return here is another matter.*

Mother Wehn gave a grateful smile before her sorrow returned and she lowered her gaze. "You must forgive me," she whispered, hurrying from the chamber. "I am remiss in not organising refreshment for such honoured guests."

"The cough was a deception," Sho Tsai said after Mother Wehn left the chamber.

"I don't believe the woman who dwelt here is capable of illness," Vaelin replied.

"And the song. You think it significant."

"Centuries spent labouring to perfect an ancient song that can conjure unbidden memories, then she has Sherin summoned here on the pretence of illness and disappears the same night." Vaelin gave a faint laugh. "Yes, I think it's significant."

"But hardly likely to lead us to them." The captain went to a north-facing window, gazing out at the vast tract of mountain and valley. "With no trail to follow, no witnesses, we could search for years and find not a trace. And I doubt the Stahlhast will allow us such leisure."

Vaelin's gaze returned to the forsaken harp of the Jade Princess. It occurred to him that it might well sit in its stand for years, even centuries to come. An untouched relic of the blessed being that once resided here, its strings forever silent. *She had a song,* he thought. *A song of the Dark, as once did I. And I was not the only singer.*

"The town where Sherin made her home," he said, turning to Sho Tsai. "Is it far from here?"

"Thirty miles due east," the captain replied with a puzzled shrug. "But what use is going there? The local Dien-Ven have already searched her home and found no clue to her destination."

"She didn't live alone," Vaelin said, trying but failing to keep the reluctance from his voice. "Did she?"

"She had rooms above a stonemason's shop. A highly skilled and respected man, as I recall."

Forgive me, old friend. "The stonemason," Vaelin said. "He can find her."

CHAPTER FIFTEEN

The town of Min-Tran sat atop a broad rise in the rolling hill country that dominated the Northern Prefecture of the Venerable Kingdom. Its buildings were taller than those Vaelin had seen so far, all constructed from stone rather than wood and nestled within walls that were even taller, also well maintained.

A place of stone, Vaelin thought, a smile playing over his lips as they rode through the main gate. *Where better for him to make a home?*

"It would be better if I talked to him alone," he told Sho Tsai. They had continued through the gate without pause, the captain leading the company along a broad thoroughfare into the town's western quarter. "He may take some persuading."

The captain turned in the saddle, squinting at him in bemusement. "We are here on the Merchant King's business. As a subject he is required to assist an officer of the king's army in any way I see fit."

Vaelin kicked his horse forward, reining to a halt in the captain's path and forcing him to do the same.

"He's no ordinary subject," he told a glowering Sho Tsai. "He's *her* friend, and mine. We owe him at least the illusion of choice in this."

The captain glowered for a second or two more, then turned and barked out, "Dai Lo Tsai!"

Tsai Lin trotted his horse forward and saluted. "Dai Shin!"

"You will accompany the foreigner to the stonemason's home. If he refuses to accompany us, you will bind him and bring him to me."

"Understood, Captain."

Sho Tsai tugged on his reins, turning his horse about and giving the hand signal for his company to follow suit. "Find us at the barracks, and don't be long about this."

"Go with them," Vaelin told Nortah and the others.

"Are you sure, Uncle?" Ellese asked. "If this man has the Dark in him . . ."

"He's no danger to me." Vaelin gave Tsai Lin a cordial nod and they resumed their passage along the thoroughfare. "You're still on cooking duty," he reminded Ellese over his shoulder. "Try to produce something edible by the time I get back."

Tsai Lin led the way, guiding them into the narrower streets of what was evidently the artisans' quarter. "You've been here before?" Vaelin asked, noting the youth's obvious familiarity with the route.

"Many times. My . . . the Dai Shin would bring me here to spend the summer when I was younger."

"So you know her? You know Sherin?"

"Of course, lord. It was from her that I learned your language and many lessons in the healing arts. Although my skills in that regard are far from expert."

Did she ever talk of me? The question rose and then faded from Vaelin's lips, for he had a sense he already knew the answer.

Upon entering the quarter the air became filled with the familiar refrain of blacksmith's hammer and carpenter's saw, soon punctuated by a rhythmic pounding that instantly brought forth memories of Linesh. *His arm's as strong as ever,* Vaelin thought as Tsai Lin reined to a halt before a shop with wide double doors. The steady thud of hammer and chisel continued to echo from within until they both climbed down from the saddle, whereupon it abruptly ceased.

"Wait," he told Tsai Lin as the apprentice officer looped his reins around a postern and started towards the doors.

"Lord?" The Dai Lo hesitated, glancing back at Vaelin. "I have orders . . ."

"Just wait." Vaelin gave him a humourless smile, keeping his gaze on the shaded interior of the shop. "Please."

The silence continued for the space of what seemed a very long minute.

There must be a back door to this place, Vaelin thought. *Feel free to use it, old friend.*

"Forgive my tardiness, Honoured Sir." The man who appeared in the doorway bowed his shaven and partially scarred head at Tsai Lin before raising it to regard Vaelin with a warm smile. "Had I known you brought such welcome company, I would have come quicker."

"Ahm Lin." Vaelin's voice was thick as he began to bow, then stopped as the mason came forward to wrap his arms, still as corded with muscle as ever, around his shoulders, drawing him into a fierce embrace.

"I knew you'd come," he said in a low whisper. "I've been waiting."

He drew back and Vaelin was struck by how little he had aged. The burns that had been so raw that final day on the Linesh dockside were faded now, the puckered flesh tanned to a leathery sheen. Grey showed in the stubble of his scalp and wrinkles webbed his eyes, but he was as lean as the first time Vaelin had met him in Linesh. An exiled former servant of the Merchant King Lol-Than, Ahm Lin had made his home in the Alpiran port seeking rest after a lifetime of travel, only for his blood-song to summon a fellow singer to his door, an invader in fact. Their friendship had been an instant thing, forged by their songs, and sufficiently threatening to the Ally's plans to send the Messenger to seek the mason's death. On this occasion, he had been thwarted by means that still remained vague to Vaelin, but the burns Ahm Lin suffered in the attack left a lasting mark. Nursed back to health by Sherin, he had been the perfect choice to take her away and Vaelin was glad her inevitable anger hadn't sundered their connection.

"Mason Lin," Tsai Lin said, his voice heavy with reluctance. "I come with . . ."

"Orders compelling me to the Merchant King's service," the mason finished. "Yes, I'm aware. Give me a moment to fetch my things."

He disappeared back into the shop, Vaelin following after a moment's bemused hesitation. He had known it would be impossible to surprise this man, but his affable willingness to forsake his home was unexpected. He found the shop's interior similar in many ways to Ahm Lin's home in Linesh, although not so spacious and the fruits of his labour were very different.

No statues, he realised as he scanned the space, seeing many rectangular marble boxes, each carved with Far Western script and the corners decorated with curved columns. But there were no gods here, no heroes of ancient legend, and no beasts of any kind.

"Mausoleums, sarcophagi and monuments to the honoured ancestors," Ahm Lin said, emerging from the shadowed recesses of the shop. He had divested himself of his apron and wore a quilted jacket and trews. A pack sat on his shoulder and he carried a sturdy yard-long stick of ash. "My stock-in-trade these days. People here are almost as in love with death as they are in your Realm."

"I thought you might have carved another wolf," Vaelin said.

Some of the cheerfulness slipped from Ahm Lin's face. His gaze grew sombre as he turned to regard the shop with the air of a man saying goodbye. "No, brother. One wolf was enough for any lifetime." He brightened quickly and hefted his stick. "Shall we go? I just need to ask my neighbour to have a care for the place whilst I'm gone."

"Your wife," Vaelin said. He had been dreading the woman's reaction upon seeing him again. His presence had never boded well for her husband. "Don't you wish to . . ."

"I sent her home," Ahm Lin said, moving briskly to the doors.

"Home?" Vaelin asked.

"Back to Alpira. It was for the best."

There was a guardedness to the mason's tone that forbade further questions, and Vaelin duly followed him into the street. Ahm Lin spent a brief moment in conversation with the wheelwright next door, the two men embracing before they parted, whereupon the mason turned his back on his shop and strode with a determined step in the direction of the town barracks.

"Come along then," he said, waving his stick for them to follow. "I'm keen to hear what you've been up to for the past ten years or so. I only caught a few glimpses and it all seemed very fraught."

◆ ◆ ◆

Sho Tsai permitted only one night's rest in Min-Tran before resuming their search. He accepted Ahm Lin's suggested north-westerly course without question, causing Vaelin to reflect that the captain may have long harboured some suspicion as to the stonemason's true nature. The fact that he hadn't disclosed this to the Merchant King owed much, Vaelin assumed, to Sherin.

After a march of over twenty miles the rolling hill country descended into an undulating plane stretching out to the northern horizon like an unbroken yellow-green sea.

"The Iron Steppe," Erlin said. "They say you can ride for a thousand miles without sight of hill or mountain, until you reach the tors, of course. Hopefully, we won't be going that far."

He raised his voice as he spoke, directing the implied question at Ahm Lin. In response, the mason merely turned in the saddle of his squat pony to offer a bland smile. Vaelin rode beside him for the first two days, myriad questions churning in his mind but somehow failing to escape his lips. Finally, on the second day Ahm Lin turned to him with an exasperated sigh and said, "You can ask her when you see her, my lord. What lies between you two, or"—he cast a meaningful glance in Sho Tsai's direction—"anyone else is not for me to say."

"Your song is as strong as ever then," Vaelin observed with a note of chagrin.

"Stronger, I'd say. I've come to understand that the passage of years does much to nurture it, like a tree nourished by the rain of many seasons." A shadow passed across his face and the usual smile turned into a reluctant grimace. "Years ago it told me you had lost your own song, and more besides. I'm sorry."

"War always takes more than it gives." Vaelin hesitated before speaking his next question, one he suspected Ahm Lin might well ignore. "Your wife. Why did you send her away?"

"Because the song was clear. She couldn't stay here any longer, not if I wanted her to live."

"So, it's told you what's coming. This kingdom will fall."

"You know that's not how it goes with the song. I do know it's louder now than it's ever been, even during those last days in Linesh when it seemed the Emperor's host would soon rend the city to rubble and flame." He lowered his head, a note of self-reproach creeping into his voice. "It first began to swell when the word came from the High Temple, commanding Sherin to tend to the Jade Princess. I did try to dissuade her from going, but not as forcefully as I should have. The song . . . it was like the long, growing note that plays before the crescendo. The night after she left it brought dreams. I saw chaos, I saw blood, I saw the walls of Min-Tran crumbling . . . and I saw you, brother. In the morning I sent my wife away. You may recall Shoala was never a woman of placid character, and persuading her to leave was no easy task." His features bunched in a frown of deep regret. "It is my hope that one day she will forgive me."

"As Sherin forgave me?"

The poorly concealed wince that flickered across Ahm Lin's face was answer enough to this long-pondered question. *Some scars never heal.* "She still lives, doesn't she?" Vaelin asked, swallowing a sigh. "Your song tells you this?"

"She lives." Ahm Lin nodded at the horizon. "Though she is far away and intent on reaching her destination."

"What is it? Where is she going?"

"I know only that it is important. I sense her urgency, and the purpose of the one she travels with, though her tune is much more serene. I should warn you, brother, neither are likely to be pleased when we find them."

◆ ◆ ◆

After ten miles the fine road they had followed from Min-Tran rapidly degenerated into a track of loose gravel, their passage birthing a tall plume of dust in their wake. The foot messengers had long since been replaced by horsemen. At least one would gallop past every hour, the riders displaying the same single-minded indifference to the Red Scouts or the increasingly infrequent north-bound travellers. The southward traffic, by contrast, increased by the mile. Thin, grey-faced people in ragged clothes shuffled clear of the soldiers' path with barely a glance. There were many children amongst them, the absence of tears or infant wailing telling a grim tale.

"Starving children stop crying after a while, my dear," Erlin explained to Ellese when she commented on the ragged people's strange silence.

"But we have food to spare," she said. Reaching for her saddlebags she extracted some of the salted pork they had been provisioned with in Min-Tran. A warning shout from the Red Scout sergeant came too late as Ellese leaned down from the saddle to offer the food to a passing woman with a hollow-cheeked, dull-eyed child lolling in her arms. Within seconds Ellese was mobbed, emaciated people thronging around her with arms out-stretched, beseeching voices raised in a collective, needful groan.

Cursing, the sergeant barked out a command and a squad of scouts spurred their mounts into the mob, striking out with riding crops. The peo-ple duly reared back, most resuming their slump-shouldered trek whilst a few dozen lingered at the side of the road. They cast shouts and raised fists at the soldiers until, inevitably, their words were accompanied by a hail of stones. From the fury and shock with which the soldiers responded, open displays of defiance were far beyond their experience.

"Insolent northern swine!" Corporal Wei spat, drawing his sword and spurring towards the small knot of protestors. Two of his comrades followed suit but all three came to an abrupt halt as Nortah wheeled his horse into their path.

"Out of my way, you barbarian fucker!" Wei commanded, the words accompanied by his usual cloud of spittle.

Nortah possessed only a rudimentary knowledge of Chu-Shin but Vaelin doubted he missed the man's meaning. Nevertheless he calmly wiped the spit from his face before reaching over his shoulder to draw his own sword. "I don't think I care for your tone," he said, resting the blade on his shoulder.

A brief drum of hooves brought Sehmon, Alum, Chien and Ellese to Nortah's side, whilst a half-dozen Red Scouts moved to fall in on Wei's flanks. Vaelin glanced at Sho Tsai, sitting apparently at ease on his horse some twenty yards away. The captain's gaze was fixed on Tsai Lin rather than the unfolding confrontation.

Vaelin kicked his horse closer to the Dai Lo, speaking softly, "An apprentice officer is still an officer. Unless you want some of your men to die today, I suggest you get them under control."

Tsai Lin's gaze flicked from Vaelin to his father and back again. Vaelin found his expression odd, more reluctant than fearful. It was clear something was expected of him here, a task he would rather not perform. He briefly closed his eyes before straightening and spurring his mount forward.

"Corporal!" Tsai Lin called out. "Sheath your sword and get back in formation."

"Piss off, third egg," Wei replied in irritation, not bothering to turn. "I answer to the Dai Shin."

"Not today." Tsai Lin trotted his mount directly into Wei's path. "Today you answer to me." The Dai Lo reached up to unclip the iron star from his shoulder guard, taking a second to look into the face of the soldiers on either side of Wei before speaking on. "This man has insulted me and impugned my honour. I forsake privilege of rank and insist upon satisfaction. Bear witness to his cowardice if he refuses."

This brought a brief round of laughter, the mirth soon fading into a nervous silence as Tsai Lin continued to stare expectantly at Corporal Wei. The man coughed and slammed his sword back into its scabbard, muttering, "My steel's too good to sully on this scum."

"Stop!" Tsai Lin barked as the corporal began to turn his horse, Vaelin seeing the man's face flush red as he froze in the saddle. "Challenge is given and has not been answered," Tsai Lin went on. "Give your answer, Corporal."

The soldiers on either side of Wei began to edge their mounts away when repeated glances at their stone-faced captain made it clear he had no intention of intervening. Wei sat in his saddle a moment longer, reddened features quivering until he let out a guttural snarl and dismounted. "All right then, whelp. You want a beating, I'll be happy to oblige."

He began to divest himself of his armour, undoing the ties on his breastplate and casting it aside whilst Tsai Lin climbed down from his horse and did the same, albeit with markedly less agitation. Soon the two faced each other bare chested, the Red Scouts forming a loose circle around them. Vaelin saw Ellese angle her head in appreciation at the sight of Tsai Lin's finely muscled torso, a lean and honed contrast to the broad stockiness of his opponent. The Dai Lo's flesh was also bare of any scars whilst the corporal's bore many.

"He's not going to step in," Wei said, jerking his head at Sho Tsai. "You know that, right, whelp?"

"Yes," Tsai Lin replied. "For which I apologise." His tone possessed no mockery, merely a faint expression of genuine regret.

Vaelin recalled a morsel of Master Sollis's wisdom from the practice ground: *Only a fool picks a fight he can't finish.* Tsai Lin, as he well knew by now, was no fool.

Wei laughed, turning to his comrades with a wink before abruptly lowering his head and charging at Tsai Lin, his right fist sweeping a punch towards the younger man's jaw. It was a standard trick of the experienced brawler, a distraction playing into the expectation of prolonged threats and banter before the real fight started. However, it transpired Tsai Lin was neither easily distracted nor a brawler.

His left arm rose in a blur, blocking the corporal's punch. Tsai Lin's right arm flicked out, moving too fast to easily follow, before he stepped back, ducking under a clumsy left swing that sent Wei into an untidy spin, blood flying from his nose, which now sat at a crooked angle on his blocky features. Tsai Lin turned away and began to don his armour as the corporal staggered about, reddened spittle pluming from his mangled lips as they attempted to form words. By the time he fell, his face producing a wince-inducing thwack as it connected with the hard-packed earth, Tsai Lin had already refastened his breastplate.

"Get him on his horse," he told the onlooking soldiers as he strode to his mount. "He'll wake by nightfall. The next man to break ranks without orders won't receive such leniency."

Climbing into the saddle he took hold of the reins, then paused to regard the cluster of beggared people still lingering on the roadside, their anger now replaced by simple bafflement. "Also," Tsai Lin continued, "each man will take half his rations and share them with these people. I think you lot could benefit from a day or two with a growling belly."

The soldiers' faces darkened at this but none raised a voice in complaint as they went about their orders, Vaelin catching a few mutters spoken in a tone of resentful awe rather than anger. "Temple of Spears, I'm telling you," he heard one murmur to his comrade as they hauled Wei's inert bulk onto the back of his horse. "Just like his pa."

CHAPTER SIXTEEN

T he sun dipped behind the fortress city of Keshin-Kho as it came into view, making it resemble the dented conical helm of some long-vanished giant. It sat atop the junction of a waterway known as the Great Northern Canal and a south-flowing river bearing the unedifying title of the Black Vein. Like Min-Tran, the city featured no buildings beyond its walls. As the company drew closer Vaelin could make out two more walls within the outer barrier, each one constructed at a higher elevation than the one before. The city streets grew denser as they rose to a summit from which a slender tower ascended, rendered needle thin by the glare of the fading sun. It stood taller even than the towers he had seen in Muzan-Khi.

"You'd see an army approaching a day away from that," Nortah commented, shielding his eyes to squint at the tower.

"Two days, lord," Tsai Lin corrected with a polite smile. "There are optical devices at the top that can see for many miles."

"Spyglasses you mean?"

"Of a sort, but much larger. The Merchant King goes to great expense to ensure the lenses are replaced regularly. There is an entire workshop in Muzan-Khi where the artisans do nothing but grind glass for the long-eyes, as they're known."

Long-eyes, Vaelin thought. *Something else to write to Lyrna about.*

A short delay ensued at the city's main gate as Sho Tsai presented his credentials to the guard captain. The sight of the Merchant King's seal ensured they were quickly provided with an honour guard and escorted through the maze of narrow streets towards the central palace where the Prefecture's governor resided. In contrast to the streets of Muzan-Khi the people here were less quick to shuffle clear of their path, some standing and staring in open hostility until the soldiers shoved them aside.

"No bowing here, I see," Nortah observed quietly to Vaelin. In recent days the wine-induced vagueness that had characterised his features for so long had given way to the careful shrewdness Vaelin remembered from their last few years in the Order. Although never as insightful as Caenis, Nortah had always possessed a faculty for quickly assessing potential threats, even if such assessment didn't always lead to the wisest response.

"Erlin tells me the Northern Prefecture was the last territory to be conquered by the Emerald Empire," Vaelin replied. "Apparently, they've never taken it well. And the prospect of war rarely makes for a happy populace."

They followed a winding course to the centre of the city. Whoever had set down the plans for Keshin-Kho had evidently known something of siege craft, for the main gates of each successive wall were positioned at opposite points of the compass. Any attacking force that managed to breach one gate would therefore be obliged to traverse numerous narrow streets under the eyes and arrows of the defenders atop the next wall.

The innermost stood taller than the others, at least seventy feet high and featuring overhanging buttresses every fifty paces, which would allow defenders to shower all manner of unpleasantness on an assaulting army. This wall also featured the narrowest gate, barely wide enough to admit two horsemen at once. Sho Tsai led the way into the courtyard beyond where he was greeted by a tall, well-built man clad in a cloak fashioned from the pelt of some white-furred, black-striped beast.

"Captain!" The tall man extended his arms in welcome as Sho Tsai dismounted to offer a carefully respectful bow.

"Governor Hushan." The captain presented the scroll bearing the Merchant King's seal. "I come on orders . . ."

"Of course you do!" The governor laughed and clapped a hand to Sho Tsai's shoulder. "Why else would the Red Scouts honour my humble city with their presence? Especially since I never requested it." He laughed again, though Vaelin saw his humour abruptly diminish at the sight of the foreigners amongst Sho Tsai's company. "You bring me strange visitors, I see," he said, quickly placing another smile on his lips. "This all bodes well for a most interesting evening."

The governor's mansion, like everything else in this city, had been built for defence rather than opulence or comfort. Its stone walls were thick and the tiered rooftops sloped at a more acute angle than usual, meaning they would be harder to climb. At Sho Tsai's request Vaelin accompanied him to Governor Hushan's private chambers. The governor listened to the captain's report with a polite attention that only deepened into genuine interest at mention of the Jade Princess's disappearance.

"She's gone?" he asked with an appalled laugh. "You're telling me she has actually departed the High Temple?"

"I am, Governor. I had hoped that your patrols might have encountered her, or at least caught word of her. We have . . . sound information that she was travelling towards this city."

The governor gave a baffled shrug. "None of my lads have caught the slightest whiff of her. I can assure you of that. Still, we've all been somewhat preoccupied of late. You may have heard."

"The Stahlhast," Vaelin said, drawing Hushan's gaze. The man's expression was very different to the suspicion or outright disdain Vaelin had thus far experienced from other Far Western nobles. It was more akin to the cool appraisal he expected from those well versed in war.

"Quite right, Honoured Sir." He gave a small grin, eyebrows raised. "I must say it is strange to find oneself confronted by a figure I had thought merely mythical. Tales of the Barbarous East are a particular interest of mine. All those many wars, bizarre beliefs and fantastical events. Tell me, is it true your dread Fire Queen has command of an entire school of red sharks?"

"Only one, my lord. And it died."

"Oh." Hushan pursed his lips in disappointment. "Pity. But they do call you the Darkblade, do they not? That is how you are known to your people?" There was a decided weight to the governor's gaze now, a gravity that went beyond mere interest in fanciful foreign myth.

"My enemies once called me by that name," Vaelin replied. "But they are enemies no longer."

"And yet the name lingers. A name my people have come to dread."

"So I've heard. We saw many on the road. They looked hungry."

"Hunger is the least a coward deserves." Hushan waved a dismissive hand though Vaelin detected a defensive note to his voice. "This city has long been a haven for all in the north. The people shelter here whilst the horse-fuckers raid for a time before we drive them off. It has long been this way. If that fool Nishun had listened to me instead of marching his forty thousand southerners out onto the Steppe to get deservedly slaughtered, this current mess would probably have faded away. Fighting the Steel Horde in open country with an army that was three-fourths infantry." The governor snorted in sombre disgust. "He may as well have walked up to the Darkblade and bared his neck for the axe. Now, thanks to Nishun's defeat and all manner of nonsense spoken about this freshly arisen Stahlhast warlord, and his fearsome name, my people flee south in ever-increasing numbers, no doubt spreading vile calumnies against their governor with every step."

"Then you do not consider the Stahlhast truly a threat?" Sho Tsai asked. "Everything we have seen and heard would indicate otherwise."

"Oh, they're a threat to be sure. But they always have been and I see little to distinguish this recent bout of raiding with others that have come before. If anything, their mischief had been tailing off until General Nishun stoked their ambition with forty thousand bundles of booty. Trust me, Captain, I've been fighting the savages of the Iron Steppe since I was old enough for my father to sit me in a saddle, and I've never lost yet. Nor will I now. Feel at liberty to inform the Merchant King of this, the messenger service is at your disposal."

"I will." Sho Tsai gave another shallow bow. "Your fortitude does you credit. However, you have no doubt received word that the Most Favoured has commanded the mustering of a far larger host which will shortly march north."

The governor laughed, coming forward to clap a hand to Sho Tsai's armoured shoulder. "And it's my intention to ensure they'll have nothing to do when they get here. Be sure to tell the Most Favoured that too. Of course, I'll assist your mission in any way I can, but we'll talk of it in the morning." His smile broadened as his gaze swung to Vaelin. "As for tonight, I've a mind to greet my most interesting guests with a feast where they can entertain me with all manner of strange and delightful tales."

◆ ◆ ◆

"And this . . . World Father, he has no wife? There is no World Mother?" Governor Hushan spoke passable if somewhat halting Realm Tongue that still managed to convey the genuine mystification in his question.

"The Father is eternal and ultimately beyond our understanding," Ellese replied, chewing on a mouthful of roasted pork, which she washed down with a hearty swig of the local wine. It was a heady brew, flavoured with diced fruit that only partially disguised the strong taste of pure spirit. Vaelin's eyes strayed constantly to where Nortah sat at the end of the table. He said little to Alum and Sehmon, who were seated on either side, and displayed no obvious interest in the numerous bottles passing back and forth.

The other guests consisted mainly of senior officers in the city garrison, career soldiers with a customary appreciation for the comforts of drink. The woman seated at the governor's left was a marked and elegant contrast, clad in finely embroidered blue silks that matched the sapphire earrings she wore and the paint that shaded her eyelids. Hushan had introduced her only as his third wife; apparently it wasn't custom for husbands to name their wives to others. Vaelin felt that she resembled a finely made mannequin, her features a porcelain mask of almost unnatural perfection, lips formed into a permanently demure smile that broadened only briefly at one of her husband's loudly spoken witticisms. She ate nothing and drank no more than a sip or two of wine. Vaelin might have paid her scant attention but for the way Ahm Lin had reacted to her upon taking his seat. The mason strove to hide it but Vaelin saw the way his back straightened in discomfort as the woman's placid gaze passed over him. Also, throughout the evening Ahm Lin kept his attention firmly on his meal, providing only nods and muttered responses to Erlin's cheerful conversation.

"But no, he doesn't have a wife," Ellese added, smothering a burp. "Such earthly notions are of no meaning when considering the Father's nature."

"Then . . ." Hushan's brows furrowed as his bafflement deepened. "How did he father the world with no womb to receive his seed?"

"By the power of his love, which knows all and sees all." Ellese favoured the governor with a grin as she refilled her goblet. So far she had displayed no offence at Hushan's prolonged and skeptical questioning on the tenets of her people's creed. In fact, Vaelin had long felt her commitment to the

Church of the World Father was at best a perfunctory shadow of her mother's unwavering, if pragmatic, form of devotion.

Hushan blinked and shook his head before raising an eyebrow at Vaelin. "I think I found the Fire Queen's red sharks a more fathomable notion than Heaven being home to but one all-knowing soul."

"Oh, my uncle is far above such things, my lord," Ellese said. She blinked bleary eyes and reached again for her goblet, spilling a drop or two of the contents as she raised it to her mouth. "The Father, the Alpiran gods," she went on, staining her sleeve as she wiped it across her lips, "the wisdom of ancient scripture, the serenity of prayer. It's all just dung to him. Mother always forgave him for it though. 'A life of loss and grief will make even the kindest soul close his heart to the divine,' she told me."

"You've had enough," Vaelin said, halting Ellese's hand as it reached once again for the wine bottle. She stared at him, a measure of the old defiance creeping into her gaze, lips twitching as she fought the drink-fuelled impulse to speak some no-doubt-choice words.

"Do you have something to say?" he asked, tone mild as he met her glowering gaze. "A decision regarding my tutelage, perhaps? I am happy to forgo any further lessons if you wish."

She clenched her fist and drew it back from the bottle, lowering her eyes, albeit with some obvious effort.

"Master Sehmon!" Vaelin called to the young outlaw, who quickly scrambled to his feet.

"My lord?"

"Lady Ellese is tired. Please escort her to her chamber." He fixed Sehmon with a hard stare. "And be sure to return swiftly."

"Of course, my lord."

Ellese allowed Sehmon to take her arm as she rose from her seat. She bowed stiffly to the governor, and the two of them made a carefully paced exit from the meal hall.

"Always a sound practice to remind them of their place, I find," Hushan commented. "In these lands a girl her age expressing such strong opinions would find herself locked in a hut for a month. I allowed it tonight in deference to your custom. The men of your lands do, after all, permit yourselves to be ruled by a woman."

"No," Vaelin replied. "She permits us to be ruled by her. And we find it a more than fair arrangement."

The evening wore on for another hour, dominated by Sho Tsai's continual quizzing of the governor on the preparedness of his city for imminent attack.

"I was surprised to see no evidence of stockpiled provisions, Governor," the captain said. He was seated at the governor's right, presumably due to his status as a favoured servant of the Merchant King. Like Nortah, the captain hadn't touched his wine, and Vaelin judged that his relative silence until now had been carefully calculated to allow time for Hushan to drink himself into a more forthcoming mood. "Also, it is standard practice to enlist the menfolk of the city into a militia in times of crisis."

"Getting the locals to march in step, let alone wield a spear with any skill, is a thankless task, Captain," Hushan replied with a casual wave of his hand. "I have close to fifteen thousand men under my command, good soldiers all. As for provisions, given the number of cowardly swine fleeing south, Keshin-Kho finds itself with something of an abundance at present."

"Nevertheless, I feel the Most Favoured would wish me to make a tour of the defences. Perhaps I can offer some advice . . ."

"Oh, don't trouble yourself, good sir. It's all well in hand. Besides, I wouldn't wish to delay a mission of such importance. The sooner you find our wayward treasure the better, eh?"

Sho Tsai forced a smile and let the matter drop. Apparently, being one of the Merchant King's favourites didn't equate to unlimited authority.

◆ ◆ ◆

"The governor's third wife," Vaelin said to Ahm Lin. The gathering had finally broken up close to the midnight hour and they were making their way to the rooms they had been given in the eastern wing of the mansion. "She's Gifted isn't she?"

The mason glanced around before replying with a nod. They had been provided a discreet escort of four guards, though they seemed indifferent to conversation spoken in a foreign tongue.

"Does she have a song?" Vaelin persisted.

"I don't think so. The sense I had of her was . . . unusual. Something I haven't encountered before. I do know she was both surprised and displeased by our appearance here."

Ahm Lin fell silent as they came to a suite of adjoining rooms linked by a central courtyard, the roof open to the stars. Sho Tsai and the Red Scouts had been quartered in the main barracks but the governor had seen fit to house his foreign guests in an opulently furnished suite reserved for esteemed dignitaries from the south. Ahm Lin waited for the guards to close the heavy double doors before moving to a small fountain in the centre of the courtyard, lowering his voice so that it was barely audible above the cascading water.

"There's something else, brother," he said. "The governor, he lied."

"About what?"

Ahm Lin gave a wary grimace as he scanned their surroundings, clasping his hands together in a manner that made Vaelin remember that, for all his gifts, this man was not a warrior. "Everything," he said. "The song was clear. Every word that man spoke tonight was a lie."

CHAPTER SEVENTEEN

It had been many years since Vaelin had endured a night in certain expectation of an attack. Nevertheless, he found the sensation an unpleasantly familiar mingling of irritation and anticipation. The journey to Keshin-Kho had been long and the governor's feast something of a trial, so he would much rather have spent the hours in slumber. *Yet another reminder*, he reflected, feeling the aches in his back and legs with aggravating keenness, *the years pass and are kind to no one.*

So, when it finally arrived, the faint grind of metal on metal that told of the lock on the door to his chamber being picked, it was something of a relief. He continued to lie under his blankets, face turned away from the door as it swung open, the creak of hinges muted by the slowness with which the lock-picker entered the room. *Two of them,* Vaelin concluded, hearing dual scrapes of steel sliding from leather sheaths.

He tracked their movements by their breath, low and well controlled, but even the best-trained assassin is unable to remain completely calm when the killing moment looms closer. One moved to the left side of the bed whilst the other approached from the right. A pause, then a quick intake of breath as the one on the left readied himself for the thrust, the soft gasp then abruptly transformed into a scream as Chien lunged from her position beneath the bed, knife slashing across the assassin's ankles.

Vaelin cast the blankets to the right as he surged fully clothed from the bed, sword in hand, the covering entangling the second attacker. "I need him alive," he reminded Chien, glancing down to see her wrapping her arms around the other assassin's neck, legs encircling his waist as he writhed and bucked, still shouting in pain. The man was clad entirely in black cotton, features concealed behind a leather mask.

Vaelin turned away, spinning aside as the assassin's comrade, having divested himself of the encumbering blanket, leapt forward, the faint edge of a black-bladed knife glittering as he brought it up and down. Vaelin's sword flicked out, the edge catching the knife blade before sliding along the metal to meet the guard. Twisting his wrist, Vaelin sent the knife spinning into the dark. Its owner hissed in mingled fear and rage. The latter evidently outweighing the former for instead of taking the wiser course and attempting to flee, he drew a second knife from the small of his back before promptly stiffening in death as Vaelin's sword point slipped between his ribs, piercing lung and heart with expert precision.

"No, you pig-fucker!"

Chien had released her hold on the first assassin and torn away his mask, one hand fisted in his sparse hair, the other on his chin as she shook him. His slack, bleached features showed no response, and Vaelin quickly divined that his body possessed no more life than a doll.

"Poison?" he asked, crouching at Chien's side.

She prised the man's jaw apart, revealing intact teeth and none of the bloody froth that would usually accompany a self-administered toxin. "No sign," Chien said, leaning closer for a sniff and shaking her head. "It was strange. He struggled, then I felt the beat of his heart stop. It didn't slow first, it just stopped."

"Let's see if he brought any more-talkative friends," Vaelin told her, rising and stepping out in the courtyard. He found Nortah and Alum flanking the fountain with weapons in hand. Ellese crouched in the doorway to the room where they had secluded Ahm Lin and Erlin, an arrow nocked to her bow and features tensed by the effects of being rudely woken from a drink-induced sleep. She bore it without complaint, however, and the grip on her weapons was firm.

"No other guests tonight, brother," Nortah mused, scanning the rooftops edging the courtyard. "They don't know you very well, only sending two."

"No . . ." Ahm Lin said, appearing at Ellese's shoulder. The mason's eyes were half-closed and his head tilted at an angle, as if straining to hear a distant call. "No that's not it. This"—he gestured at the body visible through Vaelin's doorway—"was just mischief, a distraction."

"From what?" Nortah asked.

Ahm Lin's forehead creased in concentration. "The Red Scouts," he said, eyes snapping open. "They're the true target . . . or, one of them is. The song is loud tonight, but imprecise."

"Sehmon," Ellese said with a poorly concealed note of alarm. Vaelin had ordered the outlaw to scale the courtyard wall and make his way across the mansion rooftop to the barracks in order to warn Sho Tsai of the possibility of an impending attack. That had been more than an hour ago and neither the captain nor any of the Red Scouts had yet appeared.

"Stay here," Vaelin told Ellese, pointing to Ahm Lin and Erlin and adding, "guard them," as she began to voice a protest. Gesturing for the others to follow he moved to the door, tearing it open to step over the bodies of the two guards lying outside, then sprinting along the corridor.

◆ ◆ ◆

Vaelin counted another dozen slain guards littering the tiled courtyard that separated the governor's mansion from the squat, two-storey structure that comprised the barracks. Each soldier had been pierced through the neck by a crossbow bolt or slashed across the throat from ear to ear. The tumult of combat grew loud as they drew nearer, finding the corpses of more black-clad assassins amongst the pile of dead soldiers crowding the entrance. Vaelin picked out two red-armoured bodies amongst the pile and drew some comfort from the fact that they had at least had time to arm themselves before the attack. It appeared young Sehmon may have arrived in time.

Leaping over the bodies, he found the interior mostly in darkness apart from the glow of a few fallen lanterns, the meagre light illuminating yet more corpses and the streaks of blood on the walls. Vaelin charged along the broad hallway, drawn by the familiar sound of battle, screams and shouts mingling with the ring of steel.

As he approached a set of wrecked doors a black-clad body abruptly sprang to its feet, whirling towards Vaelin with a curve-bladed sword. He ducked under the stroke and slashed his sword into the assassin's leg. The man responded with impressive swiftness, apparently immune to the pain of his wound as he whirled again, bringing his sword up in a swift stroke aimed at Vaelin's groin. He stepped clear of the blade's sweep, his own already drawn back for a countering thrust at the man's face, which proved unnecessary as Nortah's gore-covered sword point appeared under the assassin's chin.

"Tricky buggers, aren't they?" he said, drawing the blade clear and letting the corpse fall.

Vaelin kicked his way through the remnants of the doors, emerging into a huge meal hall where a battle raged amidst a chaos of overturned tables and dead or dying men. The Red Scouts were clustered into a ragged but solid line alongside a much less orderly group of soldiers from the garrison. They numbered perhaps fifty men in all but were battling a force almost twice their strength. Vaelin could see Sho Tsai in the centre of the Red Scouts' line, barking orders with a bloodied sword in hand that blurred with precise and deadly regularity as he fended off repeated attacks. Sehmon stood at his side, jabbing frantically with one of the six-foot-long spears favoured by Far Western soldiery. Tsai Lin was closer, positioned at the end of the Scouts' formation where the enemy seemed to have clustered. The Dai Lo battled two assassins at once, his armour spattered with a copious amount of blood, although from the skill and swiftness with which he moved, Vaelin doubted he was wounded.

By the time Vaelin had closed the distance between them, the Dai Lo had despatched one assassin and maimed another, the man kneeling in silent shock as he regarded the blood pumping from the stump of his wrist. He recovered with what seemed an unnatural rapidity, regaining his feet and drawing a knife that he prepared to throw at Tsai Lin, who had turned to face a trio of fresh enemies.

Vaelin hacked down the one-handed man before he could throw his knife, kicking the corpse aside and moving to stand at Tsai Lin's left. The three men before them paused for a brief second, Vaelin sensing a mutual unspoken decision before they surged forward in unison. He dodged a thrust, flicked his sword at the assassin's eyes, then followed up with a punch to his chest as the man raised his arm to block Vaelin's blade. It was a precisely aimed blow to the sternum, capable of leaving a man senseless if delivered with sufficient force. This man, however, was stunned for only an instant, letting out a hard grunt before lowering himself into a crouch and charging forward, sword held in a two-handed grip and aimed at Vaelin's belly. He sidestepped the charge and spun to one knee, ready to lash at the assassin's legs, but before he could do so Alum's spear jabbed into his guts. The man staggered as the hunter withdrew the spear, adjusted his grip and delivered a fatal thrust to the neck with enough force to split his enemy from larynx to spine.

The Moreska shouldered the collapsing corpse aside, spear jabbing once again, this time into the thigh of one of the men facing Tsai Lin. The Dai Lo took full advantage of the distraction, stepping forward to bring his sword around in a single fluid arc that slashed open the throats of both attackers.

"Form line!" Tsai Lin called out to a nearby group of garrison soldiers who were busy hacking at a partially dismembered corpse. "If you would care to cover my left, Honoured Sir . . ." the Dai Lo said to Alum, who apparently failed to notice, charging straight into the midst of the assassins, spear whirling left and right.

"I don't think he's much for tactics," Nortah observed. He hefted his sword, nodding at the now-frenzied melee with a raised eyebrow. "Shall we?"

Vaelin nodded and they launched themselves in Alum's wake. As Vaelin had noted before in moments like this, the more heated the combat became, the more time seemed to slow. Sound and sensation slipped away as mind and body became fixated on the need to kill and survive. He and Nortah moved together as they had learned to do all those years ago, back-to-back, swords cutting through flesh and bone in repeated blurring strokes as they described a lethal dance through the disordered ranks of the assassins.

Despite the chaos caused by their attack and Alum's ferocity, Vaelin saw no sign of panic amongst their enemies, responding to this new threat with a uniformity that put him in mind of Volarian slave soldiers. They drew back from the Red Scouts to form a tight defensive knot in the centre of the meal hall. A series of barked orders from Sho Tsai soon had the Scouts and surviving soldiers marshalled into a circle, spears and swords levelled as they closed in for the kill.

Hearing a guttural shout at his back, Vaelin whirled in time to see Chien withdrawing her staff-sword from the guts of an assassin who, having feigned death, had reared up and attempted to drive a dagger into Tsai Lin's back. The Dai Lo gave her a stiff and very brief bow of gratitude before moving to stand alongside his father.

"Crossbows, Dai Shin?" he asked, nodding at the increasingly tight knot of assassins.

"Dead men don't talk," the captain replied. "And I've a yen to meet who-ever organised this reception."

As if in response the clustered assassins became instantly still, all move-ment vanishing and not a breath uttered. Then, as one, they collapsed, weap-ons clattering to the floor from lifeless hands. Sho Tsai quickly moved to the nearest body, checking for a pulse or movement to his chest, then cursing when he found nothing. A quick examination of several more bodies re-vealed the same result.

"Check the wounded!" the captain ordered, but a thorough examination of every assassin in the hall confirmed that none remained alive.

"Gone to their ancestors and taken their secrets with them," Chien observed, using her sword to lever away the mask of one assassin. "Same as the other one," she told Vaelin. "His heart wasn't stopped by poison."

"Other one?" Sho Tsai demanded of Vaelin.

"There were two, actually," he said. "And as for who organised this, the stonemason has a very clear notion."

◆ ◆ ◆

They found Governor Hushan in his rooms, weeping beside a pool in a bath-ing chamber, the deep red of the water a stark contrast to the finely illus-trated porcelain tiles covering the walls. He whispered barely audible entreaties as he wept, fingers playing in the red-stained water, eyes fixed on the body of his third wife.

No poison for this one either, Vaelin thought, seeing the deep gashes the woman had slashed into her arms, single cuts reaching from wrist to elbow. Her blood would have drained in seconds. In death she appeared more human now, the doll-like visage rendered empty and ugly. Just a dead woman floating in a cloud of her own blood. Vaelin doubted she could be more than twenty years old.

"No shame . . ." the governor sobbed in a thin voice, crimson water rip-pling as he reached deeper into the pool. "He teaches there is no shame in failure . . . He would still have welcomed you home . . . welcomed us . . ."

"Who?" Vaelin asked, tone deliberately soft, solicitous. The discordant shrillness of the governor's voice, and the wild cast in his eyes as they snapped to Vaelin, told of a man with a greatly weakened grip on reason. "Who would have welcomed you?"

Hushan stared at him in blank silence for a time, tears streaming from unblinking eyes to his beard. Then he laughed, a thin, grating giggle that soon built into a hearty bellow of genuine mirth.

"Traitorous cur!" Sho Tsai spat. Hushan barely seemed to notice, his unabated laughter causing the captain to step forward, sword raised for a killing blow.

"Wait," Vaelin said, moving between them. "Dead men don't talk, remember?"

He crouched at Hushan's side, offering a good-natured smile to the governor's continuing mirth before pointedly shifting his gaze to the dead woman in the pool. "She wasn't really your wife, was she?" he asked.

Hushan's laughter stopped at that, expression abruptly shifting into a mask of grief. "She was bound to me," he murmured. "And I to her . . . in His sight. Our bond went beyond the mere formalities of marriage. Through her, I heard His voice from across the Steppe . . . Such clarity she brought, such wisdom . . . What am I now?" His gaze swung back to Vaelin, beseeching, earnest in its desperation. "Without her, what am I?"

Mad, to be sure, Vaelin concluded, looking deep into the void behind the governor's eyes. *But there must still be knowledge in there somewhere.* "She heard his voice," he said. "The Darkblade. Through her, he spoke to you."

"More than mere words . . ." Hushan got unsteadily to his feet, Vaelin gesturing for Sho Tsai to stay put when the captain once again readied his blade. "Through her I saw so many things."

The governor slipped into the bloody pool, the white and silver pelt of his cloak staining red as it trailed in the water. Fresh tears fell as he enfolded the dead woman in his arms. "She showed me what will be. The fire and fury of it all. The destruction of the southerners who made us their whores."

A defiant glint crept into Hushan's eye as he cast a glance at Sho Tsai. "For which my family have beseeched Heaven for so long. And finally they answered us, with Him." The expression drained from his face once again as he looked at the woman in his arms. "With her. Your whoremaster king can send all the armies in the world, it won't matter, for I have seen what will come. This"—he pulled the woman closer still, crushing her limp form to his chest—"was but the first taste."

"He told you to kill us, didn't he?" Vaelin asked, careful not to employ too demanding a tone. "Our arrival here was unexpected."

"You?" The governor's voice regained a measure of mirth as his eyes flicked from Vaelin to Sho Tsai. "Him? The Thief of Names and the Merchant King's errand boy." He began to weep once more as he cradled the woman's head against his shoulder. "You are not worth a single drop of this precious blood. He will deal with you in time, for his minor amusement."

"Then why?" Vaelin pressed. "Gathering so many assassins here must have taken weeks. Preparing this place to ensure its fall when the Stahlhast come without arousing suspicion couldn't have been easy. Why gamble it all now?"

"Ask the errand boy." A disgusted, almost pitying grin played over Hushan's features as he jerked his head at Sho Tsai. "Does the Temple of Spears really think it can remake the past . . . ?"

The captain moved too fast for Vaelin to have any chance of stopping him, leaping high with his sword raised, bringing it round in a swift arc as he landed in the pool. Vaelin saw Hushan's eyes give a final curious blink as his head tumbled from his shoulders. Blood painted the tiles as both bodies collapsed into the water, entangled in death.

"He still had more to tell us!" Vaelin grated at Sho Tsai as the captain hauled himself from the pool, crimson water dripping from his armour. He gave no answer and started toward the door.

"What did he mean?" Vaelin demanded, stepping into his path. "About remaking the past."

"I have no idea," Sho Tsai replied. "Just the babble of a corrupted mind. Whatever that witch did to him evidently overthrew his reason."

"He spoke of the Temple of Spears," Vaelin said. "Where you once studied. I think it's time I learned more about it."

Sho Tsai's features, liberally decorated with the governor's blood, twitched as he matched Vaelin's stare, before his anger abruptly leeched away. "My thanks for your assistance this night," he said, wiping clean his sword before sliding it into the scabbard. "But there is nothing more to discuss. And, with the governor's demise, I find myself with a great deal to do."

He moved his head in the briefest of bows and stepped around Vaelin before making his exit.

CHAPTER EIGHTEEN

It took only a few moments in the company of Governor Hushan's deputy to understand why, unlike the city's garrison commander and several other well-regarded officials, he hadn't attracted an assassin's blade the night before.

"The governor . . . a traitor?" Deputy Governor Neshim mopped his brow with a silken handkerchief. Like Hushan he was of northern stock with a similarly broad-shouldered build that somewhat belied a less than resolute character. "His third wife a witch. It's impossible, surely."

"No, Honoured Sir, it is not," Sho Tsai told him, his patience clearly starting to wear thin. "Governor Hushan conspired with an agent of the Stahlhast against the Venerable Kingdom."

"But she was always so . . . nice. Three years since he brought her back from a northern patrol, a slave rescued from the savages' clutches, he said."

"Three years," Vaelin said. "A good stretch of time to lay the ground for their attack. Gather intelligence on the strength of the defences, seed the city with assassins under her thrall. The Darkblade is careful, it seems, and patient."

"The Darkblade," Deputy Governor Neshim repeated, silk swatting at his brow with renewed energy. "So he's coming? The war is actually upon us?"

"As I explained," Sho Tsai said. "I also explained that the title of governor, and its responsibilities, now falls to you."

"To me?" Neshim began to chew on the corner of his handkerchief, which had somehow found its way into his mouth. "Really?"

"Yes, Governor." The captain gritted his teeth and forced a smile. He fell to an expectant silence, one Neshim seemed to harbour no desire to fill, continuing to chew on his handkerchief in consternation.

"Perhaps," Vaelin said, "the governor would be better placed to formulate his orders if he were given a fuller picture of the current situation." He knew such an intervention was probably a severe breach of etiquette but every hour spent in this city meant Sherin would be slipping further beyond his reach. That morning Ahm Lin had advised his song had taken on a subtle but discernible note of warning.

"She continues to journey north, brother," the mason said. "But the danger she faces grows by the day."

A flicker of annoyance passed across Sho Tsai's brow before he sighed and turned to the other man in the room, a blunt-featured figure wearing the unadorned iron-grey armour of the local soldiery. "Subcommander Deshai," Sho Tsai said, providing the required bow of an officer greeting a superior. "As I understand it, command of the city's defences now rests with you. Perhaps you have a report for the governor?"

Deshai gave a stiff nod, Vaelin discerning a degree of understanding in him that greatly surpassed his newly ascended superior. A subcommander outranked a captain, but this captain had the favour of the Merchant King.

"We lost over a hundred men last night," Deshai told the governor. "More than half were officers and senior sergeants. The rest were mostly skilled archers and engineers. Damage was also done to the main lock where the canal meets the Black Vein, meaning we'll have trouble moving cargo at a decent rate until it's repaired."

"Which will take longer than usual because we lost so many engineers," Sho Tsai mused, rubbing the faint stubble on his chin. This was the first morning since their journey began that Vaelin had seen him unshaven. "Officers, sergeants, engineers, the garrison commander and the most able administrators in the city. Clearly, this was a blow long in the planning."

"And delivered early," Vaelin reminded him. "Meaning there may well be sufficient time for these capable gentlemen to put it right whilst we continue our most vital mission."

Sho Tsai frowned at his pointed tone but it was plain the need to delay here chafed on him also. "What messages have been sent?" he asked Neshim, who blanched at the question.

"Messages?" he said, the handkerchief finally slipping from between his teeth.

"Yes, Governor, messages," Sho Tsai repeated. "Messages warning the other strongholds in the region. Messages to the bordering Prefectures. Messages to the Merchant King."

Neshim spent some time gaping at the captain before summoning a modicum of inner resolve. "I, ah—" He coughed. "I shall see to it immediately. Though I may need some small assistance with the formal phrasing. Hushan always took care of that sort of thing . . ." Neshim's voice faded, as if the mere mention of the traitor's name might herald some form of censure. Sho Tsai paid it no mind, however.

"I shall be glad to help," he said. "But our honoured guest"—he inclined his head at Vaelin—"is correct in reminding me of the urgency of our mission. I shall take my company north before the day is out and return as soon as possible. When I do, I hope to write to the Merchant King informing him of your fulsome preparations to meet the coming assault. Subcommander Deshai, I *suggest* you ignore the former governor's stricture against forming a militia and start recruitment and training without further delay."

The subcommander's blunt features betrayed a wariness that evidently overcame any resentment at the clear instruction in Sho Tsai's tone. "A suggestion happily accepted, Captain," he said.

"Excellent." Sho Tsai moved to Vaelin, speaking in Realm Tongue. "I won't tarry with these fools any longer than I have to. Get your people ready to ride and tell the Dai Lo to muster the Red Scouts. Any wounded will have to be left here. The stonemason will be at the head of the column from now until we find them."

◆ ◆ ◆

Sho Tsai ordered the company to proceed north in battle formation. Outriders scouted the flanks and the rear whilst the main body rode in a broad column four abreast. At Ahm Lin's instruction they followed a loose gravel track along the eastern bank of the Black Vein. The river was rich in boats crowded with people in much the same beggared and dishevelled state as those they had encountered on the road to Keshin-Kho. Despite their evident hunger they worked their long-bladed oars with a determined energy, gazes fixed on the promise of refuge that lay over the southern horizon. Vaelin saw many wounded amongst them nursing bandaged heads and limbs, some with raw and recent burns. Whatever the delusions of the late Governor Hushan, Vaelin doubted the Stahlhast's newly risen god had come to the borderlands as a liberator.

They rode until dusk and camped for the night within a tight perimeter with the Red Scouts standing double watch in two-hour relays. The soldiers slept fully clothed with their weapons close at hand and horses remained saddled. Vaelin found sleep beyond him and lay for a time on his bedroll, listening to Erlin's snores, which soon found a muted accompaniment in youthful voices engaged in muted conversation.

"Never seen a sky so big," he heard Sehmon say. "Stars are much the same, though."

"'We walk beneath a shared sky on a shared earth,'" Ellese murmured in response. "'And so, should share our hearts as we share this world.'" A quote Vaelin recognised from the Tenth Book of the Cumbraelin god, the Book of Wisdom, her mother's favourite.

"What's that?" Sehmon asked.

"Never mind," she told him in a half-irritated mutter, grunting as she turned on her side. "Best sleep. There'll probably be fighting tomorrow."

There was a short pause and a sigh before Sehmon said, "So, you're doing this again."

"Doing what?"

"Pretending this, us, doesn't matter."

"I'm not pretending. It doesn't matter." A brief but potent silence followed before she spoke again, voice softer. "I know you want something from me, something I can't give. It's just not in me . . ."

Beset by a sudden sense of intrusion, Vaelin rose, gathering up his sword and walking away until their voices faded. He wandered the outskirts of the camp for a time, eventually coming to the riverbank, where he found Alum crouched, using the butt of his spear to scrape symbols in the dry earth.

"A message for the Protectors?" Vaelin asked him.

"For the children," the Moreska replied. "When a hunter's trek takes him far from the tribe, he will mark the earth with his True Name to let them know he still lives. The Lord of Sand and Sky will carry the message home so his kin will not worry."

"True Name?" Vaelin crouched at Alum's side to survey the symbols he had drawn. They were more complex than the marks he had seen him make in the ash back at the outlaws' mine, three swirling pictograms bisected by various lines, some straight, others curved.

"The name by which the Protectors know me," the hunter explained. "The name I craft with every step on the journey of life. This"—he pointed to the leftmost symbol—"the stars under which I was born. This"—his finger tracked to the next symbol—"the lives I have taken in the hunt or in war, and this," he continued, his voice growing softer as he turned to the third, "what I hope to leave behind when the Protectors speak my True Name."

"A story," Vaelin realised with a smile. "Your True Name is a story." He looked closer at the third symbol, the most complex yet, formed of interwoven spirals interspersed with small circles. "Your children," he said.

"The children of the tribe." Alum's gaze dropped and his voice grew soft. "The children I made with my wives were very young when we set out for your Realm, and the journey was long. Hunger always takes the young first."

"I'm sorry."

Alum grunted, forcing a tight smile. "All children of the Moreska call each man Father and each woman Mother. Those that remain, somewhere in the world . . ." He splayed the long fingers of his hand over the third symbol. "They will call me Father when we find them."

"Every step we take on this journey takes us further away from where they're most likely to be. And I have a sense that tomorrow will bring battle, the first of many, for war is coming to these lands. It's not too late for you to walk your own path. You should feel no obligation . . ."

"The path to the children lies with you." Alum's voice held no doubt, and the hard gaze he turned on Vaelin lacked any glimmer of uncertainty. "And I'll fight any number of battles to see them again."

Vaelin nodded, clapping the Moreska on the shoulder before rising and moving away, pausing when Alum added, "They will call you Father too. You walk under the Protectors' gaze now, whether you believe it or not."

He turned back to his symbols, hefting his spear to add more details, and

Vaelin sensed it would be best to leave him to what was essentially a form of prayer. He moved to tour the picket line, exchanging clipped conversation with the Scouts. Their manner was markedly less hostile now, as he would expect from men he had fought alongside. But the tension of being on the enemy's ground was palpable.

"Six years since I last rode the Iron Steppe," Corporal Wei muttered in response to Vaelin's greeting. Despite his well-expressed disdain for foreigners, Wei seemed more willing to talk than the other Scouts, which Vaelin suspected was due to an innate inability to still his tongue rather than any softening of prejudice. "Hoped I'd never set eyes on it again. Not a place for civilised folk to fight a war. A man can die of thirst or hunger out here just as easily as he can fall to a savage's sabre."

"You fought the Stahlhast?" Vaelin asked.

"Once." A shadow passed over Wei's battered visage before he grunted out a bitter laugh and traced his thumb over his mangled upper lip. "One of the fuckers gave me this. Stuck a lance through his neck by way of thanks; even then the bastard kept fighting. That's the worst thing about them, see? Yes, they can ride better than most, fight better than most, and they got all manner of cunning tricks when it comes to battle. But what makes them near impossible to beat is that they just refuse to die when they should."

The corporal fell silent as a sound came drifting across the featureless plain. It was faint and high pitched, somewhere between a howl and a yelp. The sky was clear tonight, and the light of a half-moon cast a dim glow, revealing much of the terrain to their front. However, Vaelin still failed to pick out whatever animal had produced such a cry.

"Wild dogs?" he asked Wei, who replied with a grim shake of his head.

"Stahlhast hunters," he said. "They mimic the call of the wild dog when they find prey. We've been seen. Only a matter of time, I s'pose."

"I'll tell the captain," Vaelin said, turning away.

"No point. He's probably heard it already. Anyway, the Stahlhast will always find you when you ride their Steppe. A long-standing truth known to those who patrol the northern border."

"Won't they bring others?"

"Surely." Wei shrugged. "Just a question of how many. I'm guessing we'll find out tomorrow."

♦ ♦ ♦

Come the morning Ahm Lin once again had them following the river for
several hours until he drew his pony to an abrupt halt. "What is it?" Vaelin
asked, seeing the mason's features bunched in mingled fear and discomfort.

"They . . ." He winced and shook his head. "They've been found."

Vaelin took a breath to still his racing heart, forcing calm into his voice
as he asked, "Are they . . . ?"

"They're alive." A measure of fear slipped from Ahm Lin's face. "Unharmed
too, I believe. They . . ." He trailed off, lips forming a puzzled grimace. "They
wanted to be found."

"How far?" Sho Tsai demanded.

"I can't say exactly but they're close." He turned his pony towards the
north-east and spurred it into a fast trot. "This way."

The company proceeded at the speed of the mason's pony, which Vaelin
found ever more frustratingly sluggish with each passing mile. His gaze was
locked on the horizon, tracking back and forth for the smallest silhouette.
They had covered another ten miles when Alum suddenly spurred his horse
to the front of the column, arm raised and attention focused on the ground.

"Sign?" Vaelin asked him. The hunter nodded and slipped from the saddle, crouching to inspect a cluster of hoof-prints. After a moment he grunted
and moved off, eyes roving the sparse turf until he came to a stop some
twenty yards away.

"A half-dozen riders there," he said, pointing to the first set of prints.
"Joined by a dozen more here." He nodded at the more disturbed sod beneath
his feet before turning to face due north. "They're moving fast," he said, raising an eyebrow at Ahm Lin and his pony. The animal's breath had become
ragged and it tossed its head in fatigued annoyance.

"Can you track them?" Vaelin asked the Moreska.

"This land is like scripture," he said, swiftly climbing back onto his
mount. "So easy to read."

"I'm not waiting," Vaelin said, turning to address Sho Tsai. "Leave sufficient men to guard the mason. I've a sense we'll need his talent again
before long."

He kicked his horse into a gallop without waiting for an answer, Alum
and the others quickly following suit. The hunter spurred ahead to lead the
way, eyes continually tracking the earth. After half a mile Vaelin glanced

back to see Sho Tsai following with half his company. *At least we won't be outnumbered,* he thought, suppressing uncomfortable notions of what the Stahlhast might do to their captives when it became clear they were about to be intercepted.

It took over an hour of hard riding before a plume of dust rose on the horizon. With no more need for Alum to read the signs, Vaelin spurred his horse to greater efforts, voicing thanks for having been provided with a beast bred for the hunt rather than battle. A warhorse would never have matched such a pace. He drew away from the others, ignoring Nortah's shouted warning that they should stay together. Gradually the dark specks of men on horseback became visible at the base of the plume, resolving into a band of close to twenty riders. The dust rose thicker as they reined to a halt, wheeling their mounts around with the effortless swiftness of those born to the saddle. They spread out as Vaelin galloped closer, drawing sabres and unhooking lances to stand in readiness.

He knew the wisest course would be to halt, wait for the others, perhaps even try to talk to these people, but all such thought fled his mind at the sight of two smaller figures beyond the line of Stahlhast. They both rode sturdy ponies like Ahm Lin's, both clad in dark cloaks although one wore a long white scarf that trailed in the wind. But it was the other that captured his gaze. Even though it was too far to make out her features, the rush of recognition was immediate, made fierce by the fear and concern that accompanied it.

The Stahlhast spurred forward to meet him as he closed in, drawing his sword and bringing it down on the lance point of the lead rider. The blade turned the weapon aside, sliding the length of the shaft to bite deep into the forearm of its owner. Vaelin angled the blade so that it slashed across the rider's neck before his horse brought him clear. The swish of a sabre caused him to lean low in the saddle, feeling the rush of wind on his back as the blade cleaved the air.

He tugged on the reins, bringing his mount to a halt and then wheeling about, sword extended in a thrust. The sabre-wielding Stahlhast wore an iron helm decorated with what appeared to be metal thorns but lacking a face guard. The speed of his charge left no time to dodge and the star-silver-edged sword point sank deep into his cheek, Vaelin pushing it deeper still until he felt it meet the unyielding iron of the helmet.

He withdrew his sword, letting the corpse tumble from the saddle. The Stahlhast had encircled him now, faces dark with fury, every lance and sabre levelled at him. "They," Vaelin said, pointing at the two figures beyond the circle, "are all I want. Ride away and you can live."

He spoke in Chu-Shin, assuming they must have some knowledge of the tongue, but if they did the words evidently had no effect. As one they let out a war cry and charged. The closest, a woman with striking red hair streaming from beneath the edges of her helm, bared her teeth in a snarl, sabre extended in a perfectly aimed thrust at his chest. She wore a breastplate that would have been proof against most arrows, but Nortah had always been expert at finding gaps in armour. The woman's snarl turned into a shocked grimace as the arrow pierced the thin chain mail below her extended arm, driving into the flesh beneath. Vaelin had time to glimpse Nortah loosing another arrow as he galloped closer, sending another Stahlhast tumbling to the ground, and then the rest were on him.

He parried a lance thrust, then pulled hard on his reins, causing his horse to rear. The animal didn't lash out with its hooves as a warhorse would, but by rearing it woke an instinctive reaction in the mounts of the Stahlhast. Several reared in response, whilst others let out shrill whinnies of challenge. The resultant interruption to their riders' assault was only momentary, but it was enough.

Vaelin palmed a throwing knife and cast it at the nearest Stahlhast, aiming for his face. The man's reflexes proved keen and he managed to jerk his head aside, the knife careening off his iron helm, but it distracted him long enough for Nortah to close and hack him down with two well-placed strokes of his sword. Alum was close behind, leaping from the saddle as he rode into the midst of the Stahlhast, whirling in midair and landing with blood trailing from his spear.

Then the Scouts arrived in a tight charging mass, cutting down the remaining Stahlhast in a frenzy of slashing swords and stamping hooves. They went about the subsequent slaughter with grim but evident relish. The few remaining Stahlhast, still vainly trying to fight despite hopeless odds, fell to a flurry of crossbow bolts after which the Scouts dismounted, drawing daggers to finish any wounded.

Vaelin turned his horse away from the ugly spectacle, sheathing his sword and trotting towards the two figures still sitting on their ponies a short distance away.

The woman with the long white scarf offered him a demure, welcoming smile as he reined to a halt, dismounting to offer a bow, which she acknowledged with a small incline of her head. The stories of her beauty were clearly not exaggerated, although her features possessed a warm vitality very different from the doll-like mask of Governor Hushan's third wife. However, Vaelin found himself sparing her little more than a glance before his gaze was drawn to the woman at her side.

She's barely changed, he thought, drinking in the sight of her. The same dark eyes, the black curls of her hair tied into a neat, sensible ponytail. The same angry scowl that told of a deep and unwelcome judgement.

"Oh." Sherin sighed in a tone of infinite weariness. "Go away. You're spoiling everything."

CHAPTER NINETEEN

Vaelin found his tongue incapable of forming words as she continued to stare at him, the judgement in her gaze cutting deep. "I . . ."
he began, then promptly faltered to silence before trying again. "I
thought you were in need of help . . ."

"Then you were misinformed." Her gaze softened fractionally as it shifted
to Sho Tsai reining to a halt nearby. He dismounted before striding forward
to offer a deep, respectful bow to the Jade Princess.

"Blessing of Heaven," he said before bowing to Sherin. "Good woman
Unsa. I come on the orders of the Merchant King . . ."

"I'm sure you do," Sherin cut in and Vaelin watched the captain do some
faltering of his own. He also saw Sherin's expression soften further as she
took note of the hurt her tone provoked. "Your concern honours me, as
always," she said, slipping from the back of her pony and moving to clasp his
hand. "But you shouldn't have come."

"How could I not?"

Watching their eyes meet, Vaelin suddenly knew himself to be the worst
of fools. *Come halfway across the world to save a woman who no longer knows
me,* he thought. He wondered if this had been the Messenger's final barb, a
last ugly jape before he slipped into the void. Vaelin's gaze tracked from
Sherin's hand entwined with Sho Tsai's to the mutual affection he saw shining in their eyes. *She's right; I was misinformed. He wanted me to see this.*

He was therefore grateful for the distraction when the Jade Princess let out a laugh and leapt from the saddle, clapping and jumping in girlish delight as Erlin guided his horse through the carnage of the Stahlhast's demise.

"Young wanderer," she greeted him as he dismounted, throwing her arms around his waist and pressing herself close. "You came to see me again and it's barely been two decades!"

Erlin winced at the strength of her embrace before laughing and gently easing her back. "Careful," he said. "I'm not so young now."

"Oh." The Princess reached up to pluck at his greying hair, her fingers moving on to play over the deepening wrinkles in his forehead. "How?"

"A very long story." His smile turned to a frown of concern. "And you? They said you might be ill."

"Just a small ruse." She shrugged and giggled. "I had to go on an adventure with my new friend."

"Dai Shin!" Vaelin turned at the sound of Tsai Lin's voice, finding him pointing to the eastern horizon. Squinting, Vaelin managed to make out the silhouette of a lone rider who promptly vanished a heartbeat later.

"Gone off to tell his friends all about us, I assume," Nortah said. He wiped a rag along the length of his sword before sliding it into the sheath on his back. "Sister," he said, inclining his head at Sherin. "Good to see you again."

It took Sherin a moment before her brow creased in recognition. "Brother Nortah. It seems I am beset by not one but two ghosts today. You are supposed to be dead, are you not?"

Nortah spread his hands. "A long-settled misunderstanding."

"You cut the Battle Lord's hand off, as I recall."

"I did, and later served under him in the Liberation War. The world is ever a place of contradictions, don't you find?"

"Contradictions," Sherin agreed, casting another glance at Vaelin. "And lies."

"To your mounts if you would, honoured ladies," Sho Tsai said, preparing to resume the saddle. "That scout will be hastening to bring word of our presence to his kin. We need to be many miles south before nightfall."

"You have my leave to depart," Sherin told him. "As for myself and the Princess . . ."

"You will mount up and ride!" Sho Tsai snapped. The set of his shoulders told of a reluctant harshness, but one he wouldn't shirk. "Or I will have you bound to your saddles."

"We are not here on some mad jaunt," Sherin shot back. "Our mission is of great import."

"And what exactly is your mission?" Vaelin asked, watching Sherin turn to the Jade Princess in exasperation. The ancient woman gave a tight smile accompanied by a fractional shake of her head that seemed sufficient to still Sherin's tongue.

"There is no time for this." The captain hauled himself into the saddle. "You can explain yourself when we make camp." He stared down at her, matching her defiant glare with implacable determination. "Now, Honoured Grace of Heaven, please resume your mount and follow me."

◆ ◆ ◆

They reached the riverbank by dusk, Sho Tsai insisting they push on until the sun had almost fully dipped below the flat line of the horizon. He organised an even tighter perimeter than the night before, fully half the company standing watch with crossbows primed. Tsai Lin was also set to keep a close watch on the river.

"Order any passing boat to heave to," the captain said. "We'll get the ladies and foreigners aboard, then lead the Stahlhast away whilst they make safe passage to Keshin-Kho."

As the Dai Lo bobbed his head in acknowledgement and hurried off towards the riverbank, Vaelin noticed how the Jade Princess's gaze tracked him. Her eyes were narrowed in a shrewd appraisal that contrasted greatly with the near-childlike manners she had exhibited so far. He watched her move closer to Sho Tsai, asking a question in a voice too soft to hear. There was a palpable wariness to the captain's nod of response, though she seemed satisfied, the warm smile returning to her lips as she touched a hand to Sho Tsai's armoured forearm. This time Vaelin was able to catch her words: "He is a credit to you. The Servants of the Temple chose well."

Sho Tsai merely nodded again and moved on, snapping out orders forbidding any fires to be lit. Consequently, the evening meal consisted of hard-tack and dried beef. The Jade Princess and Erlin maintained a softly spoken and cheery conversation throughout the night, which contrasted with Sherin's stern and unyielding silence. She sat opposite Vaelin, moonlight catching the outline of her face but features unreadable in the gloom. He could, however, feel her anger and took some small comfort in the fact that it wasn't directed entirely at him. Sho Tsai had attempted to question her on the nature of her mission only to receive a curt and loudly spoken response: "It doesn't matter now." She hadn't said a word since.

"This is worse than the supper I had with Mother after she caught me with that stable hand," Ellese muttered.

Vaelin heard what may have been a laugh from Sherin, albeit a very small one. "A Cumbraelin accent," she said. "You've journeyed far for one so young."

"My uncle needed me," Ellese replied.

Sherin's face tilted toward Vaelin, then away again. "Uncle?"

"Well, not in blood. He and Mother won the war together, you see."

"Not without the help of several thousand others, my dear," Nortah pointed out.

"Yes." Sherin's voice was faint but Vaelin could hear the bitter resignation in it. "I had heard the Realm had suffered another war."

"This one needed fighting," Nortah said. "Rest assured of that."

There was a pause, Sherin's head lowering a little. "Aspect Elera, is she well?"

"When last I saw her. It has been a good long while now." Nortah turned to Vaelin. "You would know better than I, brother."

"I had a letter from her not long before we sailed," Vaelin said. "She writes every month to advise on my sister's well-being. Aspect Elera continues to head the Fifth Order, which has grown in size and import under the queen's patronage. These days there is not a village in the Realm without a healing house."

"Lyrna." Vaelin could hear the smile in Sherin's voice. "They call her the Fire Queen here. The woman I knew wanted little more than to read, write and tend her garden. War transforms us all, it seems."

She wasn't transformed, Vaelin thought. *When you knew her, she was just waiting.* He didn't bother voicing the notion. Sherin had always been more inclined towards perceiving the best in people. "Caenis died saving her," he said. "He was Aspect of the Seventh Order by then."

"Seventh Order? You mean to say it was real?"

"It still is. An entire Order of the Faith dedicated to study of the Dark, now openly acknowledged and recognised by the crown after centuries in the shadows. The Realm is greatly changed."

"It must be markedly more peaceful at least, for the queen to permit this intrepid quest of yours."

The sardonic lilt of her voice kindled a small heat in his chest. He had forgotten how easily she could stir his pique. "She didn't permit anything," he said. "I am here on my own agency, as are my companions."

"Apart from Sehmon," Ellese pointed out, chewing on a mouthful of beef. "He used to be an outlaw but he's Alum's servant now," she explained to Sherin. "Uncle spared him the hanging he gave his relatives. Well, some of them were beheaded actually . . ."

"Ellese," Vaelin said, bringing her verbal torrent to a halt.

"So." Sherin's face turned away from him once more. "The Realm is greatly changed, but you are not."

"Much has happened," he said. "And I have much to apologise for . . ."

"I don't want your apology, Vaelin. I want you to go back to your tower and leave me alone."

She got to her feet and moved away, a slender shadow in the dark. He watched her walk to where the Jade Princess sat talking quietly with Erlin. There was a brief murmur of conversation before Sherin disappeared fully into the gloom.

"Captain!" the Princess said, tone bright with enthusiasm as she got to her feet, clapping her hands. "Gather your men. In payment for their brave service I would like to sing them a song."

"A song, lady?" Sho Tsai said, his tone one of utter bafflement. "I don't think . . ."

"But I do!" she cut in with a laugh. "And I speak with the authority of Heaven, don't forget." She clapped her hands again and wagged a finger at him. "Hurry now."

Sho Tsai hesitated a moment further before calling to his sergeant. The Red Scouts were duly drawn into a yet smaller perimeter. Half were ordered to keep facing the Steppe, whilst the rest all stood staring at the Jade Princess, eyes rapt in expectation of hearing a song blessed by Heaven.

"They look like worshippers in the cathedral," Ellese whispered.

"That's because they are," Vaelin whispered back. "Hush. I suspect you're about to hear something quite special."

He watched the Jade Princess run a hand through Erlin's thinning hair. He couldn't see her smile in the dark but the fondness and the sadness in her voice were unmistakable. "It was truly wonderful to see you again, young wanderer," she said, dipping her head to press a kiss to his cheek. Rising, she straightened, drew a breath and sang her first note, and the world turned to utter blackness in an instant.

◆　◆　◆

He awoke with the dawn, finding Sherin looking down at him with an impatient scowl. "She says you're needed," she told him in a flat voice, touching her toe to the sword lying at his side. "So is that, apparently. Pick it up and let's go."

Vaelin blinked and got to his feet, scanning the camp and finding himself surrounded by slumbering bodies. Corporal Wei lay with his head resting on his sergeant's breastplate, snores loud in the morning air and a contented smile on his misshapen lips. The only exception was Ahm Lin. He gave a grim smile as Sherin embraced him. "Please," she said, drawing back and blinking damp eyes, "get away from here. Go and be with your wife. You have cared for me long enough."

"True friendship is rare," he replied. "And not easily forsaken. You know I had to come."

Sherin wiped her eyes and nodded, enfolding him in a final fierce embrace before turning away and striding towards where the Jade Princess stood holding the reins of their ponies.

"She did this," Ahm Lin said, nodding to the princess. "One note of her song and they all fell into the soundest sleep."

"But not you," Vaelin observed.

"I have a song of my own." He shrugged. "It's no match for hers to be sure, but I believe it protected me."

Spying Nortah, Vaelin moved to grasp him by the shoulder, shaking it hard.

"They won't wake until she allows it," Sherin called from the back of her pony. "And she won't allow it until we're many miles north of here."

"Why do this?" Vaelin demanded, advancing towards the Jade Princess. "These men came here to save you. They'll be defenceless like this."

She replied with an aggravatingly coquettish smile, raising an eyebrow at Sherin. "Is he always so . . . forceful?" she asked.

"It varies according to circumstance," Sherin said before fixing Vaelin with an expectant glare. "The sooner we're gone from here the sooner they'll wake. If you care about their well-being, you'll get your backside on a horse and come with us."

"What about him?" Vaelin's finger lashed towards Sho Tsai's unconscious form. "Don't you care about him? Leaving him here for the Stahlhast to slaughter . . ."

"Rest assured they'll soon forget about this incursion when they have me."

Sherin raised her hand at Ahm Lin in farewell, a sad smile on her lips. The mason raised his own hand in response, though it appeared his wariness of the Jade Princess forbade him coming any closer. "Stay or go," Sherin told Vaelin, tugging her reins to turn her pony and kicking it into motion. "I'm tired of this."

The Jade Princess lingered a moment before following her, casting a wistful glance at where Erlin lay slumbering. "I would have done this sooner," she said with a note of apology. "But I so wanted to talk to my old friend for a time."

"Wait," Vaelin said as she gathered her reins. He felt a sore but unwise temptation to wrest them from her grip, knowing if he did he would find himself waking with the others some hours later. "Why are you doing this? Why willingly place yourselves in the hands of the Stahlhast?"

"Come along and find out," she laughed, spurring her pony into a canter.

Vaelin watched her ride off into the dust raised by Sherin's pony, biting down a curse before hurrying to his horse. "Brother," Ahm Lin said, moving to his side. "I would come, but . . ."

"She scares you," Vaelin finished. He tightened the saddle's cinch before hauling himself up. "And well she should. Better if you stay here in any case. The captain will have need of your song."

"You wish us to follow?"

"No." Vaelin scanned the Steppe, wondering how many eyes had already witnessed this bizarre waking. "The princess won't allow it, and the Stahlhast are sure to bring greater numbers to meet us. Tell him he should go south and wait until your song brings a clear notion of where to find us."

"And if it doesn't?"

"Then he'll have a war to fight . . . and a lover to avenge."

He paused to survey his companions, arranged in a loose circle of unconscious bodies around the smoking remnant of their fire, his gaze settling on Ellese. In slumber her features were even more youthful than usual, birthing a sense that he was about to abandon a child in hostile country.

"I ask you to have a special care for my niece," he said, leaning down to clasp the mason's hand. "She is not as strong or worldly as she appears."

Ahm Lin returned his grip with fierce assurance. "I will."

Vaelin felt a pang of gratitude for the way the mason kept his features as expressionless as possible, though the moistness of his eyes was a clear sign of his thoughts.

"I trust your song, old friend," Vaelin said, forcing a smile before kicking his horse into a gallop, riding hard to catch up with Sherin and the Princess.

◆ ◆ ◆

They came upon the battlefield when the sun had reached noon. At first Vaelin thought the ugly dark smear marring the yellow-green blanket of the Steppe was the result of a summer grass fire, but his experienced eye soon picked out the bones. They lay blackened or bleached upon the dry earth, many pierced with arrows, withered fletchings making them resemble cornstalks growing from between ribs or sprouting from empty eye sockets. Shattered lances and broken crossbows lay about the field, and many of the bodies still wore armour. Some had been reduced to nothing but bone whilst desiccated flesh still lingered on others. Vaelin paused at the sight of a man lying beneath the remains of a horse, drawn by the gleam of his breastplate. It was more elaborately decorated than the others littering this ground, with inlaid swirls of silver and Far Western script etched onto the steel. One half of the man's face was a grinning skull and the other a mask of leathery flesh. The crows had taken both his eyes, however.

"General Nishun, if I'm not mistaken," the Jade Princess said, reining her pony to a halt to peer at the corpse. Her tone was light and not entirely respectful, as if she were greeting a casual acquaintance of little regard.

"You knew this man?" Vaelin asked.

"He came to hear my song some years ago. It's long been customary for newly appointed luminaries to come to the High Temple. I suppose they think they might glean some favour from Heaven if they hear me sing." Her small nose wrinkled a little. "This man just stood there without the slightest change to his craggy old face. Then he bowed and left. Plainly the man had no ear for music."

"Or much in the way of good sense," Vaelin said, raising his gaze to scan the surrounding carnage. He found he could track the course of the battle from the position of the bodies. About half were arranged in an untidy line facing north, the rest scattered over the space of half a mile with more concentrated on the western and eastern flanks. It was clear this had all happened very quickly.

The main line broken in several places whilst cavalry assaulted both flanks, he concluded. *Then a slaughter. They had no time to run.* The amount of burning was a puzzle, however. As was the condition of the bodies, some of which appeared to have been dismembered, although when he dismounted for a closer look he saw no sign of cutting on the flesh or bones. *Blasted apart,* he decided. *So, the Stahlhast have Gifted in their ranks.*

"Is there a point to lingering here?" Sherin enquired, watching from the saddle as he continued his examination of the site.

"I would know my enemy," Vaelin said, plucking an arrow from between the ribs of a fallen soldier. It had a head of good if blackened steel rather than base iron, and had been fashioned with no small amount of skill, the twin barbs near perfectly symmetrical and the edges still sharp to the touch. "They didn't bother gathering their arrows," he murmured.

"Does that mean something?"

"This is well made and still useful," he said, holding up the arrow. "But they were happy to leave it behind, along with all this armour and these weapons. A rich people by most measures, yet still greedy for more."

"It's not greed that drives them," the Princess said. "It's love."

"Love?" Vaelin asked, gesturing at their grim surroundings. "Love of slaughter?"

"Love for their god. Or terror. I've often found they're much the same thing."

"Whatever drives them," Sherin said, "it will end soon. We will end it."

"By what means?" Vaelin enquired, turning to the Jade Princess. "I know your gift is powerful, but I doubt even you have a song that will put their entire horde to sleep."

"I have many songs," she laughed. "There is great power in music. The power to seduce, to enrage, to bring sorrow, and also rest. But I have spent many years perfecting one in particular, and it doesn't bring sleep. When their faux god hears it . . ." She cast a sorrowful glance around the field. "This will all be over."

"That's your mission?" Vaelin's gaze veered between them, incredulity loud in his voice. "You will sing a song to their leader? Will it kill him?"

"Certainly not!" The Princess stiffened. "I do not take life."

"Then what? It will . . . transform his soul somehow? Turn an evil man into a good one?"

"No one is truly good. But it will change him." The Princess paused and raised an eyebrow. "As it will change you, Vaelin Al Sorna."

"Look at this." He pointed the arrow at the disassembled corpse nearby. "I imagine you have lived long enough to know what this means. This man, this Darkblade, has enrolled Gifted into his army. They will know what you are. They will sense your gift and kill you before you can voice a note."

"I don't think so. I have a sense the Darkblade has a curious mind, not to mention a towering arrogance. He will hear me."

"Sherin." Vaelin moved to her, striving to keep any note of anger from his tone, knowing it would only stir her own. "You have to see this is madness. It's not too late to turn back . . ."

"Oh," the princess interrupted, shielding her eyes to gaze off to the east. "I'm afraid it is."

CHAPTER TWENTY

Vaelin estimated their numbers at around two hundred riders, all armed and armoured though they refrained from drawing blades or levelling lances as they closed in. He resumed his mount and sat with his hands clamped on the pommel of his saddle. "Do nothing," Sherin had instructed as the dust cloud rose to the east.

The Stahlhast fanned out to encircle them as they drew nearer, closing in on all sides and drawing to a halt at a remove of only a few yards. Vaelin's gaze slid from one face to another, seeing either the tension of imminent violence or the part-lustful grin of those who enjoy the taste of anticipation.

"Which one is the healer?" one of the Stahlhast asked in accented but passable Chu-Shin. She kicked her horse forward as she spoke. Like the woman Vaelin had seen fall to Nortah's arrow the day before, she had red hair that swirled like copper threads in the stiff winds of the Steppe.

"I am," Sherin replied.

The woman's eyes scanned her from head to toe before moving on to the Jade Princess. "So you would be *her*, then? The Blessing of Heaven."

"I suppose I would," the Princess replied with a small laugh.

The Stahlhast woman grunted and turned her gaze on Vaelin. "We were told there would be only two of you," she said. Vaelin noted how her eyes snapped from his face to the sword hilt jutting over his shoulder and then back again.

"This man is our escort," the Princess told her. "A fine and trusty sword to guard two defenceless ladies on their travels."

"Is that right?" The woman's features hardened further as she guided her horse closer, eyes still locked on Vaelin's. "He guard you from the riders sent to fetch you, did he? We found them last night, all cut down and not by the hand of one man."

"An unfortunate misunderstanding," the Princess insisted.

"Misunderstanding." The red-haired woman's lip curled. "Found my own sister with an arrow through her. Not the kind of arrow used by the Merchant King's soldiers either. An arrow from far away, I'd say." She leaned closer, Vaelin maintaining a blank expression as she bared her teeth. "You're not from the southlands," she hissed. "And you're not Stahlhast either. Do they make arrows where you're from? I'd bet they fucking do."

The knife appeared in her hand as she lunged closer, Vaelin's hand gripping the sword hilt and half drawing the blade clear before Sherin's voice stopped the Stahlhast woman cold. "Kill him and your Skeltir's son dies!"

The woman's fingers twitched on the knife handle as she drew in a few ragged breaths before turning her enraged gaze on Sherin. "On the Iron Steppe, bitch," she grated, "threats are not forgiven."

"I threaten nothing," Sherin replied. She swallowed hard but refused to look away as the woman continued to stare. "I merely state the truth. Kill this man and I will not heal your Skeltir's son."

The woman straightened, head tilted back as she dragged more air into her lungs. Once a modicum of calm had been recovered, she slid her knife back into its sheath and barked out a short series of what were unmistakably commands to the surrounding Stahlhast in their own language. The entire group immediately turned their mounts towards the south-west and spurred to a gallop.

"They'll find your friends," the woman promised Vaelin. "I told them to keep any archers alive. If you're lucky, I'll let you say goodbye before I flay them." Tugging her reins, she pointed her stallion's nose north. "We ride for the tor. And you," she added, casting a baleful glance over her shoulder at Sherin, "had better pray your skills match your legend."

◆ ◆ ◆

The tor rose from the plain into the late evening sky, resembling the long-rotted stump of a great tree. The Stahlhast woman had maintained a rigid silence throughout the three-day journey north, ignoring Sherin's cautious attempts at conversation and spending the evenings sitting at a separate fire. Vaelin could read the depth of the woman's bloodlust in every glance she shot his way, causing him to ponder the wisdom of allowing himself to sleep. However, after the first night passed without incident, he concluded she was as bound by duty as Sho Tsai or any other soldier. Despite their supposed barbarism, it seemed the Stahlhast didn't lack discipline.

"So, this is where they get their iron," he said, eyeing the flanks of the tor, scraped raw and pale by what must have been the labour of generations.

"Metal from the tors, meat from great herds of deer and musk oxen," the Jade Princess confirmed. "As you said, they want for little and yet strive for more."

The Stahlhast woman led them towards a dense cluster of stone houses guarding the south-facing approach to the tor, passing a few cultivated fields along the way. Vaelin was struck by the fact that the people tending the fields were all of Far Western appearance. He assumed they must be slaves but saw no guards or whip-bearing overseers. Also, the people were all clad in cloth of good quality and went about their labour with an energetic diligence, many singing songs as they worked.

"Who are they?" he enquired of the Jade Princess.

"Slaves once," she said, a line appearing in her usually flawless brow as she surveyed the fields. "But no longer, I fear."

"Why fear it? Liberation is always to be celebrated."

"A slave in body can still be a slave in mind," she replied. Her usual flippancy was gone now, her voice possessed of a grave surety that spoke to the vastness of her experience. Sometimes it was easy to forget she had walked this earth for more years than he could imagine. "A slave won't fight for an owner, but they will fight for a god, especially a god who breaks their chains."

They skirted the houses where the close-packed streets were rich in the babble of children at play. The town also lacked the stench typical to a place reserved for the lowest orders. Smiling faces were everywhere as people greeted neighbours or chided their offspring. Vaelin noticed that their happiness was not matched in the caustic gaze the Stahlhast woman afforded them, her lips twisting in open contempt. He also saw how the smiles faded and the townsfolk averted their gaze as she passed by.

"It must be hard," he said to her, "having your property stolen by the Darkblade."

"Shut your mouth!" she snarled, hand twitching as she resisted the urge to reach for her knife. "*His* word is not to be questioned by the likes of you."

She spurred her horse to a canter, aiming for a large encampment in the eastern lee of the tor. The tents were elaborate constructions of animal hide, all patched with numerous repairs that told of many years' use. They were arranged in an arc around a large corral where a herd of horses raised dust as they gambolled and grazed. Vaelin estimated the camp must be home to at least a thousand people. One of the riders posted in a loose picket line came galloping to intercept their approach, then reined to a halt as the Stahlhast woman waved him aside.

She slowed to a walk as they entered the camp and people emerged from their tents to stare at the strangers she had led into their midst. Vaelin saw little of the curiosity that had coloured the faces of those in the Venerable Kingdom when they beheld foreigners, but plenty of the same suspicion. Men and women of fighting age stared at Vaelin with expressions of naked challenge, whilst others leered at Sherin and the Jade Princess and called out no doubt lustful insults in their own language.

"Calm down," Sherin told Vaelin as he bridled at the sight of one man holding his crotch as he shouted something at her, much to the hilarity of his fellows. Vaelin quelled his rising temper and dragged his gaze away, keeping it fixed on the Stahlhast woman as she guided them to the largest tent in the encampment. An unusual banner jutted through the tent's roof, a circle of burnished steel set within a wrought iron frame. The steel circle was engraved with a skillfully executed depiction of a hawk, wings spread and talons extended.

The man standing in the entrance to the tent was shorter than many of the other Stahlhast that Vaelin had seen so far, and several years older with streaks of grey showing in the untidy black mane of his hair. He held a sheathed sabre in one hand and a flask in the other, taking a long drink from it as the Stahlhast woman dismounted, holding up both hands in what was evidently a gesture of respect.

"Skeltir," she said, jerking her head at the three foreigners before continuing in the Stahlhast tongue. The man nodded as she spoke, continuing to drink as his eyes tracked over Vaelin and the Jade Princess before coming to rest on Sherin, where they lingered.

He halted the woman's words with a raised hand and murmured something before disappearing into the gloomy confines of the tent. "The Skeltir of the Ostra doesn't like to be kept waiting," the woman said, gesturing impatiently at the open flap.

The Jade Princess and Sherin quickly dismounted and proceeded inside, Vaelin following at a more cautious pace and halting a foot or two inside to allow his eyes to adjust to the gloom. The Skeltir sat alone on a low seat covered in oxhide, sabre resting on his knees and flask still in hand. Before him an iron stove cast a steady stream of smoke up to the opening in the tent roof as coals glowed within. Vaelin's eyes roved every corner of the tent, finding no one else.

"A Skeltir of the Stahlhast doesn't lure folk into his tent to kill them," the woman muttered, coming to Vaelin's side. "If there's a need for killing, he does it openly in front of the eyes of his Skeld. Now sit."

Vaelin made another pointed survey of the tent before moving to take a seat on a pile of furs alongside Sherin and the Princess.

"Thirus tells me you killed her sister," the Skeltir began in Chu-Shin. His voice had the quality of a nicked blade grating on a stone. His gaze was steady on Vaelin's, hard with scrutiny rather than anger. "And more besides. Loyal riders of the Ostra Skeld sent forth on my word."

"They drew blades on me and my companions," Vaelin replied. "So we fought, and so they died."

The woman, Thirus, stiffened at this, a thin hiss escaping her lips as she moved to stand at the Skeltir's shoulder. Dipping her head she spoke rapidly in their shared tongue, her tone beseeching and slightly choked.

"*Eta!*" the Skeltir snapped in his dry rasp, cutting her off. Thirus straightened and retreated, head lowered in either shame or concealed fury. "She just offered to trade her life for the chance to kill you," the Skeltir told Vaelin. "The bond between sisters is always a strong one."

"Skeltir Varnko," the Princess said, "you know our mission and we know your price. Perhaps we should proceed to paying it and we can be on our way."

The Skeltir's eyes shifted from Vaelin to Sherin. "The southlanders call you the Grace of Heaven, do they not?"

"Yes," Sherin replied. "Although I'd rather they didn't."

"Why? Do you not enjoy the favour of Heaven? Is your power a lie?"

"My power amounts to knowledge and skill acquired over many years of study and practice. Heaven had nothing to do with it."

A small glimmer of amused satisfaction passed across Varnko's face before his stern mask reasserted itself. Apparently, he had heard what he wanted to hear. "I wish to ensure our bargain is fully understood," he said. "You will cure my son. Once I am satisfied he is returned to health, I will take you to the Mestra-Skeltir."

"That is what we agreed," the Princess said with a polite smile.

"If he is not cured," Varnko went on, gaze still steady on Sherin and paying no heed to the Princess, "your life and the lives of these two are forfeit. I'll allow Thirus to do as she wishes with all three of you."

Sherin's features grew hard as she turned to the Princess. "That is not what we . . ."

"She agrees!" the Princess stated in a bright and casual tone. "And so does her tall friend from across the sea."

Vaelin saw Sherin grit her teeth as the Skeltir raised a questioning eyebrow at her. "I agree to your terms." She sighed, getting to her feet and continuing in a brisk tone Vaelin remembered very well. "Fetch my saddlebags and take me to the boy. From what I've heard of his condition, time is against us."

◆ ◆ ◆

"A bolt in the gut from sixty yards," Varnko said. "Punched through his mail but didn't sink in all that deep. He plucked it out and laughed, even kept it as a token. Then this . . ." The Skeltir trailed off and gestured at the youth lying on the furs. The boy had perhaps fifteen years, though his emaciated condition and hollowed cheeks made him appear simultaneously older and younger. He lay with his eyes half-closed, breathing shallow and ragged. A thin film of sweat covered his body, naked but for the bandage on his stomach.

Sherin crouched and gently removed the bandage, unleashing the sweet, throat-catching stench of corruption. Vaelin thought the boy's injury the most festered wound he had seen on a living soul, a dark irregular circle an inch across, oozing with pus. Purple tendrils of infection radiated from it, snaking across the lad's belly and no doubt deep into his innards. Vaelin knew the Fifth

Order had many remedies that would ward off infection and, if administered swiftly, might save a limb from the bone saw or a wounded brother from the pyre. But he had never seen a soul so riven with it live more than a few days. The fact that this boy had lingered for weeks seemed miraculous.

"Filth on the bolt, presumably," Sherin said, peering close at the wound. "Perhaps some form of poison too."

"Our healers tried packing it with maggots," Varnko said. "Seemed to clear up for a bit, then worsened."

"Maggots work on wounds to the extremities," Sherin said, reaching for one of her saddlebags. "Where the infection can't get too deep. Try them on an injury like this and there's a chance they'll eat their way into his gut. It's fortunate your healers didn't kill him."

She extracted a small thin-bladed knife from the bag along with a number of bottles. "I need more light in here," she said, glancing around the small tent. "Also, a steady supply of freshly boiled water, preferably in copper pots. Plus sheets of gauze, or any fine material to ward off the flies."

"You're going to cut him?" Varnko asked.

"Some of the infected flesh needs to be cut away." Sherin pressed a hand to the boy's feverish forehead and grimaced. "But his chance of survival lies with the curatives I've brought, and it slips further from his grasp with every second I waste talking to you."

◆ ◆ ◆

"You have a name?"

Vaelin looked down at the flask the Skeltir offered him and decided refusing would be impolite. The liquid it held was both surprisingly pleasant and familiar. "Cumbraelin red," Vaelin said, handing it back. "You have expensive tastes."

"So that's where you're from. The Land of Wine, my people call it. Not very original, I know, but they only heard of the place recently. Tell me, is it true it rains there every day?"

"Not every day. Just most."

The Skeltir grunted and drank again, turning to regard the large herd of horses in the corral. Having left Sherin to her ministrations, the Jade Princess had abruptly adopted a demeanour of regal authority and announced she would be taking up residence in Varnko's tent, demanding refreshment and attendants as she strode away, nose held at an imperial angle.

Varnko watched her go and called out instructions to a nearby Stahlhast, the man swiftly mounting up and riding off towards the town. "He'll find a maid amongst the slaves," he said, then frowned and corrected himself. "The artisans, I mean to say. You strike me as a man with a good eye for horses. Come take a look at mine."

Vaelin had to admit the horses were remarkable, all tall at the shoulder and long of leg and neck, mounts suitable for both hunting and war. "See the grey," Varnko said, pointing. "Derka, the pride of my herd. The finest blood runs in his veins. Centuries of breeding to produce the perfect mount."

"An impressive beast," Vaelin agreed, watching the way the other horses veered from the grey's path, long silver mane trailing as he galloped back and forth with the energy of a youth.

"He was to be Lotzin's mount in time." Varnko's gaze darkened as it tracked the stallion. "My son."

"He'll ride your horse," Vaelin assured him. "My friend is very skilled."

"Friend?" Varnko's eyebrows curled in amusement as he drank again. "That what she is? The way she looks at you reminds me of my first wife. Got a scar an inch north of my cock from where she tried to geld me. She did catch me fucking her sister, so I suppose she had cause. Always felt it a bit on the excessive side though." He laughed at Vaelin's evident discomfort and drank again. "Still haven't heard your name, I notice. Any reason for that?"

"Vaelin Al Sorna." He turned and gave a formal bow. "Tower Lord of the Northern Reaches and Humble Servant to Queen Lyrna Al Nieren of the Greater Unified Realm."

"The Fire Queen," Varnko said with a shrug, turning back to the horses. "Heard of her at least." He fell silent, Vaelin sensing a brief hesitancy before he asked his next question. "Why did you come here, Vaelin Al Sorna? I know you rode with the Merchant King's soldiers, but you're no more in thrall to him than you are to me. It was for *her*, wasn't it? The healer." He shook his head and drained the last few drops of wine from his flask, tossing it aside with a sigh. "Came a very long way for a woman who can't stand the sight of you, if you ask me."

"Some debts have to be paid," Vaelin replied. "Regardless of distance, or price."

"That they do." The Skeltir rubbed a hand over his chin, stepping closer. Vaelin took note of the fact that his hand lingered close to his mouth to conceal the shape of his lips as he spoke. "As you said, he's a fine horse," he said, eyes flicking to the grey stallion. "Could carry a man many a mile before dawn."

Vaelin's gaze tracked from Varnko to the array of tents as the sense of being observed increased. This man was supposedly the leader of these people and yet he made efforts to conceal his speech.

"You wish me to leave," Vaelin said, turning his back to the tents. "Out of concern for my well-being, perhaps?"

"No." The Skeltir also turned to face the corral, his words softly spoken. "You killed my kin so I'd happily shit on your bloodied corpse. But I know this for certain: no good can come from you meeting the Mestra-Skeltir. The Stahlhast will suffer for it."

"And how do you know this?"

Varnko shifted in discomfort, fingers stroking his lips in a manner that reminded Vaelin of Nortah when the thirst was upon him. "Suffice to say that I trust the source completely," he said. "Wait for darkness and take the horse. No one will stop you. Leave the women with me and I will honour our bargain. Come the dawn there will be nothing I can do."

His voice had now fallen to a fierce, urgent whisper, Vaelin seeing a glint of desperation in his eyes. It was clear he believed every word he said, and the belief frightened him.

"The Mestra-Skeltir," Vaelin said. "He is the one they call the Darkblade, is he not?"

"The artisans do. And his own Skeld, other Stahlhast who believe his legend."

"And you do not?"

"Some of it, because I've seen it. As for the rest." He let out a snort. "A man cannot be a god. The Unseen are not of this earth and so they deserve our worship. A man who eats, shits, bleeds, and fucks like the rest of us does not."

He turned and stalked away, leaving Vaelin in silent regard of the grey stallion. As if sensing his scrutiny the animal came to a halt, turning his head to meet Vaelin's gaze. Breath streamed from his flared nostrils as his forehooves scraped the ground.

Little older than a colt and the herd is already his, Vaelin thought, seeing how the other horses shied away in anticipation of the beast's ire. *How fierce you must be.*

The grey snorted again and spurred to a sudden gallop, letting out a shrill whinny as he charged. Vaelin stood his ground, continuing to meet the stallion's gaze as he drew ever closer. Dust rose in a thick pall as the animal came to a halt barely a few feet from the rope that formed the edge of the corral. He reared and stamped, teeth bared as he whinnied once more.

Vaelin gave a small laugh as he dipped under the rope and approached the horse at a slow walk, both hands held out to his side. "You remind me of an old friend," he said, the grey betraying a small measure of alarm now, his stamping ceased as he stood, muscles twitching. His eyes grew wide as Vaelin's hand reached out to smooth the hair on his neck. "Are you a biter, I wonder?" Vaelin murmured, watching the grey's mouth open and close reflexively. "I'd wager you are."

The grey's teeth snapped and he wheeled away, hooves pounding the earth as he sped back into the ranks of his fellow horses. *Fast and strong*, Vaelin thought, making his way back to Varnko's tent. *Strong enough to carry two, though riding whilst bound hand and foot won't be comfortable.*

◆ ◆ ◆

"Will he live?"

"The curative seems to be taking hold." Sherin blinked tired eyes and wiped a clean cloth over one of her tiny-bladed knives. "It seems I was right about the poison. A nasty concoction I haven't seen before. Luckily it was similar enough to nightshade to enable me to formulate a counter." She glanced over her shoulder at the sleeping boy behind the veil of silks she had erected around his bed. "Youth is on his side, and he's a strong lad. However, it'll require a few days' observation before I know for sure."

Vaelin stepped closer, ignoring her forbidding frown and lowering his voice to a murmur. "We don't have a few days. It's time we were gone from here."

"I have a patient to care for. And a mission, unless you've forgotten."

"Your part is done. Varnko will take the Princess to meet their man-god. She can sing her song perfectly well without you, or me."

Sherin sighed and met his gaze squarely, speaking in soft but intent tones. "Understand this, Vaelin. I am not leaving her. We began this journey together, and we'll end it together."

Vaelin began to reach for her arm but stopped himself. However, the gesture drew her gaze to the rope he held in his other hand. "Well," she said, eyes narrowing in understanding. "At least you're not going to drug me this time."

"You can hate me if you wish, but I didn't journey all these miles to watch you die."

Her eyes flashed at him. "I already died, years ago when I woke on a ship to find the man I loved had betrayed me. Ahm Lin told me the Alpirans had killed you, as I assume you instructed. I knew it was a lie, of course. I knew you lived. Through all the years it took me to come back to life, I knew you were still breathing, still somewhere on the other side of the world fighting yet another filthy war."

"There were reasons. Something I had to do. Something that needed doing."

"*This* needs doing. I need to be part of it and so, she insists, do you."

Vaelin steeled himself against the implacable resolve in her gaze and hefted the rope. "Please don't make me."

Her eyes, bright with fury, slipped from his to the rope and back again. He knew there was a risk she might scream but was confident he could clamp a hand to her mouth in time, although he fervently hoped he wouldn't have to. Finally, she looked away, taking a deep breath. "Let me gather my things," she muttered, mouth set in a hard line as she began collecting her knives and bottles.

"Be quick." Vaelin glanced at the open tent flap, the Skeltir's warning ringing louder in his mind with every passing second. *Come the dawn there will be nothing I can do.* "I doubt we have lo—"

His words became a hiss as something small but very sharp stabbed into his neck. He whirled, instinctively batting away Sherin's hand, though managing to stop himself from following up with a punch. She stepped back quickly, avoiding his flailing grip, her stern features blurring as a deep, liquid heat spread from his neck through his shoulders and into his chest. Reaching up he felt the long thin needle still embedded in his skin, positioned precisely to find the biggest vein.

"I know," Sherin said as his legs failed him and her face dissolved into darkness. "Hurts, doesn't it?"

CHAPTER TWENTY-ONE

H e seemed taller in my dream, like a giant."

"Oh, I think he's big enough for the task."

"A task I thought we had agreed was unnecessary."

"I recall no such agreement. But then, for me our shared dream was so long ago. Perhaps the details have dimmed with time."

The voices were faint and discordant, as if heard through water. Vaelin attempted to blink and found he couldn't, his eyelids having apparently become much heavier during his involuntary slumber. He could feel his body swaying as the surface he lay on moved, like the deck of a ship suffering particularly choppy seas. However, the faint squeal of a poorly oiled axle made it clear he lay in a cart.

"You saw what I saw. *He* brings ruin . . ."

"And what does your brother bring?"

Vaelin summoned his strength and forced his eyelids open, grunting with the effort. A smear of dull grey light slowly resolved into the dry splinters of aged wood as he blinked his way to consciousness. His hand splayed on the wood, fingers numb at first but flaring with pain as he tried to lever himself up.

"See?" the Princess said. "He's strong. She said he would sleep for another day at least."

Vaelin's arms shook as he raised himself to his knees, staying upright despite the cart's continual judder. The Jade Princess sat opposite him, the small buds of her lips forming a smile of welcome. "My lord," she said in perfect Realm Tongue. "I trust you are well rested."

"Speak in Chu-Shin, if you please."

Vaelin's gaze went to the source of the second voice, finding a woman glancing down at him from the cart's buckboard. She was a few years shy of his own age with sharp features that put him in mind of a fox, as did the reddish brown hair tied back from her face in a series of tightly woven braids.

"I think our enterprise will benefit from shared understanding at all times," she added to the Princess.

"Quite so," the Princess said, slipping back into the Far Western tongue. "I was remiss." She smirked a little at Vaelin as the woman turned away, snapping the reins she held against the rumps of the two dray horses pulling the cart.

Vaelin's hands were unbound but he noted that his sword was nowhere in sight. Resting his back against the side of the cart for a second to gather his strength, he hauled himself up to look over the edge. Sherin rode alongside on her pony, sparing him a brief glance before spurring ahead. Glancing around he saw they were escorted by about fifty Stahlhast. They were garbed much the same as Varnko's people but the subtle differences to the motifs with which they decorated their armour led him to conclude they must hail from a separate Skeld. The passing Steppe was as featureless as ever, giving no clue as to how far they might have travelled.

"Three days," the Princess said in response to his unasked question. "The Grace of Heaven brews a strong tea."

Vaelin's hand went to his neck, feeling a small scab and the tenderness of what was surely a livid bruise but no serious injury. "She always did," he said, inclining his head at the woman driving the cart. "Aren't you going to introduce me?"

"Of course, please forgive my rudeness. I present Luralyn Reyerik, Druhr-Tivarik to the Cova Skeld and sister to the Mestra-Skeltir. Luralyn, this is . . ."

"I know his name," the woman cut in, not turning, and adding in a low whisper, "one of them, at least."

"Mestra-Skeltir," Vaelin repeated. "You are sister to the leader of the Stahlhast?"

The woman replied with only a short nod, keeping her gaze firmly on the way ahead. The set of her shoulders told of a deep aversion to his presence that he might have ascribed to her people's prejudice if he hadn't heard her words to the Princess. *He brings ruin . . .*

A loud snort drew his gaze to the rear of the cart. Derka, the grey stallion, trotted in the cart's tracks, led by a long tether. Seeing Vaelin, his eyes took on a wider cast and he tossed his head in either greeting or challenge. Vaelin suspected it might be both.

"Skeltir Varnko was suitably grateful," the Princess explained. "The boy seemed well on the way to health when we left. The horse is yours now, in body and soul. I sang to him, you see."

"Sang to him?" Vaelin asked.

"Just a small tune to bind you together. It didn't take much. I think he had developed a liking for you already. Varnko was sorry to lose him, but felt honour demanded some form of parting gift."

"I have been wondering," Vaelin said. "How you came to know of the boy's condition, and that his father would be open to your bargain."

"The ways of Heaven are ever mysterious," the Princess said, arching an eyebrow.

"Really?" Vaelin's gaze tracked to Luralyn's rigid back.

"Sherin warned me you always saw more than anyone realised." The Princess laughed with a note of genuine delight before her humour faded and she leaned closer. "It matters not how we came to be here, only that we are."

"And where, exactly, is here?"

"The Great Tor," Luralyn replied, hauling on her reins to bring the cart to a halt. "Heart of the Iron Steppe and home to the Sepulchre of the Unseen."

Vaelin got to his feet, gazing at the vast wedge of stone rising from the plain a mile distant.

"Also," the Stahlhast woman added with a sorrowful note, "where you will most probably meet your end, Thief of Names."

◆ ◆ ◆

Derka allowed himself to be saddled without demur, saving his revenge for when Vaelin put a foot in the saddle whereupon the stallion reared. Vaelin managed to disentangle his foot before the grey wheeled about, but the beast still contrived to catch him with his rump. Vaelin sprawled in the dirt, much to the amusement of the watching Stahlhast.

Swatting dirt from his trews as he got to his feet, he cast a questioning glance at the Princess. "Your song appears weak," he observed.

"It bound him," she said with a shrug. "But it didn't change him."

Vaelin approached Derka with a determined stride. Catching hold of the reins, he pulled the stallion's head around, looking directly into his baleful eye.

"Enough!" Vaelin told him, holding his gaze. Derka snorted and stamped a hoof but didn't rear again when Vaelin mounted up.

"You should have whipped him," Luralyn advised, now mounted on her own horse, a tall white stallion. "Still too much of the colt in him."

"I think I like him as he is," Vaelin replied, running a hand along Derka's neck and causing him to toss his head in irritation.

Luralyn shrugged and kicked her horse into motion, setting off towards the Great Tor at a fast gallop. Sherin and the Jade Princess quickly followed on their ponies whilst the Stahlhast guards closed in around Vaelin.

"*Beskar!*" one of them snarled, jerking his head impatiently.

Vaelin sat still in the saddle, blinking placidly at the man's reddening face. He was a veteran warrior with pale channels running through a thick blond beard, and clearly unused to disobedience from captives. "*Beskar, uhm levrik!*" he said, hand going to the sabre on his belt.

Vaelin remained still, watching the blond man half draw his sabre and then stop. The scars tracing through his beard became paler still as his features darkened with impotent fury.

"So, you have orders," Vaelin said. "No harm comes to the Thief of Names."

He gave a bland smile and spurred Derka into a gallop, the encircling Stahlhast scattering from his path.

Derka proved a fast mount, easily closing the distance to Sherin and the Princess. As they drew nearer to the Great Tor, they passed by an increasing number of encampments. Each was roughly the same size as the one where Skeltir Varnko held sway, but some were much larger. The camps grew into a vast sprawl of tents surrounding a ring of tall free-standing monoliths that formed a circle around the tor. Uncountable Stahlhast were visible amongst the tents, most going about their chores whilst a few stood to watch the foreigners ride past.

A people great in number, Vaelin concluded as his eyes roved the densely populated tents. But he doubted even this many could hope to take the lands of the Merchant Kings, whatever recent triumphs they might have scored.

Luralyn slowed as they neared the circle of monoliths, guiding them through the maze of encampments to the eastern flank of the tor. She reined to a halt before two huge slabs of stone, taller than the others by several yards, and dismounted. A young man stood between the two stones, well-muscled arms crossed and a lopsided grin on his face. Unlike most of the other Stahlhast men Vaelin had seen, he wore no beard, and his features, smooth and youthfully handsome, were free of scars.

The Mestra-Skeltir? Vaelin wondered but quickly discounted the notion when he saw the unconcealed disdain on Luralyn's face as she strode towards the young man. He was also several years her junior.

"Babukir," she said before continuing in Chu-Shin, "what are you doing here?"

"You know I can never resist a celebration, dear sister," he replied, a frown accompanying his grin. "Why are we speaking the pig-language, pray tell?"

"In deference to our guests." Luralyn nodded at the Jade Princess. "And because our brother has ordained it be so."

The young man's gaze settled on the Princess for a time before moving on to Vaelin, whereupon his grin faded. "Can this really be him?" he asked, stepping past his sister to approach Vaelin, arms still crossed, an expression of mock incredulity on his face. "The Thief of Names? Surely not." He shook his head. "I was going to beg my brother for the honour of killing you. Now I think I'll leave it to one of my bastards. The oldest is about five, I think."

Vaelin smiled and nodded before tightening his grip on Derka's reins. The grey's head abruptly jerked to the left, catching the young Stahlhast full in the face. He reeled away, letting out a yell accompanied by a gout of blood from a broken nose.

"Apologies," Vaelin said, reaching forward to scratch behind Derka's ears. "He's young, still somewhat unruly."

Babukir stood regarding him with blood streaming down his face, every inch of him quivering with the desire for immediate and violent revenge. However, he made no move to reach for the sabre at his waist. *No harm to the Thief of Names.* An injunction that apparently applied to all Stahlhast, regardless of blood or rank.

"Where is our brother?" Luralyn asked him, apparently indifferent to his injury.

Babukir's eyes continued to blaze at Vaelin as he reached up to grasp his nose. "In communion," he said, grunting with pain as he reset the bone with a quick shove. He snorted more blood and grinned again. "Feel free to disturb him, if you like."

Vaelin watched Luralyn turn to regard a small grey structure beyond the two stone slabs. It was completely featureless save for a single open doorway. Her gaze lingered on that doorway for some time, fox-like features unreadable.

"Come," she said finally, turning and beckoning to Vaelin and the two women. "It seems we have some time to wait. We might as well do it in comfort."

◆ ◆ ◆

Luralyn's tent was one of only three within the monolithic circle. The other two were large and grand arrangements of hide and canvas, festooned with various banners, some, Vaelin noted, bearing Far Western script. *Trophies from their recent battle,* he concluded, remembering the blackened, corpse-strewn site to the south. Luralyn's tent lacked any banners and was markedly smaller, albeit finely furnished with couches and tables that wouldn't have looked out of place in a Far Western palace.

The Princess immediately arranged herself in a languid pose on one of the couches, waving a hand at the two other people already present in the tent. "I will have tea, thank you." The pair, a man and a woman of Far Western origins, exchanged glances before looking to Luralyn for guidance.

"This is Eresa and Varij," she said. "They are not servants. If you wish tea, you'll find a kettle and leaves in the adjoining tent. Make it yourself."

"She has the Divine Blood," Eresa, the Far Western woman, said. She regarded the Princess with a deep frown that mixed suspicion with a suppressed sense of awe. "I feel it . . ."

"I told you she was powerful," Luralyn interrupted.

"Your brother," Eresa went on, her frown becoming fearful. "He will feel it too . . ."

"As is expected. Stop worrying." Luralyn looked at Vaelin. "We have a distraction for him. The Thief of Names is here after all."

"Why is that so important?" Sherin asked.

"My brother is jealous of his name. And your arrival," she added, turning to Vaelin, "has been long awaited."

"You didn't tell me that," Sherin said to the Jade Princess.

"Two warriors of great renown, both named the Darkblade." The Princess shrugged her slender shoulders. "Did you imagine it was no more than an insignificant coincidence?"

"You said the Stahlhast warlord only has to hear your song for this all to be over."

"I did. And for him to hear it the Thief of Names must also be here."

"You didn't . . ." Sherin trailed off, shooting a guarded look at Vaelin before speaking on. "You didn't say I would be leading him to his death."

"No, I didn't. But I must confess surprise that you care." The Princess got to her feet. "You know, I think I will try to brew some tea. It's been several centuries since my last attempt."

She made a suitably regal exit into the adjoining tent, leaving a thick silence in her wake.

"So," Vaelin said to Luralyn, "it appears you have gone to great lengths to embroil us in a plot against your brother. Is that not sacrilege?"

Eresa let out a small whimper of alarm, reaching out to clasp the hand of the man at her side. He drew her close, cradling her head against his chest and whispering soft words of comfort.

"If I believed him to be a god, then it would be sacrilege," Luralyn said. "Instead, it is a vile betrayal that will haunt my heart for the rest of my days."

From outside there came a sudden uproar, thousands of voices raised as one in a storm of thunderous acclamation.

"What is that?" Sherin asked, obliged to shout over the continuing roar.

"Kehlbrand has completed his communion with the Unseen," Luralyn said. "Now we will have two full days of revels to celebrate our great victory over the southlanders and gird our souls for the conquests to come."

She made for the tent flap, Eresa and Varij close behind. "We are needed to guard the artisans against any overly excited revellers." She paused before leaving, regarding Vaelin and Sherin with grave eyes. "My brother will send for you soon enough. I suggest you use the time to settle any differences. It's an ill thing to meet your end with a bitter heart."

◆ ◆ ◆

"I heard you lost your woman in the war."

They stood outside Luralyn's tent watching the celebrations rage beyond the stone circle. Night had fallen now and the glow of innumerable campfires and torches played over the spectacle of the Stahlhast in the throes of celebration. They cavorted in various states of undress, drank liquor in copious quantities and sang their oddly melodious songs to the beat of drums or skirling pipes. Several brawls had broken out in the last hour, though no blades were bared and Vaelin noticed how men and women who had been assailing each other with balled fists moments before would soon after dance together in happy abandon. Whatever their faults as a people, the Stahlhast were plainly not joyless.

"Stories of the Fire Queen's great crusade fly far and wide," Sherin went on when Vaelin didn't answer. "Though some are so outlandish I afford them scant credit." She paused, her expression displaying more sorrow than resentment as she asked, "Who was she?"

"Her name was Dahrena Al Myrna," he said. "First Counsel to the North Tower, greatly beloved of the Reaches and the Seordah Sil."

"The previous Tower Lord's daughter. I heard a great deal about her when I visited the Reaches. Much was said of kindness."

"Kind she was. Also fierce in battle and wise in counsel. Without her the war may well have been lost." *And she died with my child inside her.* "If it were permitted by the Merchant King, Sho Tsai would be your husband now, would he not?"

"I expect so, although it's a question he's never formally asked." She gave a smile, faint but still rich in the compassion he remembered so well. "It seems time insisted on passing for both of us. I am not the same me, you are not the same you. And, though I wish you had never come here, I am sorry for what you lost."

"And I am sorry for what I did. But I won't lie, Sherin. I would do it again, for so much depended on it. So many lives, including your own. As bad as the Alpiran war was, worse was coming. I needed to be there to meet it."

She looked out at the unconstrained revels beyond the stones. "So many lives stand to be lost here too. These people seem so . . . human now. But the Princess has left me in no doubt as to the evil they will wreak upon the world. That's why I came, Vaelin. I had to, but I didn't know you were ever supposed to be a part of it. Our journey was rich in delays and distractions, taking far longer than it should have. I put it down to her fascination with the world beyond the temple she had escaped after so many years. What a fool I was not to realise. I was bait to lure you here."

She stepped closer, lowering her voice although the continuing din of the Stahlhast celebration would surely prevent their being overheard. "The Princess lied to me. Which means she may be lying about everything. For all we know she's been driven beyond reason by her endless years. This entire enterprise may be just the grand folly of an ancient madwoman." She moved closer still, voice dropping to a whisper. "Slip away. It'll be easy for you amongst all this chaos."

"You know I can't."

"You won't be able to protect me whatever happens. Not here. Please." She reached out to grasp his hand. "Go."

His eyes lingered on her hand for a moment, struck by the warmth of it, familiar even after so many years. Then he caught sight of two figures standing between the great stones. They were both of impressive stature, although one was taller than the other by several inches. They stood motionless for a brief moment, then approached at an unhurried walk. Both were bare chested and bore no weapons, the taller of the two drinking from a large flask, his unruly mass of hair twisting in the stiff breeze that swept through the monoliths. The other man's hands were empty and his hair was tied into a long tail that stretched down his back. His features had the pleasing angularity that seemed typical to the Stahlhast, the sharpness of his nose and chin an echo of Luralyn's features. In contrast, his taller companion had a blunt, brutish aspect, marred by several recent bruises.

They came to a halt a few feet away, the shorter man executing a precise bow of respectful depth. His companion squinted at this with a half-amused grimace and continued to drink from his flask.

"Good evening," the other man said, straightening. "Allow me to introduce myself."

"You are Kehlbrand Reyerik," Vaelin said. "Mestra-Skeltir to the Stahlhast."

"I am indeed. But I'm sure you know I have another name. And you"— the man's smile broadened to reveal a set of perfect white teeth—"have stolen it."

CHAPTER TWENTY-TWO

Vaelin said nothing, his gaze switching between Kehlbrand and the larger man. They both exuded an aura of physical strength and contained violence he had seen in only the most dangerous of people. He also suspected that, despite his repeated gulps from whatever beverage his flask contained, the taller man was very far from drunk.

"This is Obvar," Kehlbrand said, noting Vaelin's scrutiny. "My saddle brother and anointed Champion of the Darkblade."

Obvar inclined his head at Vaelin. "You broke Babukir's nose," he said in heavily accented Chu-Shin. "Why do such an uncivilised thing?"

"I didn't like him much," Vaelin said. "And I've rarely been considered civilised."

The large man's lips betrayed a grin as he drank again, saying something to Kehlbrand in the Stahlhast tongue. Whether it was a witticism or an insult Vaelin couldn't tell, but it failed to bring a smile to Kehlbrand's face, merely a nod of satisfaction.

"You're the healer my sister told me about?" he said, bowing to Sherin. "Come all this way to heal Varnko's boy."

"I am," she said, returning the bow. "Sherin Unsa."

"My people will have work aplenty for you, two mornings from now." Kehlbrand gestured to the revelry beyond the stones. "Our celebrations tend to become more fractious as they go on. Blades will be drawn, blood will be spilled. Those who survive will need their wounds tended and stitched."

"I shall be happy to lend a hand."

This brought another grin to Obvar's lips, though it was more sour than his first and the words he spoke held a tinge of disgust.

"'Only the weak give succour to their enemy,'" Kehlbrand translated. "One of the lessons the priests would teach us. And one of many I've now forbidden to be spoken." He fixed Obvar with a steady eye, Vaelin noting how the big man's jaw clenched tight before he looked away. Kehlbrand's gaze, however, continued to linger.

"Tell me, brother," he said in a low, intent voice. "What do you make of our visitors from across the wide water?"

Obvar's throat swelled as he took a series of hard, deep gulps from his flask, Vaelin noting how he still failed to meet Kehlbrand's eye. *He's terrified of him*, Vaelin realised.

"They look like us," Obvar said, wiping a hand across his mouth as he lowered the flask. "But they are not us. This one has killed many, to be sure." He jerked his head at Vaelin. "But still, they are not of the Hast, and any not of the Hast are weak and worthy only of conquest."

Kehlbrand gave a weary laugh and returned his gaze to Vaelin. "You must forgive my brother, for his mind is so very limited. Mighty though he is, he has in truth seen little of this world, whilst you must have seen a great deal of it. Many lands, many wonders too, I imagine." He extended a hand towards the unremarkable grey building Luralyn had called a Sepulchre. "Would you like to see another?"

Vaelin's eyes lingered on the black rectangle of the Sepulchre's entrance, knowing with certainty that if he still possessed his song, it would be very loud at this moment. "Isn't that a holy place?" he asked. "A place where your gods reside?"

He saw Obvar stiffen at this, perhaps in indignation at some perceived blasphemy, although Vaelin suspected it owed more to his fear of Kehlbrand's reaction. The Mestra-Skeltir, however, merely laughed.

"My people have but one god now," he said, starting towards the Sepulchre. "The healer can stay here and tend to those scratches on Obvar's back. Our womenfolk tend to get overexcited on nights like this."

Vaelin stared hard at Obvar, but if the hulking champion saw any threat in it, he failed to bridle, merely shrugging with a placid smile.

"You have another needle handy, I assume?" Vaelin asked Sherin in Realm Tongue.

"Two, actually," she said, eyeing Obvar, who had returned his attention to his flask.

"Good. Don't hesitate should the need arise."

◆　◆　◆

Kehlbrand paused at the Sepulchre entrance to strike flint to a torch propped against the outer wall. "Not long ago," he commented, extending his arm so the torchlight illuminated the interior, "it would have been death for one not of the Hast to step within the circle, never mind approach the Sepulchre of the Unseen. One of the priests' many stupidities. For a faith to grow, it must be open to all. I have guided exiles, outlaws and artisans here. Even southland captives wise enough to give me their allegiance and join the ranks of the Redeemed. All have left enlightened, filled with devotion to the Darkblade and his sacred mission. How will you leave, I wonder?"

He stepped inside without waiting for an answer. Vaelin followed to find himself confronted by a rectangular hole in the ground and a series of stone steps descending into the absolute gloom below. Kehlbrand started down without pause, his torch soon fading to a small yellow ball and obliging Vaelin to hurry so as not to lose his footing in the dark.

"This place once sat beneath the Great Tor," Kehlbrand told him, voice echoing long in the slanted tunnel. "Revealed after generations of labour as we dug away ever more rock to harvest the ore it held. These stairs are not our creation, however, begging the question of how they came to be constructed under a lump of rock that must have stood here since the world's birthing. Clearly, whoever crafted them expected it to be found one day."

The play of the torch's glow on the walls abruptly disappeared as the stairs came to an end, Kehlbrand leading him into a large chamber. The air was musty and unpleasant, possessing a familiar sting of decay.

"Sorry about the smell," Kehlbrand said. "Never seems to fade. Still . . ." He paused, lowering the torch to reveal a withered corpse on the chamber floor, "this lot stank just as badly in life."

Vaelin judged the body to be perhaps four years since death. It was not completely denuded of flesh, the skin blackened with corruption, and teeth grinning from flaked and ragged lips. The cause of his end was easy to discern in the sundered rib cage and sternum, a single stroke from a long-edged blade delivered with impressive force. Vaelin's gaze settled on one of the bisected ribs, jagged and sharp, sharp enough to pierce flesh. *Kill him and then what?* he asked himself. *Fight my way through tens of thousands of enraged followers with Sherin in tow?*

"I had Obvar give him a quick death, finding myself impressed by his bravery at the end," Kehlbrand said, Vaelin forcing his gaze away from the jagged rib to regard yet more corpses. They lay close to the walls of the chamber in a disordered, often dismembered state that told of a massacre. They had all plainly been left where they fell with no regard to whatever death rituals these people might observe.

"But I didn't feel so kindly disposed to him," Kehlbrand added, the glow of his torch falling upon a skull lying apart from the other bodies, the light drawing a gleam from a patch of revealed bone. "Behold," he said in a tone of mock reverence, "the Mestra-Dirhmar of the Stahlhast, last priest of the Unseen."

He crouched to touch a contemplative finger to the skull, voice becoming thoughtful. "I often wonder why I felt the need to torment him so. Perhaps because he killed my older brother, but that was a necessary act, one Tehlvar and I orchestrated, in fact. Or it could be what he tried to do to my sister, she being so precious to me. But no, I made him watch as I slaughtered the others. I flayed him, I bled him, I visited all manner of humiliations on his flesh and left him a broken old wretch because I just didn't like him. Much like you and Babukir, eh?" He grinned up at Vaelin. "I imagine he's not the first man you disliked. Did you torture any of them to death?"

"No," Vaelin said, "despite often sore temptation."

Kehlbrand gave a soft laugh and rose, gaze still lingering on the head of his murdered priest. "But all the torment wasn't the worst of it. I wanted him to know. I wanted him to see the great lie of his existence. And so I made him touch it. After that, he begged for the blade and I gave it to him."

"Touch what?"

Kehlbrand angled his head, gaze narrowing. "You already know, I think," he said in a very soft voice, extending his arm so the torch's glow illuminated something in the centre of the chamber.

It stood about four feet high with a wide base that narrowed as it rose before widening into a flat top. Vaelin's heart lurched at the sight of it, pulse throbbing his temples as he moved closer. *How foolish we were,* he thought, *to imagine there would be only one.*

As his gaze roved over the stone, he saw it wasn't entirely a twin of the one that had lain beneath the arena in Volar. Whilst its surface was mostly black, there were veins of reddish gold running through it that flared with unnatural brightness when the torchlight caught them.

"You have seen one like this before," Kehlbrand said, moving to stand on the opposite side of the stone. He attempted to conceal it but Vaelin could hear the hungry note in his voice. "If there is another somewhere in the world, I would dearly like to know where."

"There was," Vaelin said. "Pounded into dust and cast into the ocean. It's gone forever."

A thin hiss escaped Kehlbrand's lips as he shook his head. "A terrible waste. A crime in fact."

"No. An act of dire necessity." Vaelin nodded to the stone. "If you truly care about your people, you will do the same with this *thing.*"

"It is thanks to this that my people prosper. With this I have freed thousands from bondage and will soon free thousands more from the greedy yoke of the Merchant Kings."

"Killing how many in the process?"

"Only as many as is necessary. Unless"—Kehlbrand's mouth twitched as his eyes flicked to the priest's skull—"I happen across some I dislike along the way."

The humour slipped from his face and he focused a hard, inquisitive gaze on Vaelin. "You stole my name, Darkblade."

"It was given to me. I didn't choose it and I never wanted it."

"Nevertheless, you carry it with you. The name is part of your legend, and names are important, names have power. Some years ago there was a man, a Skeltir of great renown whom the tale-tellers had dubbed the Blade of Darkness, whereas the priests had named me the Darkblade. You see the problem, I assume?

"I was kind to this man, at first. For I knew I would have use of his battle skill in years to come, and so sent a gift of gold and horses with a polite request that he choose another name. He took my gold and my horses, and sent my messenger back minus his tongue. He was an older man, you see, this Blade of Darkness, his pride swollen by never having tasted defeat.

"I killed his sons so that he might know the taste. One by one in single combat they fell to me, and each time I sent the same request and the same gifts, and each time he took my gifts and the tongues of my messengers. Taking him alive required a war of many weeks and a great deal of blood, but finally I had him, bound and kneeling before me. I made the same request and a promise: 'Choose another name and I will restore you. I will give you horses, I will give you warriors, you will stand high in the Hast and we will be brothers.' He cast his spit at my feet and said, 'If I have not my name, what am I?' Names, you see, are important and I will have no rival for mine."

Vaelin's mind immediately returned to the dead priest's jagged rib. Kehlbrand bore no weapon that he could see, save the torch, but his confidence told of a far from defenceless man. *A fair fight is often the one you lose*, Master Sollis had told him once, and the years since had proven him right time and again.

"That would be foolish," Kehlbrand said. "Bones grow soft as they age."

Vaelin looked again at the stone, a germ of understanding building in his mind.

"There is love between you and the healer," Kehlbrand went on. "An old love, born in youth, but now stained by bitterness and regret. The wounds left by betrayal never truly heal." He frowned in calculation. "You were content to leave her with Obvar because she has the means to defend herself. A drug of some kind?"

"You have touched this," Vaelin realised, eyes still on the stone. "It gave you a blood-song."

"Blood-song? A good name. I just call it the Gift of the Unseen." Kehlbrand's eyes narrowed further in understanding. "You had this once, didn't you? It sings to me a tune of envy, of grief at something lost. How did you lose it?"

"It was taken from me."

"And yet"—Kehlbrand's hand hovered over the stone, trembling slightly—"you once had the means to restore it, and you didn't. Why?"

"I have seen enough to know that whatever these stones are, their power is fickle, the effect of their gifts unpredictable, dangerous. Once they brought down a realm that spanned half the world in peaceful concord, fallen to war and slaughter because one man grew greedy for the gifts the stone would give. Perhaps it would have restored my song. Or perhaps it would have given me the power to heal, or to kill with a touch, or to know every thought in every head. I wouldn't risk it just for the chance I might regain my song."

"What if I were to promise you it would?"

Vaelin's gaze snapped up, finding Kehlbrand regarding him with an expression of honest sincerity. "This is no trick," he said. "Touch the stone and regain your blood-song. Then"—he raised his arms to his sides, open in invitation—"you and I will fight for the name we both bear."

"No trick?" Vaelin gave a humourless smile. "You think I don't know what waits on the other side of this thing? After doing murder under my roof, its servant told me a great deal. Something vast and hungry, and you're intent on helping it eat the world."

"It will save the world, rescue it from greed and disunity, through me. I will give the world a god. A real, living god. One they can see and hear. A god that will make them tremble in fear and weep in gratitude. To do that, all other gods must die and all other faiths must perish. But first, I need more to my legend. For a god's legend to endure he needs an adversary, a terrible villain to overcome. Did you think that vile ghost of your dead friend journeyed all that way to kill a pair of functionaries to the Merchant King just to redeem himself with a final service to you? He called you here on my instruction, tempted you with the healer's peril should she fall into our hands. You are here to play a role, Thief of Names. Your dread Fire Queen has sent her greatest assassin to murder me, for she sees that only I can stand against her tide of conquest. It's a fine tale. Touch the stone and you'll have a chance to write your own."

Vaelin looked at the gleaming veins tracing through the fabric of the stone, feeling a growing certainty that somehow this one was different. A conduit to something far greater in power and malice than the gifts offered by its plainer cousin. Even so, he was appalled to find the urge to touch it was strong. *So many years without it,* he thought. *You would think the ache would have faded by now.* But it was an ache he knew he had to endure, for every instinct warned him that this man, this would-be god, was lying.

"No," he said, looking again at Kehlbrand. "I don't need a song to fight you."

"True," Kehlbrand said. The humour returned to his face and he lowered his arms. "But you would need one to win. Fighting you as you are would be like fighting a child. Hardly grist for a legend. Come." He turned away and started back to the stairs. "I think I should like to hear the song of the Jade Princess. She's come such a long way, it would be rude not to."

CHAPTER TWENTY-THREE

Most of those gathered under the roof of Kehlbrand's palace-sized tent regarded him with faces of rapt awe. He seemed oblivious to it as he moved amongst them, clapping some on the back, offering brief witticisms to others. He reminded Vaelin of an affable noble meeting trusted retainers rather than a man with pretensions to godhood.

The assembly was about sixty strong in all and surprisingly varied. Stahlhast warriors in full armour, some with red eyes and hollow cheeks from the previous night's carousing, stood alongside plainly garbed artisans. Others were dressed in the quilted, fur-lined jackets worn by the folk Vaelin had seen in the border country. Some wore leather armour and clearly hailed from one of the Steppe tribes, although their features and colouring were more akin to the border folk. He saw plenty of mutual detestation in the glowering looks each group showed the other whenever Kehlbrand's gaze was elsewhere, but the awe they shared was disconcerting in its uniformity.

How many have touched the stone? Vaelin wondered as he surveyed the group, recalling Kehlbrand's words from the night before. *And what gifts did they receive, besides blind worship of this man?*

The only exception he could discern was Obvar, who stood amongst a cluster of fellow Stahlhast, his face a dark, masklike contrast to their evident devotion.

"Little colt!" Kehlbrand said, smoothly disentangling himself from the throng to enfold his sister in a warm embrace. Like Vaelin, Sherin and the Jade Princess, she stood apart from the assembly. He saw some of the worshipful congregation regard her with a similar level of reverence, mostly amongst the artisans, but the majority either ignored her or were conscientious in avoiding her gaze.

"Did you miss me?" Kehlbrand asked, easing Luralyn back to sweep a stray lock of hair from her forehead.

"Of course not," she replied, reaching up to clasp his hand, Vaelin finding himself struck by the genuine warmth in her eyes. *She truly loves him.*

"Well, your dream didn't fail us, at least," Kehlbrand said, glancing at Vaelin. "Nor your little stratagem. I'll confess I was skeptical at first, but it got him here. True love in peril, promise of deliverance from an ancient princess. It was all rather perfect, I must say."

Seeing a sudden anger creep over Sherin's face, Vaelin clasped her forearm before she could speak, shaking his head in warning. She lowered her gaze, teeth gritted and jaw clenched.

"Friends, we find ourselves honoured this day!" Kehlbrand said, turning to address the gathering. "For here stands the fabled Blessing of Heaven." He gestured for the Jade Princess to come forward, which she did without particular haste or hesitation, smiling demurely at the assembly.

"Can there be a truer sign of the righteousness of our cause?" Kehlbrand asked his audience, each face now riven with fascination. "The Jade Princess herself has journeyed many miles to bless us with her song."

The Princess raised an eyebrow at this but said nothing as every onlooker sank to one knee, heads bowed low.

"Heaven, as you know, my friends, is a myth," Kehlbrand said. "A vile lie concocted by emperors past and kings present to keep their subjects in bondage. This poor woman, this being of wisdom and power, has spent countless years dwelling in a prison her captors chose to call a temple. Now she stands before you freed by the hand of the Darkblade's sister and we are honoured to hear her voice."

A hiss of whispered affirmation rose from the kneeling throng. Vaelin saw some were weeping, tears leaking from tight-shut eyes as they voiced their devotion. He could hear several different languages amongst the murmuring babble, but the sentiment was clear; they all felt themselves to be present at a moment of huge significance.

The murmuration died away, however, when the Jade Princess let out a small but audible giggle.

"Sorry," she said, covering her mouth as Kehlbrand turned to her. Her cheeks dimpled as she fought down further mirth before coughing and forcing her features into the same demure smile. For the briefest second there was a flicker of bemused annoyance on Kehlbrand's brow before he too laughed.

"What a delight you are," he said. Stepping back, he extended his arms in grand invitation. "And how keenly we await the sound of your treasured voice."

The Princess inclined her head before pausing and turning to Sherin and Vaelin. The smile had changed now, becoming something far more sombre, but the impish light in her eyes remained, although Vaelin saw how they glistened with budding tears.

"Tell my dear friend the young wanderer," she said in perfect Realm Tongue, "that he was right. The time for the old ones has gone. We must make way for the new."

She returned her gaze to the kneeling audience, all faces now upturned in grave expectation. The Jade Princess took a breath and began to sing.

Vaelin thought the first note perhaps the purest and sweetest sound he had ever heard. It was pitched high but not piercing, possessed of a sense of command he knew could only come from the Dark. This was a song no ear could be closed to, as addictive and captivating as the most potent drug. Further notes followed, each as pure and compelling as the first, and each seeming to sink into his mind. The world changed as the song continued, the varied hues of the tent's interior becoming more vibrant whilst edges blurred and extraneous detail slipped away. The faces remained, however, like masks floating in a radiant fog, all the supplicants to the Darkblade wearing the same expression of utter rapture he knew must colour his own.

As the song continued, he realised it had lyrics, but the language was unknown, perhaps unknowable. Ancient words sung by an ancient being, but although he could never know their meaning, the song left no room for doubt as to their intent. Every note sank deeper into his mind, cutting through fears and memories like a surgeon's blade through muscle and sinew. The song was like a hunter, tracking down the events of his life and bringing them forth in vivid, often unwelcome detail, and each was accompanied by a question.

Why? the song asked as it showed him the outlaw hanging in Ultin's Gulch, legs twitching as the effluent of death dripped to the ground.

The law, he answered, then winced as the song's answer overwhelmed his own.

Anger, it told him, summoning Dahrena's dead face, the chill of her forehead against his. The truth cut him, forcing a cry from his lips. He had spent years harrying outlaws and any others who aroused his ire, killing where he could and sparing only where he had to. Not for the queen, not for the Reaches, just to sate his own rage.

The song grew louder and more memories burst forth, collapsing into each other in a fearsome collage of image and feeling. There was joy in this maelstrom, brief flares of light in the red and blackness of it all.

Why? it asked as Reva arose from the storm, that first night in the forest when she had attacked him. He watched their dance again, seeing her blade slice and jab at the air as he refused to do what the Cumbraelin priests so wanted of him.

My song's guidance, he replied. *And she needed me.*

The answer this time was less painful, but just as contradictory: *You were lonely.*

On it went, his every self-deceit revealed and dismissed. Some were obvious, petty self-delusion to guard his pride, others unveiling lies that had become part of him, necessary shields to preserve his sanity. Pain blossomed as they were wrenched away, leaving him reeling in confusion.

Why? it demanded once more, the whirlwind slowing to coalesce into Sherin's face, the drugged, unconscious face from all those years ago when he placed her in Ahm Lin's arms.

Various answers flitted through his head. *I had no choice ... The Ally had to be stopped ... Prophecy ... Duty ... Destiny ...* All lies. The pain diminished as he summoned the resolve to give a truthful answer.

Fear, he told the song of the Jade Princess. *She would never have known peace with me. However far we travelled, whatever corner of the world we hid in, war would always find me, and in time she would hate me for it. I feared her hate.*

The pain dwindled away then, leaving him staggering. The fog had dissipated to reveal the Darkblade's followers, all still captured by the Princess's song. From the stricken look on every face it seemed the effect was universal.

All their lies were being stripped away, leaving only truth. *Truth is the enemy of faith. She didn't come to sing to him. She came to sing to them. A god without worshippers is nothing.*

His gaze snapped to Kehlbrand. Having been driven to his knees by the song's effect, the Mestra-Skeltir now rose unsteadily to his feet. His face was a continually changing mask of black rage and unalloyed fear. Spittle flew from his lips as he gabbled, a hand going to the sabre at his belt.

"No!" Vaelin started forward, the lingering confusion causing him to stumble and fall. He gathered his strength and surged upright, head lowered as he barrelled towards Kehlbrand. But the distance was too great, and the Darkblade's sabre too swift. It came free of the scabbard in a blur of silver that birthed a blossom of red as it sliced open the throat of the Jade Princess, blood arcing from the wound in a crimson torrent as she collapsed.

Kehlbrand stood staring at the spectacle in apparent shock, oblivious to Vaelin's charge. He swung a fist as he closed, aiming for the temple, a stunning blow to send the Stahlhast to the ground whereupon Vaelin would claim his sabre and take great satisfaction from driving it deep into his guts.

His fist juddered to a halt less than an inch from Kehlbrand's temple, Vaelin's arm jarring with shock as if he had punched a solid wall. He began to raise his other arm but found it rigid and unresponsive, his feet no longer able to gain traction on the ground. It was a sensation he had felt before, back in the tunnels beneath Varinshold and again in the arena at Volar when the Ally revealed his gift. This was the binding touch of a Gifted.

"Don't kill him!" Kehlbrand said, raising a hand to the artisan who stepped from the crowd. He was portly and middle-aged, otherwise undistinguished but for the rage that dominated his quivering features. Vaelin's eyes, unconstrained by the binding, roved over the other devotees, finding each face set in the same fury. *Her song wasn't finished,* he realised. *She tried to take their god away, and failed.*

"Such a waste," Kehlbrand went on, gaze lowered to the Princess's body. The mingled rage and fear had gone now and he appeared merely sorrowful, his voice possessed of a reflective tone. "It would all have been so much easier with her at my side, for who amongst the Merchant Realms would question the word of one who makes the Jade Princess his queen? Still." He turned to Vaelin with a half grin. "At least I still have my villain. Obvar!"

The hulking Stahlhast stepped forward, face grave and speaking in a formal tone. "Mestra-Skeltir."

"This"—Kehlbrand waved a hand at Vaelin's frozen form—"wretch evidently seduced the Jade Princess with some evil magic and forced her to attack me. He has come here to strike down the Darkblade in accordance with the wicked design of his dread Fire Queen. He is her champion. You are mine. Will you answer this insult?"

Obvar's gaze settled on Vaelin. Alone amongst the devotees, his features were untouched by rage, his complexion paler than before and eyes possessed of an almost wild cast that made Vaelin ponder what questions the Princess's song had asked of him. Blinking, he turned back to Kehlbrand and sank to one knee. "I will, Mestra-Skeltir."

Kehlbrand inclined his head in solemn gratitude before moving closer to Vaelin. The Stahlhast's fingers stroked his cheek as he whispered, "I told you to touch the stone."

CHAPTER TWENTY-FOUR

In the Unified Realm, duelling was typically a semi-ritualised business. Seconds were appointed and the precise location, time and nature of the contest agreed. Great care was taken to ensure both parties were identically armed and enjoyed no unfair advantages, although negotiations over the precise terms were known to drag on for days or weeks. On occasion such discussions could become so protracted that one or both of the parties either forgot the suffered insult or decided extracting just retribution wasn't worth risking their life after all. The Stahlhast, it transpired, had a much less prolonged and elaborate approach to such things.

"No rules," Luralyn explained. "You get a horse and a blade. So does he. You fight. One dies."

They stood alongside Sherin on the edge of the encampment of the Cova Skeld, watching the flames consume the body of the Jade Princess. Kehlbrand had given permission for a brief ritual observance of her passing before the duel commenced. Sherin advised that cremation was common amongst the people of the Far West and asserted a pronounced distaste for having the Princess's remains buried in this place. So Luralyn had her artisans gather wood into a tall pyre atop which the small, still-youthful body of an ancient woman was placed, doused with oil and set aflame.

"She lied to me," Sherin said, frowning as she watched the rising smoke shroud the silk-covered corpse. "But I find I can't hate her."

"I'm not sure she did lie," Vaelin said, turning to Luralyn. "His followers were supposed to turn on him, I assume, once they heard her song."

Luralyn stared at the flames and nodded. "We shared a True Dream over a year ago. How she found me, I do not know. But she offered hope, a hope that we could end this before it began. A hope that lived in her song."

"True Dream?"

"A . . . vision, you would call it. I prefer to think of them as dreams that hold truth, about the past, or the future. Sometimes . . ." She lowered her gaze, eyes closed. "Sometimes they are nightmares."

"That's why you conspired against your brother. You saw his future."

"Yes, and it was worse than any of my fears made real. Of course, when I awoke the next day he knew something had changed. So I told him of the Jade Princess and her desire to sing for him, a dutiful sister warning her brother of danger. And I told him of the healer, and her connection to you. The Jade Princess would bring her to us and you would follow. The Thief of Names within his grasp. As for her song, 'Let her come,' he said. 'I like music.' Godhood has made him arrogant, made him imagine he can withstand all threats." She closed her eyes, adding in a bitter sigh, "Perhaps he's right."

Vaelin looked around at the sound of an impatient grunt. Their hosts' previous indifference had abruptly transformed into close and careful scrutiny. They were encircled by a dozen Stahlhast guards, the portly artisan with the binding gift also standing close by. The veteran Stahlhast with the scars marring his beard had charge of the escort and stepped forward to heft Vaelin's sword with a raised eyebrow. Kehlbrand evidently had no intention of forsaking the chance to enhance his legend.

"Don't," Sherin said, reaching out to clasp Vaelin's arm. He saw how she forced herself to meet his gaze, shame bright in her eyes. She began to say something else, then faltered.

"The Princess's song was hard to hear," Vaelin said.

"Yes," she whispered. "This is all because of me. My pride, my stupidity, my anger . . ."

She trailed off as Vaelin raised a hand to cup her cheek. "I think I have enough of those for both of us," he said before turning to Luralyn. "All eyes will be on the duel. Take her and ride south for Keshin-Kho. You'll find refuge there."

Luralyn let out a hopeless, mirthless laugh. "There is no refuge to be had now. Not from him."

◆ ◆ ◆

A large patch of ground beyond the encampment had been roped off to provide a site for the duel. It lay in a shallow depression in the otherwise featureless Steppe, providing the mass of spectators a decent view of the proceedings. The veteran Stahlhast led Vaelin through a dense throng of onlookers, the guards forcing a path with ungentle insistence. Judging by the hungry malice on every face, word had clearly spread of Vaelin's supposed perfidy. Many muttered as he passed by, presumably curses, obscenities or wards against his heretical evil. It soon built into an ugly growl, the crowd becoming more agitated, one woman lunging forward to hurl her spit into Vaelin's face. The veteran Stahlhast swiftly drew his sabre and cut her down with a stroke that sundered her from shoulder to breastbone.

He barked something at the suddenly quiet throng, Vaelin hearing the words "Mestra-Skeltir" amongst the angry torrent as the veteran levelled his bloodied blade at them in warning. The other guards all drew their sabres, and the gap between Vaelin and the crowd widened by several yards. Given their numbers he doubted it was fear of the guards that kept them at bay; the Darkblade's word bound them all, and his legend would hardly be enhanced should the villain of the story be torn apart by an angry mob.

Once clear of the onlookers he found Derka waiting, stamping his hooves and tossing his head in irritation. The artisan holding his reins stood as far from the stallion as he could, a fresh bruise on his cheek. He quickly scurried off when Vaelin took the reins.

"Chek," the veteran said, tossing Vaelin's sword onto the ground at his feet. He glanced over his shoulder at the mounted warrior some fifty yards away and spared Vaelin a thin smile before stomping away.

"Eager are you?" Vaelin asked Derka and received a snorted spatter of mucous in response. "Then I'm sorry to disappoint." Vaelin dropped the reins and stepped away. "I always fought better on foot."

He strode forward several paces, drawing his sword and casting away the scabbard. He scanned the crowd until he found Kehlbrand, standing amongst his ardent coterie of disparate followers on a raised platform at the edge of the makeshift arena. Vaelin had expected more speeches, more righteous condemnation of the Fire Queen's assassin. But none came, the Mestra-Skeltir standing with his arms crossed and watching Vaelin with an expression of solemn rectitude.

Coming to a halt, Vaelin rested the sword's blade on his shoulder and stood regarding the mounted warrior in expectant silence. Obvar remained immobile for a time, a frown of consternation drawing his heavy brows together. He wore no armour, only a loose jerkin of black cotton, a large, broad-bladed sabre in hand. With a grunt he kicked his tall stallion into a trot, coming to a halt a dozen yards away.

"You think I won't ride you down?" he asked Vaelin. "You think I have any interest in giving these worthless fucks a show?" He jerked his head at the crowd. "The sooner I kill you the sooner we march for the Merchant Realms, the one thing I wanted all my life . . ."

"What did the song show you?" Vaelin broke in.

Obvar's mouth clamped shut, throat swelling as he choked down fresh words. Vaelin suspected this may have been the first time in his life he had tasted true fear, but not of combat.

"It told me many truths," Vaelin went on. "Truths I didn't want to hear . . ."

"Shut up," Obvar murmured, his bemusement rapidly turning to anger.

"That was her gift," Vaelin said. "She came all this way knowing it would cost her life, just to reveal the truth to your people."

Obvar's fingers flexed on the hilt of his sabre, his horse letting out a shrill whinny of anticipation. "Shut up," he repeated through gritted teeth.

"He is not a god." Vaelin's finger stabbed towards Kehlbrand. "You are not part of a divine mission. All the slaughter you have done is worthless. You are a killer in service to a liar . . ."

"*Shut up!*"

Obvar scraped his heels against his stallion's ribs, spurring him into a gallop. Earth rose in clods as he closed in, leaning low in the saddle, teeth bared and sabre drawn back for an upward sweep. He was a skilled rider and swordsman, but his rage made him incautious, his charge too fast to allow for a change of course as Vaelin dived to the side, rolled to his knees and brought his sword round to slash the stallion's rear leg. The animal managed to veer away a little before the blade connected, so it failed to sever the limb, but still left a wound severe enough to send the beast into a panicked stumble. It whirled, screaming and legs flailing, before collapsing several yards away.

Vaelin sprinted towards the thrashing animal, leaping over it with sword raised high, bringing it down with enough force to tear open Obvar's rib cage.

The sword's star-silver edge sparked and gave forth a near-musical ring as it met Obvar's sabre. He was on one knee, having rolled clear of his struggling mount, staring up at Vaelin through the crossed blades.

"Nice trick," he hissed through gritted teeth.

He moved with a swiftness that should have been beyond a man of his size, jerking Vaelin's sword free of his own, then twisting and lashing out with his boot. It caught Vaelin full in the chest, sending him into the midst of the stallion's still-flailing hooves. He suffered two glancing blows before scrambling clear, dragging air into winded lungs. Obvar leapt over the horse, sabre held level with his head in a two-handed grip. He lunged as his feet met the ground, the sabre aimed at Vaelin's neck. The thrust was strong and Vaelin grunted with the effort of forcing it aside, feeling the sting of the edge as it scraped over his shoulder. He ducked as Obvar whirled, the sabre slicing air, then flicked his sword point at the Stahlhast's eyes. He dodged in time to avoid a blinding wound, though not without suffering a deep cut above his jaw.

Cursing, Obvar jerked to the side, avoiding the follow-up slash Vaelin aimed at his shoulder. Blood sprayed from the face wound as Obvar cursed again, although the rage-fuelled clumsiness Vaelin hoped for proved unfounded when the Stahlhast's obscenities transformed into a laugh.

"Not bad," he said in a wet rasp, Vaelin seeing the gleam of his teeth through the red mess of the wound. "Not bad at all."

Moving with the same unnerving swiftness he launched into a series of attacks, lunging and slashing, sabre and sword ringing as Vaelin fended off the blows. Obvar advanced with every stroke, forcing him back, attempting to close the distance and gain the advantage of his greater bulk. Vaelin continued to back away, parrying every blow and watching for an opening. It came when Obvar fractionally overextended a thrust, allowing Vaelin the split second he needed to open a cut on his forearm.

You can't fell a tree with a single stroke of the axe was Master Sollis's advice from Vaelin's earliest days in the Order. *Skill can beat strength, but only when married to patience.*

Obvar grunted in rage and pain before launching another flurry of attacks, this time advancing too fast. Vaelin allowed him to close the distance, tempting Obvar into making a grab for his sword arm. As the fingers closed on his wrist, Vaelin let the blade fall from his right hand, caught it with his left and slashed it across Obvar's belly.

The Stahlhast danced back with his typical speed but not before suffering a foot-long cut from abdomen to chest. It wasn't deep enough to do serious injury, but still bled profusely. Seeing him wince in pain Vaelin slipped under Obvar's flailing counterstroke and delivered another cut to his upper thigh. He felt the sting of the opposing sabre's tip score his back as he whirled away, a shallow cut only.

He began to circle Obvar, sidestepping his repeated blows and administering wound after wound to his limbs. Soon a circle of spattered blood surrounded the Stahlhast, his head beginning to sag as his strength seeped away.

"Give it up," Vaelin told him, deflecting another thrust, the slowest so far, and replying with a slash to Obvar's bicep. "You don't have to die today, not for him."

The Stahlhast staggered back, red vapour leaking through his face wound with every laboured breath. "Die?" he asked, words slurred by blood although Vaelin heard the bitterness they held. "I already died." He stumbled and slumped to his knees, propping himself up with his sabre. "When I heard that bitch's song."

"What was it?" Vaelin asked, pausing. Despite Obvar's growing weakness, he kept a sword's length between them. He knew this was foolish, that he should finish the Stahlhast now, but the need to know overrode his caution. "What did you hear?"

Obvar gave a weary jerk of his head at Kehlbrand, who was still watching the contest with his unmoving vigilance. "He . . . has no love for me," Obvar said. "He never did. Not when we were boys, not now. I was only ever just . . ." He bared crimson teeth in a smile. "Useful."

There was no warning before he lunged, no change of expression or renewed tension to his form. It was his swiftest attack yet, the sabre sweeping up from the ground as his legs propelled him forward, the blade angled expertly towards Vaelin's waist. He saw in the brief instant before the blade bit home that there was no chance of blocking it, but in his haste Obvar had allowed him a killing blow of his own.

The sword sank into Obvar's gut just below the rib cage at the same instant the sabre cut deep into Vaelin's side. But for the shock caused by the sword thrust, Obvar might have cleaved all the way to Vaelin's spine. Instead, the sabre stalled, having cut deep enough to birth an explosion of agony that sent Vaelin to his knees, sapping all but the last vestige of strength and forcing his hand to slip from the hilt of his sword. But it wasn't deep enough to kill, at least not immediately.

"A god . . ." Obvar said, grunting with the effort of tearing the sabre free of Vaelin's flesh, "is still a god . . . even if he despises you." He stumbled back a few feet, Vaelin's sword still skewered through his midriff. "And," he said, raising the sabre above his head for the killing stroke, "my people need their g—"

Derka's hooves raised a thick pall of dust as he rode Obvar down, concealing the subsequent ugly spectacle of the Stahlhast champion's demise. The stallion reared and stamped amidst the dust for some time, so long in fact that Vaelin found himself lying on his side with darkness encroaching his vision by the time Derka was done. He could feel his life seeping away into the soil of the Steppe, feel the hard-packed earth beneath his cheek as the dust cleared to reveal Obvar's corpse, a broken bundle of sundered flesh and bone.

"Bloody nag," Vaelin muttered as the stallion's head dipped to nudge him. "I expected you sooner."

Derka snorted and nudged him again. With victory achieved he apparently expected them to ride away, but the icy chill creeping into the core of Vaelin's being left no illusions that he would be riding anywhere. Despite his infinite weariness, he felt a burgeoning panic. With death so close he wanted to remember so much, bring so many faces to mind, but time conspired against him and he could only summon one before the shadow claimed him.

PART III

For those of us who spend our days attempting to parse meaning from the myriad enigmas of existence, one essential dilemma will forever remain unresolved. Life, you must understand, is dependent upon death. For new life to flourish, what has gone before must perish. The deer must die so that the tiger may live, the tiger must die so that it does not eat all the deer and its cubs will have prey to hunt. We, in our arrogance, imagine ourselves removed from this cycle. Have we not crafted wonders? Have we not divined the course of the stars and measured the weight of the world entire? Have we not cloaked our-selves in this concordance of trickery and comfort we choose to name "civilisation"? Yes, we have done all these things, and yet in essence we remain no different to the tiger or the deer. For a new concordance, a new civilisation to rise, the old must and will fall. The Emerald Empire may call itself eternal, but it is no more than rice paper drifting ever closer to the flame.

—FINAL STATEMENT OF THE MOST ESTEEMED KUAN-SHI, PHILOSOPHER AND POET, EXECUTED FOR TREASON AND HERETICAL TRANSGRESSION, EMERALD EMPIRE, C. LATE FIRST CENTURY OF THE DIVINE DYNASTY

Luralyn's Account

The Third Question

My people have no calendars, at least none that have ever been written down. The obsession with carefully tracking the passage of days amongst those who live beyond the bounds of the Iron Steppe is seen as baffling and pointless by the Stahlhast. Can they not see the stars in the sky? Can they not feel the chill of a coming winter or the warmth of summer? When the days grow warm it is time to hunt or fight. When frost sparkles on the Steppe it is time to pitch tents for the long camp and guard your food stocks well.

But there is one particular day that must be marked, its arrival being so important. When the star the priests call the Herald of the Unseen appears between the two stones that form the gate to the Great Tor, it is time for the one considered worthy of elevation to Mestra-Skeltir to face the question of the Unseen. And so, as the wind took on the bite of winter and the first icy jewels beaded the grass, we gathered to watch the Herald crest the horizon so that my brother could answer the third and final question.

There was a sense of inevitability to the whole affair, the great swath of encamped Skeld possessed of a celebratory mood that left little room for doubt. Regardless of what rituals the priests might insist on, Kehlbrand was now acknowledged as Mestra-Skeltir by almost all who called themselves Stahlhast. Furthermore, he was the chosen Darkblade of the Unseen, greater than any mere man. All Skeltir followed his word and the artisans considered him a god, or at least godlike in his generous and merciful deeds. I was as lacking in uncertainty as any other that first night; as the songs grew loud and the

Stahlhast fell to their revels, there was no doubt in my mind. Tomorrow my brother would answer the third question, ascend to Mestra-Skeltir and the great southward march would begin. What I didn't know, what the True Dream had never revealed to me, was that the Mestra-Dirhmar also had a question for me.

I spent the evening in the company of my small coterie of Divine Blood, keen to stay clear of the carnality and inevitable violence as the celebrations wore on. There were six in all now, each one plucked from the ranks of the artisans and given a new name to go with the Darkblade's favour. There would be more to come over the course of the following year, Gifted souls found amidst the ruin of town and camp, but they were different from these first six. Being born into the Stahlhast had provided me with siblings aplenty, and more cousins than I can easily remember, but apart from Kehlbrand I had never known the true nature of family, not until I crafted my own.

"Ouch!" Varij cursed, snatching his hand away from Eresa's, much to the hilarity of the others. It was a game they played, holding her hand for as long as possible as she steadily increased the flow of power through her fingertips. Varij, for reasons that were becoming increasingly obvious, always held on the longest.

"You made it worse that time," he accused, flexing his hand and blowing on the flesh.

"A man who can crush stone can't stand a little extra tingle?" Eresa chided in response. She held her hand out to Shuhlan, a chunky former slave from one of the more northerly tors. She had been a scrawny thing when I found her, charming mice into the snares she set without understanding how. In those days she would have happily sworn loyalty to a mange-ridden dog if it meant a full belly, and her appetite had barely abated since.

"No thanks," she said around a mouthful of freshly roasted goat haunch.

"You're no fun." Eresa pouted and extended her hand to me. "Divine One?"

She gave an impish smirk at my glare of annoyance. Much as I insisted on being addressed simply by my name and nothing more, they continually contrived ever more grandiose titles for me.

I was about to rebuke her, yet again, when I saw Juhkar's tall form rise and move towards the tent flap. He was unusual amongst the former slaves in that he had never laboured at the tors. Instead the Skeltir who captured him as a boy had quickly discerned his uncanny facility for tracking game, often without benefit of tracks. So he had been spared labour over the succeeding years but not the lash, as his master was an impatient hunter. Consequently, it hadn't troubled my conscience when Kehlbrand ordered Obvar to cut the fellow's head off for refusing to give up what he termed his best dog.

"Someone's coming," Juhkar said, turning to me with warning in his eyes. "Someone like us."

I felt the familiar sensation of gathering power as the others all swiftly rose from their mats to assume a well-practised formation around me. Eresa and Varij moved to place themselves between my person and the tent flap, whilst Kihlen, the youthfully pretty master of flames, moved to my left. His identically Gifted and equally pretty twin sister, Jihla, fell in on my right and Juhkar moved to guard the rear. Shuhlan, meanwhile, concealed herself in the shadows at the far end of the tent where a massive hunting dog waited for her command. Kehlbrand's ascendancy had done much to quell the fractious nature of the Hast, but occasionally deadly feuding continued and I had never been so secure in my position as to consider myself immune from such things.

The man who stooped to enter the tent was tall, near as tall as Obvar in fact, but considerably thinner. I recognised him as one of the lesser priests, often seen in the background whenever the Mestra-Dirhmar conducted a ritual. Like all those called to the priesthood he had a gaunt aspect, hollow cheeks below sunken eyes and skin prematurely lined with age. I could feel the power in his veins that marked him as one of the Divine Blood, but it was a small thing in comparison to those he faced in this tent, like a song whispered into a gale.

"What do you want?" I said.

His gaze roved over each of us in turn, narrowing momentarily into an unmistakable grimace of purest envy before the usual impassivity returned. "The Mestra-Dirhmar . . ." he began, hesitating before mouthing the next word with distasteful reluctance, ". . . requests your presence."

"What for?"

"His intentions are not for me to know. I serve the Unseen and they speak through him. Will you deny their word?"

The old man is just a liar and you are his deluded slave. I caged the words behind my clenched teeth. The priests had always possessed the power to arouse my anger, an anger I knew would cloud wits I needed this night.

"I'll deny anything that would obstruct my brother's divine path," I said.

The lesser priest's grimace returned for an instant, this time mixed with palpable anger. But, however great his frustration and whatever power lurked in his veins, he must have known he couldn't hope to match the combined gifts of those who shielded me.

"The Mestra-Dirhmar," he continued, tone hard but rich in unspoken meaning, "bid me tell you that he wishes to share a dream with you, a dream of truth."

Did they always know? I wondered, meeting his stare. If so, why did they spare me?

"Where?" I asked, hating the uncertain grate of my voice.

Seeing my fear, the corners of his mouth twitched in what I suspected had been the closest they had come to a smile in decades. "The Sepulchre."

◆ ◆ ◆

I refused to meet him alone, taking Eresa and Varij with me as I trod the stone steps into the darkness. I told the others to wait in the Sepulchre itself, commanding in the southland tongue that they exact a bloody and fiery punishment on the assembled lesser priests should any screams or commotion sound from below.

I knew what lay beneath the Sepulchre, of course, all Stahlhast did, though few ever saw it and when they spoke of it they did so in whispers. I had long assumed it must be a monstrous and wondrous thing, so was faintly disappointed by the sight of a black stone plinth veined in gold rather than the multi-hued and glowing column of my imagination. Still, there was a power to it. I could sense it as I drew closer. It was similar in some ways to the feeling of being in proximity to another of the Divine Blood, but less constant, bringing to mind a hornet's nest in its constant, discordant thrum.

The Mestra-Dirhmar stood with his hands clasped together and head lowered in contemplation of the stone, remaining still and failing to acknowledge my presence until I voiced an impatient cough. Even then it was the space of several heartbeats before he spoke, surprising me with the sorrow that coloured his voice.

"Do you know what you have done?" he asked.

"Served my brother in his divine mission," I replied promptly, suspecting some form of trap in his question.

"His divine mission," he repeated, speaking each word with soft, bitter precision. He fell silent once more, eyes lingering on the stone before slowly raising them to mine. "You saved him, didn't you? The battle with the Wohten all those years ago. Your vision, your dream of truth."

I scanned the chamber as my unease deepened, Eresa and Varij stepping closer to me as they sensed my agitation.

"We're alone here," the Mestra-Dirhmar assured me. "At least," he added, extending a hand so that his palm hovered over the stone, "as alone as one can be in this place."

"How long have you known?" I asked. "About the dreams?"

"Since your first visit to the Great Tor." A tic of amusement showed in his gaze as he watched my hand move instinctively to the tiger's tooth beneath my robe. "You think that kept you from us? A worthless trinket carved with gibberish. No, it was your brother's threats that stayed my hand, coward that I was. And when I realised the depth of my folly, you had already gathered this lot." The priest jerked his chin at Eresa and Varij.

"And yet, with my nature revealed, you never demanded I be brought here. Why?"

"Because it would have given him the excuse he so desperately wants to destroy our order and claim the Sepulchre for himself. That was at least partly his reasoning in having you find these others. Useful as they have been, they were bait in his trap." He angled his head, eyebrow raised into a mocking arc. "Didn't you know?"

"All lies." I voiced a scornful laugh, shaking my head. "That's all you ever had to offer, old man."

I turned to leave but stopped when he spoke on. His voice lacked any particular urgency but the soft sincerity it held, so rich in fear as well as sorrow, was enough to freeze me in place.

"He was supposed to die that day."

I turned back to find him once again contemplating the stone. His features were a mix of weariness and something it took me a moment of puzzled scrutiny to recognise, it being so unexpected. Hate. He hates this thing.

"What do you mean?" I demanded.

"The battle with the Wohten. It had been foreseen. The warrior on the white horse, the warrior you warned him against. Your brother was supposed to die. It was why we hadn't acted against him before, allowing his strength to grow, allowing him to build his alliances. He was useful in that, bringing the Stahlhast together, uniting us. So we let him live, assured in his eventual demise, despite the danger he posed."

He trailed off into a thin sigh, the hate on his face subsiding into shame.

"The arrogance of power is a terrible thing. It blinds you, succours the illusion of control, but there is no controlling this." He flicked a hand at the stone. "As there is now no controlling your brother. Tell me, what do you imagine he will do when he is named Mestra-Skeltir?"

"Fulfil the divine mission ordained by the Unseen centuries ago. Isn't that what you want?"

"Ah, yes. The great march to the Golden Sea. You called me a liar, and you were right. It is the role of priests to lie, and our divine mission is perhaps the greatest of lies. Long ago, when the danger posed by this thing was first realised, our forebears faced a quandary. How to bind a fierce and very pragmatic warrior people to something they could never see? A god whose word they could never hear? With lies, of course, lies that promised everything. One day the great lord of the Stahlhast will arise and lead us to claim the southlands for our own, so that all might know the blessings of the Unseen. And it worked. The mere promise of a divine leader and a glorious future sufficed to keep the Skelds in bondage to the Sepulchre for more than a thousand years. But it was a promise never to be fulfilled, until your brother made it real."

He fixed me with a glare then, hard with judgemental accusation. "You must have known what he would be, or at least suspected. He will soon unleash an ocean of blood, much of it our own. All because you stood in the way of destiny. Why?"

Once again I was tempted to leave, simply walk away and deafen myself to his questions. What right did he have to demand answers? This bitter old man. But I didn't leave. Liar though he was, I had heard enough truth in his words to keep me standing there, facing his judgement.

"Love," I said. "I saved him because I love him."

"Then you are as much his victim as we will be. He has no love for you, for anyone. It is beyond him. Power." He nodded at the stone and I felt the hornet's nest pulse for a second, as if sensing his enmity. "The power that rests in this. That is all he wants. Power we have long sought to contain, for that is the true mission of the Stahlhast. Fierce we were and we became fiercer still, spurred on by generations of priests, for we knew that to secure this thing would require strength, cruelty even. Countless slaves have died to make us great, all to ensure no other hand can lay claim to this."

"The stone is the source of the Divine Blood," I said, a disorientating ache of incomprehension building in my head. Furthermore, a deep, painful nausea was growing in my belly. It occurred to me that the old man intended to inflict harm upon me after all, that he possessed a gift capable of inflicting illness. But the suspicion was banished by another pulse of power from the stone and I knew he wasn't making me sick. It was.

"We dug it from the earth generations gone," I went on, voice thick with rising pain. "Through this has come the guidance of the Unseen . . ."

"Guidance?" His laugh was loud and full of mockery, abruptly silencing my rote recital of dogma. "The Unseen offer no guidance, child. They didn't choose us as the agents of their ascension. They do not bless us any more than a herdsman blesses the beasts he leads to the slaughter pen."

"Liar!" I rasped as the pain in my gut redoubled, causing me to stagger. Varij and Eresa came swiftly to my side, she catching me before I could fall. Varij must have possessed some instinctive understanding of the source of my distress for he crouched in front of me, hand extended towards the stone.

"Stop that!" the Mestra-Dirhmar snapped as I felt Varij begin to summon his gift. The priest's voice possessed such a note of accustomed command that Varij hesitated, though his arm remained raised.

"You might be able to crumble stone, boy," the priest said, "but you won't even scratch this. For countless years many have tried, but it resists all injury." When Varij still failed to lower his arm the priest gave a disgusted snort and shrugged. "Very well," he said, standing back. "Feel free to try, just don't expect to survive the experience. They'll surely appreciate a meal like you."

Varij turned to me, confusion and indecision on his face. I shook my head and he nodded, lowering his arm and assisting Eresa in helping me to my feet. The nausea had lessened a little, allowing me to make a faltering step towards the stone.

"Then what is it?" I demanded of the priest. I recall now just how much I wanted him to be lying, for this all to be yet more deceit. Everything I knew, everything I felt, railed against this old man's words. Kehlbrand has always cherished me, he has given me a family, a mission . . . All my inner protestations slipped away as I looked into the eyes of the Mestra-Dirhmar and knew him to be speaking only truth.

"It is a lock," he told me, "on a very old and rotten door, one your brother intends to break to pieces and unleash what waits behind."

"What . . ." I staggered again as a fresh wave of sickness swept through me. "What waits? What are the Unseen?"

"Endless hunger and depthless malice. We fed them, all these years, we gathered the Divine Blood into the priesthood and we fed them, thinking it would keep them sated. It drains us, bleeds our gifts from us and turns us into these wasted souls you see now. Sometimes I wonder if we were the ones being lied to, a lie we told ourselves. We imagined the Unseen would be satisfied with morsels when, beyond their prison, there was a whole world to eat. Some years ago something changed, their hunger grew. It was as if they had woken from a torpor. However much we fed them it wasn't enough. They always wanted more than we could give, our gifts diminishing with every feeding so that when your brother failed to meet his appointed end, we had not the power to oppose him. More than that, we could feel them reaching out, into the realm where the shadows of lost souls linger, and there they found servants. Somehow, what lurks beyond the door found a way to engineer its release."

As he spoke his voice grew dull, the words still audible but faint, as if heard from far away. My gaze was locked on the stone now, eyes tracking continually over its red-gold veins. The pulses of power were more frequent, beating in time with my heart and birthing an upswell of sickness each time. It was the pain that saved me, cutting through the fog clouding my mind to reveal the sight of my hand, lowering slowly towards the stone.

Gasping, I snatched it back and began to turn away, but the priest, despite his age and the sticklike emaciation of his form, possessed enough strength and swiftness to reach out and snare my wrist. I tried to pull it free but another series of pulses from the stone sent me to my knees, retching in agony.

"Eresa!" I rasped, turning to find both Varij and Eresa standing immobile, faces slack and void of consciousness.

"Withered it may be," the priest said, pulling me closer, breath rank on my face, "but my gift lingers, child. I have just enough left to give them one last meal."

I snatched the dagger from my belt and sought to drive it between the stark bones of his chest, but the sickness made it a feeble attempt. The blade scored his skin down to the ribs before he batted it away with an angry grunt.

"Your gift is great," he said, dragging me towards the stone. "Perhaps great enough to sate them for years."

I fought him as best I could, scratching at his eyes, trying to thrash as his bony arm encircled my waist, but I felt like an infant struggling in the grip of an adult.

"Know that I take no pleasure in this," he said, his hand like a vise on my wrist as he forced it closer to the stone. "But it must be done. It will buy time, send them back to their torpor. We can gather strength to oppose him . . ."

His words were interrupted by a hard wet thud from behind us. Jerking me around, the priest let out a plaintive whimper at the sight that confronted us. The tall lesser priest who had summoned me slid slowly down the rough rock of the chamber wall, entrails spilling from a wound that had sundered him from shoulder to groin. By some whim of chance he was still alive, sunken eyes bright now as he stared at the Mestra-Dirhmar with abject contrition, a dying man begging for forgiveness.

"Best let her go, you old fuck," Obvar said, stepping from the shadows, his outsize sabre dripping blood as he twirled it with casual skill. "It's going to get ugly enough for you as it is. It'll get uglier still if he notices any bruises on his sister."

Behind him more figures resolved from the shadows, Stahlhast of the Cova Skeld dragging priests across the floor, each one bound and gagged. Some wept, some pleaded, but most were silent, kneeling with heads bowed as Kehlbrand strode from the stairwell. The Mestra-Dirhmar's grip slipped away as my brother came fully into the torchlight. The old man staggered back, his features a curious mix of defiance and terror, bony chest heaving as he dragged in one ragged breath after another.

I went quickly to Eresa and Varij, both crouched on their knees and blinking in confusion. Checking their eyes I saw whatever control the priest had exerted gone, though they both remained pale and trembling.

"Before we get started," Kehlbrand said to the Mestra-Dirhmar, "I believe you have a question for me."

The old man's features twitched as he fought to master himself, resolve eventually winning the struggle against fear as he set his jaw and stared back at Kehlbrand in silence.

"Disembowel one of these," Kehlbrand told Obvar, waving a hand at the bound lesser priests. "Doesn't matter which."

"Stop!" the Mestra-Dirhmar said as Obvar hefted his sabre. The priest took a shuddering breath and straightened, speaking to Kehlbrand in the formal tones of ancient ritual. "Kehlbrand Reyerik, called the Darkblade, do you wish to gain the blessing of the Unseen and be named Mestra-Skeltir of the Stahlhast?"

"Mmmmm." Kehlbrand rubbed his chin in mock contemplation that drew a deep-throated chuckle from Obvar. "After due consideration," my brother said, "I believe I do."

"Then touch the stone," the old man said, a sneer creeping into his tone and defiance still shining in his gaze. His finger stabbed at the stone, shrill and desperate triumph in his voice as he spoke on. "You were born to one of the Divine Blood, but you have no gift. There is no power in your veins. You are merely mortal, and throughout all the ages any mortal who touched the stone has received only a swift death. That is the purpose of the third question, the question that, even if one who pretended to lead the Stahlhast had a chance to answer it, ensures there will never be a Mestra-Skeltir."

"You're a fool," I told the priest, rising to my feet and advancing towards him. "You and these others will die here. As far as our people will ever know, my brother answered the third question, for who would ever claim otherwise?"

I allowed myself a laugh at the abject frustration on his face and turned to Kehlbrand. "I'd prefer you make it quick. Have done and let's be gone from here."

He wasn't looking at me, his gaze instead focused on the stone. The faux calculation from moments before was gone now, replaced by deep and grave consideration.

"You can't be thinking it," I said, laying a hand on his arm when he failed to answer, gaze still locked on the stone. "Kehlbrand. You heard what he said . . ."

"Yes." He clasped my hand and smiled before stepping away. "I heard him. Obvar, take my sister and her companions away from this place. I wish to commune with the Unseen alone for a time. Oh, and leave me your knife."

◆ ◆ ◆

So we come at last, honoured reader, to the decisive event that would in time earn me my most famous soubriquet as the Darkblade's Betrayer. Were I a less honest soul I would ascribe my change of heart to Kehlbrand's bloody vengeance upon the priests. It is true that the screams emanating from the Sepulchre were terrible, and prolonged, conjuring all manner of unwelcome conjecture as to my brother's actions below. It is also true that the sight of Kehlbrand when he eventually emerged from the building birthed a chill in my heart that has never truly faded. But it wasn't the blood that slicked his arms *from wrist to shoulder, nor the gore-covered knife he tossed to Obvar that began my journey from sister to traitor, it was my brother's eyes.*

He had always possessed the piercing gaze of one granted both intelligence and insight, not to mention cunning. Consequently, becoming the object of his scrutiny was often an unsettling experience for those not so blessed. But that night it was different. Now there was a knowledge that accompanied the scrutiny, a sense that he already possessed the answer to any question he might ask.

So, when I asked him if he had touched the stone, the reply was no surprise. "Of course I did, little colt." He laughed and drew me into his blood-soaked arms. "And here I stand, hale and whole. It was just another lie from a best forgotten corpse."

"What happened? What did you . . . ?"

I fell silent as he drew back and put a finger to my lips. His smile was as warm as ever, but his knowing gaze also possessed a glint of warning I hadn't seen before. "I entered into communion with the Unseen," he said. "As would be expected of the Mestra-Skeltir. They gave me such gifts, dearest sister. The stone is a source of power—that is what the priests were guarding for so long, festering away in their greed and privilege. Ask of the Unseen with an honest heart and they shall reward you."

I wanted to believe him as much as I had wanted to disbelieve the Mestra-Dirhmar, but found I couldn't. It was there in his eyes when he released me and turned to Obvar, the sense of knowing, birthing a certainty in me that my brother had emerged from the Sepulchre changed, and it was a change in the core of his being for, in addition to his altered gaze, there was the power I now sensed in him. Kehlbrand had received a gift.

"We'll take a tour of the camp," he told Obvar. "The priests were never loved but there are still those who harbour unwise loyalties to the old ways."

"True," Obvar conceded. "But, after this they're hardly likely to say as much out loud."

Kehlbrand started towards the gate with a purposeful stride, his tone one of brisk cheerfulness. "They won't have to. Little colt, I'll find you in the morning. See if you can come up with a ceremony of sorts to mark the occasion. Some form of ritual will be expected." He turned back for a moment, arms wide and voice exultant. "For tomorrow the great march to the Golden Sea begins!"

◆ ◆ ◆

The commencement of the great march, in truth, proved something of a misnomer for what was in effect a series of campaigns and alliances conducted over the course of the next two years. Although we had achieved dominance over the Iron Steppe, the Stahlhast were not the only people to ride across its vastness. Many tribes to the south and east had been driven off to face annihilation in the southlands generations before, but those that remained were still substantial in number even if they couldn't hope to match us in battle. Kehlbrand, however, desired no battle with other Steppe folk, considering them far too valuable as warriors.

Therefore, he was swift in rejecting Obvar's suggestion that the first act of the great march should be to destroy the Tuhla, a confederation of tribes who ranged across the western Steppe as far as the coastal mountains.

"The Skin Riders?" Obvar said in disdain when Kehlbrand gave voice to his intentions, an appellation referring to the Tuhla custom of cladding themselves in armour of hardened oxhide.

"I have a sense," Kehlbrand replied, "there is one amongst their elder chiefs with a keen eye for opportunity, and a deep hatred of his rivals. After all, they look to the Merchant Realms with just as much envy as we do."

He refused to engage in the traditional practice of sending emissaries on the grounds that "they'll just come back tied to a saddle and headless. I'll go myself." And so he went, alone with no escort into the heart of the Tuhla dominion despite voluble protestations from both Obvar and myself. The exact details of his journey and negotiations remain unknown to me, but I have little doubt his newly acquired gift was the principal reason why he returned three months later with thirty thousand Tuhla warriors at his back.

Their chief was a wiry man of middling years named Heralka, which he insisted meant Grey Falcon in the Tuhla tongue, although I heard his warriors use it as an insult on numerous occasions. He rode with four part-rotted heads tied to his saddle and a permanent smirk of triumph on his lean features. The heads had belonged to his rivals for dominance over the Tuhla confederation, slain as a result of some convoluted scheme of subterfuge and betrayal I never fully understood, except to note that Kehlbrand was key in orchestrating it. Despite his evident triumph, as the subsequent campaigns unfolded, I often witnessed Heralka sitting alone at a campfire, the four heads arranged around it in a circle as he engaged them in animated, sometimes jocular conversation.

As the night wore on, and his consumption of ale grew, his humour would eventually subside into tears and shouted accusations before he finally passed out.

At Kehlbrand's behest, and with Heralka's permission, I sought out others with the Divine Blood amongst the ranks of the Tuhla, finding two. One was a foul-tempered old man with a facility for summoning rain, the other a sturdy woman of forty summers who could bend and mould metal with her bare hands as easily as if it were clay. Both agreed to join my coterie only at Heralka's insistence and accepted my authority with a stern resentment that never faded. Consequently, I didn't name them, nor any of the others discovered in the aftermath of our first victories. I had my family now, and it would grow no larger.

With the Tuhla alliance firmly secured, Kehlbrand launched the first of his campaigns into the border country, breaking with tradition by choosing to fight in the wet season. This was a deliberately restricted series of raids against trading caravans and small-scale harassment of Merchant Realm soldiery, designed to gauge the strength of the enemy whilst confusing them as to our intentions.

Having destroyed our foe's most northerly stronghold years before, the Stahlhast now enjoyed unfettered reign over the southern reaches of the Iron Steppe, enabling us to raid almost at will. The varied garrisons of the Merchant Kings responded with increased patrols and some punitive expeditions consisting of a few thousand mounted soldiers. These were left alone at Kehlbrand's command and would spend days or weeks riding across an empty Steppe before lack of supplies forced them to return to their strongholds, whereupon the raids would resume at a yet greater tempo.

When the last rains faded and the Steppe grew dry and hot, Kehlbrand, having gained as complete a picture of the enemy's disposition as he could hope for, chose the fortress town of Leshun-Kho as the target for his first full-scale assault. The assembled host was ordered to encamp beyond range of the garrison's spyglasses whilst Varij, in company with Obvar, stole forth under cover of darkness to approach the town's high walls.

Varij had made careful study of various captured architectural texts and knew just the right places to employ his gift so as not to cause an immediate collapse. Instead, he weakened the foundations in three different places, ensuring they would crumble under their own weight within hours. Consequently, when the town garrison saw the approaching host come the dawn, they rushed to man the battlements in time to watch the breaches appear in their walls. Attempts to improvise barricades met with little success as the Stahlhast and Tuhla streamed through the gaps, cutting down the desperate defenders and galloping on into the streets beyond. The town fell within two hours, despite some suicidally courageous stands by the Merchant King's soldiers.

It was the fall of Leshun-Kho that brought the next step on my traitor's journey. Troubled though I was by the changes in my brother, I did not yet fully understand just how profound his transformation had been. Thinking back on my tour of the conquered town, I wonder now at my own indifference to the destruction and suffering all around. Kehlbrand had forbidden the customary rapine and wanton murder that accompanied the fall of a settlement, but still the slaughter of both soldiers and townsfolk had been considerable. The Tuhla had been particularly savage, this being their first opportunity for many years to fully indulge their love of looting, displaying no hesitation in cutting down any householder who dared to protest the theft of their valuables. So, although most of the population survived the fall of their town, its corpse-strewn, blood-streaked avenues still made for a pitiful sight.

"Mercy is weakness, compassion is cowardice," I heard Eresa mutter continually as we passed by successive scenes of tragedy. A young widow sobbing over the corpse of her gutted husband whilst her two children stood by in numb, wide-eyed shock. A brawny man crouched in the shadow of a smithy, face set in a stoic mask against his pain as he wrapped a bandage around the stump of his left hand. A well-dressed woman of striking beauty stood by a fountain, completely unharmed but screaming at the top of her lungs. She uttered no words that I could discern, just repeating shrieks of desolate grief.

"Mercy is weakness . . ." Eresa murmured on, turning away from the screaming woman.

"Stop that," I snapped. "It was the priests' creed. We no longer have need of it."

Attempts to quiet the woman proved fruitless so we left her to her screams and moved on, finding a massacre at the turn of the next corner. The Tuhla had herded the remanants of the city's garrison into their own parade ground, roping them together in a long line. Each man was dragged forward in turn to be beheaded, his bonds cut and the body pulled aside before the next in line was forced to kneel at the feet of a tulwar-wielding warrior of impressive stature. As was their custom, the Tuhla were making sport with the heads, using pincers to pluck out teeth to craft the trophy necklaces they cherished. The still-dripping, slack-jawed heads were then impaled on spears that would be arranged in a circle around their camp for the victory feast that night.

I was struck by the dumb obedience of these doomed souls, the line shuffling forward in dull-eyed, stooped servility, their faces sagging in utter exhaustion rather than fear. As my eyes traversed the line, I straightened in surprise at seeing a number of civilians amongst the ranks, older men in robes rather than uniforms, some women and youths too. Unlike the soldiers, most were far from compliant, weeping out entreaties to their indifferent captors or assailing them with curses. Others were more stoic; one older, bearded man in a plain brown robe in particular caught my eye in the way he stepped forward in straight-backed, expressionless rectitude, somehow maintaining a dignified air even as he knelt beneath the tulwar's blade.

"Scholars and their students mostly," a Tuhla warrior explained in answer to my query. It was common for captured soldiery to face execution in the aftermath of victory, but the variety of victims here was unusual. "The Darkblade's order," he added, grunting as he used iron tongs to lever a tooth loose from a recently severed head.

Scholars and their students, I repeated inwardly, finding it easy to discern Kehlbrand's reasoning. Those with knowledge and wisdom are not so easily swayed by the Darkblade.

We pressed on, traversing more horrors until we came to the broad square where the Temple of Heaven resided. I was surprised to find it unscathed, the central three-storey building of slanted roofs unmarked by fire or arrow, the surrounding park of shrines and statuary intact and almost serene in the smoke drifting from the streets. But, whilst the temple itself had been spared, I discovered as I ventured inside that its inhabitants had not.

The monks lay around the largest shrine in a jumble of bloody faces and limbs, the blood stark against their pale robes of grey and white. An exact count of the dead was impossible, but it appeared that the entire order of this temple had perished, save two.

The old monk stood facing the shrine, head bowed and lips moving as he recited his cantos to Heaven, hands clasped together and a string of black beads entwined about his wrists. He paid no heed at all to my brother, who stood nearby, nor to the youthful monk who knelt to his left. Obvar stood behind the boy, a meaty hand under his chin and a knife pressed to his throat.

"One left," Kehlbrand told the old monk, then gave an amused, slightly exasperated snort when he received no response. The monk's chanting continued uninterrupted, his bearing never wavering.

"I know this is all mummery," Kehlbrand said. He moved closer, speaking softly into the old man's ear. "I feel your fear, your hatred, your despair. There is no serenity in you. And this"—he cast a hand at the shrine—"is just old stone carved into meaningless abstraction. Heaven is a lie, and I need you to say it."

No response, just the same unchanging pose and murmured prayers.

"As you wish." Kehlbrand nodded at Obvar, who promptly opened the young monk's throat with a swift flick of his knife.

Much as I would like to nourish any admiration you may harbour towards me, honoured reader, I will offer no lies as to my actions at that moment. I did not call out to stay Obvar's hand. Nor did I rush to my brother, eyes streaming tears and heart riven, demanding answers and cursing him for his cruelty. No. I simply stood and watched as Obvar cut the boy's throat whilst Kehlbrand drew his sabre and hacked the old monk's head from his shoulders. I didn't need to ask why, for in that moment I knew. Kehlbrand was no longer playing the role of a god. Now he was a god, a living god who would tolerate no worship of any other. He had become the Darkblade, and so was no longer my brother.

◆ ◆ ◆

The monks were not the only servants of Heaven to die that day. Nuns from the nearby convent also met the same fate, as did any townsfolk who refused to renounce what was now termed "the great lie." When the killing was done, Kehlbrand ordered the Tuhla to leave the town and set the artisans to work cleaning up the mess and tending to the wounded. "The Darkblade does not come as a conqueror," they would say as they repaired roofs and stitched cuts. "He comes as a redeemer. He comes to break your chains. No longer will you suffer under the greed of the Merchant King."

Perhaps as a consequence of the death toll, fully one-fifth of the town's population by my reckoning, I recruited only one soul with the Divine Blood in Leshun-Kho. Having reported a futile search to Kehlbrand, he suggested I try the magistrate's dungeon. I found her chained in a cell, clad in rags and covered in dirt that failed to conceal her beauty. The gaoler, somehow spared the slaughter that had claimed the lives of the other civic servants, called the woman "the vilest of witches," and refused to go near her even when threatened with execution.

As I approached the bars the woman slowly raised her dirt-covered face, blinking eyes that were both rich in understanding and bright with madness. *You think your brother is not truly a god,* her voice said in my mind, causing me to stagger back in alarm. The woman rose and approached the bars, standing expectantly at the lock and smiling as she effortlessly pushed another thought into my head. *You are wrong.*

I never discovered her true origins, though she told many tales of noble birth and exile due to her gift. These stories changed on a whim; one day she would be the daughter of a general, the next a merchant. Her mother was a famed courtesan to the Merchant King of the Enlightened Kingdom or a warrior maiden from the Opal Isles. These cannot be considered lies, for I suspect she believed them as they escaped her lips, but every story she told would inevitably trail off into confused mumbling and be forgotten soon after. Consequently, her true name would be lost to the ages, but Kehlbrand named her Dishona, which means Grass Snake in the older tongue. She never seemed to see it as an insult, however, for she hung on my brother's every word with all the devotion of a newly whelped pup to its mother. I believe Dishona was the first to worship the Darkblade out of love rather than fear.

"She's mad," I told him some days later. We had ridden south with a small escort, Kehlbrand being keen to scout the approaches to the hill country that marked the borderlands. "And her gift is . . . extremely unnerving."

"But she uses it only sparingly, you notice?" he replied. "Her mind may be broken but some measure of caution remains, not to mention cunning. All useful traits wouldn't you say?"

We reined to a halt atop a hillock that afforded a view of a broad winding river that traced through plain and hill to a misted, jagged cone on the horizon.

"Keshin-Kho," Kehlbrand said. "The key to unlocking the Venerable Kingdom and all that lies beyond."

"Our next target?" I asked, trying to quell the roiling unease the notion provoked in me. Kehlbrand, however, either failed to sense it or thought it of little account.

"We don't have the strength yet," he said. "Other towns along the border offer easier pickings, not to mention fresh adherents."

"They have to be alive to worship you."

"And they will remain so, for the most part. For our mission to succeed, dearest sister, I require an army of believers, not mere soldiers, an army of those redeemed in the sight of the Darkblade."

But for that maddening knowledge in his gaze, I would have thought this the old Kehlbrand, letting the godly mask slip to share a confidence with the only soul he could truly trust. This is the mask now, I realised, matching his sardonic grin with a forced smile.

"Did you know," Kehlbrand went on, fixing his gaze on the distant city, "that our agents tell me the governor of Keshin-Kho has two principal traits, great ambition and desperate loneliness. I believe, with Dishona's help, we can unburden him of both."

◆ ◆ ◆

That night, for the first time since childhood, I wept. I had pitched my tent apart from my Gifted family, telling them I needed to be alone. They assumed I intended to delve into the True Dream, but instead I felt an overwhelming need to surrender to my sorrow, at least for just one night. The tears fell freely and I choked my sobs with the wolf-pelt hem of my cloak, fearing they might draw Kehlbrand's attention.

Does he know? I asked myself over and over. Does he know that I see him, see what the others do not? It seemed incredible that he had failed to sense my despair, which raised the question of why he hadn't sent me away, or . . . killed me.

He will never do that. I knew this with as much certainty as I knew Kehlbrand was no longer my brother. Whatever changes had been wrought upon him when he touched the stone, the ability to murder his sister was not amongst them. The kernel of our love remained whole, but would it survive all that awaited us?

Eventually the tears faded and I lay on my mats, exhausted and mind churning endless unanswerable questions. Usually the black veil will descend only when my mind is at its calmest, but that night it fell when it had reached the pinnacle of despair. The world disappeared and the True Dream unfolded, my skin prickling with the unfamiliar sensation of a chill breeze accompanied by warm sunlight. I blinked and immediately swayed on my feet, stomach lurching at the sight confronting me.

Mountains, so many, so tall. A lifetime on the Iron Steppe had provided scant familiarity with high places, although I had glimpsed the western coastal peaks from a distance. But never had I seen mountains so close, nor from above.

Looking down, my stomach lurched with greater urgency, summoning a dizziness that threatened to tip me over.

"Careful," a soft, pleasant voice advised, small but firm hands grasping my arms until I steadied. I found myself confronted by a diminutive woman with as perfectly fashioned a face as I ever expected to see. She wore fine robes of bright, intricately embroidered silks, her hair arranged in an elegant but complex display of combs and pins.

"Thank you for coming," she said. "I thought it was time we talked."

"Talked about what?" I grimaced in confusion, my gaze flicking from her face to the mountains, then the balcony on which we stood, clearly part of some far larger structure. "Who are you?"

"My mother gave me a name a very long time ago," she said. "But it will have no meaning now. These days they call me the Jade Princess. And we have a great many things to talk about. Principally your brother, and a man I believe he refers to as the Thief of Names."

CHAPTER TWENTY-FIVE

D ying, Vaelin knew, was not akin to falling into a gentle slumber. The onset of death inevitably summons pain and terror, stripping away the self-deceits of courage and resolve to leave only the instinct of survival, the need to clutch to life.

This was easier the last time, he concluded as a fresh wave of agony swept through him. His vision was an alternating haze of shifting black clouds parting occasionally to reveal barely comprehensible glimpses of the living world. A blue expanse of sky, speckled in cloud. The sparse grass of the Steppe as he felt himself being lifted and carried. Then more drifting clouds, more pain. Time stretched and contracted in concert with the various agonies that wracked him, each respite a brief precious moment until the long hours of pain returned.

He could hear voices through the fog that enveloped him, speaking in Chu-Shin, which his distressed mind lacked the ability to translate. But he could hear the conflict in those voices, one rich in caution, the other in implacable purpose. It was the purposeful voice he recognised, along with the face that swam into view when the clouds parted one last time, the same face he had called to mind after Obvar's cut left him bleeding his life away.

Sherin didn't say anything. Nor did she offer a smile of reassurance. Her expression was one of grim determination, diminished only slightly by the glimmer of fear he saw in her eyes. Then the clouds closed in again, leaving only the pain until that too faded to a small angry flame.

◆ ◆ ◆

He awoke to Derka's breath on his face, a hot and unpleasant blast that left him coughing. For a second he wondered why his vision was full of a slowly passing tract of earth and grass before realising he lay across Derka's back, secured to the saddle by ropes about his wrists and ankles. The stallion came to a halt, continuing to twist his head round to nibble at Vaelin's face, either in an expression of affection or, more likely, because he somehow divined how annoying it was.

"Get off, you bloody nag," Vaelin groaned, moving his face clear of the stallion's muzzle.

"Hold, he's awake!"

Vaelin craned his neck to see Sherin cantering towards him on her pony. She dismounted and quickly moved to sever his bonds with a small knife, Vaelin sliding clear of the saddle. To his surprise he didn't stagger as his boots met the ground, his legs apparently free of the expected weakness. Also, he felt no pain. If anything he found himself possessed of a refreshing vigour. He laughed at the feel of the Steppe wind on his skin, and raised his face to smile as the sunlight bathed it. His smile faded, however, when he lowered his head and caught sight of Sherin's guarded gaze. There was a sunken look to her eyes that hadn't been there before, a tension and paleness in her features that put him in mind of one recovered from a recent illness.

His hands went to his shirt as a suspicion began to build in his mind, drawing the fabric aside to reveal Obvar's cut, finding only a pale line in otherwise unmarked flesh. *Weaver's gift,* he recalled, thinking of the healing he had received all those years ago in the Fallen City. Weaver had been the most powerful Gifted he had ever met, even before draining the power from the Ally and ensuring all the sacrifice of the Liberation War hadn't been in vain. But Weaver was not here, nor did Vaelin ever expect to see him again.

"What did you do?" he demanded of Sherin.

Her pale features formed a brief, tremulous smile. "What I had to."

"We can't linger."

Vaelin's gaze snapped to Luralyn, mounted on a white horse. Behind her rode the man and woman he had met on first arriving at the tor along with four others all clad in the garb of the artisans. Glancing around he saw only the empty Steppe with no sign of any Stahlhast.

"Here."

Vaelin caught his sword as Luralyn tossed it to him, strapping it across his back. "How?" he pressed Sherin, who just shook her head and hurried back to her pony.

"My brother will have a thousand scouts ranging in every direction," Luralyn said. "We have no time."

She gathered her reins, preparing to kick her horse into a gallop, but paused as Vaelin reached out to catch hold of the bridle. "I must know," he said. "How did she do this?"

Luralyn looked at Sherin, now climbing stiffly onto the back of her pony. Luralyn's face was stern but Vaelin saw the shame in it. "She touched the stone," she said.

Tugging her reins she jerked the bridle loose from his grip. "We must ride." Spurring her horse forward she galloped off towards the west, her companions close behind.

◆ ◆ ◆

Luralyn allowed no rest, only short intervals every few hours during which the horses were walked. They rode into the evening and through the night, finally stopping at noon the following day when it became plain some of the horses were close to collapse, as were most of their riders. Luralyn bore scant signs of fatigue but her companions all slumped from their mounts to stumble into near-instant slumber.

"The advantage of being born to the saddle," she said, dismounting alongside Vaelin. "Stahlhast will sleep mounted if the need arises."

Vaelin's gaze was focused on Sherin. Having lagged behind for several miles, she brought her pony to a halt a dozen feet away and climbed slowly from its back. "Don't!" Luralyn said when Sherin unfastened a bundle of sticks from her pack and began to build a fire. "The smoke will be seen for miles."

"Your brother's gift has already told him where we are," Vaelin said.

"But not his scouts," she returned, casting a wary glance at the horizon.

"Assuming he won't come himself."

A spasm of worry passed over her features. "That's certainly a possibility. But still, I'd prefer not to take the risk."

Vaelin took a blanket from his own pack and walked to where Sherin sat on the ground, settling it on her shoulders. She gave a listless nod of thanks but said nothing.

"You touched it," he said. "That was not wise."

"She tried to stop me." Sherin glanced at Luralyn, now unfurling her bedroll on the ground. "But the Princess told me it would be this way. After all her scheming I had hoped it might be another lie, but as you were . . . dying, I saw it must have been part of her design all along. So I had Luralyn take me to the stone and I touched it. I needed to. As the Princess needed to sing her song and you needed to fight that animal."

"I lost," Vaelin pointed out. He wanted to reach out and clasp her hand but restrained himself. Even given what she had risked to save him, he still doubted her current regard would allow for such intimacy. "What concerns me now is what *you* lost," he said. "Gifts always exact a price."

She raised both hands, turning them and flexing the fingers. "Pain, I suppose. Healing you hurt a great deal and it was not simply a matter of laying my hands upon the wound and watching it mend itself. Your flesh needed to be remade, skin, muscle, nerves and veins all woven back together. Without my knowledge I doubt I could have managed it. It was like I was feeling it as I healed it, like the wound was part of me. It left me . . . drained."

"I'm sorry. I would never have wished . . ."

She waved him to silence, shaking her head. "The healing wasn't the worst of it. When I touched the stone, it . . . took me." Her face clouded in confused remembrance. "It was like being drawn through a door, dragged, in fact. Taken to another place, a place where all is chaos. Like a storm made of screams, each one a different voice. I thought it would drive me mad, but then it changed, found form. I saw . . ."

She fell silent, closing her eyes as a shudder ran through her. Vaelin made no effort to prompt her, finding he feared what she might say next. "Once, years ago when I journeyed to the western coast," she said, eyes still closed, "I had the luck to glimpse a tiger. I thought it the most beautiful creature I would ever see. White fur striped in black, eyes like opals. We stared at each other for a time, then it bared its teeth at me and bounded off into the forest, and I never forgot it. That's what I saw, Vaelin. All the swirling chaos and fury of that place formed itself into that tiger and that forest. I believe whatever lurks there plucked it from my head and made it real. For it was real. That place beyond the stone is as real as anything in this world.

"It came for me, not snarling, but sniffing, tasting the scent of my terror and wonder. I could feel its hunger like a bottomless well, and when I dared to look into its eyes I saw understanding there. It knew what I was, it knew what

I wanted. And it had no desire to give it to me, it just wanted to sate the empti-ness inside it. Then . . ." A baffled tone crept into her voice, along with the faintest note of amusement. "It seemed to smell something it didn't like. Snarl-ing and rearing back. I felt hate along with its hunger then, and fear. Somehow, by impossible chance, I had actually made it afraid."

Sherin opened her eyes, blinking tears that she quickly wiped away. "Then it was gone, the forest, the tiger all vanished in a heartbeat and I was back in the Sepulchre. Luralyn told me only a few seconds had passed. I—" She looked at her hands again. "I could feel it, the change in me. It was like a bright, burning flame, and I knew what I could do, what I had to do."

"Did you bleed?" he asked, noting again the pallor of her skin.

"Some," she replied with a note of irritation. "Enough to leave me in this irksome state. Don't worry, the body will recover from loss of blood in time."

"Your gift is dangerous. Not just in the price it exacts, but in the passions it stirs in others. You must be cautious in how you use it . . ."

"Thank you, my lord." A measure of the familiar animus returned as she shot him a warning glare. "But this gift is mine, and I will decide how best to employ it."

He quelled the compulsion to argue, but not without difficulty. Her com-passion worried him. How could one such as her resist using this gift, regard-less of what hazards it entailed?

"I offer only guidance," he said, tone as gentle as he could make it. "For most of my life I bore a gift. I would not have you make my mistakes. Many and grievous as they were."

She looked away, pulling the blanket more tightly around her shoulders. "I need to sleep."

Vaelin watched her settle onto her side, back turned to him, then rose and moved to Derka. He removed the bridle to allow the stallion to partake of the grass but left his saddle in place, suspecting they might need to ride on quickly. He felt only a faint fatigue after so many hours' hard riding so stood guard whilst the others slept. He knew this invigorated state must be an effect of Sherin's healing, making him wonder how long it would last. All the aches that had begun to beset him over the course of the past couple of years were gone now and, had he a mirror, he fancied he might see fewer lines around his eyes.

"Youth is not appreciated by the young," he told Derka, scratching his nose as he munched a mouthful of grass. The stallion gave an indifferent nicker and lowered his head to the ground.

◆ ◆ ◆

They rode on come nightfall, Luralyn maintaining an unerringly westward course. "I assume you have some destination in mind?" he asked her as they cantered across the darkened plain.

"The Steppe turns to marsh on the southern shore of Materhein Lake," she said. "Beyond the lake lies the foothills of the coastal mountains."

"You intend to navigate a marsh?"

"There is a passage, known only to a select few of the Cova Skeld. Once clear of the marsh we'll head south to Keshin-Kho. Hopefully, the high country will slow any pursuit. My people are masters of the Steppe, but not the hills."

"This path through the marsh, your brother will surely know of it."

"He will." She slowed her horse to a trot and Vaelin followed suit. She waited until the others had ridden out of earshot before speaking again. "I have a notion of how to forestall further pursuit," she said, speaking in the clipped tones of one imparting knowledge with great reluctance. "My family . . . these people we travel with, will resist it. When the time comes I shall need you to lead them on."

"Meaning you will not be coming with us."

"My brother doesn't want you. It suits him to have his great enemy out of reach, a goal for his worshipful army. But not me. Me he will never let go."

◆ ◆ ◆

The marsh proved to be some of the worst ground Vaelin had ever seen. Flies swarmed in dark clouds above pools of stagnant, algae-covered water amid islets of tall rushes, all wreathed in a perennial mist. Even the supposedly safe path Luralyn led them along was a waterlogged sponge of moss and peat that forced them to dismount lest the horses become mired. Twice they were obliged to pull one of Luralyn's companions from the water after a wayward step sent them stumbling into one of the pools.

"We expected to lose a rider or two whenever we used this path," Luralyn explained. "Traversing it was a rite of passage of sorts. Any Cova who successfully made it through to raid the caravans bringing ore from the mountains had many years' boasting to look forward to."

"Did Kehlbrand make it through?" Vaelin asked.

"Eight times. Twice as many as any other, as you would expect. He never could resist outshining the achievements of others."

They traversed the marsh for a full day, eventually stopping at a large islet formed of the firmest ground so far. A solitary tree grew in the centre of the islet, spindly branches reaching up into the misted sky as if in forlorn hope of grasping sunlight.

"Kihlen, I think we can risk a fire," Luralyn said to one of the pretty-faced twins. "If you would be so kind."

"Won't that reveal us to the scouts, mistress?" he asked, exchanging a worried glance with his sister.

"Oh, I doubt it, and don't call me that."

They assembled the bundled sticks from their packs to fashion the fire, there being no dry timber to be had. Kihlen flicked his hand towards the piled wood, sending an egg-sized ball of flame into it. The blaze took hold immediately, birthing a warmth that banished the dank chill of the marsh air.

They ate a meal of dried venison as night descended to shroud their surroundings in an impenetrable black curtain. With the meal complete Luralyn reached into her jerkin to extract a small scroll, which she handed to Vaelin. Unfurling it he found a rudimentary map tracing a westward course through marshy ground into a series of hills.

"Two miles on you'll come to another tree," Luralyn said. "It's important you take the path on the right. Keep to the route marked until you see a mountain rising above the mist. Head straight towards it and you'll reach the hills before nightfall."

Eresa, the diminutive woman seated next to Luralyn, frowned at her in utter confusion that slowly turned to fear as the meaning of her words sank home. "You mean for us to leave you?" she asked in a small choked voice.

Luralyn didn't look at her, eyes steady on the flames of the campfire and tone flat. "I do."

Varij, the sturdy young man on her right, got slowly to his feet, staring at Luralyn in frank disbelief. "You can't mean that . . ."

"I can. I must." She took a hard breath and shifted her gaze from the fire, looking at each of her companions in turn. "You have followed me for years now. I commanded and you followed. Now I have another command for you. Go with this man." She nodded at Vaelin. "Follow his word as you would follow mine. It is my wish that you journey to Keshin-Kho and do everything in your power to resist my brother's assault, for it is surely coming."

"And you?" Varij asked.

"My brother will not harm me. You know that. I guided you here to secure your escape. I never deluded myself that there would be any escape for me. This is my final command to you. Come the morning you will go with this man and leave me here."

"We never followed you because you commanded it," Eresa said.

"No, you followed me because you were slaves, beaten and starved and grateful for the slightest kindness. You thought I freed you. I didn't. Just because you couldn't see the chains I bound you with doesn't mean they weren't real. It was all farce, all lies. The Darkblade needed you for his army, needed you to counter the power of the priests. You were useful, that is all."

"If that is all," Varij said, "why are you letting us go?"

Vaelin saw her begin to speak, no doubt intending to voice some more caustic lies designed to force them to hate her, but the words died on her tongue. He could see as well as she could that there was nothing she could say that would sunder these people from her.

"When they come," she said, "they will bring other Gifted with them, those who truly believe in my brother's godhood."

"Then we'll fight them," the twins said with unnerving uniformity of both voice and conviction.

"As we have fought before," Eresa added. "We stood together against the Merchant King's army, as you taught us to."

"It's hopeless!" Luralyn shouted, rising to her feet. "Can't you see that? There will be too many, Stahlhast and Gifted. Too many to prevail against." She turned to Vaelin, a desperate plea in her gaze. "Tell them," she said. "You know war. You know if we stand here we'll surely meet our end."

Vaelin pursed his lips and glanced around. "If we stand here, yes," he said. "This is a poor place to defend. The marsh will hamper our enemy to be sure, but it hampers us just as much. So many Gifted assailing each other on a narrow patch of ground will bring only disaster." He raised the map she had given him, pointing to a spot amidst the hills to the west. "What is this?"

"Just a gloomy ruin," she said, squinting at the map in bemusement. "My people call it the Ghost Shacks. It used to be home to people who worked a copper mine in the nearby hills. They all fell victim to some form of plague years ago. The bones still litter the houses."

Vaelin's gaze returned to the fire, brows knitting as his mind resumed the familiar practice of formulating a stratagem. "Wooden houses?" he asked, glancing at the twins.

"Yes," Luralyn replied, voice cautious.

"Then that's where we'll stand." Vaelin rose and hefted Derka's saddle. "Can you guide us clear of the marsh in the dark?"

Luralyn remained still for a moment as she regarded the determination on the face of each of her companions. Sighing, she said, "If Kihlen and Jihla can light the way as we go, yes."

"Then let's not linger." Vaelin hauled the saddle onto Derka's back. "Leave it burning," he said, seeing Varij prepare to throw water on the fire. "You can't trap a fox if he won't follow the scent."

◆ ◆ ◆

The marsh grew more perilous the further west they went, their feet sinking deeper into the waterlogged earth with each passing mile. The twins led the way with torches fashioned from their few remaining sticks, sometimes casting bursts of flame ahead to enable Luralyn to gauge their course. Despite the painful slowness with which they moved, and Luralyn's careful navigation, it was inevitable that the marsh would attempt to claim at least one victim.

Juhkar strayed a few inches from the path and soon found himself flailing in water up to his chest. From the bubbles surrounding his struggling form and the rapidity with which he sank, it was clear he had contrived to discover a patch of quicksand.

"Ropes!" Vaelin said, quickly unhooking a length of cord from Derka's saddle. It was too late, however, Juhkar's head slipping beneath the oily blackness of the water whilst his long arms waved frantically.

A loud splash drew Vaelin's gaze to the rear of the column, where he saw one of the horses leaping into the water. Shuhlan stood on the shore in utter stillness, staring at the animal with absolute concentration. The beast swam quickly to Juhkar, snaring his wrist with its teeth just before it could slip beneath the water. Turning about, the horse struck out for firm ground, dragging Juhkar with it. He emerged into the air, sputtering and clamping his arms around the horse's neck as it bore him to safety. Once within arm's reach of the shore, Vaelin and the others dragged both horse and man clear of the water.

"I think," Vaelin said, seeing Shuhlan wipe a trickle of blood from her nose, "it would be of considerable assistance if I had a full understanding of the gifts of everyone in this company."

◆ ◆ ◆

They cleared the marsh come the dawn, straggling free of the sucking mire with all heads save Vaelin's lowered in near exhaustion. He allowed a short rest on the gentle slope they had emerged onto, peering into the misty depths of the marsh for any sign of their pursuers. For all Luralyn's certainty, he had yet to see any firm evidence that her brother had set hunters on their trail. Nor could he see any now, just grey-green murk unblemished by torchlight or the silhouettes of men.

"They're coming," Juhkar said, moving to Vaelin's side. His features were dark with fatigue but his eyes remained bright and alert as he scanned the marsh. "I can feel it."

"Your . . . song tells you so?" Vaelin ventured. Although he had been provided with a brief description of their abilities, the true nature of this man's facility for tracking game and sensing danger had been described in the vaguest terms.

"Song?" Juhkar frowned. "No. I *feel* it. Like the wind on my skin or the heat of a fire. Sometimes it's strong, sometimes weak. Today"—he met Vaelin's gaze—"it's very strong."

"Do you know how many? How far off they are?"

"A half day's ride over firm ground, so at least a day in that muck. As for how many . . ." The tall man shrugged. "More than a few, less than an army."

Vaelin inclined his head at the strongbow lashed to the saddle of Juhkar's horse. "How well can you use that?"

"As well as any slave who faced a whipping if he were caught practising. But I've got better since Luralyn raised me up."

"If you can hit a mark from fifty paces, it'll suit our purposes well enough."

He harried them onto their horses after barely a half hour's rest, following Luralyn as she traced a path into the hills that became steeper as the day wore on. Vaelin worried over Sherin's condition, seeing her diminished strength in the sag of her head and the slump of her shoulders. He hoped it was due to the fetid air of the marsh rather than any lingering effects of her gift or, more worrying, some consequence of touching the stone.

The journey to the village Luralyn called the Ghost Shacks took a full day and a half of difficult riding through craggy, rock-strewn hill country. By the time it came into view, Juhkar advised that their pursuers were now clear of the marsh and rapidly closing the distance to their prey. The village consisted of a dozen houses of varying dimensions, clustered in the lee of a south-facing ridge. The buildings were aged and mostly roofless with long-vanished doors and empty windows. True to Luralyn's description each house featured a collection of human skeletons, rotted of flesh and the bones jarringly white and clean in the drab ruin of their former homes.

"Old and young," Sherin observed with a wince as she and Vaelin surveyed the largest house. It was the only two-storey construction in the village, presumably the home of the village leader or official from whichever Merchant Kingdom had established this place. Sherin stood regarding two entwined skeletons in what Vaelin assumed had been the kitchen, judging by the rusted iron stove in the corner. Both skulls, one large and one small, were bowed towards one another, the bones of their arms overlaid in a parody of an embrace.

Sherin crouched to peer at the upper spine of the larger figure, grimacing in recognition. "The Red Hand," she said. "Or at least a highly pernicious variant of it. The infection leaves a honeycomb mark on the neck bones, but I've never seen them so pronounced."

"Does it still pose a danger?" Vaelin asked, keeping a good distance from the bones as memories of Linesh sprang to mind.

"Bones don't hold plague." Sherin's mouth curled a little in amusement at his trepidation. "Both female," she mused, turning back to the embracing skeletons and running a hand over their brows. "A mother and daughter, perhaps? It must have swept through this place in a day or two. Pity there's no time for me to study these."

"That there isn't," Vaelin assured her. He took some comfort in the sudden absence of dullness from her eyes, now bright with a familiar and particular interest. It had always struck him as strange that a soul so rich in compassion should also be fascinated with death and its innumerable causes.

"Luralyn tells me the mine these people worked lies a few hundred paces further on," he said. "You and she would be better off sheltering there until this is done."

"No." She rose, shaking her head firmly. "There may be need of me here."

"That's what concerns me."

She returned his steady gaze with one of her own, placid but also unyielding. He was considering the distinctly unwise but also guiltily tempting notion of binding her hand and foot before depositing her in the mine, when a shout from outside made further discussion irrelevant.

"They're coming!" Juhkar called. "No more than an hour away. And there are far more than I thought."

CHAPTER TWENTY-SIX

Vaelin navigated a somewhat dilapidated stairwell to climb to the building's upper floor, scanning the eastern approaches to the village and swallowing a curse at what he saw. The Stahlhast approached in single file, making it a relatively easy matter to gauge their numbers as his experienced eye tracked over the column from end to end. Over a hundred warriors in armour, the Gifted adherents of the Darkblade riding at their head along with a muscular figure in a tall plumed helm. Vaelin might have mistaken him for Kehlbrand himself but for the eagerness with which the warrior spurred his horse up the incline, all the while casting ill-tempered exhortations to those following.

Babukir, Vaelin concluded. *Still smarting over a broken nose.*

"How many?" Luralyn called to him from the street below, her family clustered around her in a tight, protective circle.

"Too many."

Vaelin climbed back down, drawing his sword as his eyes roved this village of the dead, marking each hiding place and shadowed alcove. "We can't beat them," he told the others in frank admission. "But we can delay them long enough to escape, also kill the Gifted amongst them, which will hopefully prevent further pursuit."

"Or I could just go and surrender to them," Luralyn pointed out. "I can bargain for your safe passage . . ."

"It's your younger brother that comes," Vaelin cut in. "Do you really think you can bargain with him?"

She let out a hard sigh and slowly shook her head.

"The map shows a narrow track along a mountainside some miles west," Vaelin continued, turning to Varij. "Take your mistress and the healer there. If we fail to follow within the hour, bring as much stone down as you can to block the path."

"I'm not . . ." Sherin began.

"Enough!" Vaelin barked. "There's no healing to be done here today, only fighting. And I can't fight and watch over you too."

"He's right," Luralyn said, voice grating with reluctant acceptance. She took hold of Sherin's arm and tugged her towards the horses. She resisted for a moment, regarding Vaelin with a mixture of anger and concern before allowing herself to be pulled away. She mounted her pony and rode off without a backward glance whilst Varij and Luralyn lingered for a moment, raising their hands to their fellow Gifted.

"Don't linger a second longer than necessary," Luralyn said before wheeling her horse about and riding away. Varij paused to exchange a stricken glance with Eresa, and for a moment it seemed he was about to dismount until she sternly shook her head and pointed at their mistress. He gave a pale-faced nod and turned his horse to gallop in Luralyn's wake.

"Start at the rear of the village and work your way forward," Vaelin told the twins. "Ride away as soon as the last house is alight. The wind comes down off the ridge so it'll sweep the smoke into their eyes and cover your escape. Shuhlan, set every horse you see against its rider. Eresa, keep her alive whilst she does so. Juhkar, fetch your bow and come with me."

"And what is our role?" the tall man asked, having retrieved his bow and a quiver of arrows.

"You were a tracker," Vaelin said. "Today you're a hunter, and we hunt the Gifted, assuming you can find them in the smoke."

"I can find them."

The roar of erupting flames drew Vaelin's gaze to the upper portion of the village. Fire burned bright in the belly of the two-storey house, the flames soon licking up the walls to consume the upper floor, birthing a thick pall of grey smoke in the process.

"Hide there until they're upon us," Vaelin told Shuhlan and Eresa, pointing his sword at the well in the centre of the village. "When you see us run, it's time for you to do the same."

He led Juhkar to a rectangular enclosure constructed from loose stone, presumably once a pigsty or animal shelter of some kind. The walls had tumbled in places, creating small gaps that afforded him a view of the lower reaches of the village. He could see four riders through the gathering miasma, Babukir in the centre, unmistakable in his armour, flanked by three unarmoured companions. *Using the Gifted as his vanguard,* Vaelin surmised, letting out a small grunt of annoyance at the realisation that Kehlbrand's brother was not altogether a fool.

Another upsurge of flames sent fresh gusts of smoke across the village, obscuring the riders from view. Vaelin waited until fully half the village was alight before turning to Juhkar with a raised eyebrow. The tall man drew an arrow from his quiver, nocking it to his bowstring with impressively steady hands. Shuffling forward in a low crouch, he paused at the edge of the wall, eyes lowered for a second then abruptly raising his head in a manner that put Vaelin in mind of a cat scenting a mouse. He moved to follow Juhkar's line of sight as he slowly drew his bow, thankful for the continuing roar of the flames that smothered the creak of the stave. Vaelin could see no targets in the grey pall that now covered the village, but noted how Juhkar's arrowhead tracked steadily from left to right, then stopped.

The tall man loosed his arrow and immediately sprinted from cover, Vaelin close on his heels. The smoke swirled around them then parted to reveal a stocky man lying on the ground, hands clutching at the arrow jutting from his shoulder. Seeing them he let out a furious snarl and Vaelin recognised the man who had bound him in Kehlbrand's tent after the murder of the Jade Princess. Mouthing curses, the stocky man raised a bloody trembling hand towards them, then died as Juhkar stepped forward to put his second arrow through his throat.

"Down!" Vaelin said, shoving the Gifted aside as a large silhouette loomed out of the smoke, sabre raised for a killing stroke. The blade whistled close to Juhkar's head as he ducked, then grated on Vaelin's blade as he turned it aside and thrust at the Stahlhast warrior's face. The man was swift, however, dancing back, sabre angled to parry another thrust. Vaelin feinted a swipe at the man's arm, then whirled to the right in a crouch, the sword sweeping in a broad arc to bite deep into the Stahlhast's leg.

Vaelin left the man yelling and bleeding, pulling Juhkar along as they fled into the smoke. He could hear shouted commands above the flames, accompanied by the dull thrum of bowstrings. Arrows snapped the air as they ran, finding refuge behind a tumble-down hut the flames hadn't yet reached.

"Where?" Vaelin asked Juhkar in a whisper but the Gifted's answer was swallowed by a rumbling crash of thunder. A second later Vaelin felt the damp kiss of moisture on his skin and looked up to see dark clouds roiling above the drifting smoke.

"That old Tuhla bastard!" Juhkar cursed, nocking another arrow to his bow. Rain began to fall in thick sheets, the smoke soon thinning to a wispy mist. Fortunately, the rain was so heavy it provided a measure of continued cover, Vaelin watching a trio of Stahlhast sprint heedlessly by their hiding spot. Even so, with the flames now diminishing to a dull orange glow, it was clear their time here was over.

"Make for the ridgetop," Vaelin told Juhkar. "I'll guard your back." The tracker didn't seem to hear, eyes lowered once more as his gift brought fresh prey.

"Leave it," Vaelin hissed, reaching out to restrain him but it was too late. Juhkar's head snapped up and he was gone, charging off to be swallowed by the shifting grey curtain of unceasing rain. Vaelin grunted in annoyance and ran in pursuit, hearing the snap of a bowstring some yards ahead. He rounded a corner to find Juhkar back-pedalling and frantically attempting to nock another arrow to his bow as a Stahlhast woman advanced on him, sabre moving in rapid arcs. Beyond them lay the body of an elderly man in patchy leather armour. Juhkar had made sure with his first arrow this time, spitting the fellow through the neck. As the old man coughed blood and shuddered to stillness the rain ebbed into a thin drizzle.

A shout of frustration again drew Vaelin's gaze to Juhkar, finding him on his back, bow raised like a staff as he made ready to ward off the Stahlhast's killing stroke. Vaelin snatched the hunting knife from his belt and sent it spinning towards the warrior, the blade finding the gap below the rear of her helm and sinking up to the hilt.

Vaelin hauled Juhkar to his feet, pushing him towards the upper end of the village. The rain had stopped altogether now, the unnatural clouds fading to bathe the scene in unwelcome sunlight. He glimpsed Stahlhast on all sides as they ran, arrows thrumming the air around them. Patches of smoke still drifted between the blackened houses, providing sufficient protection for them to make it to the well.

Eresa and Shuhlan stood back to back in the centre of the village, the muddy earth around them littered with half a dozen Stahlhast corpses. A lone horse stood nearby, shivering in distress as it nuzzled at the trampled body of its rider. As he and Juhkar neared the scene, Vaelin saw a Stahlhast charge towards Eresa, thrusting with a lance. She ducked under the weapon's narrow-bladed point and clamped a hand to the wielder's forearm. A bright plume of sparks brought tears to Vaelin's eyes and when he blinked them clear he saw the Stahlhast lying dead, smoke leaking from a blackened steel arm guard.

"Go!" Vaelin shouted. "To the horses!"

Before either woman could respond the air was filled with a rushing shriek, the village disappearing in a welter of raised grit and swirling debris. Vaelin's legs were swept from under him and he found himself cartwheeling across the ground, brought to a sudden and jarring halt as he collided with the well. The gale raged for several seconds more, Vaelin seeing Shuhlan's body tumbling past, limbs slack and head lolling atop a snapped neck.

The whirlwind died as swiftly as it had been born, detritus showering down as the last of the smoke faded away. Vaelin saw Eresa propped against the wall of the well, but there was no sign of Juhkar.

"Where," a youthful and enraged voice demanded, "is my fucking sister!"

Babukir guided his horse through the remnants of a ruined house, sabre in hand. Behind him rode an unarmed woman clad in the garb of the border country, gaze fixed on Eresa. Her face, streaked with blood from recent and extensive use of her gift, was set in the hateful mask all true believers reserved for the heretic. "Betrayer!" she called out in a near scream. "How could you offend our lord so?"

"Oh," Eresa responded in a weary sigh, "go and rut with a goat, Drehka."

"Shut your mouth, you traitorous whore," Babukir snapped. He walked his horse forward, furious gaze shifting between Eresa and Vaelin. Stahlhast, mounted and on foot, were at his back, thronging the village. "Where is she?" he demanded, levelling his sabre at Vaelin. "I won't ask again, Thief of Names."

Vaelin rose, working his neck to banish the ache of connecting with the well. "Then don't," he said, raising his sword.

He saw bloodlust vie with fear on Babukir's face. Having witnessed Obvar's end, he seemed to possess enough wisdom to calculate the likely outcome of single combat, nor did his pride compel him to risk it. "Kill them," he said, waving the Stahlhast forward. "Then scour this place . . ."

A blast of heat and displaced air drowned his words, Vaelin whirling to see a fireball erupt amongst a group of Stahlhast. They fell writhing amidst the flames, screams high and piteous. Another fireball streaked towards Babukir, although he dragged his horse aside in time to avoid it. The Stahlhast behind him took the full brunt, a dozen flame-wreathed figures performing a crazed dance.

Vaelin saw Kihlen and Jihla advancing from the upper end of the village, marching in perfect step as they cast fireballs into the ranks of the Stahlhast. Drehka, the Gifted believer, spurred her horse forward, arms raised and fresh blood leaking from her nose and eyes. A vicious invisible whip swept the twins off their feet, quickly enveloping them in a small whirlwind that sent them spinning. Something buzzed the air close to Vaelin's ear and he jerked aside, lowering into a crouch, but the arrow hadn't been meant for him. It took Drehka in the belly, doubling her over to collapse from the saddle, the whirlwind that embraced the twins dying along with her a heartbeat later.

"Pity," Juhkar said, emerging from the tumbled stones of the pigsty with bow in hand. "I always had a sense she rather liked me."

"Help me," Vaelin said, rushing to help Eresa to her feet. Together, he and Juhkar bore her up the slope, making for the horses. Kihlen and Jihla were back on their feet now, keeping the Stahlhast at bay with their fiery projections. From the twins' increasingly bleached pallor and the blood streaming down their faces, Vaelin doubted they had the strength to last much longer.

"Get to the horses," he commanded. "You've done enough."

They fled past the steaming remains of the two-storey house, making for the rope line where they had corralled the horses, then coming to a halt at the sight of mounted warriors atop the ridge. *Knew enough to send a flanking force too,* Vaelin thought, his grudging respect for Babukir's tactical nous increasing further. He put the riders' number at close to forty, too many to have a hope of fighting their way through, at least not without Gifted assistance, but one look at the twins told him they were close to collapse.

"We can try, at least," Jihla said, reading the unspoken question in Vaelin's gaze. She and her brother staggered a short way up the slope, holding on to each other for support as they raised their hands. The riders on the ridge seemed to take this as some form of signal for they spurred into an immediate charge, streaming down the slope in two companies, a narrow wedge at the fore. Vaelin was about to run to Derka, hoping to mount up in time to assail the charge from the flank, but halted as they drew nearer and he was able to discern the colour of their armour.

"Don't!" he said, rushing to stand in front of the twins before they could unleash their fire. "These are friends."

He pulled them aside as the first of the Red Scouts swept past. He recognised Corporal Wei and Tsai Lin amongst the vanguard, Sho Tsai, Alum and Nortah close behind. His brother grinned and lifted his sword in greeting as he rode past.

The leading contingent of Red Scouts met the pursuing Stahlhast head-on, riding down those on foot and disordering the ranks of the mounted warriors, cutting their already depleted and scalded force in two. As an ugly melee developed in the heart of the village, the following Scouts split into two wings, wheeling left and right to assail the Stahlhast with a flurry of crossbow bolts before driving home their charge.

"Did you miss me, Uncle?"

Ellese appeared beside him on foot, grunting out the last word as she loosed an arrow into the mass of thrashing riders. He might have rebuked her for recklessness if he hadn't been certain the shaft would find its mark.

"We had companions," he said. "Sherin . . ."

"Back there." She jerked her head to the ridgetop. "Sehmon and Chien are watching over them. The stonemason led us to you. It's been a hard ride, I must say."

"Get these people clear of here," he told her, climbing onto Derka's back. He expected some argument, seeing her habitual keenness for combat. Instead, she gave a terse nod and began to usher the Gifted up the hill, hectoring them in her far from elegant Chu-Shin, which reflected many days spent in the company of soldiers.

"Run, lazy bastards! Run!"

The fighting was mostly over by the time Derka brought him into the midst of the melee. Perhaps twenty Stahlhast remained, fighting in three separate knots with a determined ferocity that told of an acceptance of imminent death. At least a dozen Scouts lay dead amongst the ruins, though Vaelin was relieved to see Alum and Nortah still fighting. Never a keen horseman, the Moreska had dismounted at some point, though it didn't seem to have disadvantaged him greatly, judging by the slick of blood covering his spear. Vaelin felt a swell of pride as he watched Nortah deftly guide his horse clear of the path of a Stahlhast's desperate charge, his sword delivering a precise and deadly cut to the neck as the warrior swept past.

Another Stahlhast, eyes wild and face blistered by fire, came staggering to hack at Vaelin with an iron mace. Unbidden, Derka reared and smashed the fellow's skull with his forehooves before he had the chance to deliver the blow. Vaelin spurred the stallion on, searching for Babukir. Catching a flicker of shadow in the lower reaches of the village, Vaelin urged Derka to a faster gallop. They cleared the village quickly, but the loose footing forced Vaelin to rein the stallion to a halt. Babukir had no such qualms, Vaelin finding himself impressed with the man's horsemanship as he drove his horse down the slope and into the valley below with barely a pause. Within seconds he was beyond hope of reaching, a lone figure galloping hard for the dubious safety of the marsh.

"What happened to your hair?"

Vaelin turned to find Nortah reining in close by, brows furrowed as he looked Vaelin over.

"My hair?" Vaelin asked.

"There was grey in it when you left us. Not a great deal, but it was there." He squinted, coming close to tease at Vaelin's hair with his sword point. "Now there isn't."

"Haven't washed in days, that's all." Vaelin batted the sword away and met Nortah's grin with one of his own. "It's good to see you, brother."

"That makes a welcome change." Nortah inclined his head at Babukir's fast-diminishing form. "Friend of yours?"

"One I expect I'll see again." Vaelin tugged on Derka's reins and together they started back up the slope. "Assuming his brother doesn't flay him to death."

CHAPTER TWENTY-SEVEN

The journey to Keshin-Kho required ten days of hard riding. The hills fringing the coastal mountains were sparsely populated, but more settlements began to appear when they veered to the south-east, the hills becoming verdant downs of rich grass interspersed with numerous plantations of rice and wheat. According to Tsai Lin, the region was known as Keshin-Ghol, the Garden of the North, and served as the principal source of food for the Northern Prefecture. The people they encountered were well fed and cheerful for the most part, although their good humour would evaporate in the face of Sho Tsai's warnings regarding the Stahlhast.

"But they have never raided here," one village elder protested after the captain had gathered them together to hear his word. "The Tuhla will sometimes attack the caravans on the eastward road, but never the Stahlhast."

"All is changed," Sho Tsai told him. "They do not come to raid. They come to conquer. They will kill any who refuse to bow to their false god. And should they spare your life, they will surely not spare you the theft of your crops. An army must be fed, and they know they'll find supplies in this province."

"What would you have us do?" the old man asked, cutting through the alarmed chatter of his fellow elders.

"Harvest all the food you can and cart it to Keshin-Kho, where it will be sorely needed. Burn or spoil the rest. Nothing is to be left that might succour the enemy." Sho Tsai paused, allowing the resultant babble of protestation to continue for a time before barking out, "I speak with the authority of the Merchant King Lian Sha, and you will abide by my word!"

This had the effect of silencing the protests but, from the shared expressions of doubt and distrust on every face, Vaelin surmised that little in the way of persuasion had been achieved.

"Do you think they'll do it?" he asked once they had departed the village. "Flee homes they've known all their lives and burn everything they leave behind?"

"Most won't," the captain admitted. "And I have not the numbers to compel them. It's in the nature of man to ignore the tiger at his door until he sees it with his own eyes. All I can do is warn and command in the hope at least some might heed me."

Sho Tsai's gaze strayed to Sherin, as Vaelin noted it often had during their journey. The captain's brief display of relieved joy upon finding her alive in the hill country had subsided into something more guarded, not to say troubled. To Vaelin's eyes she had recovered much of her former vitality, though a shadow remained in her eyes and her smile was a rare thing now. Despite his protestations, she had insisted on using her gift to heal the Scouts who had suffered severe wounds in the skirmish with the Stahlhast. All had recovered well save one man with a severed spine who proved beyond her skills. Even so, she had kept on trying, blood flowing freely from her nose and eyes as she clamped her hands on the gaping wound in the man's back. Had he and Sho Tsai not pulled her away Vaelin suspected she might have bled herself white in her efforts to save him.

"She is changed, it is true," he told Sho Tsai, reading his expression. "But not so much as to make her someone else."

A brief flush of anger passed over Sho Tsai's face. Clearly he wanted no advice from the former lover of the woman he had long wished to make his wife, but his concern for her apparently overrode any ill-tempered response. "This particular . . . blessing," he said. "You have seen it before?"

"Only once. A man I knew. He was no warrior but nevertheless did great service in war."

"Did he fall?"

"No. But his gift exacted a high price. It made him . . ." Vaelin faltered, trying to find words to describe what Weaver had become when he healed the Ally. The term "inhuman" seemed cruel, given the man's selflessness, but neither was it inaccurate. "Made him unable to live amongst others."

"He was so dangerous then?"

"Partly, although he was a kindly soul at heart. But it was more the danger posed by others. Such power begets fear, and envy. The desire to control it is strong, even amongst the wisest rulers."

He saw Sho Tsai's frown deepen at this, no doubt as he pondered the likely reaction of his own ruler.

"The Merchant King is wise," Vaelin said, choosing not to add "but also ruthless," as he was aware the captain knew this far better than he. "Do you think he will punish you?" he asked instead. "We failed to retrieve the Jade Princess after all."

"He will do what must be done," Sho Tsai responded, straightening his back. "And I will accept his peerless wisdom and Heaven-blessed authority. The Princess may be gone, but the Enlightened Realm lives on, and will do so whilst I still have strength to hold a sword."

◆ ◆ ◆

The iron matrix of the west-facing gate of Keshin-Kho rose to reveal at least three thousand soldiers in full armour crowding the courtyard beyond. Vaelin could see yet more thronging the streets of the city's lowest tier and on the battlements of each successive wall. The soldiers' armour varied in colour from grey to blue to green, but each contingent stood in well-ordered ranks beneath the banner of the Merchant King.

As Sho Tsai rode through the gate, the entire host let out a uniform shout Vaelin recognised as the formal salute of a superior officer. Newly promoted, Governor Neshim and Garrison Commander Deshai strode forward to greet the captain as he brought his horse to a halt, regarding the assembled soldiery in evident bemusement. The Governor wore an ornate but ill-fitting set of armour that clanked somewhat as he and the commander both bowed to Sho Tsai.

"General Tsai," Governor Neshim said, rising but keeping his head lowered as he approached Sho Tsai, proffering a scroll-tube bearing the Merchant King's seal.

Sho Tsai took the tube and extracted the scroll within. For the briefest second a profound shock registered on the man's face before he forced it back into a stern officer's mask. "I see," he said, beckoning Vaelin and Tsai Lin forward.

"It seems," he told them, handing the scroll to his son, "the Merchant King has appointed me General of the Northern Armies, and sent thirty thousand men to reinforce the garrison of Keshin-Kho."

"Congratulations," Vaelin told him, speaking in Realm Tongue to keep his words from the assembled soldiers. "But you know thirty thousand won't be enough."

"The Merchant King assures us more are on their way," Tsai Lin said, glancing up from the scroll. "But it seems there has been trouble in the middle provinces. So many people fleeing south and not enough food to feed them. Riot and even rebellion are mentioned."

"Besides," Sho Tsai added, taking back the scroll, "if I had but fifty men, I would still endeavour to hold this city, for that is what the Merchant King commands." He angled his head at Luralyn and her Gifted companions. "And let's not forget our new and very useful allies."

He turned back to the governor and commander, both still standing with heads bowed. "Governor," he said, "I require a complete inventory of all supplies and a full and accurate count of every living soul within these walls. Please ensure I have both by noon tomorrow."

The governor bobbed his head. "Of course, General."

"Commander Deshai," Sho Tsai went on, "I hereby give you command of three regiments of cavalry and order you to proceed to Keshin-Ghol with all urgency. The inhabitants are commanded to harvest their crops and bring them here. Anything that might aid the enemy is to be burnt or destroyed. All wells are to be spoiled." The new general gave an almost imperceptible pause that Vaelin doubted anyone but he and Tsai Lin noticed. "Any subjects who refuse this order are to be executed on the spot."

◆ ◆ ◆

"My brother will send the Tuhla to Keshin-Ghol," Luralyn said. "Theft and terror being their principal attributes as a people. The Stahlhast and his army of faithful adherents will be coming here."

"When?" Sho Tsai asked, not raising his eyes from the large map spread out on the table. They were in what had been the late Governor Hushan's library. From the surprisingly small number of book-scrolls but preponderance of maps, Vaelin concluded Hushan's interests had been more military than literary.

"As soon as he can march them across the Steppe," Luralyn replied. It seemed to Vaelin she had aged since the skirmish in the village, the last vestiges of girlhood fading into the drawn features of a grief-stricken woman. Vaelin suspected it wasn't just the death of Shuhlan, although the pain of losing one she looked on as family lingered in her eyes. *She lost her brother,* he knew. *All ties to the man who now believes himself a god are severed. She can never return to her people.*

"He no longer has any reason to wait," she continued, face grim as she surveyed the southern reaches of the Iron Steppe. "There are no more strongholds to subdue, towns to capture or competing tribes to conquer or suborn. Also . . ." She gave a half-apologetic, half-regretful shrug. "He knows that I am here. It might be better if you sent me away."

"No." Sho Tsai gave a firm shake of his head. "Having you here means I can read his intentions. Provided you're willing to stay, of course."

Luralyn blinked in surprise. "You would let me go?"

"It strikes me it would be best not to antagonise your Heaven-blessed friends, and I'll need their help as much as I need yours. Better if it were given willingly."

"They'll give it," she assured him. "As will I."

His lips twitched in what might have been a smile of gratitude before he turned to Vaelin. "And you, my lord? Failure or not, your mission for the Merchant King is complete. I can issue a pass guaranteeing free passage through the Venerable Kingdom. You could be on a ship home within weeks."

Vaelin's surprise was the equal of Luralyn's and he found himself replying with a rueful laugh. However, he sobered quickly as he discerned the unspoken suggestion in Sho Tsai's steady gaze: *Take Sherin and go.*

"She won't leave," he told the general. "You know that. And neither will I. I've seen enough to know this man has to be defeated. If he's not stopped here, it's likely I'll find myself fighting him on the walls of my own tower in the space of a few years."

"Very well." Sho Tsai turned to an unfurled scroll on the table. "Governor Neshim may not be the most resolute of men, but his bookkeeping skills are exemplary and he's been sufficiently astute to have begun stockpiling supplies in our absence. By his reckoning we can subsist here for at least three months, longer once Commander Deshai returns with the supplies from Keshin-Ghol."

"Kehlbrand will not try to starve us out," Luralyn said. "You could have filled your storehouses ten times over and it won't matter. My people have little patience or ability for siege-craft. When he comes it will be as a storm and it won't stop until he has this city."

"How many more Gifted does he have?" Vaelin asked.

"There are only three others that I found. Sehga is a border country woman who can plant lies in men's minds, lies they believe utterly to be true. Lehkis is Tuhla and has a special way with metal. Useful for crafting but not much else. Morheld is Stahlhast, spared the priests' attentions by pretending madness for all his life, so much so that it came to be truth. He can draw blood from any living thing, leaving only empty skin and dry bone. But there are more, those I had no hand in recruiting. Once Kehlbrand had his own gift he no longer needed me to find others with the Divine Blood. Exactly how many and what they can do, I know not."

And he has the stone, Vaelin added inwardly. *How many have touched it at the Darkblade's command and, if it didn't kill them, what gifts did they receive?* "They'll have to be dealt with," he said. "And quickly if we're to have any chance of holding this place."

"I'll leave the matter in your hands," Sho Tsai told Luralyn. "Dai Lo Tsai will take over command of the Red Scouts and see to your safety, with Lord Vaelin's assistance."

"We'll need more," Vaelin said. "Kehlbrand will know the value of our Gifted as well as we know his."

"I'll need every trained soldier for the walls. Commander Deshai has been assiduous in recruiting and drilling the militia companies, however"— the general looked again at the governor's scroll—"it appears there is one as yet untapped well from which we can draw. Lord Nortah had tales aplenty to share on the trail. One in particular caught my attention. I believe, my lord, you are experienced in taking scum and moulding them into soldiers."

◆ ◆ ◆

"Why do they always stink?" Nortah's features bunched as the heavy doors swung open to reveal the dark vaults that served as the dungeons of Keshin-Kho. "Surely, somewhere in the world there must be a clean prison."

"Stinks because people shit in it," Sehmon said, apparently bemused by Nortah's failure to perceive the obvious.

"Of course." Nortah clapped him on the shoulder. "My lad, you've clearly missed your calling. Such powerful insight makes you a fine candidate for acceptance into the Third Order. I shall be sure to write a letter of recommendation the moment we return to the Realm."

"Don't want to join the Third Order," the former outlaw said, his frown deepening.

"By the Father's arse," Ellese muttered, wearily shaking her head. "Why do the pretty ones have to be dullards?"

"How many in all?" Vaelin asked Governor Neshim, who seemed even less immune to the fetid emanations of the dungeons than Nortah.

"Three hundred and forty-eight," he replied, face pale and eyes blinking against the miasma's sting. "At the last count."

"Their crimes?"

"Oh, the usual. A few bandits, though not so many as they're usually executed immediately. The rest are thieves and beggars, plus a few smugglers. They're the worst. All part of the same brotherhood so they never inform on one another and band together if there's a fight down here. We generally leave them to it. Less work for the headsman."

"Does this brotherhood have a name?"

"The Green Vipers. They've been a scourge on the border country for as long as any can remember. Some say they date back to the early days of the Emerald Empire."

Vaelin turned a questioning glance on Chien. "You know this name?"

"I know it," she said. "Their reach is long. The Crimson Band has done business with them in the past, and also fought them, as is the way of things."

Vaelin nodded and turned to the governor. "You have the document?"

Neshim plucked a small scroll from his sleeve and began to hand it to Vaelin.

"No," Chien said. "They'll need to hear him read it." She gave Vaelin a mostly empty smile of apology. "The word of a foreign barbarian is unlikely to carry so much weight."

"You want me to go in there?" The governor's skin paled yet further as he peered into the gloomy recesses of the vaults. A few beams of sunlight bisected the otherwise complete darkness and the only sound was the murmur of many softly taken breaths. The denizens of this place were apparently keen not to attract the attention of whoever might have opened these doors.

"You'll have our protection, sir," Vaelin assured him. He stepped through the doors, pausing to regard the governor with an expectant smile. Neshim, however, only consented to follow when Alum and Nortah moved to stand close on either side, nudging him forward with polite but firm insistence.

Vaelin heard the mingled breaths grow deeper as they proceeded into the dungeon, bare feet scraping on stone as the inmates stirred. He could see them only as vague shapes in the gloom, the meagre light revealing glimpses of tattered rags and unwashed skin. He waited for Nortah and Alum to bring the governor to his side and gestured for him to read the scroll.

"I . . ." Neshim began before his voice cracked, the trickle of sweat on his brow telling Vaelin that it wasn't only the odour of this place that disturbed him. "I," he tried again after a hard swallow, "having been duly appointed Governor of this city by the wise beneficence of the Merchant King Lian Sha . . ."

"Just tell us what you want, you greedy fuck," a voice called from the darkness. It had a weight and confidence to it that seemed alien to these surroundings, heralding a brief flurry of laughter from the unseen inmates. But it was the laughter of fearful men and soon faded.

"Um," Neshim said, the scroll fluttering in his hand as it began to shake.

"The Stahlhast are coming," Chien said, moving to stand in front of the governor. "The law-dogs want you to fight in their army to defend this place. Anyone who fights will be pardoned. Say no and they'll leave you to rot and there'll be no more food."

"You expect us to trust this man's word?" the same voice asked, stilling the subsequent upsurge in whispers. "Half of us are in here only because we couldn't afford his bribes."

"Lies!" Neshim cried, although a quavering voice and increasingly sweat-covered brow explained much about his earlier reluctance. "I say leave this scum here, my lord," the governor went on, drawing himself up and attempting an authoritative air. "They don't deserve the honour of fighting for the Merchant King . . ."

"Be quiet," Vaelin told him. He took the scroll from Neshim's hand and jerked his head at the doors. "Leave. I'll deal with this."

Relief warred with aggrieved pride on the governor's face for a moment before he turned and walked from the vaults, his stiff-backed stride proving a poor attempt at a dignified exit.

"You don't know me," Vaelin said, raising his voice so that it echoed through the vaults. "I, as you can see, am a foreigner. And this"—he held up the scroll—"is just a piece of paper. So, you will ask yourselves, why should you trust me?"

"Why indeed?"

This time the voice's owner stepped into view. Vaelin was surprised by his youth, perhaps a year or two past his twentieth year. He was of average height but remarkably lean with well-honed muscle showing through the rents in the rags he wore.

"You belong to the Green Vipers?" Vaelin asked him.

The lean man's eyes narrowed and his mouth twitched in defiant amusement. "Never heard of them," he said.

"Have you heard of the Crimson Band?" Chien asked. As she spoke she raised her hands, making a fist of one and tapping two fingers to it with the other before slowly tracing them to her wrist. The man kept his face impassive but Vaelin saw a definite glimmer of recognition in his eyes.

"I speak as one who has walked the nameless road all her life," Chien went on, casting her voice into the depths of the vaults. "And I speak true. This is no lie. What would be the purpose? I have no love for this man." She pointed at Vaelin. "His arrival in this land caused my father's death and the fall of the Crimson Band. But, he is a warrior of great renown in the Barbarous East and, having seen him fight, I can attest to his skills and that he does not break his word. I swear as the daughter of Pao Len of the Crimson Band that you can trust him. The choice is yours: take a chance on his word and you might live, or most likely die fighting. Don't and you'll certainly die starving in your own filth."

A multitude of voices babbled in the shadows and more prisoners came into the light. Many were bowing in servile obeisance whilst others glared in suspicion. Whatever their willingness, the ragged and emaciated state of most caused Vaelin to wonder what use they might be as soldiers. He did spy some sturdy specimens amongst them, but most of these stood behind the lean man who remained as impassive as before.

"Shut it, you fawning shits!" he barked out, instantly silencing the other prisoners. "I've heard of Pao Len," he said to Chien. "Heard he died on the Merchant King's order."

"He did," Chien said. "And the Merchant King himself told me how impressed he was that my father never gave up a name in the long hours he suffered before the headsman ended him, even those he had called enemies all his days. Know this and know that his blood runs in me. The word of the Crimson Band is never broken."

The smuggler turned to the cluster of sturdy men at his back, voice lowered in swift discussion. "If we fight we get paid," he said, turning back to address Vaelin this time. "The same as any other soldier. And"—a smile played over his lips—"I get to be captain."

"Yes to the pay," Vaelin said. "No to the captaincy. You can be a corporal." He held the young man's gaze, looking for a sign of challenge. If it came to it he would have to be beaten down, most likely killed to ensure the others fell into line. As Sho Tsai had noted, Vaelin had done this before.

"Corporal then," the young man said, proving at least that his defiance didn't extend to stupidity.

"You have a name?" Vaelin enquired.

"Cho-ka."

Dagger or thin-bladed knife, Vaelin translated, doubting it was the name this man had been born with, not that it mattered. "Corporal Cho-ka," he said. "Get these men into some semblance of order and march them from this place. You will follow me to the canal. I feel a bath is sorely needed."

Chapter Twenty-eight

F orm a circle!"
    Boots stamped and armour clinked as the company attempted to
    perform the manoeuvre they had been taught over the course of
three torturous days. Vaelin saw several collide with their comrades, dropping their spears in the process. The contrast to the other regiments drilling
in the central square was stark. Even the relatively raw militia troops were
given to laughing openly at the outlaws' clumsy attempts at soldiering. The
overall sense of disorder was not helped by the decidedly non-uniform
appearance of his troops. With much of the garrison's armoury already
denuded of kit, Vaelin's command had been obliged to make do with the
leftovers. Consequently, the men marched in armour of varying hues wearing helms that ranged from plain to extravagantly ornate. The only real uniformity was in their weapons, a six-foot-long curve-bladed spear and short
sword for each man. Vaelin had hoped to find some archers amongst them
but the armoury had been stripped of its crossbows.

"I'd say it was like herding cats," Corporal Wei told Vaelin with a sour
grimace, "if I didn't think cats would make better soldiers."

It took a full two minutes before the company had managed to form a
semblance of a circle and another two before it conformed to something that
might actually withstand a cavalry charge.

Vaelin swallowed a sigh, taking in the sight of sweaty faces beneath the
mismatched helms. For all their amateurish ineptitude, most at least were

making an effort. As he had seen before, desperate souls facing certain execution often responded with gratitude and loyalty when offered deliverance
and a chance at redemption, not to mention regular meals and a bed to sleep
in. *They could be good soldiers one day,* he knew. *Had we the time.* But time
was against them, and these men would not be saved by a soft-hearted commander.

"Too slow," he told Wei. "Twice round the square at the run. A beating
for any man who falls out."

He stayed for another hour, drilling and punishing them until they
began to sag with exhaustion. "One hour for rest and food," he told Wei.
"Then take them beyond the walls and march them south along the canal for
ten miles. Any who don't make it back by nightfall will sleep in the open."

"You sure, my lord?" Wei asked. "Plenty of likely deserters amongst
this lot."

"Make sure they know the Stahlhast's scouts will make great sport with
any runners," Vaelin replied. "Besides, any who do take to their heels will be
doing us a service. If they run now, there's little chance they'll stand later."

He found Ahm Lin receiving a lesson in the spear from Alum. The mason
had always been a sturdy figure, and the muscles on his forearms bulged
impressively as he thrust the spear into a grain sack. But, strong as he was,
he was no longer young and had never been a warrior. His first thrusts were
swift and well placed, but grew notably slower and less accurate after only a
few minutes' effort.

"You don't really have to do this," Vaelin told him. "Alum and Sehmon
will guard you close when the time comes." In truth he had wanted to keep
Ahm Lin as far from the fighting as possible, but the potential advantage
offered by his song was too great. Also, the mason showed a marked aversion
to avoiding what he saw as his due share of the danger.

"A man should always be open to new skills," Ahm Lin said, smiling and
panting as he hefted his spear for another try.

"Killing isn't in his soul," Alum advised Vaelin in Alpiran. "He tries hard
but he's no fighter."

"He also speaks your language fluently," Vaelin said, seeing Ahm Lin
wince. He put a hand to his shoulder as Alum coughed in embarrassment.
"Any change?" he asked the mason, who shook his head.

"A tune that tells of approaching trouble only. But you don't need my song to know that, I'm sure."

Vaelin nodded and moved away. "Find me when it changes."

Ellese and Nortah were on the north-facing battlement of the city's outer wall. An ample supply of arrows surrounded them as they drew and loosed at a target some two hundred paces out on the scrub plain that surrounded the city.

"Missed again, my lord," Ellese told Nortah with a brief grin before forming her features into a frown of mock concern. "Perhaps your eyes are failing. A common trait amongst the elderly, I'm told."

"I've caned students older than you for insolence," Nortah replied, though his tone remained mild. He nocked and loosed again, his whole body moving with the effortless combination of strength and precision of a lifelong archer. Vaelin followed the arc of the shaft as it sank into the centre of the bristling target.

"Good," he told them. "Now move it another fifty yards out."

"We can't be sure of a kill at such a range," Nortah pointed out. "Not to mention the difficulty of finding a particular target in the confusion of battle."

"You'll have Juhkar to guide your aim," Vaelin said. "As for being sure of a kill, I have a notion about that."

◆ ◆ ◆

At Sho Tsai's urging, Sherin had established a makeshift healing house in the largest of the city's temples, joined by an assemblage of the local healers. Most of these were monks and nuns from various Heavenly orders, one of whom proved to be a familiar face.

"Wait a moment," Vaelin told Chien, who shrugged and found a shadowed corner as he went to greet the handsome woman bearing a basket of laundry.

"Mother Wehn," he said, bowing. "You are far from the High Temple."

The smile she gave him was faint, her handsome features tense with suppressed grief. "My order spent many hours in contemplation after your visit," she said. "We decided it was unseemly to continue to sit idle in her home when we could journey north in the faint hope of providing her some measure of assistance." She lowered her face. "We waited too long."

"It's my belief the Jade Princess set her own course many years ago," Vaelin told her.

"But it was all for nothing. She failed to halt the Stahlhast, failed to heal the heart of their false god." Mother Wehn's tone was one he had heard before, the voice of a soul nearing the limit of their faith.

"Their false god is beyond any healing," he said. "I think she knew that. She didn't come to stop him, but to show others that they needed to."

Mother Wehn smiled at this, but it was a tremulous thing, gone quickly as she briskly gathered laundry into a basket and went about her chores.

He found Sherin at a table in the temple's scriptorium, cutting strips from a plain cotton sheet to increase the stock of bandages. "I don't craft poison," she told him with a hard glare, her knife making another precise lateral cut through the fabric. "War is your province, not mine."

Her response didn't surprise him, but the anger it provoked in him did. "Do you want this place to fall?" he asked, voice growing heated. "See every soul within this temple slaughtered for failing to bow down to the Darkblade? And what do you imagine Sho Tsai's fate will be should the Stahlhast take this place?"

Her knife came down hard, the blade sinking deep into the surface of the table. Her fist lingered on the handle for a time, knuckles white before she snatched it away. It occurred to him that she had spent relatively little time in the general's company since arriving in the city, and he knew she would have had hard words for him regarding his orders when he sent Commander Deshai to Keshin-Ghol.

Taking a calming breath, she said, "That was unfair."

"War is never fair," he returned. "You've seen enough of it to know that. You heal so that others may live. I fight to do the same. It's what we've always done. Will you help me or not?"

She lowered her gaze, a small, bitter laugh escaping her lips. "Were we like this before?" she asked, voice soft with reflection. "Have I misremembered all these years? I cast you in the role of betrayer for so long perhaps it obscured how you really were, how I really was. Sometimes I think we were mere children playing at love."

His anger faded with as much swiftness as it had arrived, leaving a small but painful ball of regret in his gut. "I wasn't playing," he said, turning away and gesturing for Chien to come forward. "I have asked Mistress Pao to see to your safety. She will be at your side for the duration of the siege."

Sherin glanced at Chien, who replied with a cautious nod. "No disrespect to you," Sherin said, "but I don't require a bodyguard."

"Yes," Vaelin insisted, "you do. You are Gifted now, which makes you a target."

Sherin sighed and forced a smile at Chien. "Do you have any healing skill?"

"I can sew a cut," Chien said. "If it's not too deep. Also, I know how to mix poppy essence so it will banish pain without killing."

"Very well. You can stay. As to your mission, my lord . . ." she added, turning to Vaelin.

"Never mind," he said. "I'll find an apothecary somewhere in this city . . ."

"Come back tomorrow," she cut in, grunting as she worked the knife loose from the table. "Around noon. It'll be ready then."

◆ ◆ ◆

Commander Deshai returned two days later. Watching the cavalry approach the western gate, Vaelin reckoned its strength was perhaps one-third what it had been when it set out. They moved in a ragged formation, two wings flanking a central column of people towing carts or labouring under the weight of heavy bundles. As they filed through the gate, he saw the faces of both people and soldiers were blackened by smoke and sagging in exhaustion.

"We'd barely made it halfway through the province when the Tuhla came," Deshai reported to Sho Tsai. He had dismounted in the courtyard to offer the general a smart salute, but stood at attention on unsteady legs and voice dripping with fatigue. "Just a few hundred at first, we drove them off in short order, but they brought a swarm of their brethren back a day later. We burned all the crops we could, dumped animal carcasses in the wells. I doubt the enemy will glean much in the way of supplies from Keshin-Ghol. But it cost us, General." He turned his weary gaze on his men, many of whom were sinking to their knees the moment they slid from the saddle. "As you can see."

"I couldn't ask for more, Commander," Sho Tsai told him. His gaze tracked to the bedraggled farmers setting their burdens down. Perhaps half were men in their twenties or thirties, the rest a mix of younger women and a few children. "This is all?" he asked Deshai.

"The old folk either chose to stay or fell away on the trail," the commander replied. "Most of the people fled directly south, ignoring our offers of protection. I don't think much for their chances in open country. The Tuhla were in no mood to spare anyone. We even found children . . ." Deshai choked, face twitching before he mastered himself and coughed. "Your pardon, General."

"See to your men," Sho Tsai told him. "Then get some rest."

The commander gave another smart salute and marched unsteadily away, rousing his men with orders to stable their horses and clean their kit.

"So," Vaelin observed to the general, nodding at the beggared farmers. "No more supplies."

"And more mouths to feed into the bargain." Vaelin saw a decision flicker in Sho Tsai's gaze. "It's my intention to make this city the grave of the Stahlhast," he said. "To do that it must become a trap, a battlefield unencumbered by useless mouths and those who cannot fight."

A seed of worry crept into Vaelin's heart as he took in the stern resolve on Sho Tsai's face. "What do you intend?" he asked.

Some measure of his concern must have coloured his voice because the general replied with a short, caustic laugh. "Why, kill all the civilians in Keshin-Kho, of course. Is that what you expect me to say?" He shook his head. "The Barbarous East must truly be a terrible place. No, my lord, I have another plan in mind."

◆ ◆ ◆

"I have to say, I think I'd much rather walk."

Erlin's brows bunched in dubious appraisal as he looked over the barge. Vaelin had to admit it seemed incredible that the barges could remain afloat, so crammed with people were they. Most were women, mothers with children and as yet unwed daughters. The men were all old and few in number. The Great Northern Canal met its terminus in the lowest tier of Keshin-Kho, opening out into a circular harbour equal in size to anything Vaelin had seen in a mid-sized port in the Realm.

The useless mouths of the city clustered in a weeping but otherwise quiescent multitude on the quay, many saying hurried tear-soaked farewells to their husbands and sons before walking the ramps to the barges. Once a barge had sunk low enough that the water obscured the white line painted onto its hull, ropes would be cast and sails raised as it began its southward voyage.

"You wouldn't get more than a few miles before their scouts picked you up," Vaelin told Erlin. "And I'm keen for our enemy not to read this." He handed over the sealed scroll-tube along with the letter of free passage signed by Sho Tsai. "You have the gold secreted, I assume?"

"In my boot-heels and the lining of my jacket," Erlin assured him. "If a bandit should find one, hopefully they'll miss the other. Besides, I think any passing outlaws will find easier pickings elsewhere," he added, gesturing to the fleet of heavily laden barges.

Thanks to a low-key but constant exodus of civilians in recent months, the city was only two-thirds as populous as it had been before the crisis. Consequently, there was sufficient space aboard the long, deep-hulled barges to accommodate every soul in need of escape. Some had been given a choice, mainly men considered too old for military service but not so infirm that they had no use. Most of these elected to stay, Sho Tsai forming them into companies of porters who would distribute supplies and ferry wounded from the walls once the fighting started. But for most their departure had been decreed by the order of the Merchant King's General, and none had been left in any doubt regarding the consequences of refusal. Even so, Vaelin found their obedience strange. Had he ever attempted such a thing in North Tower, or any town in the Unified Realm, this would certainly have been a scene of chaos and angry remonstration, if not riot. But here the people made their farewells, heart-rending though they were, and meekly trooped onto the barges to be carried away south.

"Were I a braver man I'd be begging to stay," Erlin said, meeting Vaelin's gaze with a grimace of self-reproach.

"And were you a wiser man you'd already have left," Vaelin pointed out.

"An interval of self-delusion, I'm afraid. I had visions of joining the fight, repelling the savage horde, as much as my old bones would allow me, until I met my valiant end. It would have been a fine epitaph, don't you think?"

"You are commanded by the Tower Lord of the Northern Reaches, as a loyal servant of the Realm, to undertake a mission of vital importance and no small amount of peril. In truth, I feel shamed in not sending anyone with you."

"Your niece refused to leave, I take it?"

"Sehmon, too."

"I walked these realms alone for many a year, in times of war and in times of peace. Have no worries on my account, I will reach a port and find a ship."

Erlin hefted his staff and started towards the plank linking the barge to the dock. Before stepping aboard, he paused, voice faint with reflection as he said, "The Princess said I would be the last of us, you know. The old ones. I knew there had to be others somewhere in the world, but she was the only one I met. She told me of our fellow ancients, how, one by one, they had all come to seek her out, journeying from the far recesses of the world entire to hear her song. I was the only one who came back, because she and I were the only ones left now. She told me something once. I'm not sure if it matters amidst our current trials, but something tells me it does. She told me that whatever kept death from our door was not born of the black stone, for she was old before the first stone was ever dug from the earth."

He smiled and shrugged. "Something to ponder on the trail, I suppose." All humour faded from his face as he turned back to Vaelin. "Don't die here, brother," he said before striding onto the barge.

Vaelin watched the craft draw away from the mooring and join the line of barges, soon slipping beneath the huge iron portcullis that guarded the entrance to the harbour. The portcullis fell as soon as the final barge departed, chains rattling and iron squealing. It birthed a tall wave as it crashed into the water, causing the few remaining barges to bob at their moorings.

"Won't the Tuhla try to block the canal?" Vaelin asked Sho Tsai.

"Commander Deshai assures me they could never cover the distance in time," the general replied. "Why would they when they have so many other fleeing people to amuse themselves with in Keshin-Ghol?"

Sho Tsai called out to his son, who duly hurried over and snapped to attention. "General!"

"Burn those." Sho Tsai pointed to the bobbing barges. "Any avenue of retreat, however slight, may weaken the men's resolve."

"At once, General."

"I thought you might have promoted him by now," Vaelin said as the apprentice officer hurried off, shouting orders for the Red Scouts to light torches. "He's performing the duties of a captain, after all."

"He has been a soldier for less than two years," Sho Tsai replied. "The

Merchant King decrees at least five years' service before promotion can even be considered."

"You still cling to such things? Even now?"

"Do you throw off your Queen's Word simply because times are troubled?"

"No, but I will endeavour to find room for interpretation."

"Brother!" Vaelin turned at the sound of Ahm Lin's call, finding the mason hastening across the quay. "The tune," he said, coming to a halt, face grim. "It changed."

◆ ◆ ◆

"How many?"

"See for yourself." Sho Tsai stepped back from the spyglass and gestured for Vaelin to take his place. Peering through the eyepiece, he was struck by the clarity of the image, the steadily approaching riders appearing close enough that he could make out the details of their armour. Taking hold of the glass's tripod, he tracked the device across the ranks of the Stahlhast, making careful note of the banners he saw.

"I count six different Skeld," he said, pausing the glass in surprise as it alighted on a familiar sigil, a hawk, wings spread wide. "All told, over thirty thousand strong, I'd say. The Ostra amongst them," he added to Luralyn.

Together with Ahm Lin, the three of them had climbed the tall tower rising from the centre of the city to view the Stahlhast's arrival. The spyglass, a giant tubular contrivance far larger than any Vaelin had seen before, sat atop a brass tripod in the centre of a bare platform covered by a tiled roof but open on all sides. As a result, a constant northerly wind swept through the chamber, buffeting those inside and forcing them to converse in raised voices.

"I was expecting the horde entire," Sho Tsai said.

"This is just the vanguard," Luralyn told him, her braids whipping in the wind. "They will scout the surrounding country, kill any patrols you send beyond the walls, watch for reinforcements from the south. You can expect the full army within a day or so."

Vaelin raised a questioning eyebrow at Ahm Lin. The mason, still feeling the effects of the climb, rubbed at the ache in his back as he spoke. "I'm not sure," he said.

"Sure of what?" Sho Tsai enquired, his face intent. Ahm Lin's success in guiding them to Sherin's location had apparently convinced the general of the usefulness of the man's gift.

"The song speaks of imminent battle," Ahm Lin said. "And deceit. There is more at work here than just the scouting of an advance guard."

Vaelin stepped aside as the mason moved to press his eye to the glass, grunting softly. "Can't see them, but I also sense at least one Gifted soul amongst this lot."

"Deceit," Luralyn repeated. "It could be Sehga. Deception is her art. But she needs to be in close contact with a victim for it to work. She can't just cast it out like a torrent."

"Then who?" Vaelin asked.

"Someone I've yet to meet." Luralyn gave a helpless shrug. "If they are going to attack, it'll be tonight. My people will battle in open country in daylight, but they always attack a stronghold under cover of darkness. Also, they won't attack in one place. You should expect at least three separate assaults, probably launched at the same time."

Sho Tsai moved to the edge of the platform, brows furrowed as he surveyed the city below. "We double the strength of the regiments on the outer wall," he said. "Master mason, you will patrol the battlements under guard to gauge the point of attack."

"Whatever their stratagem they'll still need to scale the walls," Vaelin pointed out. "Cavalry can't charge a stone barrier twenty feet high. And they no longer have Varij's gift to crumble them."

"They'll have grapples and ropes," Luralyn replied. "Ladders too most likely."

"Ropes burn, so do ladders," Vaelin said, meeting her gaze. "So do people."

She gave a sober nod. "I'll warn the twins to be ready."

"What of your own abilities?" Sho Tsai asked. "I'm given to understand you can see the future."

"I see what the True Dream chooses to show me, and it shows me both past and future. But it has always been capricious. I have tried to summon it every night since we came here, but all I see are fragments, usually chaotic and meaningless. It's as if the future is in flux somehow. That could be a good thing. If the outcome of the battle is uncertain, then at least we have hope."

"Prophecy is all too often a liar," Vaelin said. "It lies to the prophet as much as the believer."

"I'll keep trying," Luralyn promised the general.

He nodded and started for the stairs. "Lord Vaelin, muster your scum and guard our allies close."

"Skulls," Vaelin said, the hardness of his tone causing the general to pause. "Not scum."

"What?" Sho Tsai asked.

"They've taken to calling themselves the Skulls," Vaelin explained. "Considering themselves already dead men. Soldiers do like their names, and that is what they are now. Soldiers. And I'd thank their general to refer to them as such."

Sho Tsai locked eyes with him for a moment, perhaps perceiving some form of challenge, but then grunted and began to descend the tower. "As long as they fight, I'll call them whatever name they wish."

Luralyn lingered a moment before following him down, gazing out at the expanse of the Iron Steppe to the north. The spyglass might have revealed her people's approach, but to the unassisted eye the horizon remained bare. "The Ostra were always his least ardent followers," she said. "Strange that he should choose them to lead his vanguard."

"Skeltir Varnko tried to convince me to leave," Vaelin recalled. "I assumed at your urging."

"No, that was his own act. He has long known that Kehlbrand's rise means potential destruction for the Stahlhast. If the Darkblade wanted you, it couldn't be good."

"And yet the Ostra still came to do the Darkblade's bidding."

"The dream of riding to the Golden Sea resides in the heart of every Stahlhast. Perhaps even Varnko couldn't resist it in the end."

Luralyn gave a sorrowful sigh and started down the stairs. Vaelin began to follow but stopped at Ahm Lin's mutter. "She lied, brother."

Vaelin turned to see the mason once again looking through the glass. "What a marvellous thing," he said, shaking his head as he stepped back to run an admiring glance over the device. "What I wouldn't give to open it up. The lenses must be ground with incredible precision."

"She lied?" Vaelin prompted.

"Oh, she didn't lie to us," Ahm Lin said. "She lied to herself, about her True Dream. It showed her far more than fragments."

"What did it show her?"

"Something her mind can't accept. Not yet at least. But I have a sense we'll all need her to remember very soon."

CHAPTER TWENTY-NINE

Handle it only when wearing gloves." Vaelin handed one small vial to Nortah, Ellese and Juhkar. "Even the smallest drop on bare skin could be fatal. And I'm told you shouldn't sniff it unless you want to permanently lose your sense of smell."

"What's in this?" Nortah asked, holding the vial up to the fading late evening light. The liquid inside seemed to have the viscosity of plain water and was mostly clear with a yellowish tinge.

"She wouldn't tell me," Vaelin said. "But you can be sure that any penetrating wound with a blade or arrowhead coated in this will undoubtedly prove fatal. Remember your instructions. Stay with Juhkar. He will guide your aim. Corporal Wei's squad will guard you. No haring off on your own, regardless of how tempting it might be." These words were addressed solely to Ellese, who began to reply with a roll of her eyes before noting the hardness of his gaze.

"I understand, Uncle," she said.

He left them at the north-facing gate and sought out Ahm Lin on the western battlement. The mason was flanked on either side by Alum and Sehmon with the full company of Skulls arrayed in two ranks behind. Vaelin paused to straighten the stance and spears of a few, taking a measure of satisfaction from the controlled trepidation he saw on most faces. A complete absence of fear would be more worrying than outright terror. Contrary to expectations, none had deserted during their forced march beyond the walls, although he suspected this was due to pragmatic self-preservation rather than any dutiful impulse.

"Corporal," he said, coming to a halt before the man known as Cho-ka.

The outlaw came smartly to attention with a well-practiced salute. "My lord!"

"You know your orders?"

"Preserve the mason's life at all costs."

The strict formality of his tone and bearing contrasted with the defiant smuggler Vaelin had met in the dungeons, causing him to wonder if the man might be harbouring some hidden mockery. However, careful scrutiny of the fellow's rigid features revealed nothing beyond soldierly resolve.

"Quite so," Vaelin said. "If he falls, so does this city. Make sure your men know that."

"I will, my lord."

"What tune do you have for me tonight?" Vaelin asked, joining Ahm Lin at the shoulder of one of the triangular crenellations that topped the wall, looking out into the gathering dark.

"The low growl of an approaching storm," the mason replied. His pensive gaze tracked from east to west, Vaelin noting how his hand twitched on the haft of the spear he insisted on carrying. "All around. The Stahlhast woman was right. They won't strike in just one place."

"And the Gifted?"

Ahm Lin could only shake his head. "They're out there somewhere, but as to their ability . . ." He trailed off with an apologetic shrug.

They began to hear the enemy as twilight faded into full darkness. The sky was clear, revealing a half-moon and a vast swathe of stars that would have been captivating at another time, but the gloom beyond the walls betrayed no sign of the Stahlhast. Instead, their approach was signalled by the drum of hooves and the weirdly musical jangle of massed armoured riders on the move. Vaelin saw Ahm Lin straighten as the noise abated, his head snapping to the west.

"What is it?" Vaelin asked.

"The song is loudest there." Ahm Lin pointed in the direction of the west-facing gate. His features bunched as if in pain and he added in a hiss, "There's a truly ugly note to it, brother."

"Stay here," Vaelin told him. "Guard him well," he added to Alum before sending one of the Skulls running to fetch Juhkar, Nortah and Ellese. He ordered the rest to follow as he made for the west gate. This section of wall was held by regular troops from the city's garrison, all hard-faced men with more than one battle in their past. He found Commander Deshai atop the small diamond-shaped bastion that housed the gate, sword already drawn as he peered at a row of flickering lights a few hundred paces from the wall.

"Torches?" Vaelin asked, coming to Deshai's side.

"Looks like it." The stocky commander rubbed his broad chin in consternation as more torches blazed to life until at least a hundred bobbed in the gloom. "Can't see the purpose to it. Stone won't burn and the gate is made of iron."

A series of shouts sounded along the wall as the bobbing torches seemed to blaze brighter in unison, each one growing into a large fireball. As the glow increased, Vaelin was able to make out the sight of large bundles of what looked like entangled gorse or sapling branches, each one bursting into flame at the touch of a torch. The lighted bundles glowed brightly for only a second or two before becoming dimmed by a thick pall of smoke. It swirled and eddied in a dense mass, its apparent immunity to the prevailing northerly wind convincing Vaelin that what he witnessed was far from natural. Some unseen hand had command of this miasma.

"Well, that complicates things," Nortah observed, coming to a halt at Vaelin's side, Ellese and Juhkar close behind.

"Can you sense them?" Vaelin asked the tracker.

"They're close," he confirmed, grimacing in frustration as he viewed the thickening smoke. "But not close enough."

More shouts rippled along the battlements as the smoke seemed to convulse, throbbing and expanding as if possessed of life. It grew paler as it spread, coalescing into vague, ghostlike shapes that began to drift towards the walls. The smoke gathered pace as it drew nearer, the shapes within it taking on clearer form, seeming to lope across the plain with swift, predatory energy. The shouts rose in volume, taking on a panicked edge that was only partially quelled by Deshai's barked orders commanding silence. The commander himself seemed only slightly less alarmed than his men, wide-eyed horror creeping over his face as he gaped at the fast-approaching host, a single word slipping from his lips in a fear-laden whisper: "Harbingers."

They were fully formed now, snarling as they sped towards the wall, each one the size of a horse, striped in black with eyes that glowed like silver orbs. "These are not the Harbingers of Heaven!" Vaelin called out as fresh panic swept through the ranks. "They are illusions! They cannot harm you!"

Such reassurance, however, found no purchase on the soldiers as the oncoming monstrosities reached the base of the wall, sweeping up and onto the battlement with hardly a pause. Shouts became screams as men reeled back from the slashing, snapping phantoms, well-ordered companies dissolving into chaos in the space of a few seconds.

"Stand where you are!" Vaelin barked at the Skulls, seeing them begin to waver, the first rank starting to edge back from the wall. "Smoke cannot pierce armour!"

Vaelin turned back to the wall to face a tiger as it clambered into view. "Watch!" he ordered, rushing forward to meet it. The tiger whirled towards him as he closed, mouth gaping in a roar that emerged as a howling gust of choking smoke. The sight of the cat's seemingly solid fangs and scythe-like claws birthed a momentary doubt regarding its harmlessness, but it was too late to avoid the collision. Vaelin found himself enveloped by the smoke, the tiger's blows like hard gusts against his armour, but inflicting no wounds. It dissipated as he wafted his sword about, leaving him coughing in the fading tendrils.

"You see?" he called to the Skulls, all staring in blank amazement. "These are phantoms. No more than mummery—"

Vaelin's exhortations died as Ellese sprang forward, bow fully drawn and aimed directly at his face. He instantly dropped to his knees, the arrow snapping the air above his head. Jerking around he was confronted by the sight of a tall Stahlhast warrior with an arrow jutting from the visor of his helmet. Sherin's poison swiftly fulfilled its promise, the warrior immediately collapsing onto the battlement, blood frothing from his mouth as he twitched once and lay still.

The corpse was quickly dragged from sight as another Stahlhast clambered to the top of the wall, teeth bared as he hauled himself up using the iron grapple lodged onto the crenellation. Seeing Vaelin, he reached for the sabre on his back, stiffening in death a heartbeat later as the Order blade speared him through the throat. Vaelin drew the sword clear, letting the man fall, casting his gaze left and right to take in the sight of the Stahlhast labouring up the wall wherever he looked. The battlement above was now fully shrouded in smoke, the soldiers within it milling in confused fear.

"Forward!" he called to the Skulls, pausing to hack the hand off another Stahlhast as they crested the wall. He saw the one-time outlaws hesitate, some still distracted by the smoke-crafted tigers wreaking chaos amongst the other soldiers. But then Corporal Cho-ka lowered his spear, gave a brief shout of command and charged forward. The Skulls followed, the carefully drilled tactic of repelling attackers with a disciplined advance of two well-ordered ranks forgotten as they surged in an untidy mass. Despite its lack of cohesion, the speed and violence of the Skulls' attack was enough to dislodge a score or more of Stahlhast at the first thrust of the spears.

"Cut the ropes!" Vaelin shouted, kicking another Stahlhast loose from the wall and slashing his blade through the rope the woman had been climbing. A series of enraged shouts from below indicated at least a dozen others were now plummeting to the ground. More followed in quick succession as the Skulls obeyed his command, all ropes within reach cut through in the space of a few seconds, although some were dragged to their deaths by the final desperate grabs of the enemy.

Robbed of their ability to scale the wall, the Stahlhast lingered at the base to assail those above with a hail of arrows from their strongbows, half a dozen Skulls reeling back with shafts embedded in face or neck.

"Oil and rocks!" Vaelin called to Cho-ka, who quickly organised a party to cast their baskets of heavy stones over the wall, followed in short order by the contents of several large clay jars filled with boiling oil. Screams of rage and pain from below indicated the tactic's success, and a brief glance over the edge revealed the sight of a hundred or more Stahlhast fleeing into the darkness, leaving behind twice the number of corpses and flailing wounded at the base of the wall.

"The gate!" Juhkar appeared at Vaelin's side, bow in hand. He pointed to the floor of the bastion. The entire structure was now almost entirely concealed in smoke as the phantom tigers continued to assail the battlements on either side. Vaelin could see no sign of Commander Deshai.

"There's more than one," Juhkar added, making for the nearest stairwell. Vaelin shouted to Cho-ka to hold in place and followed with Ellese and Nortah close behind. The tall tunnel that led into the guts of the bastion was so filled with smoke that Vaelin found it impossible to discern what might be happening within. It also roiled with phantom tigers, a wall of snarling cats that few of the soldiers nearby showed any inclination to approach.

He strained to hear the trundle of wheels that might indicate the approach of a battering ram sufficiently large to dislodge the gate, but instead heard only the din of battle and the shouts of panic from above. He was about to ask for guidance from Juhkar when he simply walked into the wall of smoke, bow raised. Vaelin started reflexively from the lunge of a smoke tiger, then steeled himself and followed the tracker into the fog. It was so thick he could barely see a foot in front of his nose, his throat catching the acrid sting, causing him to cough continually. He covered a dozen steps, then jerked aside, colliding with the tunnel wall as something fast and hard scraped over the shoulder guard of the hauberk he wore. The surrounding smoke twitched and the air thrummed with the buzz of multiple arrows.

Vaelin subsided into a crouch and pressed on, eyes streaming as he attempted to pierce the swirling, foul-tasting mist. He hissed as an arrow scored a shallow groove across the back of his hand, then flinched as another careened off the bricks an inch from his head. From his right came the hard thrum of a bowstring followed by the sound of an arrowhead striking metal. He heard Juhkar curse before launching another arrow, this time producing the hard thwack of a shaft finding flesh.

The smoke immediately began to thin, the twisting shadows of cats fading away into coiling wisps, the criss-cross edifice of the gate standing revealed. The tunnel beyond the gate was thick with Stahlhast, a brace of archers in front, aiming their strongbows through the small gaps in the iron lattice. The body of a young man lay against the gate, bloodied face pressed to one of the gaps and an arrow jutting from his shoulder. Next to him stood a sturdy woman in leather armour, very much alive and clutching the gate with a fierce grip. Blood trickled from her nose, face quivering with strain. The iron seemed to glow beneath her fingers, softening and contracting.

Lehkis, Luralyn had said. *A special way with metal.*

"Kill her!" Vaelin called to Juhkar, turning to find the tracker crumpled against the wall, one arrow in his leg and another through his shoulder. Seeing the sturdy woman tear a piece of glowing iron loose from the gate, Vaelin drew a throwing knife from his boot and cast it at her. It was a decent throw but the woman was clearly no stranger to battle, jerking her head aside as the knife came spinning through the gap, slicing off part of her ear. With a shout, she clamped her hands on the gate once more, the metal glowing and softening as if it lay within the heart of the forge.

Stahlhast arrows chased Vaelin across the tunnel as he rushed to Juhkar, retrieving his fallen bow and reaching for his quiver. Before he could nock a shaft, a pair of arrows streaked past, both expertly aimed to find the gaps in the gate. One struck the Gifted woman in the thigh and the other in the belly. This time the effects of Sherin's poison were somewhat spectacular. Blood exploded from the woman's mouth in a thick crimson flower and she spasmed with such violence that Vaelin could hear the crack of her bones breaking. She seemed to deflate as she collapsed against the iron barrier, her hands slipping from the part-melted metal.

More arrows followed in quick succession, swiftly felling three of the Stahlhast archers. But there were plenty to take their place, Vaelin shrinking low to avoid a fresh hail of shafts.

"For Faith's sake, brother, get out!" Nortah's voice echoed loudly, Vaelin glancing back to see him and Ellese crouched at either side of the tunnel's mouth, loosing shaft after shaft with typical speed and precision. Vaelin's sense of urgency was further enhanced by the sight of Luralyn approaching across the courtyard beyond, flanked on either side by the Gifted twins and the Red Scouts in close formation behind.

Grasping Juhkar about the chest, Vaelin dragged him towards the exit. Nortah and Ellese continued to cut down the Stahlhast archers, their perfectly aimed arrows creating a shield of twitching, poison-raddled corpses that prevented their comrades from taking their place. Vaelin pulled Juhkar clear of the tunnel just as the twins reached it, arms raised. Fortunately, the roar of the torrent of flame they sent into the tunnel was sufficient to swamp the screams of those inside. The twins continued to pour fire into the bastion until they sagged in exhaustion, the flames fading to reveal a blackened tunnel and gate, speckled with lingering flame but still mercifully intact. The tunnel beyond was carpeted with charred, steaming bodies.

"Get him to the temple," Vaelin said, hefting Juhkar into the arms of two Red Scouts. "Take them with you," he added, nodding at the twins.

"There's still fighting here," Kihlen said, staggering a little as he wiped the blood from his face.

Vaelin stood back to survey the walls above. With the spectral harbingers banished, the Merchant soldiery had been quick to recover their discipline. Several knots of Stahlhast had managed to gain purchase on the battlements but were being vigorously assailed on all sides, whilst scores of crossbowmen rushed to fill the gaps along the wall.

"We can hold without you," Vaelin told Kihlen. "Best conserve your strength."

"They also attacked from the north and south-east," Corporal Wei said as the Scouts carried Juhkar's unconscious form away. "Seized a good-sized portion of the wall near the north gate but the general led a countercharge that scraped them off good and proper."

A flurry of shouts drew Vaelin's gaze back to the wall. A regiment of soldiers were jabbing their spears into the air, shouting in feral triumph, boots stomping the Stahlhast bodies littering the battlements. Only one knot of attackers continued to fight on, a dark cluster of thrashing defiance amidst the tide of encroaching spearmen. One familiar figure in the centre of the melee slashed his sabre left and right with furious energy, seemingly indifferent to the certainty of death.

"Go with them," Vaelin told Corporal Wei, nodding at the retreating Gifted.

With Ellese and Nortah following he climbed the stairs to the rampart, stepping over the mingled bodies of attacker and defender, pausing at the sight of Commander Deshai, lying dead with a sabre point thrust deep into his neck. The commander's hands were wrapped around the neck of the Stahlhast who had killed him, the fingers gouged into the flesh.

"Pity," Nortah said. "A capable fellow."

An upsurge of shouts from the edge of the bastion drew Vaelin on, seeing the familiar figure now forced to one knee, the only surviving Stahlhast on the wall. Varnko's armour sported a half-dozen crossbow bolts, and the stone beneath him was slick with blood. He still had enough life left to snarl at the soldiers as they closed in, spears levelled for the killing thrust.

"Stop!" Vaelin called out, striding forward and waving the soldiers back. "This man is my prisoner."

They continued to stare at him, the bloodlust and rage of battle fading to leave a host of confused and besmirched faces. "Stop gawping!" Vaelin snapped. "See to the wounded." He gestured to the surrounding bodies, most dead but some still clinging to life.

"I . . ." Varnko rasped as the soldiers withdrew, "am not . . . giving up my blade . . . whilst there's still breath in me."

Vaelin crouched at his side, reaching out to steady the Skeltir to prevent him toppling over. "I wouldn't dream of taking it."

Varnko hunched in pain, the tip of his sabre scraping on the stone as he tried to prop himself up. Vaelin caught him before he could fall, easing him against the nearest crenellation. "Sherin is here," Vaelin told him. "She'll heal you like she healed your boy."

Varnko snorted, blood speckling his lips "My boy . . . has chosen . . . to hate me," he said in a halting gasp. "Said I stole . . . his renown . . . by sparing him a death in battle." He bared reddened teeth in a grin. "Ungrateful little . . . fucker, eh?"

"Ungrateful indeed. Come." Vaelin beckoned Nortah closer, preparing to lift the Skeltir. "We'll take you to her."

"No!" Varnko pushed his hands away. "Don't . . . sully my death."

His gaze was fierce with resolve, but Vaelin could see a plea in it too. The Skeltir of the Ostra Skeld was begging to be allowed to die. "As you wish," he said, waving Nortah back.

Varnko's body slackened against the stone and he grunted with the effort of shifting his sabre to rest it across his knees. "This . . ." he said, tracing a finger along the many nicks and scratches of the blade's curve, "was my father's . . . He wasn't Skeltir . . . died too young to make a challenge . . . But, I . . . it seems, lived too long."

He cast his gaze over the bodies littering the rampart. "Oh, my Skeld. Look . . . at what he made of us. Once we were great . . . now no more than the fanatic army of a madman . . ."

"Why?" Vaelin asked. "Why did you follow him? You know he is no god."

Varnko's eyes grew dim as his head lolled towards the plain beyond the battlement. "The lure of the Golden Sea . . . is hard to resist. For all our feuds . . . the Stahlhast are bound together . . . with steel. And he promised . . . such renown. In that, at least . . . he didn't lie."

The Skeltir's gaze slid back to Vaelin, eyes brightening as he summoned the last vestiges of strength. "My son . . . abased himself before that deceiver," he grunted, shuddering with the effort of speaking. "Begged forgiveness for . . . his father's weakness. Now he stands . . . ever at the Darkblade's side . . . his most loyal dog. This . . ." He gripped the sabre's hilt, trying to raise it. "Is not . . . for him. I gave you a fine . . . gift. Now, I ask for payment in kind. Find a suitable hand . . . to wield this." Trembling, he pushed the sabre towards Vaelin.

"I will," he said, reaching out to touch his fingers to the pommel. "Skeltir," he said, shuffling closer. "I must know, how many people with the Divine Blood does the Darkblade possess? What are their gifts?"

"More"—Varnko bared his crimson teeth once again—"than mere smoke, my friend . . ."

The Skeltir's head slumped one final time, his last breath spattering a red mist onto Vaelin's hand.

"Ellese," he said, rising and hefting the sabre.

"Uncle?" She peered curiously at the blade as he held it out to her, hilt first.

"Your mother once owned something similar, as I recall," Vaelin told her. "This man asked for a fitting hand to wield it. I think yours will fit very well."

She gave a tight smile and took hold of the sabre. "Mother taught me the sword," she said, coughing to clear the sudden hoarse note in her voice. "But I was always better with the knife and the bow."

"So was she."

"Let's see him on his way," Nortah said, nodding at Varnko's corpse. "You have some knowledge of their funeral rites?"

"No," Vaelin said, raising his gaze to the plain, where more bodies littered the ground, felled by a swarm of crossbow bolts as they fled. They were not easily counted, causing him to conclude that most of the warriors belonging to the Ostra Skeld must have perished this night. *Perhaps that's what he wanted*, he thought, looking once again at Varnko's slumped, empty form. *To spare them becoming what Kehlbrand would twist them into.*

"Just throw him over with the others," he added. "I think he would prefer that."

CHAPTER THIRTY

The Darkblade's full host appeared on the northern horizon two days later. The great mass of riders approached to within a mile of the city before spreading out to the east and west to raise their town-sized camps. The infantry arrived as the day slipped towards evening, moving in loose ranks that told of a general lack of martial discipline as did their mismatched armour and weapons. Many wore the hauberks and carried the spears of fallen Merchant soldiery, whilst others were clad in dark breastplates and mail of Stahlhast manufacture.

"The Redeemed," Luralyn named them. "Former artisans from the tors and denizens of conquered lands and tribes, all convinced of my brother's godhood."

"Not convinced enough to march in good order, apparently," Sho Tsai said. The three of them stood atop the bastion of the north-facing gate, watching the host as it continued to spread. Camps were appearing to the south-east and west, indicating that the city would soon be surrounded.

"Most are new to soldiering, it's true," Luralyn replied. "But make no mistake, many have already tasted battle and they will all happily die for the Darkblade."

"Their full number?" the general enquired.

"My people are not as fond of counting as yours." She gave an apologetic shrug. "They are many."

"I'd estimate somewhere over sixty thousand," Vaelin said. "Together with the Stahlhast and the Tuhla, we face an army close to three hundred thousand strong."

"We counted more than two thousand enemy bodies after their first attack. But we lost much the same number fighting them off." Sho Tsai exchanged a glance with Vaelin as they both pondered a grim arithmetic and arrived at the same conclusion. The defenders of this city would bleed their strength away with every attack whilst their enemy remained strong.

"An army of such size will lay waste to the Northern Prefecture," the general said. "Perhaps even menace the heartland of the kingdom."

"Kehlbrand is not interested in laying waste," Luralyn said. "Nor will he stop until he has claimed all the realms of the Merchant Kings. His army will only grow as he conquers. Everywhere he steps he finds more adherents, more Redeemed to swell his ranks."

"Then we have to stop him here. Or at least bleed his horde so white it will stand little chance against the full might of the Merchant armies."

"Meaning we'll have to kill six of them for any one of us that falls," Vaelin said. "A hard prospect."

"But not an impossible one. I've seen armies break on less formidable walls than these." Sho Tsai straightened, turning a shrewd gaze on Luralyn. "Your brother will not delay, I assume? He will attack tonight."

She nodded. "Everywhere he can."

"Then we will meet him everywhere. Lord Vaelin, I hereby appoint you in Commander Deshai's place. You will take charge of all the regiments on the western wall. Ensure your men know that there is to be no retreat. Any man who takes a single backward step will kneel before the headsman come the morning."

"This city was constructed to allow for successive retreats." Vaelin nodded at the second tier of Keshin-Kho. "We know there are more Gifted out there. Should the outer wall be breached . . ."

"Our tactics have already proven sound. Our own Blessed-of-Heaven will match theirs. You agreed to submit to my orders." His eyes grew hard as they lingered on Vaelin's and he spoke with careful deliberation. "Not one step back."

Vaelin felt a strong impulse to argue, point out that Juhkar was injured and unlikely to recover for days. In order to discern the presence of the Darkblade's Gifted, they would have to rely on Ahm Lin's song, which lacked

the tracker's precision. *You are not Battle Lord here,* he reminded himself.
And there is always merit in a staunch defence.

"As you command, General," he said with a formal bow.

◆ ◆ ◆

As Luralyn predicted there was no lull before the storm, the first attacks
coming less than an hour after sunset. They fell on the eastern flank first, ten
thousand or more Redeemed streaming out of the dark to assail the walls
with scaling ladders. Having been warned of the assault by Ahm Lin, Sho
Tsai had rushed additional reinforcements to the sector. Vaelin could hear
the din of battle even from across the city, detecting a strange rhythmic note
amidst the discordant cacophony.

"Battle prayers," Eresa explained. "The Redeemed sing them in praise of
the Darkblade as they charge." She gave a short, strained laugh at the absurdity of her former comrades as she adjusted the hauberk she wore. It had
been greatly modified to match her diminutive frame but still caused no end
of irritation. She had been placed amongst the Skulls, whilst Jihla had been
stationed on the northern bastion and her brother assigned to the eastern
wall. Luralyn, at Sho Tsai's insistence, remained atop the second inner wall
with Varij and the Red Scouts. Vaelin had made sure to leave Corporal
Cho-ka in no doubt that the primary duty of the Skulls was to protect the
Blessed-of-Heaven in their midst.

"Just don't get too close when she uses her gift," he advised.

The struggle to the east wore on for close to two hours. At any moment
Vaelin expected one of the lookouts he had placed on the intervening rooftops to come running with word that the Redeemed had broken through.
However, when a message did arrive, it was carried by one of Sho Tsai's personal company of runners recruited from the Imperial Messenger Service.

"The mason warns of an attack from the west, my lord," the man reported, skidding to a halt and sinking to one knee.

Vaelin was about to ask when he should expect the assault, when the hiss
of multiple arrows came from beyond the walls. He reached out to grab the
messenger's arm as the man began to rise from his bow, the arrow that
would have ended him flicking his hair instead.

Vaelin moved in a crouch to the battlement, risking a glance around the
flank of a crenellation to see a mass of riders galloping in parallel to the wall
less than fifty paces out. As they galloped they loosed arrows from their

strongbows with a speed and accuracy he felt would have impressed the Eorhil. Before a volley of steel-headed shafts forced him back into cover, he was able to make out the leather armour of their assailants.

"Inform the general we're under attack by the Tuhla," he told the messenger. The man bowed and descended the nearest stairwell to sprint off through the streets.

"Save your bolts!" Vaelin snapped at a crossbowman who had bobbed up to loose at the riders. "Heads down."

He cast his voice along the battlement as he moved among the assembled companies. "This is no more than a nuisance," he told them, making sure to meet the gaze of as many men as he could. He deliberately spared no glances for the few men lying with arrows embedded in face or neck. He had long learned that command in battle required a certain indifference to such sights.

The arrow storm continued for another minute and then lessened, Vaelin risking another glance over the wall to see the Tuhla had come to a halt, forming a series of loose companies. They maintained their barrage whilst a mass of Redeemed infantry bearing scaling ladders streamed between the gaps in their ranks. Gauging their number was impossible with the Tuhla shafts still raining down, but he saw enough to know they faced an assault equal in scale to that already launched against the eastern flank.

"Crossbows up!" he shouted, the command echoed by sergeants and officers the length of the wall. "Aim your first volley at the riders, then lower sights to the infantry!"

There wasn't sufficient time for his order to reach the ears of every crossbowman, but enough heard it to send a thick hail of bolts into the halted Tuhla. Riders and horses fell by the dozen, the companies losing cohesion and expanding to obstruct the charge of the Redeemed. The Tuhla arrow storm faded completely as a gap appeared between the infantry closing on the wall and those behind.

Vaelin watched a crossbowman reload his weapon with impressive efficiency. Far Western crossbows differed from those of the Realm, with a longer stave allowing for similar range to a longbow. The man placed his foot in a stirrup where the stock joined the stave, a fresh bolt clenched between his teeth as he used both hands to draw the string into the lock. He brought the weapon up, settling the stock atop his shoulder, nocking the bolt to the string and loosing with a single flick of the trigger before instantly starting the cycle over again. Vaelin tracked the bolt as it arced into the advancing Redeemed, seeing one of those bearing a ladder stumble to the ground. The ladder was swiftly recovered by a dozen of his comrades who clustered at the base of the wall to heave it into place.

Vaelin could hear their battle prayers now; the words were in the Stahlhast tongue, which jarred on the ear at the best of times and became uglier still when shouted from a fanatical throat. Officers ordered oil and rocks thrown as the ladders began to ascend and soon screams replaced prayers. Most of the ladders fell away as the crossbowmen lowered their aim further, some leaning out to loose straight down at the massing infantry below. Of the half-dozen ladders that remained in place, three were swiftly hacked clear by axe-wielding sergeants following Vaelin's instruction to chop away the top two feet of timber. The Redeemed that attempted to scale the other ladders found themselves assailed from both sides by a hail of bolts. Barely a handful managed to reach the battlements, only to be instantly speared and thrown down. The remaining ladders were all cast away in short order, meaning the second wave of Redeemed had nothing to climb once they struggled clear of the milling Tuhla.

Despite the unceasing attentions of the crossbowmen, the Redeemed failed to retreat, instead gathering up the fallen ladders and attempting to renew their assault. All the while they chanted their mad battle prayer, Vaelin seeing several still mouthing the words even as they lay pierced and bleeding. The hot oil was exhausted but each company had been provided with a large stock of heavy stones cannibalised from houses in the lower tier. Vaelin ran along the battlement, barking orders for the stones to be cast over, and soon a torrent of rubble cascaded down onto the attackers, shattering ladders and crushing skulls. Even then the Redeemed displayed a marked reluctance to retreat, lingering in a large vulnerable mob a short remove from the walls, some throwing the remnants of the stones back at their tormentors whilst others screamed in irrational defiance.

"They remind me a bit of that Cumbraelin lot from the High Keep," Nortah remarked, loosing an arrow that arced into the gaping mouth of one yelling Redeemed. "At least they had the good manners to die quietly."

Vaelin had found his brother alongside Ellese at the point where the wall angled towards the northern bastion. From the few arrows remaining in their quivers, it seemed they had done a great deal of service this night. The pair soon exhausted all but their poison-tipped arrows, adding several more corpses to the growing pile of dead. Still the Redeemed continued to stand and rail at the hated unbelievers on the walls, although Vaelin noted the plain beyond was now bare of Tuhla. He resisted the impulse to order the crossbowmen to cease their volleys. Although these people no longer posed a danger tonight, he saw wisdom in Sho Tsai's tactics. The outcome of this siege would ultimately be decided by numbers, and the more they killed now the less they would face tomorrow.

"Do they want to die?" Ellese wondered, shaking her head as the cluster of Redeemed shrank ever smaller.

"Perhaps," Nortah said in a cautious murmur, his gaze turned towards the northern bastion. "Or perhaps they just want to keep our sight from something else."

Following his gaze Vaelin saw there to be some form of commotion atop the bastion, one of the well-ordered regular companies stationed there becoming suddenly disrupted. The troops on either side appeared unaffected and he could hear none of the shouts and chants that might signify an attack. Even so he knew instinctively he was looking upon men in combat. He was about to call for one of the Skulls to go and investigate when the disordered company was engulfed in a bright sheet of flame. Screams pealed into the night and men fell and rolled amid the blaze, the soldiers on either side forced back by the heat.

"Ready your poisoned shafts," Vaelin told Nortah, starting along the battlement at the run. "Ellese, find Eresa and bring her to the northern bastion."

They were obliged to force their way through a suddenly unruly throng of soldiers, their ranks bunching as they backed away from the fiery spectacle, deaf to Vaelin's orders to get back into line. He sought out the officers and sergeants, themselves staring in shock at the flames engulfing the company atop the bastion, but all proving responsive to an authoritative voice after some judicious shouting. With their help, order was swiftly restored, Vaelin hurrying through the straightened ranks to find Jihla on the bastion. The woman was on her knees, face stricken and wet with tears as she stared at the now-smoking remnants of the company a few yards away.

"I had to," she said in a whisper. She looked up at Vaelin with eyes that begged understanding. "They just started killing each other. Some began to turn on the other soldiers. I had to . . ."

Vaelin fought down his gorge at the thick stench of men roasted in their armour, surveying the carnage as Nortah muttered a name they both rarely spoke: "Caenis."

"What?" Vaelin said.

"I saw him wreak much the same havoc on the Volarians." Nortah's face was dark with unwanted memories. "The day he died in that fucking temple. He bled himself dry saving us." His brows creased as he continued to examine the scene. "He had to be close for it to work," he added, turning back to Vaelin. "Close enough to see them."

"Move back!" Vaelin called out to the surrounding soldiers. "No man is to show himself above the wall!"

The long lines of soldiers duly retreated as the order was relayed through the ranks. Vaelin crouched with Nortah behind one of the tall buttresses that marked the outermost point of the bastion. "Don't, brother," Nortah said as Vaelin began to edge forward, hoping to spy their Gifted assailant. "One glance might be enough."

Vaelin turned at the sound of running feet, seeing Ellese arrive at the head of the Skulls with Eresa in tow. The small woman immediately went to her knees at Jihla's side, pulling her tearful face into her shoulder.

"Wait a moment," Vaelin told Nortah, keeping to a crouch as he moved to Eresa's side. "I have a task for you," he told her.

"Together we have contrived to do some very stupid things over the years," Nortah said a few moments later. He stood with his back braced against the buttress, poison-tipped arrow nocked and bowstring half-drawn. His face was tense with a contrasting mix of determination and deep reluctance. "But perhaps none so stupid as this."

"A power such as this could undo the whole defence," Vaelin said. "We have to end it now."

He glanced over his shoulder at Eresa. "Be ready," he told her. "And don't hesitate."

Her reluctance was only marginally less acute than Nortah's, face pale and eyes wide, but she nodded and pressed a hand to the rear of his hauberk. Vaelin could feel the tremble of it even through the barrier of metal and leather. He took a breath and rose to his full height, stepping out from the edge of the buttress to stand in full view of whatever waited beyond the wall. He blinked in surprise at finding the ground to the front of the bastion free of enemies, although he could see the dark mass of a poised army waiting in the gloom beyond, edged steel and armour catching the moonlight. Then he saw the boy.

He couldn't have been more than twelve, dressed in the garb of the border folk. He stood close to where the glow of the torches on the wall faded into the shadowed plain. Seeing Vaelin he put his hands to his mouth, a shrill, delighted giggle audible in the otherwise silent air. Even from this distance Vaelin could see the manic gleam in the boy's eyes, the joyful anticipation that comes from being presented with a new toy. Jumping with excitement, he darted forward, still giggling, bright, excited eyes fixed on Vaelin.

He felt the boy's gift slide into him like a narrow-bladed dagger, sinking deep into his core and birthing an instant flare of rage. It started as a burning seed in his chest, causing his heart to race and temples to throb. He let out a gasp as what felt like a nest of hornets suddenly burst into life in his head, memories of every battle he had fought flicking through his mind in a blinding torrent. With each thunderous pulse of his heart he felt the pain and fury of every wound suffered and inflicted. His sword was in his hand, though he couldn't recall drawing it. He felt his lips form a snarl as the rage doubled and then redoubled, consuming him. The world shrank, became a crimson mist of vague figures, the sight of which birthed a hate and a need . . . a need to kill.

He fought it, struggling through the fog to summon all the memories of joy and goodness he could muster. *Dahrena's smile, Dentos's stories, Aspect Elera that day in the garden* . . . His vision cleared enough to allow him the sight of Nortah. His brother stood with his bow fully drawn and aimed beyond the bastion. However, his face lacked the hard focus of an archer about to launch a killing arrow. Instead, Nortah stared at the boy below in frozen horror, lips moving in an appalled murmur. "Just a child . . ."

The rage reasserted itself then, returning the world to a hate-fuelling state, the snarl reclaiming Vaelin's features as he lunged towards his brother, sword drawn back for the killing stroke . . .

An instant of purest white banished the world. Vaelin felt his back arch, the angle of it so acute he would wonder later why his spine hadn't snapped. A thrum of power shot through his core and into his limbs, the sword falling from spasming fingers. The white faded and in the brief second it took him to fall into darkness, he saw Ellese, moving as if through thickened air, shoving Nortah aside, teeth bared as she drew her bow. Everything slipped away the moment she loosed, Vaelin hearing Nortah's despairing cry as he slipped into the black.

CHAPTER THIRTY-ONE

He awoke to the iron sting of blood in his throat and the ache of overstrained muscles. Gagging, he rolled on a hard floor, coughing out a red, globular mass. He gasped and retched for a while longer until the acrid taste faded from his mouth. Subsiding onto his back, he blinked until the tears cleared to reveal the ornate lattice of the temple ceiling.

"Here, drink."

He blinked again, seeing Sherin kneeling at his side, a cup of water in her hands. He took it and drank, washing away the last dregs of blood from his tongue. Groaning, he sat up, wincing as every sinew in his body seemed to shout a protest.

"Eresa couldn't quite believe that you lived," Sherin informed him. "It seems you're the first to survive her touch."

Vaelin looked himself over. His hauberk and boots had been removed but his shirt and trews remained. He could see no obvious injury, and the ache was fast diminishing. "Did you . . . ?" he began but stopped when Sherin shook her head.

"Not this time. Despite some violent convulsions your pulse remained strong, so it seemed likely you would recover without my assistance. There's a strange, hand-shaped mark on your back, which I suspect you'll carry for the rest of your life. But otherwise . . ."

She trailed off at the sound of panicked whimpering, rising and moving to the side of a soldier lying on a nearby bed. The man's eyes were bandaged and he flailed his arms about, groping for something as he mumbled a scarcely comprehensible demand that his wife light the lanterns.

Vaelin got to his feet as Sherin calmed the soldier, easing him back into the bed and murmuring soft reassurances until he settled. Surveying the temple, Vaelin saw every bed now held an occupant, whilst the less grievously wounded lay on blankets on the bare floor, as he had. The nuns and monks moved amongst them ceaselessly, each face showing signs of fatigue that told of a long and arduous night. He saw Chien holding a man's leg still as one of the healers stitched a deep cut in his thigh.

"How many?" Vaelin asked Sherin.

She smoothed a hand over the blinded soldier's brow and moved away, going to a neat stack of rolled bandages. "The general has ordered that a count of the casualties no longer be kept," she said, a well-controlled bitterness pervading her tone. "It's bad for morale, apparently."

She took a basket and began filling it with bandages. "Time to make my rounds," she said. "I had to tell the others to wait outside. Your niece was being a particular nuisance, I must say."

"As is her way." He reached out to take the basket. "Rounds can wait. I need something from you."

Juhkar lay on a bunk in one of the monk's chambers, skin beaded with sweat and eyes dim as he stared up at Vaelin. The bandage on his thigh was clean and spotted with a few drops of blood, but the covering on his shoulder was dark and Vaelin's nostrils twitched at the familiar scent of corrupted flesh.

"So you got another," the tracker said, pale lips forming a smile. "Seems you don't need me after all."

Vaelin chose not to tell him that the Gifted they had claimed the night before had been a child, maddened and cruel to be sure, but still a child. "Nonsense," he said, pressing a reassuring hand to Juhkar's arm. "We need you more than ever."

He moved to Sherin's side, lowering his voice. "His shoulder?"

"Gangrene," she confirmed. "I had an effective curative for it but used most of it healing the Stahlhast boy, the rest during the last few days. I've tried a few alternatives, but none work quite as well."

Sherin angled her head as understanding dawned. "You want me to heal him." She let out a short laugh and shook her head. "You assign that outlaw woman to render me unconscious if I try to use my gift—don't lie, she told me that's why she's really here—now this. Why?"

"Because I doubt this city will have a chance without him," Vaelin responded in simple honesty, knowing it would be the only tactic likely to win her over.

She sighed and nodded. "Very well, wait outside. It won't take long . . ."

"There's something else," Vaelin cut in as she started towards the bed. "He's Gifted."

"I'm aware of that."

"Something always comes back. Weaver told me that once. Every time he healed someone, they gave something of themselves in return. By the time we parted he was possibly the most powerful and dangerous being alive. If you heal this man, it's likely you won't possess just one gift."

She paused, crossing her arms as she looked hard at Juhkar's feverish form. "Why tell me this?" she asked, voice faint.

"It has to be a choice you make freely," he told her. "Knowing full well the consequences."

"Having already told me the consequences if I don't. Always the way with you, nothing but hard choices." She uncrossed her arms, moving to sit on the bed and taking Juhkar's hand. "Wait outside," she repeated.

◆ ◆ ◆

"You're alive." Eresa's small face was blank with astonishment as her eyes tracked him from head to toe.

"So it seems," Vaelin said.

"Told you," Ellese said, coming forward to embrace her uncle. "A few sparks could never put him down."

Vaelin saw mostly relief in her expression as she stepped back, but also a new shadow behind her eyes that hadn't been there before. Guilt, he supposed, had been a rare sensation for her until now.

"The boy?" he asked.

"Swift-footed little bugger, the arrow just grazed him." She shrugged, forcing a grin that didn't last long. "It was enough."

"Brother." Nortah came to Ellese's side, Vaelin seeing a depth of shame in his face greater even than in the aftermath of his most drunken excesses. "I . . ."

"It's done," Vaelin told him. "With luck, it won't need to be done again."

"No one ever lives," Eresa muttered, continuing to stare at Vaelin, a small measure of fear creeping into her gaze until Luralyn voiced a pointed cough. "Apologies, my lord." Eresa gave a bow that was a clumsy approximation of Far Western etiquette.

"For what?" Vaelin clasped her shoulder, raising her up. "You did what I commanded."

Sehmon stepped forward bearing Vaelin's weapons and armour, whilst Alum stood off to the side, a faintly reproachful scowl on his features. "You take many risks," he said as Vaelin donned his hauberk. "I'm unlikely to find our children with you dead."

"You could have left," Vaelin reminded him, looping his sword belt over his shoulder. "Continued the search on your own. As I've said more than once, you have no obligation to me."

"We both know that not to be true," the Moreska replied. "And I hold true to my cousin's word."

They straightened as one as the plaintive but resonant sound of many signal horns blowing in unison drifted across the temple precinct. "Attacking in daylight," Vaelin said, looking at Luralyn. "Your brother changes tactics."

"No," Ahm Lin said, eyes narrowed and head tilted in the now-familiar pose that told of a new tune from his song. "This is no attack."

"What else could it be?" Nortah wondered.

"Parley," Luralyn said with a sorrowful sigh. She took a breath and strode briskly towards the temple gate. "My brother wants to talk."

◆ ◆ ◆

Kehlbrand Reyerik, Mestra-Skeltir of the Stahlhast and Darkblade of the Unseen, rode alone towards the northern gate. He wore no helm but was clad in unadorned armour of pure black that caught the midday sun, the enamelled metal bare of any blemish or scratch. His army stood at his back, a dark line of steel-clad humanity and horses extending a mile in either direction. The entire army chanted prayers as he approached, Vaelin noting how Luralyn's dismayed gaze tracked from the ranks of the Tuhla to the Stahlhast.

"So he has claimed them all now," she said. "The Darkblade rules without challenge or restraint."

She rode her white stallion at Sho Tsai's left whilst Vaelin rode Derka on his right. From the way the beast tossed his head and continually sought to

spur from a canter to a gallop, Vaelin divined he hadn't taken well to prolonged confinement in the garrison stables.

Sho Tsai raised his hand to bring them to a halt just within bowshot of
the walls. A dense line of crossbowmen were arrayed on the battlements,
ready to unleash an inescapable and deadly hail at the general's signal.

Kehlbrand reined to a stop just beyond range of the crossbows, leaving a
distance of no more than ten paces between them. His expression was a
marked contrast to the occasionally sardonic and often knowing face Vaelin
had come to despise. Now he appeared every inch the grave, resolute warrior,
complete with a reluctant cast to his eyes presumably intended to convey the
sense of a soul facing a dire but necessary duty.

The chanted prayers died as Kehlbrand held up a hand, absolute silence
descending on his army in an instant. "Little colt," he said to Luralyn, the
words clipped as if to strip them of any betraying but still deeply felt emotion. "You are well?"

"No," she replied, her own voice roughened by an unconstrained pain.
"My brother went mad and killed a great many people imagining himself to
be a god. So no, Kehlbrand. I am not well."

Vaelin saw a brief flicker of something beneath Kehlbrand's mask then,
a slight shift to his eyes and bunching of his cheek that could either signify
real hurt or anger. But it was gone almost immediately, the resolute warrior's
mask in place once more.

"For so many years," he said, voice rich with regret Vaelin knew to be
entirely false, "we were all the other had. The only love I knew was the love
of my sister. What did I ever do to drive you so far from me? To render you
into this"—he closed his eyes for a second, letting out a shuddering breath—
"state of traitorous heresy."

"Everything," she said. "Every action you took since touching the stone,
if not before. I am as I am because this is what you made me. For the world
to endure, I had to become your enemy."

"I cannot accept that." He raised his arm, casting it out to encompass the
majesty of his army. "You see here thousands of souls redeemed in my sight.
No soul is beyond the Darkblade's regard, all can be gathered into the
embrace of the Unseen." He swept his arm towards her, hand extended, fingers open as if trying to grasp her. "Even the woman they now name the
Betrayer. Amongst our people it has become a curse to speak your name, a

profane and obscene thing. But I will not have it so, Luralyn. I will not leave you unredeemed. Come with me. Sully yourself amongst these wretches no more."

"Why are you playing this farce?" Vaelin enquired. "You must know we see through it."

Kehlbrand's features twitched with momentary rage but he continued to hold his hand out to his sister. When he spoke again it was in the Stahlhast tongue, his voice soft, imploring. Luralyn's only reply was a shake of her head before she palmed tears from her eyes.

Sighing, Kehlbrand lowered his arm before casting a faintly sour glance at Vaelin. "The Fire Queen's assassin lives on, I see. Your role is done, Thief of Names. Why not find a quiet corner to die in?"

"If you wish my death, then challenge me," Vaelin replied. "Since you no longer have a champion to do your fighting for you."

Kehlbrand laughed at the jibe. "I still sense no song in you, so you remain unworthy. I've a mind to leave your death to Babukir, once he's completed his penance. General"—he shifted his gaze to Sho Tsai—"does this foreign barbarian speak for you now?"

"His words are his own," Sho Tsai returned, "and mine belong to the Merchant King."

"A dutiful man then, and given how well your troops have fought, one worthy of my respect." He bowed in the saddle, Sho Tsai returning the gesture with evident reluctance. "And therefore, I would ask that you hold to your duty," Kehlbrand went on, "and march your men away from here. I guarantee you safe passage all the way to the southern boundary of the Northern Prefecture. Bear your arms and banners with you, in honour."

Sho Tsai's features remained impassive but for a raised eyebrow. "You will simply allow us to march free? As a soldier, this strikes me as being against all military logic."

"He's lost too many Blessed-of-Heaven fighting us," Vaelin said. "And wishes to preserve the rest for his conquest of the Merchant Realms." He offered the Stahlhast a bland smile. "Do you not?"

"Do not allow this foreign deceiver to lead you into ruin, General," Kehlbrand said, not sparing a glance in Vaelin's direction. "This city will fall. I know you see it. You do not have the numbers to oppose me, and your stand here will avail the Venerable Kingdom nothing but the deaths of soldiers it can ill afford to lose. I will require soldiers, you see. When I claim the Venerable Kingdom it will need to be policed, the people's fears allayed by men who speak their own tongue and know their customs. Thus will they be guided into the embrace of the Unseen. A man like you will stand high in the court of the Darkblade, lead armies against the southern kingdoms. Glory and renown will be your reward, and the reward of your men. Preferable, don't you agree, to death and the ignominy of failure, which is all that awaits them here?"

Sho Tsai pursed his lips, angling his gaze to look past Kehlbrand at the army beyond. "How can it be," he wondered, "that a man whose words are so empty of truth even a child would know him a fraud, could have gathered such a host?"

Kehlbrand lowered his gaze, the sincere mask slipping into mordant resignation. "Are you truly going to make me do this?" he said, once again addressing his sister. "You know I spoke true, Luralyn."

Luralyn's hands went to her neck as she lifted a chain over her head. It held what appeared to be a long tooth of some kind, engraved with some form of script. "You lied to me long before you touched the stone," she said, casting the chain at him. Kehlbrand caught it, a brief flicker of sadness showing in his eyes as he looked it over.

"I wanted your life to be free of fear," he said. "I still do. Come with me. Leave these fools to their fate."

"Their fate is mine now," she replied, tugging on her reins to turn her horse about. "And you have had your answer."

She started back towards the city at a gallop, followed shortly after by Sho Tsai, who saw no need to pause for a formal farewell. "You really should have touched the stone, you know," Kehlbrand told Vaelin as he prepared to spur Derka in pursuit of the others. "I'm not saying you would have had any chance," he went on, the familiar grin now returned to his lips, "but at least it would have made this all so much more interesting."

"I'll look for you on the walls," Vaelin assured him. "Or are you too craven . . ."

His words were swallowed by a sudden resurgence of the army's prayers, Vaelin seeing how they were all stabbing the air with their lances and swords to match the cadence of the chants. His gaze was soon drawn upwards at the sight of a tall, dark silhouette rising above the throng. It resembled a castle tower, but with a more jagged outline, growing in bulk as it drew closer. As Vaelin watched, a pair of towers resolved out of the noon haze on either side of the first, with yet more appearing soon after.

The army's clamour became frenzied as the towers approached, the ranks parting to reveal teams of oxen fifty strong dragging the towers across the plain, their huge wheels carving trenches in the earth. Vaelin saw how the light caught the flanks of the towers, not with the dull sheen of timber, but the hard gleam of iron.

"Did you imagine," Kehlbrand asked, shouting above the now animal roar of his host, "that I had naught but the Divine Blood to call upon?"

The prospect of drawing his sword flitted briefly through Vaelin's head, but the distance between them was too great. The Stahlhast would have time to evade the charge, and Vaelin knew Kehlbrand's skills were more than sufficient to fight him off before the army swarmed forward.

So all he could do was meet Kehlbrand's gaze and shout, "You made a child touch the stone and had us murder him! I'll have a reckoning for that!"

Turning Derka about he rode hard for the city. The Darkblade's laughter, audible even above the fanatical tumult, chased him all the way to the gate.

◆ ◆ ◆

"Towers of iron won't burn."

Sho Tsai gave no reaction to Vaelin's words, continuing to watch the towers. There were twelve of them in all, drawn by long trains of oxen in a slow but inexorable progress across the plain. As they drew closer the nature of their construction became clear, each one standing eighty feet high with walls fashioned from overlapping plates of hammered iron. Luralyn, speaking in tones of appalled admiration, pronounced them the most remarkable contrivances ever to emerge from the workshops of the Stahlhast tors.

"It must have taken a year, at least," she said. "Another secret he kept from me."

The towers had been grouped into pairs, three of which had already halted in a wide arc to the north. Vaelin knew the others would take the rest of the day to move into position, covering every approach to the city. Come nightfall they would launch a simultaneous assault, allowing the defenders no opportunity to concentrate their strength. Vaelin could see no stratagem that might prevent seizure of the outer wall.

"Retire to the second tier, General," he told Sho Tsai. "Conserve our strength. They'll never be able to manoeuvre those monsters through the streets of the lower tier."

"Thereby giving the enemy an easy victory," Sho Tsai pointed out. "And stoking their courage, whilst our men retire in shame."

"Shamed men can find dignity in fighting another day. Dead men can't."

The general's gaze grew sharp with warning but the expected stern reminder of their respective status was forestalled by Tsai Lin. "May I crave permission to speak, General?" the Dai Lo said with a deep bow.

Sho Tsai's eyes slid from Vaelin to his adopted son, narrowing yet further. "What is it?" he snapped.

"Towers of iron won't burn, this is true," Tsai Lin said. "But the men inside those towers will. I believe . . ." He paused, taking a hard breath. "Lord Vaelin is correct, the outer wall cannot be held, but neither should we allow the enemy a bloodless triumph." He turned, nodding to the mostly empty houses of the lower tier. "Not when we can greet them with an inferno birthed by the fires of Heaven."

CHAPTER THIRTY-TWO

The remaining hours before sunset were filled with frantic labour as hastily assembled work parties broke down the doors and shutters of every house in the lower tier. The interiors were stuffed with all manner of combustible material, in addition to the various furnishings left behind by the evacuated populace. Tiles were scraped from roofs to lay bare the timbers, and every spare stick of wood from the houses of the second tier was transported to the lower, whilst coal was piled in liberal quantities on every street corner. With this done, Varij set to work, using his gift to pull down carefully selected buildings at various junctions in order to create choke points. He proved tireless in his labour, staggering a little as he crumbled the foundations of the last house, the entire structure subliming into a dense pile of brick and wood.

"More?" he asked Vaelin, using a rag to wipe away the copious blood leaking from his nose and eyes.

"I think that will suffice," Vaelin assured him. "Best if you go and stand with your mistress. She'll need your protection when it starts."

The young Gifted gave a weary but grateful nod and started towards the second tier, pausing to add, "Many times I've used this gift so the Darkblade could conquer a place. It feels good to use it to save one." He gave a tired smile and moved in a determined but somewhat uneven trot.

The contents of every intact structure were then liberally doused in oil, and additional clay pots brimming with fuel were placed at the choke points, ready to be shattered when the time came. Despite the discipline and energy with which the Merchant soldiery went about the task, Vaelin was grateful for the long summer sun, which kept the Darkblade's towers at bay until the last oil had been thrown and the bulk of the troops withdrawn to the second wall.

The towers began their slow approach to the outer wall just as the sun began to dip towards the earth. Vaelin assumed Kehlbrand, or some keen mind under his thrall, had calculated the precise moment for the towers to lower their ramps onto the battlements just as darkness fell. They were no longer drawn by oxen, but pushed by people. A long narrow column of Redeemed extended from the rear of each tower's base, pushing on beams sprouting from a pole some two hundred paces in length. They chanted as they pushed, heaving the massive constructions forward in time to their rhythmic battle prayers. Behind the pushers marched a great mass of Redeemed and dismounted Stahlhast. They halted before coming into bow-shot of the walls whilst the towers kept on. Vaelin assumed the infantry would rush forward to scale the towers once they reached the wall and low-ered their ramps.

"Crossbows forward!" he barked. Whilst the bulk of the nearest tower concealed the pushers from direct assault, they could still be assailed from the flanks. He moved to the forefront of the western bastion, standing along-side the crossbowmen as they loosed their bolts. Several Redeemed fell at the first volley, mostly those near the end of the pole, but dozens of their com-rades sprinted forward to take their place, and the cadence of the chant barely faltered.

"You know the plan!" Vaelin called to the surrounding crossbowmen. "When you're down to your last two bolts, run for the second tier! Do not linger!"

He ducked as an arrow arced down from the top of the nearest tower, the steel head striking a spark as it careened off a stone buttress. The summit of each tower featured a dozen Stahlhast archers. Fortunately the hail of bolts forced them to bob up from cover only intermittently, preventing a clear view of how thinly held the walls were this night. Some ten thousand sol-diers had been spread around the battlements as the day wore on, ordered to keep marching back and forth under different banners to create the illusion that Sho Tsai had chosen to contest the outer wall with his full strength. All had orders to retire at speed to the second tier when the towers came within ten yards of the wall.

Vaelin found Ellese and Jihla waiting at the top of the stairwell, the Skulls thronging the steps below. Kihlen waited with the Red Scouts near the eastern gate whilst Eresa, whose sparks could ignite an oil-soaked timber as well as any flame, was positioned to the south with Nortah and a group of hand-picked soldiers.

"It won't be long now," Vaelin assured the young Gifted, receiving a forced, wavering smile in response. What she had done the night before clearly still weighed heavily, but he found himself impressed by her refusal to succumb to it.

"Remember," he said to Ellese, "don't hesitate if you see any sign . . ."

"I know, Uncle," she said, her own smile unwavering but no less forced. "Kill any bastard who I think might be Gifted. You've told me enough times."

He had resisted the temptation to enlist Juhkar in this enterprise. Although the tracker was now fully recovered thanks to Sherin, Vaelin knew his value was too great to risk. He felt certain this siege was not about to end regardless of what slaughter they might inflict this night, and Kehlbrand, he was equally certain, had more surprises in store.

The low thunder of many boots on stone signalled the retreat of the ten thousand soldiers on the wall, the Skulls all standing back to allow the crossbowmen to withdraw. They moved fast but Vaelin took satisfaction in the absence of panic on their faces. He crouched at the top of the stairwell, watching the tower crest the wall, seconds seeming to stretch as it inched ever closer. The archers on the summit gazed about in apparent consternation at the barren battlement below, one cupping his mouth to shout down into the bowels of the tower, but whatever warning he had intended was drowned by the pealing of a horn.

The tower's ramp detached and slammed down onto the battlement, ringing like a cracked bell as iron met stone. The Stahlhast within came storming forward in a thick mass, voices raised in expectation of battle. Vaelin waited for the first half-dozen to sprint onto the battlement, most coming to a halt in puzzled frustration at the absence of enemies. Fixing his gaze on the closest, Vaelin sent a throwing knife spinning into a gap in his armour above his thigh. The blade had been coated in Sherin's toxin and produced the now gruesomely familiar effect. As the warrior collapsed into bloody if brief agony, a shout of rage erupted from the other Stahlhast and they surged towards Vaelin in a vengeful mob.

"It's time," he said, turning back and starting down the stairs at a run. The Skulls fanned out ahead as they raced away from the wall whilst he, Ellese and Jihla stayed in the rear. As they ran, the soldiers used their spears to smash every oil pot they saw, dousing the piled coal and slicking the streets with fuel. Upon reaching a crossroads some fifty yards from the western gate, Vaelin barked out an order, bringing them to a halt. Jihla immediately turned and raised her arms to the pursuing Stahlhast crowding the street behind, all charging forward in enraged ignorance of the trap about to be sprung.

Fire erupted from the air just in front of Jihla's splayed hands, two jets sweeping down then out to ignite the oil and coal before setting the houses aflame. The resultant inferno was near instantaneous. A red-orange curtain engulfed the street from end to end, the Stahlhast rendered into dark, writhing figures that swiftly collapsed and withered to nothing.

"Come!" Vaelin said, taking hold of Jihla's arm as she stared at the carnage she had unleashed. The initial blast faded to reveal an avenue crammed with huddled, blackened corpses flanked by blazing homes. The fire had already spread to the surrounding streets, and the night sky had vanished behind a roof of smoke.

"We can't linger," he said, dragging the young Gifted along. She lit four more fires at each of the junctions they passed through, this time untroubled by pursuing enemies. Vaelin had already traced this route several times over with the Skulls, hoping to commit it to memory in the knowledge that the smoke would make navigation near impossible. The plan had been for each of the three fire-raising companies to work their way inward in a spiral to ensure the maximum number of blazes could be lit. As ever, when confronted with the reality of battle, the plan quickly fell apart. The fires were spreading much faster than expected, forcing successive changes of course as they veered away from one blazing street after another. It was the sight of flames coalescing into a fiery whirlwind, setting trees alight as it described a reeling dance across a small park, that convinced Vaelin they had wrought all the destruction they needed to.

"Corporal!" he called to Cho-ka. "Make for the second tier!"

They were required to dodge flaming debris as they ran, the inferno having birthed a swirling gale rich in burning detritus. The force of the winds grew by the second, becoming strong enough to send some soldiers sprawling. Vaelin saw one unfortunate cast into the guts of a burning house before his comrades had time to catch hold of his flailing arms. Cho-ka shouted an order to move on, forestalling any attempts at rescue as it was now obvious any delay would mean death.

The smoke and heat dissipated a little as they neared the north-facing gate of the second-tier walls. The soldiers coughed continually now, each face besmirched with a mélange of sweat and ash, several collapsing to retch onto the cobbles. Vaelin forced them to their feet, harrying them onwards with some judicious kicks and punches. This was not a time to be gentle.

Soon the smoke diminished into an acrid mist, revealing the sight of the open gate. Vaelin could see armed figures struggling free of the smoke to their right, but his alarm faded at the sight of their red armour.

"Hot work, my lord," Corporal Wei rasped, coming to a halt nearby. "Lost a few," he added, gesturing to his men. "Could've been worse. Reckon we roasted a full regiment's worth of the bastards."

"Kihlen?" Jihla asked, eyes wide and bright in her blackened features.

"Here!" the Gifted said, emerging from the pall with Tsai Lin's arm draped over his shoulder. The Dai Lo moved on stumbling legs, besmirched features sagging and eyes dim with insensibility.

"He got too close to an apothecary's shop," Kihlen explained. "Sulphur has a tendency to explode when it catches the slightest flame."

"Get him inside," Vaelin said, jerking his head at the gate.

The Gifted nodded, turned away, then stiffened with a shocked gasp as an axe came spinning out of the smoke to strike him full in the back. Jihla's despairing scream filled Vaelin's ears as he whirled, finding himself confronted with something conjured from a nightmare.

The Stahlhast came charging from the swirling fog, sabre raised and teeth bared. He was a tall, heavily built man and would have made for an impressive sight at any time, now made horrifying by the fact that he was wreathed from head to toe in flame. It trailed from his arms, his flailing braids, his boots. Vaelin could see the raw, glistening flesh of his neck, seared down to the gullet so that the man's roar emerged as a wet rattle as he closed in. Vaelin parried the sabre's slash through instinct alone, stepping under the following stroke and forcing himself to take in the reality of the spectacle. *One more horror,* he decided, bringing his sword down to hack through the Stahlhast's extended arm. *I've seen many.*

Even as the flaming limb tumbled to the ground, the Stahlhast continued to fight, launching himself at Vaelin, his remaining hand lashing out like a claw. As Vaelin danced clear, Corporal Wei jabbed his spear into the back of the warrior's neck, the curved blade spitting him from spine to exposed throat. He let out a final, voiceless rattle and collapsed, twitching.

"They must've been putting something special in this fucker's grog," Wei grunted, working his spear loose.

"Uncle," Ellese said, bow drawn and arrow pointed into the dark miasma that now covered the entire lower tier. Vaelin could see a line of red smudges in the gloom, growing in size as they drew close enough to resolve into charging figures, at least a score of them, each one blanketed in flame.

"Form a line!" he barked to the surrounding soldiers. They moved swiftly despite the depredations of the smoke, the Skulls and the Red Scouts joining together to form a barrier of armour and spears. Vaelin saw Jihla still keening over her brother's body and dragged her upright.

"Go!" he commanded, shoving her towards the gate. She staggered away a few steps, then came to a halt, stricken features staring at the fast-approaching Stahlhast. As Vaelin watched, the grief-riven mask of her face transformed into something far uglier, lips peeling back from her teeth in a snarl as rage shone bright in her gaze.

Vaelin retreated from her, snapping out fresh orders as he did so. "Stand aside!"

"My lord?" Wei asked. His puzzlement swiftly turned to alarm when he caught sight of Jihla striding forward with her arms raised. "Move!" he shouted, shoving his men aside. "Move, you laggardly bastards!"

The Scouts and the Skulls scrambled clear as Jihla unleashed her flames. She screamed as the fiery jets lashed out, blood streaming from her eyes, nose and ears. The leading Stahlhast was blasted to cinders when the jet touched her, those on either side meeting the same fate an instant later. Jihla spread her arms out to either side, sweeping them back and forth to claim every Stahlhast she could see. Within moments the entire line of charging warriors had been reduced to blackened smears on the cobbles.

Jihla went to her knees, her flames fading as she huddled, a small weeping figure amidst the ashen ruin. She fell limp when Vaelin gathered her up, feeling the chill of her flesh despite the heat of the burning city. Turning, he sprinted towards the gate with the Gifted in his arms, shouting for the others to follow. The gates swung closed behind them with a thunderous boom.

◆ ◆ ◆

"After Alltor, I had hoped never to see a city burn again."

Nortah's face was grim as he surveyed the fires below. It had continued to blaze throughout the night, three separate infernos eventually merging to form a great ring of fire. The screams were the only indication of the scale of the injury they had dealt their enemy, reaching a shrieking crescendo as the fires fully encircled the second tier. Here and there Vaelin caught glimpses of figures running through the haze, some alight, others not, but all either maddened or frantic, judging by their screams. Come the morning the fires had diminished but not died, large sections of the lower city continuing to burn as the sun became an occluded yellow disc through the smoke.

"Destruction, it appears," Nortah went on, a ghost of his old smile on his lips, "is our principal gift to the world, brother."

His company had managed to convey Eresa to the second tier after setting light to most of the eastern quarter, but had lost twenty men in doing so, some to the fires, others to the flame-wreathed Stahlhast.

"Salvation too, on occasion," Vaelin replied, nodding to the as yet undamaged streets behind. The soldiers had gathered in the various squares and parks to celebrate what they evidently saw as a great victory. Their general for once forsook the harsh discipline of Merchant soldiery to allow them a few hours' licence. Consequently, the night had been rich in song, drink and revels whilst the lower tier burned. The raucousness died away come the dawn, leaving a host of inebriates sleeping off their indulgence whilst others staggered to their billets to catch what few hours' rest they could before officers summoned them back to their banners.

"What was that last night?" Nortah said. "I've seen a great many things wrought by the Dark, but never the sight of men continuing to fight as fire eats their flesh down to the bone."

"Juhkar and Ahm Lin were both on the walls," Vaelin said. "They sensed no Gifted amongst the flames, apart from one. *He* was there."

"And that was enough to keep them fighting?" Nortah raised an eyebrow, shaking his head. "Perhaps he truly is a god after all. A joke, brother," he added, catching Vaelin's baleful glance. "Look on the sunward side. If he really was amongst all that"—he gestured to the ruined conurbation below—"maybe we killed the bastard."

Vaelin's gaze roamed the smoke-shaded streets, experiencing the kind of certainty once conveyed by his song. *I have no song,* he reminded himself, experiencing the old, raw sense of regret he knew might never fade. But still, the certainty persisted. "No," he said. "We didn't."

They made their way to the temple shortly after, Vaelin being keen to check on Jihla, whom he had placed in Sherin's care. Passing through the gate to the uppermost tier, he paused at the sight of Cho-ka and a dozen or so Skulls remonstrating with an officer of the city garrison. The officer had a squad of spearmen at his back, all mirroring his expression of disdain as he addressed the former convicts.

"I'll have you flogged, you hear me!" he growled, jabbing a meaty finger into Cho-ka's chest. "Worthless thieving scum that you are!"

A flash of annoyance passed over the corporal's face as his hand slid towards the knife on his belt but stopped when he caught sight of Vaelin's approach. "My lord!" he said, snapping to attention along with the other Skulls. The garrison officer and his men followed suit, but with markedly less alacrity.

"Is there a problem here?" Vaelin enquired.

"Found this lot up to their old ways, my lord!" the officer said. Vaelin recognised him as a former sergeant newly promoted to captain thanks to the loss of so many officers during the first attacks. He had the habitual scowl and bearing Vaelin recognised as one who had spent more time combatting outlaws than invading foes. Such men were always useful, but more so in times of peace than war.

"Caught them looting this shop," the captain went on, chin jutting at the domicile behind the Skulls.

"It's my old gran's spice shop, my lord," Cho-ka said. "Just checking to see if the place was still intact."

Vaelin's gaze tracked over the various jars and pots clutched in the Skulls' hands, and the bulging sacks slung over several shoulders.

"That's a pile of pig shit," the captain snapped. "The woman who owned this place was known to me for years, and she didn't have a gutter-scrape for a grandson."

Seeing a dangerous glint appear in Cho-ka's gaze, Vaelin stepped between them, offering the captain an approving smile. "You're to be commended for your diligence, Captain. Rest assured the general will hear of it. For now, I'd be grateful if you'd leave this in my hands. These men were recruited by me, you see? Punishment is my duty, given how dishonoured I feel by their betrayal of my largesse."

The captain straightened, jaws bunching in frustration. It was clear to Vaelin that he would have liked nothing more than a chance to indulge his law-enforcing instincts with a flogging or even a hanging. Still, mention of the general seemed to serve as ample persuasion, for he gave a stiff bow before marching off, growling at his men to fall in line.

"Is this really your grandmother's shop?" Vaelin asked Cho-ka after the captain's company rounded a corner.

"My great-aunt's, in truth," the smuggler replied with a shrug. "She was always fond of me though." He offered Vaelin a grin that faded when it wasn't returned.

"Put it back," Vaelin said, nodding at their loot.

"What does it matter now?" one of the Skulls asked in a weary drawl. "Place is gonna be a ruin soon any—"

The man's words ended abruptly as Cho-ka whirled to deliver a hard cuff to his face. The protestor staggered back, face bloodied, but confined his response to a hard glare as he stood to attention. "Apologies, my lord," Cho-ka said, bowing to Vaelin. There was a studied neutrality to his expression Vaelin didn't like, an absence of defiance that told of an urgent need for this confrontation to end.

Vaelin's gaze flicked to the shop, then back to the still-bowing corporal. "Anything in there I should know about?" he enquired.

"Just a good deal of spice, lord. We got hold of a couple of sides of pork, y'see. Wanted to flavour the meat some."

The sense that there was more to this persisted, some secret of the criminal fraternity he couldn't divine, not that he had the time or inclination to at this point. "Even so," he said. "Put it back, all of it."

Cho-ka bowed again. "At once, my lord."

"Watch your back with that one," Nortah advised as they resumed their progress to the temple. "Outlaws are only so polite when they're lying."

"As long as his men keep fighting the way they have, he can lie all he likes."

◆ ◆ ◆

At the temple Mother Wehn guided him to the nun's cell where Jihla had been taken, Vaelin pausing outside the door at the sound of tense voices within.

"I told you," Luralyn was saying, voice clipped with finality. "I don't know!"

"My song sings a different tune," Ahm Lin replied, his own tone more controlled but also insistent.

"Then perhaps your song is addled by your age. Amongst my people a man of your years would have had the decency to get himself killed in battle by now."

Her voice trailed off as Vaelin entered. They stood on opposite sides of the bed where Jihla lay in unmoving slumber. Luralyn turned her face away from both of them, arms crossed and shoulders set with tension. Ahm Lin's face betrayed no hurt at her insult, only a hard determination.

"The song is clear," he told Vaelin. "Something sticks in her mind like a thorn, but she refuses to pluck it free."

"Oh, leave me be, you old fool!" Luralyn hissed, gaze still averted.

Ahm Lin began to speak again, falling silent as Vaelin shook his head and gestured to the door. When the mason had gone, Vaelin approached the bed, touching a hand to Jihla's forehead. Her skin was cold but lacking the icy chill from the night before. "Mother Wehn tells me her heart retains a steady rhythm," he said to Luralyn. "As to when she'll wake . . ."

"She's small but strong," Luralyn said. "She'll wake soon enough. Though I would have her sleep a while longer. Her grief will be hard to bear."

Vaelin raised his gaze to meet hers, finding it wary. "Ahm Lin has heard his song for a lifetime," he said, keeping his tone gentle. "He knows it well and I trust his judgement."

"And I know the True Dream. I have told you all it has told me."

"I have seen much that makes me question the value of prophecy. But the legends of my homeland speak of it as a thing that comes unbidden, an unwanted gift. You appear to be different. Because you can summon it, can you not?"

"Usually. And, as I told you, it is . . . inconstant in what it chooses to show me."

"Have you tried since we came here?"

She looked away once more, head moving in a small shake of negation.

"Why?" he asked. "With so much at stake?"

She retreated from him, arms tightening about her waist like a shield. "It has shown me much that I would never have chosen to see," she told him in a thin whisper.

"So you fear what it might show you now?"

She blinked and a tear rolled down her otherwise impassive face. "Kehl-brand hid so much from me. For years, he lied as I loved. What . . ." She hesitated, swallowed and spoke on. "What if this, all of this, is what he wants, what he always intended? Would that not make us all just his puppets? He twitches the strings and we dance like the fools we are."

"Not puppets. Pieces on a Keschet board."

"Keschet?"

"A game from the Alpiran Empire but beloved of my queen. I doubt there is anyone in the world who could best her at it, even your brother. I asked her once what the key to victory is in Keschet. She laughed and said there isn't one, for every game is different, but the key to defeat is always the same: predictability."

"You wish me to seek another dream, divine the outcome of this siege."

"I wish you to pluck the thorn from your mind." He smoothed hair from Jihla's forehead. "So that her sacrifice, the sacrifice of her brother and so many others will not be for nothing. Will you do it?"

She unfolded her arms, wiping her tears away and muttering something in her own tongue.

"What was that?" he asked her.

"Mercy is weakness, compassion is cowardice, wisdom is falsehood." She gave a faint laugh, shrugging. "The mantra of the priests to the Unseen, spoken as truth for centuries and cast aside at my brother's whim. He saw no use in it, for a god needs no words but his own. But *I* cast it aside because I knew it to be a lie. Mercy requires strength, compassion demands courage and wisdom compels truth." Her humour faded and she moved to a stool at Jih-la's bedside, reaching out to take her hand. "I'll seek the dream when she wakes. My mind will be too unsettled otherwise."

CHAPTER THIRTY-THREE

No assaults were launched for the rest of the day, nor any the day that followed. Fires continued to burn unchecked in the lower tier, but mercifully the screams had long faded. As the fires began to dwindle, Tsai Lin, now recovered from his encounter with the exploding apothecary shop, used the spyglass atop the tower to conduct a methodical counting of the dead visible in the streets.

"Four thousand three hundred and eighty-three," he told his father, the general having summoned him, Vaelin and Governor Neshim to the library in order to plan the defence of the second tier. "But," the Dai Lo went on, "I would submit that the count can safely be doubled in light of the number of dead rendered unrecognisable by the fire."

"Call it eight thousand then," Vaelin said. He had spent the morning drilling the companies under his command whilst occasionally surveying the charred expanse beyond the walls. Only a half-dozen fires were still burning, soon to shrink to nothing whereupon Kehlbrand would surely make his next move. "A grievous blow to be sure, but hardly fatal for a host of this size."

"It must have unnerved them," Governor Neshim said. He still wore his ill-fitting armour, though it sat more easily on him now, his girth having diminished over recent days. His fear, however, had not and Vaelin found himself assailed by the sweaty stench of the man.

"Seeing so many comrades perish in such a terrible manner," Neshim continued, "would test the strongest of hearts."

"I would agree," Sho Tsai replied. "Were they an army that fights for pay or plunder. But they are not. They fight for a man they believe to be a living god, and I doubt he is done with us."

"Then where are our reinforcements?" Neshim proved incapable of keeping the whine from his voice as he stared at the general with barely restrained desperation. "The Venerable Realm can call on countless spears, yet every day dawns with no sign of them."

"I remind you that we serve at the pleasure of the Merchant King," Sho Tsai said, voice flat. "And he will only act in the best interests of the kingdom. Therefore, if he has chosen not to send reinforcements, I trust he has sound cause."

"I do not question the wisdom of the great Lian Sha. But I do appeal to reason. We have done more than enough to satisfy honour." The Governor attempted a resolute posture, forcing the quaver from his voice as he spoke on. "I believe, as duly appointed Governor of this city, it is time to plan for our escape."

"Escape?" Vaelin enquired.

"Well, yes. 'When all hope of victory is denied you, there is no shame in retreat and conservation of remaining forces.' The words, need I remind you, General, of the Most Esteemed Kuan-Shi, the greatest philosopher of the Emerald Empire."

"A remarkable mind indeed," Sho Tsai said. "So great in fact that, after he cut Kuan-Shi's head off, the emperor had it pickled."

Neshim flushed but ploughed on with a determination Vaelin found oddly admirable. "Nevertheless," the governor said, "his wisdom echoes through the ages and we should abide it. I took the liberty of consulting our former governor's books." He unfurled a scroll showing a map of sorts, the lines having been set down in a somewhat unsteady hand. "It transpires history provides a parallel for our current dilemma. The fall of Juhlun-Kho in the late third century of the Divine Dynasty. The city commander used a screen of cavalry to shield his forces, which he divided into two columns, one numerous but poorly armed and consisting of his least effective troops, the other smaller but composed of well-armed veterans. The former was, in an act of regrettable necessity, sent on a course that would place them closest to the enemy. However, their resultant destruction bought sufficient time for the more valuable troops to make good their escape."

Sho Tsai maintained a placid demeanour as he took the scroll from the governor's trembling hand. "A clever stratagem indeed," he said after a brief consideration. "One I'm prepared to consider. However," he added, freezing the governor's relieved smile, "only if you agree to take personal charge of the weaker column. Please know I ensure word of your selfless sacrifice will be spread far and wide."

Neshim's throat bulged several times before he stepped back from the map table, bowing low. "I was remiss," he said, still bowing. "Military matters are, of course, your province."

"That they are." Sho Tsai tossed the governor's map aside, gesturing impatiently for him to stop bowing. "Our supply situation?"

"We remain well provisioned. If anything, it might be worthwhile increasing the men's rations since some of the food is likely to spoil if it isn't consumed soon."

Vaelin saw no satisfaction in Sho Tsai's bearing at this, the reason being easy to divine. They had food to spare because he had lost so many men. "Very well," he said. "Please go now and see to it."

The governor bowed again, huffing in obvious relief as he made his exit.

"Respectfully, General," Tsai Lin began, "having a coward in such a high position . . ."

"He was brave enough to stay when it would have been easy for him to flee before we closed the gates," Sho Tsai interrupted. "No man is immune to weakness, which is a lesson I thought you had learned long ago."

He stared at his son until Tsai Lin lowered his gaze, a shameful frown on his brow.

"The notion of escape is not entirely without merit," Vaelin said, retrieving the discarded scroll from the table. "At least for some. With a diversion of sufficient size, the cavalry could be got away."

"Along with your companions, I assume?" Sho Tsai asked.

Vaelin saw little point in dissembling. "I doubt they would go, but yes, if I can persuade them. They've followed me far enough."

"I need every blade for the walls," the general said, shaking his head. "Besides, any cavalry force we could muster would be chased down and wiped out by the Stahlhast or the Tuhla before they could travel more than a few miles."

"Not to mention we may need the horses later," Tsai Lin added. "For meat."

"Our Blessed-of-Heaven ally," Sho Tsai said. "Does she have any fresh intelligence to impart regarding her brother's intentions?"

The thorn in her mind remains unplucked, Vaelin thought, deciding it would add nothing of value to the discussion. "Only that he will attack again," he said. "In fact she seems surprised he hasn't already done so."

"The walls of the second tier stand ten feet higher than the outer," Tsai Lin said. "They may well be constructing taller ladders."

"Weak points?" Vaelin asked. "I once took a city because its governor forgot to secure a drain."

"Keshin-Kho was constructed more as a fortress than a city," Sho Tsai said. "All drains were built too small to allow passage of a man, or even a child. If the Darkblade wants his victory, he will need to scale the walls and hold them, meaning he will have to use his best warriors. When he does, we'll cull his army of the bravest and most skillful souls he possesses. Then let him try to take the Venerable Kingdom with a mob of untrained fanatics."

◆ ◆ ◆

He was woken by Alum sometime after moonrise, the hunter taking a careful step back as Vaelin started from slumber, hunting knife in hand. "The mason had a dream," Alum said. "A bad dream."

Vaelin rose from his bedroll, reaching for his boots. He and the others had taken to sleeping in the temple grounds, making a home of sorts beneath the roof of a centuries-old shrine. The others woke with a variation of curses or resigned sighs as Alum moved to kick them awake.

"What did you see?" Vaelin asked, moving to Ahm Lin's side. The mason sat with shoulders slumped, his gaze distant, stirring when Vaelin placed a hand on his shoulder.

"A tiger," he said, Vaelin feeling him shudder as he mastered himself, speaking on in a firmer voice. "A tiger assailing a mountain, tearing at it with tooth and claw. It bled as it fought the mountain, teeth shattered, claws torn away, flesh raw and bleeding. But still it tore at the stone, growing fresh teeth, sprouting new claws and in the end it was the mountain that fell."

"We've heard no alarms all night, my lord," said Sehmon, who had been on watch with Ellese. From the tousled appearance of both, Vaelin concluded they had been doing more than just watching, but that was of scant importance just now.

"Gather your weapons," he told them all. "We'll take a tour of the walls. Sehmon, find Tsai Lin and tell him I believe we have a troubled night ahead. I leave it to him whether he wishes to advise the general so."

The walls of the second tier featured only two gates, one facing north, the other south. They were barred by thick doors of oak braced with iron. Additional defence was provided by a heavy portcullis, which had been permanently lowered since the army's retreat from the lower tier. Sho Tsai had also taken the precaution of stationing two full regiments in close proximity to each gate. These consisted of veterans rather than the recently raised conscripts that filled the ranks of most other companies.

Vaelin checked both gates in turn, finding nothing amiss, before conducting a full circuit of the walls. He had ordered the regiments mustered in full battle order, stationing the bulk of the crossbowmen on the battlements above each gate. After an hour of pacing ranks of mostly young men, who clearly wanted nothing more than a return to their bunks, Ahm Lin's tiger had failed to appear.

"What do you sense?" he asked, coming to Juhkar's side. The tracker stood alongside Ahm Lin above the north gate, both staring into the gloomy, ruined maze of streets below. The moon was full this night, silver-blue light catching the tumbled walls and debris from which smoke still rose in places.

"Just the Darkblade," Juhkar said, eyes roving the ruins. He had a poison-coated arrow nocked to his bow, fingers tensed on the string. "He's out there, waiting."

"No other?" Vaelin pressed him.

The tracker shook his head. "Whatever stirs tonight, it will be of his making."

A chorus of formal greetings sounded to the left, indicating the arrival of their general. "These men can't stand to all night," Sho Tsai told Vaelin, striding towards him across the battlement. "Not if we expect them to fight tomorrow."

"Something is coming," Vaelin assured him, nodding to the two Gifted, who continued to peer into the gloom with undaunted scrutiny.

Sho Tsai sighed, stroking his chin as his gaze roamed over the assembled troops, no doubt taking note of the many lolling heads and misaligned spears. "One more hour then," he decided. "Then the watch will be reduced by half..."

"It's starting!" Ahm Lin cut in. He pointed to something in the depths of the ruins, Vaelin moving closer to make out the sight of a large column of infantry approaching the walls. Their chanted prayers soon reached the battlement, this time voiced at a higher pitch that spoke of near hysteria.

"Two thousand?" Sho Tsai said.

"More than three, I'd say," Vaelin replied. Peering closer he blinked in surprise. "No ladders that I can see. Nor any kind of ram."

The column came to a halt two hundred paces from the gate, too far for any but the most optimistic archer to score a hit. Their chants, already discordant with fervour, now took on a more frenzied note. They were close enough for Vaelin to identify them all as Redeemed, men and women in their mismatched armour, which, to his astonishment, they all began to discard. Breastplates, hauberks and greaves flew into the air as the Redeemed cast them away, their prayer chants becoming something that resembled the baying of animals. Bared to the waist they milled together, embracing, before joining hands and reforming their ranks, this time fashioning themselves into a narrow column four abreast aimed directly at the gate like an arrow.

"They don't need a ram," Vaelin heard Ahm Lin say. "They are the ram."

The column surged forward at a run that soon became a sprint. The crossbowmen above the gate began to loose their bolts before Vaelin even shouted the order. He saw a hundred Redeemed fall at the first volley, others keeping on despite the bolts jutting from shoulders or arms. Some of those that had fallen scrambled to their feet and ran to rejoin the column as it closed on the gate. Another volley slashed down before they connected with the oak doors, Redeemed falling by the dozen. The gate heaved under the assault, wooden beams shuddering but failing to break. The surviving Redeemed below reared back, stepping on the corpses of their slain brethren, then joined their bodies to those following behind and once again threw themselves at the gate.

"This is plain insanity," Sho Tsai said in appalled wonder as the hail of bolts continued to claim yet more victims amongst the Redeemed. The column shrank as it pummelled the gate, bodies piling up before it, some rising to add their weight to the assault despite having been pierced with multiple shafts. The gate boomed as the fist of close-packed humanity struck it once more, but as yet showed no sign of breaking, Vaelin hearing the sharp crack of breaking bones amongst the tumult.

"General!" one of the sergeants called from close by, pointing at another column approaching from the north. They numbered the same as the first cohort and were also composed of Redeemed. Their screaming chants had already begun, and like their comrades they had discarded their armour. Despite their obviously unreasoned minds they kept a tight formation as they charged, running through the rain of bolts with no more regard than if it were a light drizzle. The second column slammed into the remnants of the first, another boom from the gate, more snapping bones. The dense mass of flesh roiled against the gate, pushing ever harder as they screamed out their prayers and died.

Hearing a shocked curse from one of the crossbowmen, Vaelin raised his gaze, seeing another column charging from the gloom, with another two behind. He turned to Sho Tsai but the general was already shouting orders.

"Captain, shift every crossbow from the south gate to the north! Sergeant, light the oil and throw it over!"

The third column suffered the same losses as the first two, the remnants of which were now piled against the gate in an ugly confusion of compressed, twisted bodies. Undaunted by the flaming oil that rained down from above, the Redeemed smashed their bodies into the piled flesh. Then Vaelin heard a squeal of protesting iron amid the boom of impacted oak.

"Take charge of the regiments before the gate," Sho Tsai ordered Vaelin. "They cannot break in, regardless of the cost."

Vaelin nodded, pausing at Alum's side as he moved to the nearest stairwell. "Get the mason back to the temple," he said.

The Moreska replied with a grave shake of his head, hefting his spear. "I fear you have need of me this night. The mason will go with the young ones."

Sehmon and Ellese were swiftly despatched to the third tier with Ahm Lin, though not without protest, which Vaelin had been quick to quash. "You'll have plenty of targets before the night's out," he told Ellese, moving closer to add, "and I need someone to guard Sherin. Chien's blade won't be enough if this gate falls."

She gave a reluctant grimace before running after Sehmon and Ahm Lin, calling over her shoulder, "I hope she's got more of that poison to hand!"

Vaelin took up position in the centre of the Skulls whom he had arrayed directly in front of the gate. Another regiment was stationed behind with two more positioned on either side of the gate. Nortah and Juhkar stood to his front with their bows ready whilst Alum placed himself at Vaelin's right.

"What manner of god," the Moreska wondered aloud, staring at the shuddering gate in mystification, "makes madmen of his followers?"

"Some would say all of them," Vaelin replied, allowing himself a grin at Alum's reproachful scowl. His humour soon faded, however, as the gate voiced its loudest boom yet.

The great oak doors bulged, the brackets securing it to the wall unleashing a whining groan of protesting metal as they were wrenched from the stone. The doors relaxed for an instant as the pressure retreated, then bulged again with even greater force. The heavy crossbar bent and then splintered as a narrow gap appeared between the doors, closing and then widening, first an inch, then a foot.

The grinning, wide-eyed face of a Redeemed appeared in the gap, Nortah raising his bow then stopping at the sight of the blood pouring from the man's mouth and eyes. The prayer chants grew louder as the doors were forced wider, all cadence lost now as it became a manic, continual yell. With a final heave, the crossbar snapped and the doors swung wide. The corpses of the Redeemed burst through to slam against the portcullis, unleashing a torrent of gore that washed over the cobbles to stain the boots of the waiting soldiers.

"Steady!" Vaelin called out, hearing several soldiers retch at the sight.

The portcullis began to resemble a net crafted from mere string as it buckled, the dead flesh pressed against it bursting under the pressure to unleash the contents of bowel and vein. The corpses were piled so high that Vaelin could see no sign of what transpired beyond the gate, but the unending snap of bowstrings and shouts from the battlement indicated the Redeemed continued to face a lethal assault from above. But still the pressure increased, blood leaking in torrents as the portcullis bowed, strained and then came loose from its fastenings. It was borne down in an instant, smothered by the corpses that slid clear of the gate like fish spilled onto a dockside, and in their wake came the living.

The first was a woman, naked but for a few matted rags clinging to her gore-covered skin. Her hair and much of her scalp had been singed away by burning oil, and her bared skull trailed smoke as she charged, leaping the bodies of her fellow Redeemed with feral agility. She bore no weapon but her hands were formed into claws, reaching out like talons for Juhkar's face as she closed on him, then fell dead with one of his poisoned arrows through her chest.

A score more followed immediately after, all similarly maimed and maddened. Most were swiftly felled by Juhkar and Nortah's arrows, those that weren't meeting their ends on the spear-points of the surrounding soldiers.

For one scant moment the gate appeared empty save for the red mass of bodies that crowded its base. Vaelin began to voice orders for the Skulls to rush forward and bar the entryway, but then he heard it, a sound he remembered from the day Varinshold had been reclaimed for the queen. The Renfaelin knights had charged through the streets, and the sound of their horses' shoes on the cobbles had been like the clang of a thousand anvils.

"Prepare for cavalry!" he shouted, sending the assembled regiments into a new formation. The soldiers on either side of the gate, moving with the speed and precision that confirmed their veteran status, formed phalanxes three ranks deep. The first rank knelt with spears held at a low angle, the second braced their spears on the ground to hold them out diagonally, whilst the third brought theirs to head height to jut between the shoulders of those in the second rank. The Skulls, lacking the years of drill enjoyed by the veteran regiments, were slower in forming this hedge of spear-points, the third rank only just managing to scramble into place by the time the first Stahlhast warrior charged through the gate.

He rode a tall grey stallion that forced its way through the corpses in its path with barely a pause. Upon clearing the bodies, the Stahlhast charged straight for the Skulls, whirling a wickedly spiked mace on a chain above his head. Nortah stood squarely in his path, bow aimed and drawn for what seemed to Vaelin to be an excessive delay. Nortah loosed when the Stahlhast had closed to less than twenty feet, the arrow finding the left eyehole in the man's helm. A thick crimson torrent gushed through the visor as he tumbled from the saddle. His horse, however, continued on, obliging Nortah to dive clear. The beast reared up before the stabbing barrier of the Skulls, lashing out with its hooves until Alum darted forward to open its neck with a flick of his spear.

"Straighten up!" Vaelin barked, sending the disrupted ranks back into formation just as a dozen more Stahlhast erupted through the gate. Nortah and Juhkar moved in opposite directions, loosing arrows with lethal swiftness, the poisoned-tipped shafts claiming four riders in quick succession. The others fanned out to assault the regiments on either side of the gate. Most were quickly speared down but one managed to hack his way into the ranks of the regiment on the right, disordering their lines so that they were ill prepared to meet the charge of the Stahlhast following behind. Within seconds the regiment had been shattered, its three ranks broken and its men struggling amidst the chaos of stamping horses and slashing warriors.

Vaelin's gaze snapped to the left, seeing the other regiment in marginally better straits, their ranks holding despite a ferocious assault, although it was clear they would soon falter. In the centre a score of Stahlhast riders were struggling clear of the unfolding melee and forming up for a charge. Knowing the Skulls would have little chance of containing such a weight of armour and horseflesh, Vaelin saw only one option.

"Attack formation!" he shouted, moving to stand before the first rank with his sword raised. He waited just long enough to see the three ranks become two, the soldiers all standing with spears levelled, then turned and charged for the gate. For a second he suspected the Skulls had failed to follow, wondering if they had all turned and fled as their criminal instincts re-emerged at the crucial moment. But then he heard Corporal Cho-ka's shouted order to charge followed by the drum and rattle of armoured men at the run.

The Stahlhast were quick to take note of their charge, spurring forward to meet it but only managing to cover a dozen yards before the Skulls drove their spears home. Vaelin ducked under a slashing sabre and hacked at the rider's leg, the blade cutting into both the horse's flank and the warrior's ankle. The Stahlhast screamed in pain and fury, reversing his grip on his sabre and attempting to stab it dagger-like at Vaelin's face. He jerked to the side and reached up to grab the steel guard on the man's forearm, hauling hard to pull him from the saddle. Before he could rise, Vaelin planted his knee on the warrior's breastplate, pinning him down as he drove his sword point through the slit in his helm.

Feeling the hot rush of a horse's breath on his neck, Vaelin rolled to the side, dragging his sword clear of the slain warrior's helm. Hooves pounded the corpses and the cobbled ground as they chased him. Vaelin came to his feet, lashing out with his sword, the blade scoring a deep cut on the pursuing horse's mouth. It reared, blood and foam frothing from its lips, the warrior on its back raising an axe high, ready to bring it down when his mount plunged. Before he could deliver the blow, the axe wielder stiffened, a spear-point appearing under his chin. As he tumbled from the saddle, Vaelin saw Alum withdrawing his spear before whirling away to slash at the face of a dismounted warrior.

Looking around, Vaelin quickly surmised the charge had succeeded in stalling the Stahlhast just in front of the gate, but the struggle was far from over. Riders continued to wheel amidst the chaos, hacking at the soldiers assailing them on all sides, whilst knots of dismounted warriors fought it out with the Skulls.

Seeing Cho-ka on his back, lying about with the haft of a broken spear as he fended off the sabre strokes of two dismounted Stahlhast, Vaelin rushed towards him. He cut down one Stahlhast with a thrust to the base of his spine, the star-silver edge cutting through chain mail to sever the bones and nerves beneath. The other whirled to meet the new threat with impressive speed. She wore no helm and Vaelin took in the sight of trailing red braids and a snarling face he recognised.

The sabre rebounded from his sword with a hard clang, the woman ducking under Vaelin's counterstroke and making ready to thrust at his midriff and then falling senseless to the ground as Cho-ka slammed the haft of his broken spear into the back of her head.

"Don't!" Vaelin said as the corporal drew his dagger to finish her off.

"My lord?"

Vaelin lingered a moment to take in the sight of Thirus's slackened features. He hadn't realised how pleasing her face was before, it being so riven with anger and hate during the course of their journey across the Steppe. He had thought most if not all the Ostra had perished in the first assault, meaning she may well be the last of her Skeld.

"She's owed a life," he told the corporal. "We killed her sister on the Steppe."

Gazing around he saw the few remaining Stahlhast perish beneath the soldiers' spears, leaving the courtyard clear of enemies, although the gate remained an open maw through which he could see a great host of Redeemed approaching.

"Lord Vaelin!"

Looking up, Vaelin saw Sho Tsai looking down at him from the battle-ment. "Stahlhast have scaled the southern wall," the general called, Vaelin following his pointed finger to see soldiers on the eastern battlement engaged in a furious struggle with hundreds of warriors. A glance to the west con-firmed it; the second tier could not be held.

"Fall back to the third tier!" Sho Tsai shouted. "I'll organise the retreat! Hold the gate open for as long as possible!"

Vaelin wanted to argue that the general should see to his own safety, but Sho Tsai was gone before he could voice a protest. Rallying the Skulls and what remained of the two veteran regiments, he ordered them through the gate in the walls of the third and final tier.

"Juhkar!" he called, seeing the tracker lingering in the corpse-strewn courtyard. "We need your bow on the upper wall."

Juhkar ignored him, his features set in a frown of deep concentration, a predatory gleam in his eye.

"Juhkar," Vaelin repeated, moving to grab the Gifted's arm. "We have to go."

"He's here," the tracker said, teeth bared in a hungry grin. "So close . . . I can smell his stench. Just one scratch of the arrowhead and this all ends."

"There are too many . . ." Vaelin began but Juhkar tore his arm free and sprinted away, disappearing into a nearby alley. Vaelin stared helplessly in his wake, fighting down the urge to follow, before turning and running for the upper gate.

The third tier had only one gate, smaller than the others and concealed within a tunnel some twenty feet long. Once through, Vaelin ordered one of the Skulls to fetch Ellese from the temple, knowing her bow would be sorely needed, then gathered as many crossbowmen as he could, placing them atop the battlement directly above the gate. These walls were the highest of the city's three tiers, and the thickest. The Darkblade's army would face a daunt-ing task in scaling such a barrier, but only if they faced a meaningful defence.

Soldiers came streaming in their hundreds through the streets of the sec-ond tier as resistance on the walls began to collapse. So many crowded the gate that Vaelin organised a squad of the burliest sergeants to drag them through to prevent a blockage. He also ordered ropes cast over so others could climb or be hauled up. Hearing Nortah call his name from the battlement, he rapidly scaled the nearest stairwell, finding his brother regarding the sight below with grim resignation.

"They're not going to make it, brother," he said.

Viewing the scene, Vaelin saw little reason to argue. The second-tier walls were now entirely in the hands of the Stahlhast, whilst an ever-growing number of Redeemed were pouring through the sundered gate. Only one knot of resistance remained, a cluster of denuded regiments formed into a circle that revolved continually as it tried to fight its way to the third tier. In the centre the banner of the Red Scouts could be seen alongside the general's pennant. The circle moved at an impressively steady pace despite the repeated assaults launched against its flanks, inching closer to the upper wall by the second, but also losing men with every step.

"You have work for me, Uncle?" Ellese asked, appearing at Vaelin's side. "Where's Juhkar?" she added, looking around for the tracker.

"He has his own mission," Vaelin said. Moving to the wall he pointed to the centre of the encircled infantry. "Keep the general alive," he told Ellese and Nortah. "Nothing else matters."

Vaelin watched the continually shrinking formation of soldiers fight its way step by painful step towards the gate, assailed on all sides by an ever-increasing number of Stahlhast and Redeemed. The crossbowmen laboured to hurl repeated volleys into the ranks of the attackers, but for every warrior their bolts claimed, another three would come charging from the gate or the walls. Nortah and Ellese loosed their shafts at a more sedate pace, killing any warrior who seemed likely to force a breach in the soldiers' tight-packed ranks. Whatever madness-inducing power Kehlbrand had over these people had not abated. It required two of Ellese's poisoned shafts to put down one large, bear-like man who used a blacksmith's hammer to club his way into the circle before collapsing into a wreck of bloodless flesh and bone.

Once the circle had forced its way to within twenty yards of the gate, a series of horns sounded out from its centre. In an obviously pre-planned move the circle became a diamond, the north-facing ranks charging for the gate whilst the others back-pedalled in their wake. The soldiers at the front charged with the deadly ferocity of men facing imminent death, cutting through a dense but disorganised mass of enemies to reach the wall. As they did so the ranks behind fanned out, forming a half-circle around the gate.

Vaelin ordered rocks and oil over the wall, deluging the attackers on either side of the half-circle whilst the crossbowmen continued to assail those to the front. It began to shrink as soldiers started to make their way through the tunnel. Vaelin was once again impressed by the discipline of Merchant soldiery, each squad continuing to fight until they were ordered through the gate, at which point they would deliver a final lunge of their spears before retreating, soldiers on either side moving to fill the gap.

Soon the half-circle had shrunk to a third of its former size, and still hadn't broken. Vaelin could see Sho Tsai and Tsai Lin at the apex of the arc of struggling soldiers, fighting side by side. The general fought with an economic lethality, his sword lancing out to stab at the faces and necks of his assailants, barking out orders to his men all the while. Tsai Lin had claimed a Stahlhast sabre in addition to his own sword and fought with both weapons, slashing left and right with the kind of deadly precision that Vaelin knew could only be the result of a lifetime of expert tutelage.

"Lord!"

Vaelin turned to find one of the crossbowmen stepping back from the wall, gesturing helplessly at his empty quiver. A glance at the man's comrades confirmed they had all either exhausted their bolts or were about to do so.

"General!" Vaelin cupped his hands around his mouth to call down to Sho Tsai, hoping he could be heard above the tumult of battle. "No more time!"

Sho Tsai gave the briefest glance in his direction, a Stahlhast taking advantage of his distraction to dart forward with his sabre raised before falling dead with Nortah's arrow jutting from his shoulder. Sho Tsai barked out a series of orders that sent the remaining soldiers running for the gate. The orderly withdrawal was forgotten now as they scrambled for safety. Sho Tsai and Tsai Lin continued to back towards the gate, fighting all the way under cover of Nortah and Ellese's arrows, claiming another half-dozen warriors in the time it took the pair to reach the tunnel. By then a group of Redeemed had forced their way into the knot of soldiers trying to reach the gate, killing many and invading the passage.

Vaelin didn't hesitate in shouting out his next order. There was no choice if the third tier was to be held. "Bar the gate!"

As the order was relayed down to the soldiers guarding the tunnel, Vaelin rushed towards the nearest rope, gathering it up and casting it over the parapet. The tail end landed directly between Sho Tsai and Tsai Lin. They backed against the wall to the left of the tunnel, flanked by perhaps twenty surviving soldiers, mostly Red Scouts, Corporal Wei amongst them. Vaelin saw the general push the rope at his son and then voice a harsh, implacable command when the Dai Lo shook his head. Tsai Lin paused to block a thrust from a Redeemed, using his sabre to parry the enemy's blade as his sword came round to lop the man's arm off above the elbow. Casting the sabre aside, he sheathed his sword, took hold of the rope and began to climb.

The general turned to Corporal Wei, jerking his head at the rope. The corporal drove his fist into the face of a snarling Redeemed, bowed low to his general and then, with a shout to his comrades, hurled himself into the ranks of their enemies. The soldiers formed a shield around their general, spears and swords hacking with furious energy. Seeing Sho Tsai hesitate, Vaelin shouted, "Without you, this city falls!"

With a final glance at his men, the general sheathed his sword and gripped the rope, he and his son holding on as Vaelin and a score of crossbowmen and soldiers hauled them up.

"The gate is barred," Vaelin told Sho Tsai as he helped him over the parapet. "I had to . . ."

"I know." The general turned to regard the scene below, watching the last of the Red Scouts perish beneath a tide of stabbing, hacking Redeemed.

With the slaughter complete the Darkblade's host fell to a feral howl of triumph loud enough to pain the ears. They crowded the second tier from end to end, a sea of upturned faces, besmirched by the gore and soot of battle, all screaming their hate at the silent survivors on the final wall. Then, with a jarring suddenness, the roaring mob fell into a silence near absolute but for their laboured breathing.

"He's here," Vaelin heard Luralyn say. She stood at the parapet with Varij at her side, face pale and expressionless as the host parted to allow a lone rider to walk his stallion through the blood-slicked streets.

Kehlbrand halted his mount some two hundred paces from the wall, once again displaying a keen eye for judging the range of an arrow. He sat for a time, face as blank as his sister's and just as silent as the army that surrounded him. Then he raised his hand to display the bundle it held.

Vaelin heard Varij let out an enraged hiss whilst Luralyn betrayed no reaction to the sight of Juhkar's head twisting slowly in her brother's grip. It trailed a red arc through the air as he tossed it towards the upper-tier wall. It landed just to the front of the gate, rolling to stare up with sightless eyes.

Kehlbrand and Luralyn stared at each other for barely the space of a heartbeat, but Vaelin knew for her at least it must have felt like an age. Finally, her brother blinked and looked away, turning his horse and cantering back the way he came whilst his army's roar resumed, louder and more savage than before.

CHAPTER THIRTY-FOUR

Come nightfall, with no sign of a further assault, Sho Tsai ordered the tunnel through the upper-tier wall collapsed. Ahm Lin lent his mason's eye to the work, identifying the stones that could safely be loosened without undermining the wall above. Within hours there was sufficient weight piled up behind the gate that no number of insanely inspired Redeemed could hope to breach it.

"Now he will have to sap," Sho Tsai stated. "Dig his way through ancient cobble and foundations, then tunnel towards the walls. There is no other way to bring them down and they are too high to climb."

He sat on the table where Sherin had tended to the worst of the wounded. Every surface in the room had been scrubbed with vinegar and sawdust scattered on the floor, but the taint of sundered flesh and spilled effluent lingered. The general barely winced as Sherin went about the work of stitching his various cuts, the worst of which was a deep laceration to the nape of his neck.

"He may have imprisoned us here," Sho Tsai added, pausing and gritting his teeth as Sherin tied off the final stitch. "But defeating us will be the work of months."

The general sounded confident, if tired, after the horrors of the day, but it was a confidence Vaelin didn't share. "He has contrived to surprise us at every turn," he said. "It would be folly to assume he doesn't have another prepared. And our losses . . ."

"I need no reminder, my lord." There was a shadow to Sho Tsai's gaze and Vaelin knew the loss of the Red Scouts weighed heavily upon his shoulders. He and Tsai Lin were all that remained of the Scouts and they had not been the only regiment wiped out. Governor Neshim, assiduous in his accounting if nothing else, now reported their full strength at little over ten thousand. A great many more Stahlhast and Redeemed had surely fallen, but the Darkblade's army remained strong and its unnatural devotion unbroken.

"This trap is also his, don't forget that," Sho Tsai went on. "If he were a rational man, he would have marched on, or at least left sufficient numbers to contain us whilst he moves south. But here he stays with his entire army, all so he can lay claim to a sister that hates him."

A sister with a thorn in her mind, Vaelin thought. *Or is that why he wants her back so badly? Does he fear what secrets she'll spill when it's plucked?*

"Here," Sherin said, handing Sho Tsai a small bottle. "For the pain. Two drops in a cup of water three times throughout the day."

"I can't have my senses dulled . . ." the general said, making to return the bottle.

"Just take it and spare me your posturing," Sherin ordered with a tired sigh. She moved to a bowl of water and began scrubbing her hands. "There's a sergeant on a stretcher outside with an axe wound to the gut. I need the room."

Vaelin sensed that the pain on Sho Tsai's face had little to do with his cuts. He made no effort to rise, continuing to stare at Sherin's unyielding back. It was clear to Vaelin that more was about to be said in this room and, feeling no desire to witness it, voiced a murmured excuse about checking the sentries and left.

◆ ◆ ◆

He found Eresa and Jihla guarding the door to Luralyn's cell. The younger woman surprised Vaelin with a warm embrace whilst Eresa continued to regard him with the frowning bafflement that had become typical since surviving her touch.

"We regret we cannot let you in, my lord," Jihla said. Apart from the dark circles beneath her eyes and a somewhat pallid complexion, she seemed fully recovered, although the forced aspect to her smile told of a profound grief. "Our mistress's order." ·

"You're not supposed to call her that," Vaelin reminded her, glancing at the closed door. "She seeks the True Dream?"

"She does," Eresa confirmed. "It may take hours, or even a day or more. There's no way to tell."

"You're welcome to stay with us," Jihla offered. "Varij has gone to fetch some food."

He replied with a polite refusal and went to the shrine where his companions sat sharing a stew of Ellese's concoction, which smelt surprisingly appetising. "It turns out horse meat benefits from an excess of spices," she said, handing him a bowl.

"Horse?" he asked, now regarding the stew with dubious eyes.

"The governor forgot to transport the salted pork to the upper tier," Nortah explained. "Meat is in short supply. Eat up, brother. We've certainly had worse."

Seeing Tsai Lin sitting apart from the others, Vaelin had Ellese pour out another bowl of stew and took it to him. "Your father's wounds are slight," he said, handing the Dai Lo the bowl and sitting down next to him on the steps of the shrine.

Tsai Lin gave a nod and stared wordlessly at the stew before setting it aside. He hadn't yet removed his armour, which still bore the dirt of battle, as did his face. "Losing men is hard . . ." Vaelin began.

"A life lost in a righteous cause is to be celebrated, not mourned," Tsai Lin cut in. His voice was mostly toneless but Vaelin caught the formal note that indicated this to be a quotation.

"Kuan-Shi?" he asked.

Tsai Lin shook his head. "A line from one of the Mystic Scrolls, a collection of lore that dates back to long before the rise of the Emerald Empire. My principal teacher was always fond of employing them in his lessons. The Mystic Scrolls make mention of a race of people with oddly coloured hair and skin that were once carried across the western seas by a mighty fleet. They are said to have worshipped nameless gods and displayed such savage habits that the other tribes of the era fled before them in terror. In time they settled on the Iron Steppe, mined metal from the tors and became known to the people of the south as the Steel Horde. The Stahlhast, you see, are just as ancient a people as we are."

"So they teach more than fighting at the Temple of Spears."

"A great deal more. 'Not even a butcher wields a blade unguided by knowledge.' *That* was Kuan-Shi." Tsai Lin's mouth formed the faintest curve but it faded quickly, eyes darkening with guilt. "I didn't like my men, Lord Vaelin. I thought them brutish and ignorant. But they gave their lives for my father without hesitation. Their example shames me."

"Men are not well led by shameful leaders, and there are other men here in sore need of leadership. In the morning you will form a fresh regiment from the remnants of those destroyed today."

"Only a captain can command a regiment."

"True." Vaelin took a small metal star enamelled in silver from his belt and handed it to Tsai Lin. "Your father's order. Congratulations, Dai Shin. You'll need to come up with a name and a banner," he went on as Tsai Lin stared at the star in his hand. "Soldiers need such things . . ."

He trailed off at the sound of a bowl shattering on the stone floor of the shrine, turning to see Ahm Lin on his feet. The mason's features were blank with shock, eyes wide as they snapped to Vaelin.

"It couldn't see him before now," he said. "The song . . . he was hidden from it. I don't think he knew . . ."

"Who?" Vaelin said, striding towards Ahm Lin.

The mason blinked and Vaelin saw a terrible resignation creep over his features, a certainty of imminent catastrophe. "The stonebreaker," he said, shaking his head, voice dropping to a whisper as he repeated, "I don't think he knew."

◆　◆　◆

"Where is Varij?" Vaelin demanded, the two Gifted women outside the door to Luralyn's chamber exchanging baffled glances as he advanced towards them.

"He still hasn't returned," Eresa said. "What is . . . ?"

Vaelin stepped past her and delivered a hard kick to the door, stepping inside to find Luralyn on a narrow bed. His alarm quickened at the sight of her slack, open-mouthed face, but a touch to her chest confirmed she was alive, although her breathing was shallow and she uttered no sound as he shook her.

"This is not the True Dream," Eresa said, moving to press a hand to Luralyn's forehead. Her next words were choked with a mingling of bafflement and fear. "She's been drugged."

"Take her to Sherin," Vaelin said. "Tell her to do everything she can to wake her. Go with them," he added to Sehmon and Alum. "Tell the general to rouse the entire garrison."

He went outside, looking to Ahm Lin for guidance. "There," he said, pointing to the southern stretch of wall. Vaelin noted that the doom-laden expression remained on his face.

"Dai Shin Tsai, take charge of the Skulls," Vaelin told Tsai Lin. "Bring them and every spare man to the south-facing wall."

He told Ahm Lin to stay with Alum and started off at a run for the wall with Ellese and Nortah following close behind, bows ready. He heard no shouts from the battlement as they approached the wall, indicating no approaching enemy on the other side, but he had learned appearances meant nothing where the Darkblade was concerned.

"There," Nortah said, bow raised to point at a solitary figure at the base of the wall. Varij stood staring at the stonework with his hands at his sides, showing no sign of having heard their approach.

"Varij," Vaelin called out. "Step back from the wall."

The Gifted turned his head slightly, Vaelin glimpsing a piteous smile before he returned his gaze to the stone. "The Thief of Names," he said. "I had hoped for a death at more worthy hands."

"Step back from the wall," Vaelin repeated. Both Nortah and Ellese had their bows levelled at the Gifted, poison-coated arrowheads gleaming in the moonlight.

"Why do you seek to spare me, Thief of Names?" Varij asked, this time turning to face them. His expression was one of mild curiosity, but Vaelin saw a familiar cast to his eyes. He had seen it in the face of every Redeemer he had fought. Varij belonged to the Darkblade. "Is it my mistress you worry for?" he went on. "How her betrayer's heart will break . . ."

"I'm told you didn't know you were doing the Darkblade's bidding," Vaelin cut in. "Here you stand ready to die for a false god you detested only moments ago. I would know how this was done."

"Love," Varij said simply. "I was always his. From the moment he freed me, saved me from the whip and the endless toil. When he spoke I knew he spoke for the divine. The man you see before you is the truth, it was Varij who was the lie. I was set to watch her years ago, told that one day she would betray the Darkblade but that her betrayal was necessary. So he had Sehga craft lies in my head, birth the doubts that would win the Betrayer's trust, all so that she would bring me here." Varij smiled the bright broad smile of a contented man. "And the key to the Merchant Realms would be unlocked so that all there might know his mercy."

Hearing Ellese's bowstring tighten, Varij laughed. "Kill me, I welcome it. For I know there is only salvation in death. You cannot stop what has already been done."

Vaelin saw them then, the spiderweb of cracks in the cobbles at the base of the wall, cracks that were spreading. "Kill him!" he snapped. The twin arrows struck Varij full in the chest, punching through to protrude from his back as he collapsed. Even as all the fluid in his body flowed free in a dark tide the contented smile remained on his lips.

As Vaelin watched, the cracks at the base of the wall spread with lightning speed, powdered stone fountaining and the ground taking on a pronounced shudder.

"Back!" Vaelin said, pushing Nortah and Ellese away just as a thunderous boom sounded from below. A single deep fissure opened at the base of the wall and snaked its way to the top faster than the eye could follow. A rumble of grinding stone rose as a section of wall at least fifty feet across appeared to sublime into a cascade of small boulders. As it fell dust erupted in a thick, choking fog seeded with lacerating grit that forced them to shield their faces.

When Vaelin lowered his hand from his eyes, he was confronted by the sight of a breach he knew they had no hope of sealing. He could already see mounted Stahlhast forming up for a charge amidst the houses of the second tier, dense formations of Redeemed thronging the flanks.

"Lord Vaelin!"

Sho Tsai came to a halt nearby, three regiments of infantry fanning out behind him. Vaelin could see other soldiers quickly descending the walls to form up in the streets. The general had come to the obvious conclusion that the only battle that mattered now would be fought in this breach.

"Proceed to the temple," Sho Tsai told Vaelin. He stepped closer to meet Vaelin's gaze with steady, implacable eyes, speaking in a low voice. "Save her, if you can. If you can't, then spare her."

He turned away, beckoning Tsai Lin closer. "Go with Lord Vaelin."

"General, I must—"

"There is no time!" Sho Tsai's eyes blazed at his son, compelling him to stand at attention. "There will be chaos when they storm through," Sho Tsai added, expression softening into regret. "Perhaps enough to shield an escape. That is my last order to you, my son. Survive this place and return to the Temple of Spears. Follow their counsel, for I see the age of kings is done."

He faced the breach, drawing his sword as the thunder of Stahlhast hooves began to sound. "Now go!"

◆　◆　◆

The din of battle accompanied their flight to the temple, as loud as any storm, so loud that he failed to hear Corporal Cho-ka's greeting until the man ran from the shadows to block his path. He was flanked by the half-dozen Skulls Vaelin knew to be members of the Green Vipers.

"My lord," he said with a cursory bow. "I should like to show you something."

"What something?" Vaelin wasn't especially surprised Cho-ka and his associates hadn't chosen to stand with the general at the end, nor could he find the will to be angry. Was he not also a coward this night?

"Something in my great-aunt's spice shop," Cho-ka said, casting a wary glance around.

"Speak plainly!" Vaelin snapped, patience running thin.

"A way out," the outlaw said. "One that could not be used until now."

"But might have assisted us before."

"I owe my allegiance to the Green Vipers alone. Not to a king who might hang me on a whim or a general whose name I'd never heard until a month ago. We fought for our lives and they won't be squandered in defence of a pile of blackened bricks. But there's a debt between us that I'm keen to settle."

Vaelin turned to Ellese and Nortah. "Go with them. The Dai Lo and I have business at the temple. The pitch of battle will change once the breach falls. When it does, don't wait one second longer."

He turned away before they could argue, hastening to the temple, where he found Sherin in her treatment room waving a bottle of smelling salts under Luralyn's nose whilst Chien held the woman's head still. Eresa and Jihla stood in the corner, faces wrought with concern as their mistress moaned, nostrils twitching, but failed to wake.

"We're leaving," Vaelin told Sherin. "Get her up," he added to Chien, nodding at Luralyn. "The captain will help you."

"To where?" the outlaw woman asked, looping one of Luralyn's arms over her shoulders whilst Tsai Lin took the other.

"The spice shop on the street left of the gate. The Green Vipers have been keeping secrets."

"Trust a rat to always find a pipe," Chien grunted as they hefted Luralyn's weight.

"Go now," Vaelin told them, watching Sherin unhurriedly returning the bottle of smelling salts to her chest of curatives. "We'll be along."

Chien and Tsai Lin duly carried Luralyn from the room, Eresa and Jihla following close behind.

"It's time," Vaelin told Sherin, finding he had to swallow before continuing. "I'm sorry."

"You left him," she said in a flat, unsurprised tone, not turning.

"He ordered me to, as he ordered me to save you. And I will."

"I have patients." She closed the lid of her chest, pausing a moment to regard her hands, flexing the fingers. "And a gift to share . . ."

"If I have to knock you unconscious to drag you from this city, I will do it!"

She stiffened at his shout, eyes suddenly red, the lines of her face made sharp as she fought her pain. "Did you see him die?"

He moved to her, taking hold of her wrist and pulling her to the door. "There is no time."

She tore her arm free, red eyes glaring in accusation. "Did you see him die?!"

The lie should have been easy, a thing of utter necessity, but it died on his tongue. He had lied enough to her. "He fights," he said. "And he will do so to the death so that you can live. Don't rob it of meaning."

She turned away, drawing in a ragged breath as she moved to close the lid on her curatives chest, gathering it tight in her arms. Saying nothing else, she left the room. Outside, Vaelin found Ahm Lin, Sehmon and Alum waiting.

"Stay close," he told them. "And move fast."

He heard the sound of battle change when they had covered half the distance to the shop, the discordant medley of colliding metal becoming hushed for the briefest instant before surging into the roar of thousands of triumphant voices.

"What's that?" Sehmon said.

"They've broken through," Vaelin told him, glancing towards the south. Sherin let out a grating sob as the roar descended into a babble punctuated by shrill screams that told of a slaughter.

"I told you not to wait," Vaelin called out to Nortah as they rounded a corner to find his brother and Ellese waiting in the street.

"And, I'm sure, knew we would do no such thing," Nortah returned. He led them into the shop, where a large trapdoor lay open in the centre of the floor. "The outlaws, however, had no such qualms. Tsai Lin and the women have just gone through."

"Where does it lead?" Sehmon asked, peering into the gloomy opening with a dubious eye.

"As long as it's not here, who cares, lackwit?" Ellese said, striding forward to jump into the hole. Vaelin pushed Sherin through next, waiting for the others to follow before taking hold of the chain on the inside of the trapdoor and swinging it shut behind them as he climbed down.

The stairs below were steep, lit by a single torch in a stanchion on the rough-hewn wall, presumably left behind by Cho-ka. Alum took the torch and led the way down, the party moving as fast as they dared on the damp, narrow steps. The tunnel described a wayward course as it descended, making it impossible to gauge a direction. It finally ended in a broad chamber with a low curved roof. Moonlight reflected from the channel of water running through it to dapple silver onto the roof and walls. The light came from numerous holes in the roof and illuminated a watercourse that stretched away for at least a mile below the ground.

"My lord!" Tsai Lin's voice echoed long in the chamber as he called from a boat in the water. He sat at the stern with an oar, the three women huddled in the centre. Another boat was moored close by, complete with two oars.

"The scum refused to wait," Tsai Lin said as Vaelin climbed into his boat, taking up the spare oar and positioning himself at the prow. Ahm Lin climbed in behind him whilst the others filled the second boat. They were long, flat-hulled craft with tall sides, designed, Vaelin assumed, for the smuggling trade.

"We're alive thanks to that scum," he reminded Tsai Lin, pushing his oar against the stone bank to send the craft into the middle of the waterway.

They set off at a steady paddle, Vaelin glancing behind to ensure the other boat was following. Alum and Nortah had charge of the oars and they made good progress. Vaelin's gaze returned continually to Sherin's huddled form in the second boat, head bowed low and slim shoulders hunched in grief.

"Varij?" Luralyn stared up at Vaelin from the bottom of the boat, her eyes like dark holes in a grey mask. Whatever drug she had been dosed with had apparently faded, but he knew her pains were far from over.

"Dead," Vaelin replied, facing forward.

"He was the thorn," Luralyn persisted. "Wasn't he?"

Vaelin just nodded and worked his oar through the water.

"Did he say anything?" Luralyn's voice faltered and it was several seconds before she spoke again. "Did he . . . explain anything?"

I was set to watch her years ago . . . Her betrayal was necessary. "Nothing that made any sense," Vaelin replied. "He was quite mad. I'm sorry."

They rowed for close to an hour before coming to the end of the tunnel, the mouth of which was partially covered by a curtain of hanging weeds. Vaelin and Tsai Lin slowed the boat as they neared the opening, emerging slowly through the curtain to find themselves confronted by the long silver road of the Great Northern Canal. It stretched away to the left and right, for miles, although the southern course appeared to have no terminus whilst the northern ended in the dark bulk of Keshin-Kho.

Vaelin reckoned they were at most five miles from the city, but the noise was audible even here; thousands of voices raised in rhythmic chanting to the glory of the Darkblade's victory. He turned his gaze from it and the char-nel house visions it conjured, propelling the boat into the canal with a hard sweep of his oar, then steering a southward course.

He scanned the passing banks constantly, letting out a small sigh of grat-itude when he noticed a mist drifting in from the surrounding fields. Any-thing that might shield their escape was welcome. His gratification faded, however, when Ahm Lin shuffled closer, whispering, "This is not a natural fog, brother."

He gave an urgent nod at Vaelin's questioning look. Another glance at the mist was enough to convince him. It swirled in thick tendrils, seemingly immune to the course of the prevailing breeze. Vaelin rose, setting his oar aside and raising his hands to sign to the second boat, the old Order gesture warning of enemies close by. He saw Nortah acknowledge the warning with a brief flick of his hand before lifting his bow, Ellese doing the same.

Vaelin stooped to retrieve the oar, then paused, his gaze snared by a pale vision on the canal bank. Derka tossed his mane in recognition as he trotted through the grass, snorted breath mingling with the fog. A smile played on Vaelin's lips as he strove to imagine how the stallion had contrived to escape the Keshin-Kho stables, then faded when he saw the saddle on his back; a Stahlhast saddle.

Thirus rose from the long grass with her bow already drawn, the arrow flying free, trailing vapour as it described a perfect arc towards him. An arm slammed hard against Vaelin's chest, Ahm Lin's shout mingling with the curse Thirus screamed in her arrow's wake, both sounds choking off simultaneously as the shaft struck home.

Vaelin took in the sight of Thirus falling in a welter of blood, one of Ellese's arrows speared neatly through her neck, before his gaze slid to Ahm Lin. The mason gave a weary smile, glancing down at the arrowhead protruding from his chest, before his legs gave out and he slipped over the side.

Vaelin instantly followed him into the water, wrapping an arm around his feebly struggling form and striking out for the bank. The multiple snap of many bows filled the air, accompanied by the hiss of swarming arrows and the hard thud of iron on wood.

"No!" Vaelin shouted, seeing Ellese poised to follow him into the water, hauling herself up in defiance of the continuing torrent of arrows. She began to launch herself from the boat but Nortah, face hard with reluctance, lunged forward to catch her about the waist.

"*Let go!*" she screamed, Vaelin glimpsing her flailing limbs before the fog closed in thick enough to render both boats mere shadows in the gloom.

Ellese called out several more times, before her cries were muffled, presumably by Nortah's hand. The arrow storm faded as the pounding of drumming hoof-beats sounded from both banks. Thirus hadn't been alone.

Vaelin got a hand to the bank after a brief few moments' flailing in the water, reaching beyond it to grasp a handful of grass and haul them clear. Dragging Ahm Lin into the long undergrowth, he drew his sword, ears alive to the sounds drifting through the fog. The hoof-beats had faded now into the snorts and scraped earth that told of horses either halted or at a walk. It was impossible to tell how many.

"The . . . song . . ." Ahm Lin gasped. Vaelin shook his head, lowering his mouth to the mason's ear.

"Lie still."

Ahm Lin's eyes met his, Vaelin seeing the same weary smile on his lips. "The song . . ." he began again, voice a croaking rasp and blood welling over his teeth. "Was clear, brother. From . . . the start . . ."

"Save your strength," Vaelin whispered back. "Sherin will heal you . . ."

"No . . ." Ahm Lin's smile became a laugh, rich in irony. "The song . . . was clear. Why I sent . . . Shoala away. Why I . . . waited for you. All songs . . . end, brother. The princess . . . knew that . . ."

He reached for Vaelin's hand, grasping it with shuddering fingers as he guided it to the arrowhead jutting from his chest, pressing it into the blood welling around the wound.

"My gift," Ahm Lin said. "To you."

The blood was warm against Vaelin's skin, but he began to snatch his hand away as if he had been burned.

"No!" Ahm Lin's gaze became fierce, his mason's hand like a vise on Vaelin's, holding it in place. "You must!" he grated through teeth stained with gore. "To fight him . . . you need a song. If you don't . . . *he wins!*"

The final words emerged in a shout, Vaelin hearing the whinny of alerted horses followed by shouted voices. Stahlhast voices.

Images tumbled through Vaelin's mind as he stared into Ahm Lin's wide, imploring gaze. The assassinated emissaries in the tower. The princess's intent. The duel with Obvar. The siege. Varij's hidden truth. Thirus's arrow. Had he still possessed a song, how much of it would ever have happened?

Fighting you as you are would be like fighting a child, Kehlbrand had said. The Darkblade had said. And, in that at least, Vaelin knew he hadn't been lying.

But still the wrongness of it stopped him, disgusted him. The Volarians had made themselves slaves of the Ally by doing this thing. What would it make of him?

He heard Ellese's voice again, a distant, plaintive call drifting through the fog, soon swallowed by the sound of horses once again at a gallop. Excited shouts filled the air as the Stahlhast closed in, hungry for the renown they craved, and there was much to be had in presenting the head of the Thief of Names to their beloved living god.

"Please, brother . . ." Blood spattered from Ahm Lin's lips, his eyes growing dull. "Please . . ."

Hearing steel hiss free from a scabbard, Vaelin lowered his mouth to his friend's mortal wound, drinking deep.

Dramatis Personae

The Northern Reaches of the Unified Realm

Vaelin Al Sorna—Tower Lord of the Northern Reaches

Nortah Al Sendahl—former brother of the Sixth Order; Sword of the Realm and hero of the Liberation War; father to Lohren and Artis; brother to Kerran; renowned drunkard

Kerran Al Verin—merchant and owner of the Honoured Trading House of Al Verin, and Mistress of the Merchants' Guild of the Northern Reaches; sister to Nortah; aunt to Lohren and Artis

Erlin—former Gifted immortal; resident of Nehrin's Point

Lohren Al Sendahl—daughter to Nortah; brother to Artis; Gifted seer

Artis Al Sendahl—son to Nortah; brother to Lohren

Ellese Mustor—adopted daughter and heir to Lady Governess Reva Mustor of Cumbrael

Orven Al Melna—Lord Commander of the North Guard

Alum Vi Moreska—hunter to the Moreska Clan; friend to Vaelin

Sehmon Vek—former outlaw and indentured servant to Alum

Tallspear—Cumbraelin bowman and adopted member of the Bear People Clan

Iron Eyes—shaman to the Bear People Clan

Brother Kehlan—brother of the Fifth Order; healer to the North Tower

Cara—Gifted resident of Nehrin's Point; estranged wife to Lorkan

Lorkan Densah—estranged husband to Cara; former Gifted resident of Nehrin's Point

Kohn Shen—ambassador from the Court of the Venerable Kingdom to the Unified Realm

Gian Nuishin—commander of the Seventh Cohort of the Venerable Host and ambassador to the Unified Realm

Veiser Mortin—captain of the *Sea Wasp*, a trading vessel owned by the Honoured Trading House of Al Verin

The Stahlhast

Kehlbrand Reyerik—Great Lord of the Hast

Luralyn Reyerik—sister to Kehlbrand and Babukir; Gifted seer of the Divine Blood

Babukir Reyerik—younger brother to Kehlbrand and Luralyn

Obvar Nagerik—Stahlhast warrior of great renown; Kehlbrand's champion and saddle brother; would-be suitor to Luralyn

Varnko Materk—Skeltir of the Ostra Skeld

Thirus—warrior of the Ostra Skeld

Eresa—Gifted former slave and friend to Luralyn

Varij—Gifted former slave and friend to Luralyn

Juhkar—Gifted former slave and friend to Luralyn

Jihla—Gifted former slave and friend to Luralyn

Kihlen—Gifted former slave and friend to Luralyn

The Venerable Kingdom

Lian Sha—Merchant King of the Venerable Kingdom

Sho Tsai—captain in the Merchant King's host; commander of the Red Scouts

Tsai Lin—apprentice officer in the Red Scouts; son to Sho Tsai

The Jade Princess—immortal occupant of the High Temple

Sherin Unsa—former Mistress of Curatives to the Fifth Order of the Faith; healer of great renown known as "The Grace of Heaven"; formerly Vaelin's lover

Ahm Lin—stonemason and Gifted wielder of a blood-song; friend to Vaelin and Sherin

Pao Len—teashop owner and leader of the Crimson Band

Chien—member of the Crimson Band; daughter to Pao Len

Crab—boatman and member of the Crimson Band

Hushan Shi—governor of Keshin-Kho, capital of the Northern Prefecture of the Venerable Kingdom

Neshim Lhi—deputy governor of the city of Keshin-Kho; later promoted to governor

Corporal Wei—corporal in the Red Scouts

Cho-ka—smuggler and member of the Green Viper outlaw band; later corporal in the Skulls Infantry Company

H e felt Ahm Lin die as he drank. A faint, almost imperceptible exhalation and a final shudder, then his friend was gone.

Vaelin forced away the surge of despair to suck in the last few pulses of blood streaming from the mason's wound. The thick metallic stream flooded his mouth and caught in his throat, making him gag. Heedless of his disgust, he forced the thick torrent down. Vaelin felt the gift blossom as soon as the first few drops entered his gut, spreading through his being with lightning speed, and bringing with it a song, a song that had more in common with a scream.

The music was deafening, painfully so, filling his mind with an overlapping cascade of notes that somehow retained a tune of sorts despite their ugly discordance, a tune that held both certainty and meaning: *Death comes from all sides. IT COMES NOW!*

He sprang away from Ahm Lin's corpse, crouching low and ducking under the whistling slash of a sabre as its wielder, a hulking Stahlhast in full armour, came surging out of the long grass that covered the canal bank. The warrior cursed and tried again, both hands on the hilt as he thrust towards Vaelin's chest. The song continued to scream as Vaelin found his gaze captured by the Stahlhast's blunt, heavily creased features. The tune told the tale of a man steeped in blood and happiest in moments of violence. A man who had fought, killed, raped and looted his way across the Iron Steppe and the borderlands. A man who hungered for more when the horde swept into the heart of the Venerable Kingdom. A man who had also neglected to repair the small plate of armour that covered the space above his left hip, hacked away during the final assault on Keshin-Kho. All this the song screamed into Vaelin's mind in the space of a heartbeat.

He twisted as the Stahlhast closed, allowing the sabre to pass within an inch of his chest, then stabbed his sword point into the gap in the Stahlhast's armour. The blade sank deep, slicing through vein, tendon and cartilage to sever all connections between leg and hip. The warrior shouted in shock and fury as he collapsed, glaring up at Vaelin, lips forming a last defiant obscenity. Vaelin withdrew his blade and hacked down, the warrior's final word swallowed by the gush of blood that erupted from his mouth.

The song's shriek snapped Vaelin's gaze to a fresh threat, two more Stahlhast thrashing through the tall grass barely yards away. He hacked again at the dying warrior's neck, delivering two fast blows then taking hold of the man's helmet as his head came free of his shoulders. The first Stahlhast to clear the grass received the thrown head full in the face and reeled back on his heels, stunned and blinded by the impact and explosion of gore. He managed to scrape the red mess from his eye in time for it to receive the tip of Vaelin's sword, the blade skewering his brain before he had time to register the fact of his own death.

Vaelin kicked the twitching corpse aside, pulling the sword free in time to parry the slash delivered by the second Stahlhast. He stepped close before the warrior had the chance to retreat, delivering a swift headbutt to his unguarded nose then snatching a dagger from the man's belt before whirling and driving it into the unarmoured rear of his thigh.

More pealing cries from the song sent Vaelin sprawling into the grass as a criss-cross hail of arrows snapped the air. The unfortunate Stahlhast, still upright and staggering as he tried to pull the dagger from his leg, took a trio of shafts in the chest, evidently loosed from close range judging by the ease with which the steel arrowheads punched through mail and plate. As he crawled away, his belly scraping the earth, Vaelin heard the warrior's choking death rattle. Shouts echoed through the fog-shrouded bank interspersed by the occasional snap and whistle of a loosed arrow, but none came close.

It's different, Vaelin thought as he crawled, wincing as the song's grating tune continued. Its pitch rose and fell continually, sibilant as a snake's hiss one second then screeching like a distressed hawk the next. With every peak he felt his vision darken and his pulse quicken, accompanied by a rarely felt but familiar hunger. He had first felt it in the Martishe Forest many years ago, when his friend lay dying and Vaelin sprinted in pursuit of the archer who had felled him. It was bloodlust, a need to kill born of this song. *A different song*, he knew with growing certainty. *Not my song.* Not the song he had left in the Beyond after bleeding himself to the point of death at Alltor. Not the song he had ached for ever since.

He came to a halt as the new song's tune rose again, although the tune was not quite so discordant and the sensation it brought held no tinge of hunger. Still there was a sour note to it, a grudging thrum of welcome.

The horse's hoof came down a few inches from his head, stamping in impatience. Vaelin looked up and grimaced as Derka's snort showered hot vapour onto his face. The stallion angled his head to regard Vaelin with a single, insistent eye, shaking his neck to allow the reins to fall free.

"Yes," Vaelin grunted, reaching for the reins, "it's good to see you again too."

A fresh chorus of shouts erupted as he vaulted into the saddle, swiftly followed by another volley of arrows. They met only air as Derka bore him away, spurring unbidden into a gallop to be swallowed by the fog. The song let out another shrill cry of warning an instant before a mounted Stahlhast came thundering out of the mist directly ahead, a tall woman whirling a double-bladed axe above her head. Vaelin took a firmer hold of the reins, intending to guide Derka to the rider's left, but the stallion had a notion of his own. Earth and shredded grass fountained as he came to a halt, rearing with a whinny as the charging horse closed. The hard crack of shattered bone sounded as Derka brought a hoof down on the opposing horse's head, sending it and its rider into an untidy tumble.

Vaelin started to spur Derka forward but stopped as the song surged again, the tune not as loud this time but somehow even more painful. The notes were harsh and insistent, seeming to dig deep inside him to conjure images of the siege, all the soldiers he had commanded now dying at the hands of the Darkblade's horde, and Ahm Lin's bleached, pleading face at the end. *Please . . . my gift to you . . .*

His vision blurred as the song rose to a deafening, near-agonising pitch, turning the world into a reddish grey haze. He was aware of his hand on the reins, of the sword's handle turning against his palm and the flex of his arm, but had no control over any of it. He couldn't say how long it took for the song's tune to fade and his vision to clear—it might have been just a few seconds or an hour—but when it did he found himself staring down at the Stahlhast woman, now slumped against the flank of her slain horse. Her features were a curious mirror of Ahm Lin's at the end, whitened by blood loss and imminent death. She looked up at Vaelin and blinked once before turning to regard the jet of blood pulsing from the stump of her severed arm, watching her life drain away in rapt fascination rather than horror.

Dragging his gaze away, Vaelin slid his sword into the sheath on his back and spurred Derka into a gallop, disappearing into the fog once more. Shouts and bowstrings continued to echo through the haze but faded soon enough. Slowing Derka to a walk, Vaelin cast around for a landmark, some indication of where he might be. The fog had thinned to a low-lying mist unveiling the sun and revealing a plain of tall grass that rose into undulating hills to the south. The dim conical bulk of Keshin-Kho dominated the skyline to the north and he could see the unerringly straight line of the canal a few hundred paces to the west. The only appreciable cover consisted of a dense patch of woodland off to the east and, knowing pursuit would not be long in coming, he turned Derka towards it and set off at a steady canter.

As he rode, the sight of the dying Stahlhast woman's face lingered. He had taken many lives but always, he preferred to think, out of necessity. With the Stahlhast dismounted he could have ridden on. Killing her was unnecessary, and yet he had done it. A sharp snarl came from the song then, the tone one of harsh rebuke that carried a new thought: *An enemy is deserving only of death.*

He found his hands tightening on the reins, bringing Derka to a halt. Glancing over his shoulder Vaelin peered into the misted grass, hearing the faint but growing shouts of his pursuers. *They killed Ahm Lin*, he thought as the song's tune grew more melodious, becoming almost seductive in the promise it held. *They killed Sho Tsai and so many others, all in service to a false god. And I have a blood-song once again. Would it be so hard to kill them all? Would it not, in fact, be an insult to Ahm Lin's memory if I didn't? He gave me a gift, after all.*

Derka gave a loud, irritated nicker, breaking through his burgeoning hunger and provoking another snarl from the song. Vaelin clenched his teeth and determinedly turned his gaze east once more, kicking the stallion into motion. *No*, he decided as the hungry tune persisted, setting a continual ache in his head as he refused to answer its call. *This is not a blood-song. Blood is the stuff of life. This is a song of death. A black-song.*

◆ ◆ ◆

By the time they reached the trees the song had diminished into a sullen murmur and the ache in his head subsided to a dull throb. He brought Derka to a halt a few yards in, dismounting and crouching with his eyes closed to gauge the sounds and smells of the forest. *Earth damp from recent rain*, he concluded, fingers probing the ground. *Bird calls muted . . . Woodsmoke, drifting from the south.* There were people in these woods.

The forest was dense and the branches low, obliging him to lead Derka through the trees, maintaining an eastward course to avoid whatever lay south. He intended to reach the far end of these woods before striking out to find the canal, an easy task and following it south would inevitably lead him back to Nortah, Ellese and the others. He hoped they had had the good sense not to come looking for him and consoled himself with the knowledge that, for all his faults, Nortah was no fool and not easily swayed by sentiment, especially when sober. *He'll lead them on*, he concluded. *All I need do is find them.*

His progress, however, stalled when the song, the black-song, rose in sudden insistent volume once more. The tune remained harsh and grating but the tone lacked the vengeful hunger from before, possessing instead a note that combined warning with necessity. It also prodded him south towards the persistent scent of woodsmoke. *Something there*, he concluded, finding the song too compelling to ignore. *Something that must be dealt with.*

He led Derka through a quarter mile of thick forest until he spied wispy tendrils drifting through the treetops ahead. *At least three fires*, Vaelin concluded, eyeing the smoke then wincing as a scream sounded through the trees. This time it didn't come from within, the unmistakable product of a human throat and shot through with the plaintive terror unique to torture. It continued for several seconds before abruptly choking off, Vaelin hearing a faint ripple of laughter as it dwindled away. *Something that must be dealt with*, he repeated to himself, the scream and the laughter having dispelled any doubts about the song's course.

Derka gave a truculent snort and tossed his head in annoyance when Vaelin began to fasten his reins to the fallen branch of a yew. *I sang to him,* the Jade Princess had said during the trek across the Iron Steppe. *Just a small tune to bind you together.* "Wait here," Vaelin whispered, letting the reins fall and smoothing a hand over the stallion's snout before crouching and slipping into the concealment offered by a stretch of ferns.

The laughter grew louder and more discordant as he crept forward, making out several voices speaking a language he didn't know. Pausing to listen, he detected some resemblance to both the Stahlhast tongue and the form of Chu-Shin spoken in the borderlands, but the phrasing and accents rendered the words unintelligible. Lowering himself to the earth he began to crawl, moving with steady, practised slowness, his hands sweeping the ground free of twigs or fallen branches that might betray his presence. He stopped as a familiar hissing sound reached his ears, his eyes picking out a rising patch of steam beyond the trunk of an ash tree. A slow sideways creep revealed the sight of a man in leather armour, face set in bored distraction as he pissed into the undergrowth.

Tuhla, Vaelin concluded, recognising the man's garb. His eyes flicked left and right, finding no others whilst the laughter and conversation continued in the distance. *Never a good plan to piss alone in a time of war.* Vaelin watched the man finish his task and turn away, looking down to fasten his britches as he walked off. Vaelin rose to a crouch, moving swiftly, the sound of his footfalls causing the Tuhla to pause and turn, but too late to ward off the arms that encircled his chest and throat. Vaelin kicked the Tuhla's legs away and jerked his head up and to the right as they fell, Vaelin taking satisfaction from the double crack that told of a snapped neck. He clamped a hand over the man's mouth to stifle his death cries, pinching the nose to prevent a last intake of breath, maintaining his grip until his twitches stilled.

Rolling the corpse off him, Vaelin checked it for anything useful. The Tuhla wore a scimitar on his belt along with a flask of some foul-smelling concoction with the sting of strong liquor. He also had a bone-handle hunting knife of good steel tucked into his boot. Vaelin took the knife and moved on, once again adopting his slow, steady crawl, keeping to the densest undergrowth. He found two more Tuhla twenty paces on, both markedly less careless than their recently despatched comrade. One held a strongbow with arrow nocked to the string whilst the other gripped a drawn scimitar. Both were scanning the surrounding trees with the predatory awareness of men well versed in detecting fresh danger.

"Ulska!" the archer said in a restrained shout, presumably calling out to a man who had taken too long over a piss. Vaelin flattened himself to the soft ground as they came closer. He was partially concealed by the broad trunk of an aged oak and a covering of ferns, but this would prove scant protection when they drew within ten paces or so. Vaelin palmed one of his own throwing knives in his left hand and adjusted his grip on the stolen Tuhla weapon, waiting until the two warriors closed the distance to five paces.

He drew back his arms and threw as he rose from cover, both knives arcing towards the targets with a precision he had thought lost to his youth. The left-hand throw was marginally the less accurate of the two, the steel dart striking at the join of the Tuhla's neck and shoulder, but still managing to find a vein of sufficient import to send the warrior to the ground with blood gurgling from his mouth in a dark torrent. By contrast, the archer somehow remained standing despite taking the bone-handle knife full in the throat. He even tried to draw his bow as Vaelin made an unhurried approach, though the Tuhla's spasming limbs soon shook the weapon from his grasp. Vaelin stooped to retrieve the bow before pulling the knife free and relieving the Tuhla of his quiver when he finally collapsed and choked out his last strangled breath.

Vaelin put an arrow to the string as he moved on, the black-song growing into an ugly murmur. It was coloured by a sensation he hadn't felt for many years, the hum of recognition that meant only one thing: *Another Gifted is near.* A fresh upsurge of laughter led him to the rest of the Tuhla, a dozen standing in a loose circle around a small group of kneeling men. The kneelers were all bare chested, but a pile of discarded armoured jerkins nearby marked them as captured soldiers of the Merchant King. Also, Vaelin saw as he crept closer, men he knew.

Cho-ka knelt at the forefront of the group, flanked on either side by the prone corpses of two fellow members of the Green Vipers. His sweat-beaded features bunched in mingled hatred and frustration as he stared up with admirable defiance at the portly man standing over him.

"Where is he?" the portly man asked in Chu-Shin. Unlike the Tuhla, he was unarmoured and carried no weapons, garbed in clothing typical of the borderlands. As the man angled his head and leaned closer to Cho-ka, Vae-lin felt a blossoming of power along with a rush of recognition. *The Dark-blade's tent*, he remembered. *The day he killed the Jade Princess.* It had been this one who had frozen Vaelin in place when he tried to avenge her murder.

"Tell me," the portly man went on, playing a hand over Cho-ka's furious visage. "We know you helped him escape the city. So why isn't he with you now? Did you kill him? Steal from him?"

Cho-ka gave no answer beyond a sneering curl of his lips, which pro-voked a soft, regretful sigh from the portly man. "You have already wit-nessed the price paid by those who shun the Darkblade's love," he said, gesturing to the bodies on either side of the kneeling smuggler. Vaelin was unable to see the nature of their injuries but the ground beneath them was dark with blood and the stench was familiar to anyone who had witnessed a disembowelment. "Why suffer such a fate for a foreigner?" the portly man went on. "A vile and treacherous foreigner at that." He leaned closer, voice softening into an insistent plea. "Spare yourself and these others. Redeem yourself in the eyes of the only true living god. Tell me, where is the Thief of Names?"

Cho-ka's sneer turned into a snarl, although his teeth remained clenched and his body rigid. Vaelin saw that his arms were unbound but remained tight against his flanks. "Such a closed soul," the portly man said, shaking his head in meagre despair. "I think you should set it free from your cage of flesh." He shifted his gaze slightly, focusing on Cho-ka's bare torso. Vaelin felt another swelling of power and the smuggler shuddered, his arms coming up in a spasmodic jerk, hands forming into trembling claws. "Although," the portly man added, "the soul of one such as you will be hard to find. Dig deep."

Cho-ka's hands slapped against the flat muscles of his belly, his entire body shuddering in fruitless resistance as the fingers began to gouge at his skin. The black-song started to shriek again when Vaelin saw the first trickle of blood on the smuggler's skin, the music full of an all-encompassing rage. *There are too many*, a small, still-rational part of his mind protested as he raised the bow, the string scraping over his cheek as he drew it to the full. The song's only answer was a small, vicious trill of amusement before his fingers loosed the arrow.

Vaelin saw the shaft skewer the portly man through the chest and felt his gift dwindle and die. Before the red-grey mist descended once again to obscure the world, he was aware of casting the bow aside and drawing his sword, charging forward and throwing the bone-handle knife so that it sank into the ground near Cho-ka. Everything went away when the first Tuhla raised a sabre to parry his thrust, the last clear image Vaelin caught being the man's bisected features as the star-silver blade cleaved him from forehead to chin.

Photo by Anwar Suliman

Anthony Ryan is the *New York Times* bestselling author of the Raven's Blade novels, including *The Wolf's Call*; the Raven's Shadow novels, including *Blood Song, Tower Lord* and *Queen of Fire*; and the Draconis Memoria series, including *The Waking Fire, The Legion of Flame* and *The Empire of Ashes*. He lives in London, where he is at work on his next book.

Ready to find
your next great read?

Let us help.

Visit prh.com/nextread

Penguin
Random
House